THE MEMORY BANK

BRIAN SHEA

RAQUEL BYRNES

SEVERN RIVER PUBLISHING

Severn River Publishing
www.SevernRiverBooks.com

ISBN: 978-1-64875-602-3 (Paperback)

ALSO BY THE AUTHORS

Memory Bank Thrillers
The Memory Bank
Retrograde Flaw

BY BRIAN SHEA
Boston Crime Thrillers
The Nick Lawrence Series
Sterling Gray FBI Profiler Series
Lexi Mills Thrillers
Shepherd and Fox Thrillers
Booker Johnson Thrillers

To find out more, visit
severnriverbooks.com

1

Battery Motel, Seattle, Washington

Neon burned behind Gerald's closed eyelids. Green and red, like Christmas. Wispy tendrils of consciousness pulled at him, bringing him around to a dry mouth and bile rising in his throat. His head lolled against the back of a hard chair as he squinted at the room. Dim light from a lamp on the nightstand revealed a water-damaged ceiling, taped over cracks in the window, and vague mottled stains on the threadbare bedspread. The garish light searing his retinas was from a promo drone hawking the two-for-one drink special from the bar a few stories down. It hovered for a few seconds in front of the window, played a little hologram of an ice-cold beer pouring into a glass, and then moved on. It was night, Gerald thought. Or early morning, because he could still see the blinking lights on the tips of the buildings that spanned out into the dark beyond.

Gerald fought to remember how he'd gotten there, but he couldn't think. His head throbbed and his thoughts tangled with one another. He told himself not to worry about it. This wasn't the first time he'd woken up in a strange place feeling like crap. He just had to get home, take something for his head, and shower the stench of the room away. But when he tried to stand, he realized he was bound. Fear coiled in his gut and Gerald wrenched his arms against the duct tape holding him to the chair. He struggled until his wrists were slick with sweat and his breath came in ragged gasps.

Something underneath the city noise made him still. Beneath the rumbling of the distant traffic, the din of the bar, the hiss of bus hydraulics, there was the sound of footsteps. Close. Someone else was there.

"Hello?" The footsteps neared and a figure emerged from the dark of the hallway. Gerald reared back with confusion. "What? You—"

"Hello Dr. Price," the man answered as he dragged over a folding metal chair. He had a steel-finished briefcase in his hand and set it on the seat. "You have some explaining to do."

"Are you out of your mind? You can't do this!"

"Oh, you have no idea what I can do." The man nodded to the case. "Or what I can make you do."

"I won't tell you anything."

"I think we both know you have a hard time keeping your mouth shut, don't you, Gerry?"

"Doesn't matter. I-It's already in motion," Gerald blurted out, his fear twisting to anger. "You can't stop people from finding out what you've been doing. You're all going to—you're all going to fry!"

The man shook his head, unperturbed, and that sent a flare of panic through Gerald. Why wasn't he worried?

Squatting in front of the chair, the man opened the metal briefcase. A cloud of coolant puffed out as he raised the lid. "I'm going to ask you one more time. What did you tell the reporter, Gerry? What did you give them?"

Gerald focused his bleary gaze for the first time on the metal case and his blood ran cold. "Is that . . . how did you get that?"

"Take a guess. You think the one you stole was the only one?"

Gerald shook his head. Couldn't be true. "That project was scrapped, and you know why. The new design is safer, more stable—"

"Less effective."

"You don't know that! The trials are p-promising. It's why this whole thing is so . . ."

"Did you tell anyone about the deal?"

Gerald stared at him; his chin jutted out defiantly.

The man sighed. "Such a waste . . ." he pulled a metal half ring from the case. Smooth with a series of small flat nodes spanning the surface, it resembled the laurel wreath crowns worn by Caesar. "I'm sorry about this, Doc."

"No!" Gerald keened, eyes wide as he shook his head vehemently. He bucked in the chair as the man tried to slip the ring around the back of his head. "Don't do this, please! You know what will happen—"

A gut punch took the air out him and he wheezed, doubled over. The ring gripped his skull like a vise, tight and so cold.

"Hey, don't pass out." The man lifted Gerald's head, made him look into his eyes. They were empty, dead. "The information on Mercy, who did you give it to? Think of their face, Gerry. What's their name?"

Shaking with effort, Gerald whispered, "When I was a little boy, I had a bike."

"Don't do that Gerry. It won't work."

"It was a dirt bike, fire-engine red, I put cards in the spokes, and it sounded like—"

"Your contact's face, their name," the man said evenly as he reached into the metal case. "Where will it be published? Think of it."

"I once tried to jump this . . . this ravine and I hit the side. I broke my arm," Gerald rasped, trying to lock onto the memory. "It hurt so bad I screamed—"

"Come on Gerry, think. You met with someone. It must have been out of the way. You were scared, remember? Like now. Concentrate on that. What did you call them?" The man pulled out a syringe and plunged it into Gerald's thigh. "Look at their face!"

The serum burned up Gerald's thigh and he gasped, his body arching with the pain of it. His heart slammed in his chest as every muscle in his body tensed, holding him in rigid agony. His head shot forward from the force of the ring's filaments, and he gagged. Heated voices of an argument echoed louder and louder until his brother's words cut through him again. A flash of their fight flickered behind his eyes. Picture frames crashing to the marble steps as they struggled on the stairs. The burn of a swollen lip.

"Where did you meet the reporter, Gerry?" The man's voice came from far away. "Where?"

Gerald groaned as the tone in his head rose to a shriek and then a wall of noise slammed into him. The noise of the city, a distant horn, the ting of metal. Then the mist came. It had been heavy in the air that night. Cold on his exposed face and neck. Fish and salt odors pushed at him, and he remembered there had been a fried seafood stall nearby. It strobed into view on the boardwalk next to him. The city fell around him, framing him in perfect memory.

Gerald twisted in the chair, the wood creaking as he tried to leave, to turn away. But he hadn't that night. He'd watched her walk toward him. Wrapped against the wind in a dark coat. Sorrow and helplessness washed over Gerald, and he cried out. He couldn't stop himself from looking at her. She held out her hand and he placed something in it, folding her fingers over it gently. Her name whispered across his mind.

"I'm s-so sorry," he sobbed.

Another surge came and terrible pain ripped through him, pulling him back into the room even as it fell away. He looked out at the field from his childhood, across the whispering grass, to the fading sun. It smelled like summer. The sky turned, twisting like a record, and the stars stretched out overhead. The black sky so vast it seemed like he was falling into it. Further and further. Gerald gasped, the awe of oblivion burning through his mind like paper, and he knew then, that he was never coming back.

2

___

Seattle City College
Two Weeks Later

It really was a beautiful place to die, Detective Reed thought. Late November. Cold with waves of mist coming on the wind. An overcast sky glowing with an eerie orange sun. After an unusual hot spell around Halloween, an autumn storm washed the heat from the trees and buildings and shrouded everything in the sticky damp of autumn. He peered past his boots, dangling over the edge of the building's ledge, to the ground four stories below. Arched lampposts and ornate buildings emerged from the drifting fog like specters. Brick and sandstone façades rose out of the perfectly manicured grass. A gorgeous final view.

Icy drizzle bit at his cheeks and he buried his face in the collar of his wool trench coat. It was early, before first classes, and the campus was barren except for a few gawkers curious enough to brave the chill. Most of them weren't even students. They huddled near the crime scene tape wearing robes and jogging suits, sipping coffee from mugs they'd brought from their historically accurate homes down the street. Reed leaned over the ledge, taking in the cordoned-off crime scene, the forensic tent, the body on the pavement below, and took a picture with his phone. Peaceful now, he thought. But last night? He shook his head.

A group of cops and a campus patrol officer stood in a huddle near the forensic tent set up on the south side of the Bio Medical building. The security guard's golf cart had a plastic light the size of a coffee can on the roof, and it swiveled in the dawn, casting splashes of yellow up the street toward the student housing and down the grassy hills leading to the research labs. Reed's lieutenant, Robert "Tig" Montigliano, stood leaning against the brick wall under an alcove watching a LiDAR robot scan the crime scene as it circled the space around the body in concentric passes. Its bobbly head and square midsection always reminded Reed of old timey bubble gum dispensers. It paused, considered for a few seconds how to navigate a sprinkler head, and started off again on its fat little tires.

The victim wasn't covered, and Reed could make out the awkward way her limbs had fallen. He watched his boss chat with a young detective standing next to him. Sidearm and badge at her waist, she couldn't be more than thirty, if that. She gestured wildly as she spoke, and her voice floated up to him. He wondered what that was about. Maybe she worked the school? She looked young enough to be a narc.

Reed swung his legs back over the roof and hopped off the ledge. Something intangible bothered him. He knelt and grabbed a handful of the pea gravel that covered the area. Let it fall through his hand, feeling the weight, the grit of it. The mixture also contained weathered shards of glass, most likely from beer bottles. A place to drink with friends up and away from the bustle of the campus. A peaceful place under the stars. When the weather was good, at least. Last night's storm had left puddles on the bare spots of the roof, and they reflected the dappled sky. It would've been unbearably cold last night. Windy with rain falling in lateral sheets. Reed walked the perimeter of the roof. He searched behind a storage bin and pulled out a rusty lawn chair. Inside the bin he found a rake and some empty beer bottles. Their labels long-gone, cracked and weathered. People used to come up here, but not for a long time.

The sound of several people's footsteps on the stairs pulled him from his musing just as Lieutenant Montigliano and the female detective pushed through the roof access door.

"I'd ask if you were out of your mind, but I know the answer," Lieutenant Montigliano said as he strode over to Reed and peered down at the crime scene below. He sucked air through his teeth. Gray hair in a high and tight cut, eyes in a perpetual suspicious squint, he was one of Reed's oldest friends. "You know the students were taking bets you'd jump. The sick little bastards. What are you doing up here? We already processed the roof."

"Hey, Tig. I'm looking for a shoe."

"A shoe?" The other detective asked. She was petite, with dark hair pulled back in a soft bun. Tiny drops of mist clung to the wispy tendrils framing her heart-shaped face. Black slacks and blazer with a bright red blouse offset her dark, intelligent eyes. She hadn't worn a coat and was trying not to look like she was shivering. "The victim doesn't have any shoes on."

"Yeah, I think she lost one and so the other one had to go."

She wandered over to the ledge and peered over. "Or she came up here barefooted."

"Maybe," Reed said absently before addressing his old partner. "What pulled you from your nice warm office to brave the elements with us peasants? I thought making lieutenant meant you got to stay dry."

Tig spit out a few sunflower seed shells and shrugged. "The provost of this fine establishment, uh . . . Terrance Shuttle, is an old friend of the mayor from prep school. He called in a favor. Anyway, the crime scene is processed. You wanna come look at the body before we wrap things up?"

"Why call in a favor over this? Does Shuttle know the victim, or her family? Is he trying to head off a scandal?" Reed asked.

"More like he knows what a suicide does to enrollment. UW is bigger, better funded, and state of the art. This place looks like they still have sock hops for dances. You went here, right?"

Reed smiled. "I had my nose in books most of the time."

The humor drifted from Tig's face. "This . . . before the holidays? We don't want anyone getting ideas. Sometimes these deaths come in groups around this time. The provost wanted my best, so I bullied HR into bringing you back from injury leave early. I'm gonna need you to move fast and quiet on this one."

"When you called earlier you said there were two reasons you needed me back early. What was the other thing?"

Tig made a grand gesture to the female detective. "Say hello to your new partner. Detective Natalie De La Cruz."

She watched him quietly, a slight smirk on her face, but said nothing.

"My what?" Reed opened his mouth to complain but Tig cut him off with a raised palm.

"Don't even go there. You didn't catch a rip for storming into that building without backup." Tig nodded to the still-healing scar that ran from above Reed's eyebrow to an inch below his eye on his left side. A gift from a suspect during a raid a few weeks ago. "I guess the brass figured the souvenir would be reminder enough of how dumb that was. But you don't work alone anymore. Not on my watch."

Detective De La Cruz extended her hand. "Just up from Cybercrime Division."

"Uh . . . Detective Morgan Reed. I go by the last name." Reed shook her hand as he looked at Tig with confusion. "Where's this coming from?"

Tig handed a digital tablet to De La Cruz. "The brass wants more tech in the field and she's one of their superstars. So, suck it up. You're due to be senior partner anyways. And who knows. She might teach you how to use your phone right. Might get you over that hatred of technology."

"Cybercrime, huh?" Reed's hair, wet with mist, fell into his eyes and he flipped it back with a snap of his neck. "You must've done something spectacular to get a bump up to homicide."

De La Cruz smiled. "I shot a pedophile."

"For the love . . . she helped with that trafficking sting that crossed state lines. The missing nannies one. She's good, but green. Keep that in mind." Tig checked his watch and then pushed off from the building. He pulled open the access door and shouted over his shoulder. "Try not teach her all your bad habits, huh?"

"I thought I was your best," Reed called back.

"Yeah, well, you're the best at trouble, too." Tig said as he slipped into the dark of the building.

The door banged shut, and Reed looked at his new partner.

"Okay, Detective De La Cruz." He dropped a handful of the gravel in his suit jacket and tossed a piece to her. "Back to my question. It's all glass and rocks up here. Would *you* come out here barefooted?"

"It's Nat. And no, but I wouldn't lob myself off the edge either so, there's that."

He looked at her with amusement. "Where are you from, exactly? Am I hearing . . . California?"

"Probably. I was raised in San Diego."

"With some . . . New York in there somewhere?"

"My dad was a cop in the Bronx, transferred to San Diego before I was born when my mom got a job offer, but yeah. You probably hear some New York." She looked at him strangely. "You're acting like something's bugging you about the suicide. I thought this was a soft-ball case, being that I'm new, and you're just back from medical leave."

"Maybe." Reed shrugged. "When I passed the body, I saw there was gravel in her hair. Did you see that?"

"No, but she took a swan dive onto asphalt." Nat held up the piece of gravel and squinted at it. "However, I'm guessing your point is there's none of this stuff down where she landed."

"Exactly."

"So how did it get in her hair?"

He snapped his fingers and pointed at her. "That's the question. Any guesses?"

"I mean, maybe she was lying down on the gravel contemplating the heavens and what not before deciding to . . . you know," she made a swooping motion with her hand.

"It was a bad storm, not this weak drizzle. Windy, a buffeting force." He sat on the ledge and gestured at the gravel. "Would you lie there, on the pebbles and glass, rain falling in your face . . ."

"No . . ."

Reed got to his feet, standing on the ledge.

"Whoa! What are you doing?"

"The wind would have been frigid, spiked with cold needles of rain." He extended his arms. "She would have faced the building to land on her back like that. Rocked backward. Like a trust fall into the abyss."

"It would've been scary, I get it, but . . ." She shook her head. "Actually, I don't get what you're saying."

Reed hopped back down onto the roof and extended his hand. She handed him the tablet. "So, the gravel bothers you too?"

"I mean, it does *now*."

"Did you look at the body?"

Nat stared at him for a beat, then answered. "Yeah. Before we came up."

"What was she wearing?"

"Uh . . . T-shirt, jeans . . . socks, but no shoes."

"Yeah, that's a problem." Reed shook his head as he swiped through the files on the tablet. "Let's go take a look at Maggie."

Reed was tall, brawny like he spent a lot of time chopping wood, which he did up at his cabin. His suits were tailored for his shoulders, dark to hide stains, and nearly all the same so he didn't have to think about it. White shirts, solid-color ties, and Doc Marten boots. A non-uniform uniform. He moved with purpose, using his size to his advantage as he slid through a group of students jostling for a better view at the edge of the crime scene. He caught the scent of coffee, petrichor from the rain, and maybe a little whiff of weed. Nat followed him in, ducking as he held up the caution tape for her. They joined the group huddled under the forensic tent, which protected the figure on the ground from the elements.

"Did we talk to the roommate yet?" Reed asked Nat.

She nodded toward an adjacent building. "She's over in the lobby of the Bio Medical building warming up. A patrol cop took her statement and gave her coffee. I already went over the body with the lieutenant. Want me to go talk to her?"

"Sure."

"I'll take the glasses." Nat grabbed a pair of smart glasses to record the interview and left for the building.

Reed stayed on the edge of the crowd of technicians gathered around the victim, choosing to take in the entire scene first. She was young. The files had said Margaret "Maggie" Putnam was a freshman from Whidbey

Island, the largest of the islands that made up Island County, Washington. It sat thirty miles north of Seattle on the northern boundary of Puget Sound. He'd worked a case with the sheriff's department up there his first year as a detective. Small town life. No wonder she'd wanted to live in the dorms. Taste a little of that city excitement. Maggie was only eighteen years old. Long blond hair gone dark with the rain, T-shirt of a local band, jeans, socks, no shoes. The front of her head and face strangely serene given the damage to the top and back of her skull.

He nodded to a few familiar faces as he walked the perimeter of the body, two full circles. Then he poked his head out of the tent, stared up through the drizzle at the four-story roof before he ducked back under the tent. The edge of the roof flared outward to support an ornate cement finial. He wondered, as she stared down from up there, rain pouring down around her in the pitch dark of night, what she'd been thinking.

Technicians in white hooded collection suits knelt near her small frame. Reed stepped over to the body. Maggie stared up at him with vacant blue eyes. Flashes from a hover camera blared her pale skin white with every exposure. The whir of its rotors as it maneuvered among the forensic team was muted by the generators running the equipment set up at the scene. Reed found the medical examiner and knelt next to him near the body. Jake Sanders was a marathoner and had the gaunt, hollowed-cheek face all those maniacs have. Natural hair kept short; Jake had gray at the temples, but he wore it well. He ate like a teenager and laughed with his whole chest. Reed liked him.

"Hey, glad to have you back." Sanders squinted at Reed through his glasses. "I see they used BioBond on the cut. Nice. That's a lot of healing in a week and a half. Does it itch?"

"Like a mother."

"Yeah, don't scratch. It accelerates healing, including damage you cause by bothering it. You'll end up with a nasty gash instead of that delicate little movie scar you're rocking right now." Sanders stood, and grinned. "On the other hand, you could use some ugly on you. Give the rest of us a chance."

"I'll see what I can do but you know, it's a curse."

"Yeah, yeah." Sanders glanced at Maggie as he snapped his gloves off. All mirth left his face. "I hate this time of year, man."

Reed nodded. "The gravel was from the roof."

"Huh. I don't think the wind was blowing hard enough for a pebble that size to get kicked up. You figure out how it got in her hair?"

"I'm working on it. Does she have cuts on her feet?"

"I don't see any blood on the bottom of her socks, but I'll let you know when I process the clothing and expose her feet. Why, what're you thinking?"

"Just bothered." Reed slapped his knees and rose to meet Nat, who was walking back from talking to the roommate. A stiff wind rippled the tent material and blew the victim's hair around. Something caught his eye. He leaned forward and squinted at the strange stippling-like wound on Maggie's scalp. The size of a quarter, it left her scalp bare to the skin. He sank back down to the body. "What is that?"

"What's what?" Nat asked, walking over, and squatting next to Reed. She took a couple of photos with her tablet. "Oh wow. Did someone rip a clump of her hair out?"

Sanders leaned in with a hand lens. "Well, the skin appears to be shaved or burned. I'll sample the tissue when I get her to the morgue."

Nat looked at Reed. "It's weird, right?"

"Yeah, it's weird." Reed glanced at the skin of Maggie's arms and neck. "Let me know if you find any more of those odd marks, would you? And send me an enlarged image of that wound."

Sanders nodded.

"You think it's important?" Nat asked Reed.

"I think something's off with this one. Still no note?"

"No," Sanders said as he moved toward his bank of equipment on the portable table. "We processed her room. Nothing on any of her devices at first glance but we can get IT on it. Nothing on paper in or around her area. We're still going through her stuff, but nothing yet. Let me send you the walk-through LiDAR on the dorm room."

Reed stood, shoved his hands in his pants pockets, and caught Nat's gaze. "I think I've seen it before, the wound."

"Really? When?"

"Back when I was too arrogant to pay attention," he muttered. Nat looked at him, perplexed and he pointed to the smart glasses still on her face. "How'd it go in the lobby?"

"Couldn't really get much from the roommate. She's a mess right now. The provost was in the lobby waiting with her. He kept handing her tissues and apologizing for the trauma. I think we'll have to take a second run at them."

"Did he try to stick his nose into the interview?"

"No, but he's itching to ask his own questions. He was saying he needs to know what we're planning on doing about all this." She gestured around the place with a wave of her hand. "What *are* we doing? What's the procedure here? Do we just declare it a suicide or what?"

"We open a case to see if what this looks like is what really happened."

Nat failed to hide her excitement. "So, you're saying this is an official investigation? Is it a homicide?"

"Right now, it's suicide with suspicion."

"But you're thinking foul play?"

He looked down at Maggie and frowned. "What I'm thinking is we should make sure there wasn't any. So far, I'm not convinced Maggie went over that ledge on her own."

3

NW Precinct Station, Queen Anne District, Seattle

Downtown Seattle had a flavor all its own. Particularly Queen Anne District, one of the most affluent neighborhoods, which sat on the hill named after it. It boasted expensive homes, exclusive restaurants, art galleries, and every other accoutrement Seattle's wealthier citizen could want. Bordered on the south by the densely populated and crime-ridden Belltown, on the east by Lake Union, and the ship canals of Lake Washington to the north, the Northwest Precinct had a healthy cross section of crime and chaos.

Tig had ordered Reed to move fast, so he and Nat split up the interviews. He reinterviewed Maggie's roommate, Cara, in the dorm room, and then caught a ride with patrol back to the station, so he'd be there in time to meet with Maggie's parents when they arrived. He left the car for Nat so she could reinterview Provost Shuttle and check if Maggie had visited the health center.

They'd agreed to meet back at the station around ten thirty to catch each other up, only Reed had hit a snag. He paced the curb outside the station muttering choice words under his breath as he tried the number again. It went to voice mail for the fourth time. Wind sent a bunch of leaves and trash scraping down the gutter and Reed kicked at it with the toe of his shoe, waiting out the automated voice mail message. At least the rain had stopped. He tugged at his suit tie, the heat already returning with the storm gone.

"Listen, you're about two seconds from completely blowing it. I can't help you anymore if you do this, alright? I want to be clear. This is your last chance—"

"Are we meeting or what?" Nat called from the entrance doors. She leaned out and followed Reed's line of sight and then looked at him with a narrowed gaze. "What're you doing out here?"

"Personal call." Reed hopped up the steps, slid past her, and strode down the hallway with Nat jogging to keep up. He slowed, pulling out his leather notebook so she could catch up. "What'd you get from your second run at the provost?"

"Shuttle said the victim's parents gave us permission to see her school and health records, but they didn't help much." She navigated her tablet. "She had good grades. Great even. She was involved in the drama club, a student group called Restoration Republic, which Shuttle said was environmental or something, and she sang in the campus choir, the Madrigals. No disciplinary issues. The records at the health center showed she had a flu shot there. Other than that, nada." She looked up at him. "And you? What happened with the parents?"

Reed shook his head. "It went how you'd expect. The mother was inconsolable, the father little better. They said they had a virtual meeting with her four days ago. She was fine. A little stressed about some sort of project she was doing but not overly so. They're about as informed as we are at the moment."

"Okay, so the parents and Shuttle paint a picture of a kid doing fine, right?"

They stopped at the elevator. Reed held up his phone to Nat. There was an image of a dorm room on it. "See anything that strikes you as odd?"

Nat squinted at the photos, reaching up to swipe through them. "Besides the room being a total pigsty? No."

"Okay, the images are small. Here . . ." Reed forwarded the photos to Nat's tablet. She enlarged the images with a gesture on the screen. He pointed to one. "Right there, on the sink. A prescription bottle."

"Antidepressants?" She enlarged the image. "Label's torn off. Did they belong to the roommate?"

"No, she said they must be Maggie's."

"The roommate didn't mention Maggie was on anything when I talked to her in the lobby of the Bio Medical building." Nat frowned. "I know I asked about her mental health."

"It happens."

"No, really. I asked her. I can show you the recordings from the smart glasses."

"I don't . . ." Reed looked down at her, perplexed. "You didn't get to homicide being incompetent. You know your stuff, right?"

Nat raised her chin, her gaze direct. "Yes, I do."

"Then, I don't need more than your word." Reed pressed his palm to the panel on the elevator's wall, heard the access-granted ping sound, and waited for Nat to do the same.

"I, uh . . . appreciate that. I really do." She looked at him for a beat, and then, "Though, you know if they are antidepressants, that *sorta* ruins your argument that she didn't jump."

"I'm not trying to argue one way or another. I see what I see, and then go from there. Wherever it leads."

"Well, the health center didn't have a record of it. And she didn't see a counselor there," Nat tapped on her tablet. "I'll send a note to her parents. Maybe they know what doctor she was seeing. Could've been virtual visits with one of those apps."

The elevator doors opened on the homicide floor and Reed made a beeline to the digital wall display in the center of the bull pen. Floor-to-ceiling smart screens displayed a panoramic view of the campus crime scene, scrolling updates from labs and queries, photos of Maggie and her dorm, and aerial drone shots of her on the ground. The floor was arranged with groupings of desks peppered around the space. A coffee bar and bins of junk food sat on a table against the wall with filing cabinets on the adjoining one. The lieutenant's office took up the far side of the room, his door was shut, but the picture window looking out onto the bullpen didn't have the blinds closed. Reed shot a glance in Tig's direction. He was talking to someone on the phone, and he didn't look happy.

Support staff and mail bots shuffled between desks dropping off paperwork, files, etc. Not everything was fully digital, even after the huge endowment from the tech giants headquartered in Seattle, but they were getting there. Reed dug in his desk drawers, pulling out files and notebooks, shuffling through papers. He found the accordion file, its flap secured with a frayed string. He stared at it, wondering if he should open it. The wound bothered him. Maybe more than it should, considering where he'd seen it before.

Nat bumped his elbow with hers pulling his attention. "Hey, you wanna fill me in on the rest of what the roommate said? Did she say anything about the victim's social life?"

"It was healthy. The picture I'm getting about Maggie is light-years from the young woman we found on the ground. According to her roommate, Maggie was happy, dating, excited about the future."

"Ooh, dating? Anyone in particular?"

"No. The roommate didn't catch his name." Reed scribbled on his notepad. "She did say she got the impression he was older but couldn't really say why. Also, she didn't think he was a student. They always met off campus. One other thing. Maggie's laptop for school and her phone were in her dorm room, but the roommate said she had a mini tablet for sketching, social media, things like that. I found the charging cord, but not the device. It wasn't on the roof or on her body either. Can we see if it's on? Maybe we'll luck out and get a location?"

"If that setting is enabled, yes. I'll order a trace," Nat said, tapping on her own tablet.

An indicator light flashed on and off in the upper corner of the smart board. Reed pointed to it. "Let's go. The medical examiner's office has an update."

If the bullpen of the Homicide Division was high tech, the Medical Examiner's office was state of the art. Reed and Nat strode down the white, subway-tiled hallway to the basement morgue and pushed through the double doors to the autopsy theater. The smell of industrial cleaner hit them as they walked in. A mixture of alcohol, artificial pine, and something medicinal, Reed thought. Several robotic arms anchored to tables worked with samples in the back of the space. A scanner mounted on the ceiling made lazy passes over an uncovered body, its red beam of light following the contours of the patient's skin. Two small cleaning bots scoured the floor, beeping at Reed as he walked by. Jake Sanders waved them over to a covered body on the metal table. He was drinking boba tea and the little pearls made a slurping sound as he sucked them up the straw.

"I'm still processing your student, but I thought you'd like an update on the weird bare skin wound."

Maggie's hair peeked out from under the sheet, the pink stain of blood clinging to her ends. She looked so small on the table. "Did you figure out what it was?"

"It's a burn, I'm pretty sure. But I don't believe it's from a heat source. Maybe chemical? I'm going to excise the skin and run some tests."

"As soon as you can." Reed paced, circling outside the ME and Nat, his gaze on the display screens with x-rays and lab results hanging over the exam table. "Did you find any more of those marks?"

"No, the only one was on her head. Oh . . ." Sanders lifted the end of the sheet exposing her feet. "No cuts or scrapes on her soles."

Nat met Reed's gaze and said, "So that's a no. She didn't walk across the rocks and glass in just socks."

"No, she didn't." Reed rubbed his lips with the side of his index finger, thinking. "Let's see if we can get patrol to scour the bushes and trees around the area where she fell just in case. There's a slim chance they came off when she fell, or she kicked them off while on the ledge. I want to make sure the shoes actually mean something."

Nat nodded and tapped out a request to the lieutenant on her tablet.

Reed turned to Sanders. "Any outlier kind of injuries?"

"No. I see no signs of struggle, no scratches, bruising, etc. The only trauma I see is the one caused by the sudden gust of gravity." Sanders shook his head. "Shame. I'll let you know what I get back on the tox screen."

"Oh," Nat said. "Can you see if she was taking antidepressants? There was a prescription bottle in her things."

Sanders nodded. "Will do."

"Let me ask you something," Reed said, sidling up to the table next to Nat. "Have you come across any scalp wounds like that on anyone else? It doesn't have to be suicides."

"No, man. This is a new one for me. Not the suicides, of course, we've had a rash of them. The holidays, you know?"

"Yeah, people get depressed, miss their families, fall off the wagon . . ." Nat chimed in.

"Were there any deaths that seemed weird to you?" Reed asked.

"Weird how? Because killing oneself qualifies on its own merits as unusual behavior."

"Just . . . did anything strike a wrong note, even if you can't explain why?" Reed didn't like how he sounded like a conspiracy nut. "I heard a rumor there were more head wounds than normal."

Sanders sipped his bubble tea thoughtfully. "Hmm. We've had the usual number of overdoses, hangings, exsanguinations, etc. for this time of year, but an uptick in head wounds? Maybe. I'd have to collate some stats to be sure. Though, Rossing had one a few weeks ago. He's still working it out. Some big shot killed himself in a roach motel. Rossing said his family was connected and to keep the details out of the paper. Like I'm calling up reporters on my lunch break."

"What was weird about it?" Nat asked. "Did he jump too?"

"No, it was a self-inflicted gunshot," Sanders said. "Rossing couldn't place the weapon, a shotgun. He said the victim didn't have access to one. The guy didn't have one registered apparently. I doubt it's hard for a rich guy to get one though."

"You see strange on the daily," Reed said. "Why'd this one catch your eye?"

"It was the irony, I guess. Rossing mentioned the guy actually researched depression or the brain or something. And yet, he goes out like that. I just thought it was sort of . . . a lesson in the futility of it all."

Reed clapped the ME's back. "I really think your insights are wasted on the dead, Sanders."

"Anyway, I do remember seeing some discoloration, maybe some preda-tion on the victim's skull. I mentioned it to Rossing, but I don't think anything came of it. He didn't circle back to me about it anyway. He's waiting on some results for a substance I found under his victim's finger-nails. I thought it was blood at first, but we'll see what the spectrometer says." Sanders motioned to an expensive looking machine by the robotic arms. "To be fair, the body hadn't been found for almost a week. It could be rats."

Reed scribbled something down in his leather notebook. "Would you mind letting me know what that substance ends up being?"

"Sure. Are you folding his case in with yours or something?"

"Nothing like that. I just. Something about the scene at the campus bothered me."

Sanders was silent for a moment. "Listen, no one likes a life cut short. Especially one so young. Maybe you came back too—"

Reed snapped his notebooks shut. "Thanks, Doc. But I'm just dotting my I's and crossing my T's."

"Hey," Sanders said, his expression going soft. "I didn't give you my condolences before, but you have them. I'm sorry about Caitlyn."

Reed cleared his throat. "Uh, thank you."

"You got it. And I'll update you as soon as I have anything."

Reed caught Nat's eye. "I'm done here if you are."

They left the morgue and back on the elevator, Nat turned to Reed. "We're gonna go piss off Detective Rossing, aren't we?"

"Just a chat."

"Won't he find that insulting? You're butting in on his case and basically saying he missed something, right?"

"Rossing is close to retirement. A short timer. He barely does any work since he put in his papers. It'll be fine. Trust me."

She hit the emergency button, stopping the elevator car.

"Trust you? I just met you."

Reed took a step back, dropped his notebook to his side, and looked at her. "Is there a problem?"

"Listen, I get the feeling you get away with a lot here. And I would imagine it's because of your incredible clear rate." Reed shrugged but didn't argue. She tapped herself in the chest. "But I'm new, a woman, and younger than anyone on the squad. And I'm a person of color who literally just fought my way up to homicide. I had to get myself kidnapped by a putrid Bulgarian human trafficker to do it, too. I don't want to step on toes or rock the boat or whatever."

"You're covered. This is my call and I say we follow all leads, period. Wherever they go. I'll take the heat if feathers get ruffled." He held up his phone to her, pointed to the wound on Maggie's scalp. "I've seen this before and I intend to find out if she was right."

"Who?"

"I mean if *I'm* right."

"Nah, that's bullshit. You said 'she,'" Nat argued. "Does this have something to do with whoever Caitlyn is?" Reed's gaze snapped to Nat's. "Yeah, I caught that. You want me to trust you, then give me a chance to. Spill it."

Reed took in a long breath through his nose and let it out slowly. "Caitlyn was my girlfriend, who also happened to be a patrol cop in this precinct. She was killed in a car crash a few weeks ago."

"I'm sorry. I didn't know you were on bereavement leave. I thought you were injured on the job."

"I was on sick leave. My injury happened a week after she died."

"I'm sorry, Reed."

"I should have listened to her. I should have done a lot of things—" Reed cut his sentence short and hit the emergency button to start the elevator's descent. He shook his head. "Anyway . . . that's who Sanders was referring to."

"You said you wanted to know if 'she was right.' What'd you mean? Did Caitlyn have something to do with Maggie?"

"No, it's . . ." Reed shook his head. "Caitlyn was always looking for that career-making case. She wanted to be a detective and she'd get some conspiracy going about something she came across on patrol and she'd ask me what I thought. That's how we started talking. We were at a retirement party at Rampart."

"The cop bar downtown?"

"Yes. Before she died, she was talking about a string of suicides she thought might be linked somehow. She had a file and everything. But I didn't see it. She said I was blowing her off, but the last four conspiracies she brought to me turned out to be just . . . life. Bad luck. Whatever. We fought the night she died." He rubbed his eyes with the heels of his hands, hoping to wipe away the look of hurt she'd given him. "The last thing I did was doubt her."

"Ok, I totally see where your head's at, but I'm not clear on why you think our victim is related to Caitlyn's investigation?"

"I just . . . I owe her to look into it, that's all. If it gets ruled out. It gets ruled out."

"I can get behind that," Nat murmured. "Tell me what you're thinking."

Reed cleared his throat. "Caitlyn mentioned that so many suicides this year went down in a bad way. That families couldn't have open caskets because of the injuries. It wasn't my favorite subject and I guess she was right. I blew off the idea a little."

"But now you think she was right?" Nat asked, getting in his way when the doors opened, not letting him pass. "You legit think she was right, now?"

"I don't know. She was talking about this pattern . . . but it didn't make sense."

"And this isn't because she died, you know, with you not believing her?"

His hands dropped to his sides, and he looked at her. "You don't pull any punches, do you?"

"Crap, I'm sorry." She raised her hands in surrender. "I know I can be blunt, especially when I'm stressed. I promise, I'm not trying to give you a hard time. I just wanna know that this is not a guilt trip I'm going on."

Reed spread his arms out. "I see something there, and I need to follow it. If you want to transfer to a different partner, I'll have no beef with you." He stepped around her.

"You know people warned me about you," Nat said following after him.

"Oh yeah?" Reed laughed. "Maybe you should take heed."

"You were a star in narcotics, but you did it on a razor's edge. They said, if I was risk averse, I should steer clear."

"You don't strike me as particularly cautious." Reed said, heading down the hallway. "I think you'd find it boring."

"Yeah well, like I said, I'm not looking to ruin my career."

"What about trying to learn something? You clearly looked up my record. I do this one thing well, Nat. And I mean, really well." Reed glanced back at her. She'd stopped walking, her arms crossed over her chest. "Come on, superstar. What's it going to be?"

She sighed heavily. "Where is this Detective Rossing, anyway?"

4

Rossing was down the street at Nostimo's, a hole-in-the-wall Greek spot he went to everyday. It was a simple place with blue framed windows and white metal café tables in an alley behind the expensive coffee shops. They served traditional Greek comfort food that Reed was probably addicted to. He thought it was one of the best places to eat in the entire city, especially the gyros. Reed walked in, Nat at his side, and spotted Rossing seated at a far booth just as he was being served. The blue, yellow, and white mosaic on the wall behind him highlighted the sallow tone to his jowly skin. Soft plunky music played in the background and the scent of sizzling meat on the vertical rotisserie made Reed's stomach growl. Rossing saw them, looked confused for a moment, then annoyed. Reed let Nat sit on the bench opposite the detective and then slid in after her. Rossing stopped eating mid-bite and stared at them.

"What?" he said around a full mouth of food. "I missed lunch."

"Hey, you do you, man," Nat said with a grin. "Looks good."

"How's that suicide going?" Reed caught the waitress's gaze and raised two fingers. She smiled and disappeared into the kitchen.

"Well, you sure know how to ruin a guy's appetite." Rossing narrowed his gaze as he took another colossal bite. "What're you asking for?"

"I think I caught a case that's similar."

"Another tech executive shot themselves up with enough drugs to kill a rhino and then blew their brains out, did they?"

The waitress dropped off the two coffees and Rossing's bill. Reed slid one mug over to Nat, who proceeded to dump an ungodly amount of sugar into hers. It was hard for him to look away.

"I'm talking about forensically similar. I heard there was a mark on the victim's scalp?" Reed said.

"Oh that. *Meh*. Sanders said it was likely skin slippage or rats or something."

"But it was something." Nat held up her tablet with the photo of Maggie's wound. "Did it look anything like this?"

"I don't . . ." Rossing put his gyro down a look of disgust on his face. "The case is closed, practically. I'm doing some follow-up at the motel where he was found and I'm waiting on some tests from Sanders, but that's it. The guy was a rich junkie who fell off the wagon, felt guilty, and offed himself. He even left a suicide note. Not a lot of meat to gnaw on there, Reed."

"Where's the body?"

"It's still on ice until I close the case. Which can't come soon enough according to the vic's brother. Guy won't stop calling." Rossing pointed at Reed with what was left of his gyro. "He was a twin, and you know how twins creep me out."

"You've said." Reed rolled his eyes at Nat's questioning look.

"Anyway, the brother said the vic had a history of drug abuse and suicide attempts. Not a huge leap to guess what went down."

"Why'd you investigate then?" Nat asked. "If it was so cut and dried."

"It was suicide with suspicion because of the shotgun."

Reed leaned toward Rossing. "Yeah, I heard he didn't own one."

"It's not hard for a junkie to get one. I'm sure Sanders told you that too."

"Did anyone in his family own one?" Rossing's gaze slid from Reed's. He hadn't bothered to check. "What about motive?"

"Uh, take your pick. Depression . . . drugs . . . both." Rossing shifted in his seat, his expression tense. "The guy's brother said he had struggled for years to get on top of his addiction. He was previously treated for mental illness, too. I'm not gonna conjure up some random theory when it's obvious what happened."

"Was there anyone with him?" Nat asked. "A dealer?"

"A room like that, why have it dusted for prints, right, Rossing? Why bother with the paperwork for a place that rents hourly. The people who slither around that kind of establishment aren't worth it. I mean, there'd be hundreds of people going through that room." Reed held Rossing's gaze. "Is that how you justified not doing your job? Did you even check his hand for gunshot residue?"

"Look, Reed. The guy was alone. In fact, according to the front desk, he didn't even check in. He must have broken into the room. It's not like the locks are from this century. And like I said, he'd tried it before. There was even a note!" Rossing's voice pulled the attention of the three other patrons a few booths down. "What're you trying to do? Jam up my retirement?"

"We're not throwing shade on you or your investigation. We just wanna exclude this line of thinking," Nat said.

Rossing looked at her. "Who even *is* this?"

"I'm new." Nat extended her hand, to which Rossing rolled his eyes.

He stared at Reed silently for a moment and then said, "You never struck me as a glory-grabber, Reed. What's going on?"

"I'm just trying to do my job and clear this poor kid's death."

"And you're just ruling something out, right? That's it?"

Reed nodded "Scout's honor."

"Scouts?" Rossing chuckled, his anger dissipating. "No way you were ever a scout."

"Fine. I used to beat up the scouts. Just trust me."

"Promise me you won't somehow drag me into your usual chaos."

"You have my word."

Rossing wiped his mouth, heaved his girth out of the booth, and slid his bill in front of Reed. "You have the weekend."

He left them at the booth and Reed slipped out of the bench seat and sat where Rossing had been, facing Nat.

"What do you think?"

She sipped her coffee, added all the creamers on the table, drank some more, and then sat back. "Well, I definitely don't think you should rely on Rossing's notes if you think he's that incompetent."

Reed furrowed his brows. "What do you mean?"

"I mean, clearly you already know more than he probably bothered to write down. You should do a walk through. Data doesn't lie."

It was Reed's turn to lean back into the bench. "You mean the Virtual Depot."

"That's what I'm talking about."

"That place makes me nauseous. It's unnatural."

"The original crime scene is gone, right? The only thing that hasn't been tainted by Rossing's laziness is the virtual one."

Reed thought for a moment. She wasn't wrong. He sighed. "I need to stop off at my desk and get Caitlyn's file first.

"Awesome. I'll call ahead and reserve a viewing arena."

"Have you ever done one?"

"Done one? I helped program the system." Nat flashed a brilliant smile. "We'll be on my turf, so I guess you're gonna have to trust *me* this time."

5

The Virtual Depot sat in the heart of the Seattle Police Department's Technology Tower, a glass and chrome monstrosity erected a few years ago to much fanfare. It housed the Intelligence Office, Office of Police Conduct, and some of the more expensive forensic labs. They'd ordered two gyros to go from Nostimo's, and they ate in the car while Reed stared up at the glass and white stone building.

Once done, they headed into the reception center. A 3D banner hanging over the reception desk glowed with streaming images of community members working with police officers, clips of the St. Patrick's Day Parade, and videos of important innovations set to stirring music. Reed and Nat strode along the polished granite floor of the lobby, stopping for her to swipe her fob at the gate. The rest of the trip consisted of a secure elevator and passage by several guards with eyes like the recon guys he'd met in the army. They made him empty his pockets, scanned him with a wand, and took his photo before giving him a flimsy card on a lanyard. Then Nat led Reed down a long dimly lit hall toward a bank of rooms at the end of the corridor.

"Okay, so we're going to use the Omni-Flex room. It's better suited for viewing enclosed spaces." She pointed to the door on the left. "Take off your shoes and go inside. I'll get the equipment."

Reed kicked his shoes off and pushed through the door, and the soft blue lights of the interior glowed on slowly. He took a turn around the area, Caitlyn's folder clutched in his hand. The walk-through arena was a small, empty room outfitted with a plexiglass floor where an omnidirectional treadmill sat in the center. Cameras, lights, and surround sound speakers peeked out from behind the wrap-around virtual display screens that encompassed the entire room. It smelled like window cleaner and BO, and Reed wondered if people threw up in there a lot.

Nat came back in with a tray piled with equipment and Reed walked over.

"Where's the tech?"

"On such short notice we could get the room but not a technician. So, you're looking at her." Nat tossed him a pair of haptic gloves. "Get these calibrated and I'll grab your glasses."

The virtual viewing screens were indistinguishable from normal room walls save for a faint glow at the edges. But when Reed pulled on the rubber gloves and held his hands up, palms out, a video rendering of his gloves appeared on the wall in front of him. Calibration light points targeted and highlighted sections of his wrist and hands, then minute areas of his fingertips, pinging each area with a different color dot on the screen. Then the gloves disappeared, and the room adjusted its dimensions, glowing into a blue outline of a room with a corridor leading to a door, a sitting area, and a large bed.

"I'm all set." Reed called over his shoulder. He glanced around, and it felt like he was standing in a blueprint.

Nat walked over and slid the clear eye-tracking glasses onto his face. Three quick pulses of light flashed and then the room adjusted again to his height view.

"Lemme go start the walk-through," she said. "Remember, it's disorienting at first but the more you move, the faster your brain acclimates. The treadmill will sense the movements of your feet and adjust but don't like, move too fast. It hasn't been optimized for a jury viewing so it's a little choppy. Also, there was a lot of traffic and ambient sound on the file. I disabled it, but if you want it, I can undo that."

"No, you're right. I just want to take in the place itself, first."

She disappeared back into the bowels of the room and then the over-head lights dimmed around him. The gray walls blacked out until it seemed like Reed was standing in an endless abyss before the room rendered around him. He looked down at his feet and the floor screen surrounding the treadmill displayed a threadbare, mud-brown carpet. Bare in some areas, stiff and clumped in others, but entirely visually believable. A sagging queen-sized bed sat with its black lacquered headboard against one wall. It was flanked by dinged nightstands with chipping paint in the same color. A small table sat butted up against the wall opposite the bed. The chair was missing. Standing lamps bolted to the floor, each glowed a sickly yellow. If he didn't know better, he'd swear he was in the actual crime scene.

Some movement next to him and then Nat appeared at his shoulder, "What a crap-hole."

Reed smirked in the dark. "Go ahead and do the forensic overlay."

Nat gestured with her hands and the room populated with the informa-tion and images taken on the day the crime scene was captured. The light adjusted to early morning. Sun sliced through the room through bent plastic blinds, dusty detritus floating in the bright shards. Reed walked over to the door and leaned down, peering at the doorknob. He enlarged the rendering, looking at old scratches on the key card scanner from drunk patrons and dents from being kicked at. It wasn't jimmied though. The bathroom was fuzzy, and Nat helped him adjust the clarity before he went through drawers and pulled back the virtual shower curtain. Everything empty. All of it cleanish. Just the kind of grime that happened after years of use.

"And there's no record of him checking in?" Reed asked.

"No, but it's not hard to game the system. The front desk is automated. You buy hours of use at a kiosk, and it spits out a key card. I'm guessing for more than just convenience."

"And if someone leaves early, the room stays empty until the time runs out."

"Yup. He just had to find one unoccupied."

Her voice sounded further than before and Reed turned and caught sight of her moving behind him, but the virtual room remained empty. The technology was designed to place juries and witnesses in situ and to explain complex reenactment models in court. The point of view was of a single person walking through a space. Reed could see Nat moving around in the real-life viewing arena, but no avatars appeared in the virtual motel room itself. Designed to maximize the viewing space, avatars for multiple viewers, like juries, would crowd the area and make the whole program useless.

"The bed doesn't look slept in, but it was estimated he died at three in the morning." Reed turned in a circle, surveying the room. "I don't see any luggage."

"There's a list of his belongings. Hold on a second."

He heard her muttering to herself and then an itemized list floated over the bed.

Reed read it and shook his head. "They didn't find a wallet, either."

"Notes say facial rec was bust for obvious reasons." She touched a virtual page and it expanded to actual size. "Apparently he was identified by fingerprints, but that was a rigamarole in itself because of predation of the fingertips."

"Who called it in? Did someone hear the shot?"

"No. The motel cleaning bot alerted the desk that a human with no pulse was in the room. It never entered though and the ME didn't think it contaminated the scene."

"It's probably the only thing that didn't," Reed muttered. "Let me see the body in situ."

Nat tapped his arm. "Look over to your right."

In what might be considered a sitting area, backlit by the only window in the room, was a chair with a body slumped over in it. Bright white identification lines and notes hovered over the victim as the VR program pointed out evidence collected by the forensic team. Blood and tissue markers appeared, indicating splatter on the dingy ceiling, the curtains, a lampshade. Reed walked the perimeter of the space slowly, letting the room come to him as he strode on the omnidirectional treadmill. The rendering was smooth, and it felt like he floated across the carpet. The figure was a man, mid-forties, balding with light brown hair. He seemed to be leaning against one arm of the chair, his head flung back on his shoulder, gazing up at the ceiling. A dark blue identification tile rose over the body as Reed got close. *Dr. Gerald Price, 43, 168 lbs.*

"Nat, can you find out what kind of doctor Gerald was? We should check with the medical board and see if he's been disciplined or had any issues with substance abuse."

"Sure. There should be something on him. Rossing said he was an addict."

"Yes, but he didn't say what kind. I see no track marks. He's a healthy weight. It looks like he's been practicing good hygiene." Reed moved around the body, the room stuttering as it changed viewing angles to match his gaze. The top of Gerald's head was blown off from his eyebrows up. His soft brown eyes, however, stared up at the heavens with vast emptiness. Reed leaned in further, and then used the haptic gloves to grab ahold of Gerald's virtual head. He spread his hands, enlarging the rendering. The back of the head was intact. "His hair was trimmed, recently."

"Maybe he fell off the wagon, like Rossing said. Could be a recent slip up, right?"

"Addicts who take up again are more likely to overdose. He didn't. He shot himself." Reed frowned and stood up. "Can I have a projected trajectory of the bullet?"

"Yeah, hold on," Nat said and moved next to him, her arms waving as she brought up menus and selected another file from the medical examiner. "So, the note here says that his family didn't want an autopsy because of it being a suicide, so we only have an estimate."

A solid green line appeared and hovered in front of Reed. He stepped back and the line angled itself like a wand, positioning the path of the bullet from inside Gerald's mouth through to the back of the head. A probability of thirty-two percent glowed next to it. The line repositioned itself pivoting downward and entering Gerald's cranium from underneath the chin and angling up through the top of the head. Another percentage indicated eighty-five percent.

"That one seems to be closest to what we're seeing with the exit wound." Nat flicked her wrists and three documents appeared on the wall. It was the field report from the patrol who answered the call. "A shotgun was found on the ground at the victim's feet."

Reed saw the shotgun. It fell with the barrel away from the body and he imagined Gerald's body and arms moving in the opposite direction, back into the chair. Which is how he'd fallen.

"Let me see the cleaned body and personal effects."

The room faded to pitch black, and Gerald's clothes and shoes appeared. They were on a flat surface that Reed couldn't see with virtual forensic rulers and measuring gauges next to each article of clothing. A long-sleeved T-shirt with crimson at the neck and along the front, jeans with additional organic material, and blood splattered white tennis shoes. He glanced at them before going to the body suspended in the air before him.

Prone as if lying on a table, white light washed over Gerald's badly mottled skin. Though his tissue had decayed, his fingernails were shiny, buffed. He'd had a recent manicure. Gerald's hair was wet where the skull hadn't been blown away, his eyes closed, bottom half of his face almost serene. Naked except for the virtual modesty cloth draped across his genitals, put there in the event of jury viewing. Gerald turned on an axis like a lazy Susan as Reed gestured with his gloves.

"You're right, I see no track marks," Nat murmured. She pointed to a ragged wound on Gerald's thigh. "Just the one that would've caused an overdose had he not shot himself. The ME says that a cut obscured the needle mark on his thigh. It wasn't on the radar until the tox screen came back positive. Sanders went back to look for a point of injection and found it on a second pass."

Reed pivoted Gerald until he was looking down the length of the body from the feet up to the head. "What kind of measurements are taken if the family refuses an autopsy? There has to be standard intake procedures, right?"

Nat flicked through the notes she'd called up. They fluttered away as she discarded them. "Okay, they scan the face for identification, also the fingerprints, all the usual stuff. Uh, they clean the body . . . oh, we have some deep tissue scans, optical renderings of the exterior, stuff like that, but nothing surgical. Looks like there're x-rays, though."

"Can I have uh . . . sections?" Reed asked. "Articulated, like in a medical book."

"Gotcha." Nat put her hands together like she was holding a ball and then drew her hands apart quickly in an exploding motion. "Do that."

Reed copied her gesture and the body of Gerald separated horizontally midair into its component parts like a layer cake. Skin, muscle, and skeletal systems floated apart from each other.

"Whoa," Reed breathed. "That's . . . awesome."

"Okay, Jack the Ripper. Check this out." Nat flourished with her hands and then glowing lines indicating scalp and head injuries popped up around Gerald's head.

"You are like a wizard in here, aren't you?"

"I prefer goddess, but yes." Nat chuckled.

"That's a lot of damage," Reed said, walking around the suspended body of Gerald. He peered at the exposed brain and bone. "Can I sort for injuries by size and depth?"

"Uh . . . hold on." Nat scrolled through menus and settings in the air in front of her. A flurry of data points swarmed around Gerald, appearing, and disappearing, and then grouping together. "Yes, we can. These are all the documented injuries taken by the table scanner upon intake."

Reed knelt and pulled out the photos and papers from Caitlyn's folder and spread them on the floor. They were crime scene photos of the bodies in situ. Mangled. Bloody. Wide shots not particularly focused on the head. He squinted at one photo. A faint, pale spot on the back of another victim's head was too far to make out detail, but Reed could tell from the context of the ears the approximate size. It matched the size of the wound on Maggie's scalp.

"Okay, let's get rid of anything larger than, I'd say, a quarter. The mark on Maggie's head and the pictures I saw from Caitlyn's files are small. Also, not deep. It's surface damage, I don't even think it went through all the dermal layers."

"Just touch the ones you want to get rid of." Nat flicked away the shimmering points with a gesture of her hand. "Bone damage should go then."

"Let's do anything along the trajectory of the bullet too." Reed moved the data points and they tumbled away, disappearing. Finally, a data point highlighted a close up of a flap of scalp. The image hovered in front of Reed. He grabbed it with the gloves and tilted it.

"You want a filter or something?" Nat asked, tapping at the open space. "The standard ones are near-infra, UV, and a high-definition lens."

"Sure, okay." Reed stepped back. The skin flap flashed to a near black with neon purple highlights. Nothing jumped out at him. "See anything?"

"No, let's do the next one."

The second flash rendered the skin in gradients from yellow to dark red. Again, nothing popped as important.

"I really don't know what I'm looking for." Reed paced, rubbing his eyebrow scar with his thumb. "Can I make a call in here?"

"Yeah, the wall phone over there. Who're you calling?"

"The ME, Sanders." Reed went over and dialed the extension. He picked up after a few rings. "Hey, it's Reed. I'm in the Virtual Depot looking at a body. What kind of lens would show subcutaneous damage to the skin?"

"I'm fine," Sanders chuckled, his keyboard clacking in the background. "Uh, CAT8. But it's not standard during intake."

"Can it be applied to an already existing virtual rendering of a body? Even if it wasn't done initially?"

"Well, the CAT8, could be, I suppose. But it's tricky, you'd have to have someone who knows what they're doing."

Reed glanced at Nat through the eye tracking goggles. She was poking at Gerald's clothes with a furrowed brow. "I think we've got that covered."

"Listen, maybe don't go stepping on toes your first day back."

"Did Rossing call and cuss you out?"

"No, but he was complaining. Loudly. You need to watch your step on this one. I heard there's been pressure from the top to handle this like it's TNT."

"I will. I'm just poking around," Reed said.

He hung up and watched Nat as she fiddled with the controls. Fifteen minutes later, he had a nice image of a half of a circle on the bare scalp of Gerald. Nat made a doubtful harumph when she saw it.

"You don't think it matches?"

"It's only half and way more decayed than our jumper. That's a worse example of the wound. And the photos from Caitlyn's files aren't much clearer." Nat moved into his line of vision. "You need more data, not less."

Reed scratched at his chin with a gloved hand. "Ok, how about this? Caitlyn's 'pattern,' what made her take a second look at the deaths, was that they all had excessive head wounds. Even for the mode of death. What if we pull up all the deaths in the past month that resulted in head injuries?"

"Give me a second. That's a different part of the database. I have to request that from the ME's office." Her tablet pinged. "Oh, Dr. Gerald Price isn't a medical doctor. He holds a doctorate in engineering. You gotta read this file. This guy had awards for things I've never even heard of."

"Huh. What was he working on?" Reed noticed an unclicked data file next to Gerald's body. He opened it and several x-ray images fanned out in front of him. The table scanner had picked up artifacts in Gerald's brain not consistent with shrapnel. Reed zoomed in on the images with an opening pinch of his hand. The pieces were metal, he knew that from the way they registered in bright white, but they were angular. Almost square.

"Something having to do with memory augmentation." Nat pointed toward a virtual file collating in the corner of the room. The status indicators blinked rapidly in the dark. "Our search for head injury deaths is coming back with massive results."

Reed opened the query and scanned some of the possible cases. One head injury death ended up being an accidental shooting. The guy's friend turned himself in. They'd been drunk, shooting at cans, and the gun went off. The second one was also a dud. A guy who at first appeared to have been attacked with an ax had instead turned out to have wandered out from his metal shop after a piece he was working on flew at his head. He died in his backyard. The third was a guy who'd been dragged beneath a light rail car out by Angel Lake. He'd not left a note and appeared to be homeless. Reed thought that one had possibility. He saved it for later.

"See?" Nat said. "Way too much data. We've got thousands all over the state. Snow mobile accidents, hiking mishaps, car crashes, you name it."

"Too many variables," Reed muttered absently, his gaze going back to the artifacts on the x-ray. "You're saying we need more data on Gerald and Maggie to narrow down our search."

"That's what I'm saying. Better images of those weird wounds, more information on how their suicides are alike, that kind of thing."

"I think we need to go and talk to Gerald's brother."

Nat walked over, looked at what Reed was staring at. "You figured something out?"

He pointed to the metal squares. "These are deep brain stimulators. They're used for conditions like epilepsy, depression, and Parkinson's disease."

"I think one of the awards on the list was a patent for some kind of brain stimulator. The award sounded like he practically invented the modern version right out of college."

"State of the art neurology . . ." Reed stared at the virtual evidence laid out before him, and a slow dawning knotted in his gut. "I think Caitlyn was on to something, Nat."

"I'm not sure you can know that yet—"

"You *have* to see it now. There are definite similarities between the two suicides. You have to admit that. Gerald does have a similar mark on his scalp. He is also a head injury suicide," Reed put his hand up at the doubtful look on Nat's face. "Like Maggie, he was found in a suicide scene that doesn't match the narrative it's trying to tell. She had no cuts on her feet though she walked in socks across glass and rocks. No shoes and no coat . . . in a storm? And, sure, Gerald may have been a junkie in the past, but he was healthy at the time of his death. And if he's as successful as you say, then he had much better places to die. Remember how gross the motel room was. Now look at Gerald. He was pampered and cared for. Do you believe he really *chose* to kill himself in a hovel? Tell me honestly . . . none of this seems sketchy to you?"

Nat sighed and pulled off her eye tracking glasses. "You're sure about this?"

"Something's wrong here. I can feel it. If you want to walk away, I'll understand, but I need to know what's going on."

"Rossing isn't going to be happy." She waved her hand at Gerald's body. "Neither is this guy's brother. Rossing said they asked for discreet. Opening up an investigation is the exact opposite of what the brother wanted. And honestly, from what I'm learning from the file, the guy's got juice. He can be a problem."

"Scared?"

"Now I'm insulted. Takes more than a couple of pasty tech dudes to do that. And anyway, you're gonna need backup. Apparently, they're loaded. Money means muscle. Rich guys always have personal security. And lawyers."

Reed pulled off his gloves with his teeth. "That's why we're dropping by unannounced."

6

Neurogen Bionics, Elliot Bay, Seattle

Fiercer and fiercer storms over the past decade had led to a wave of interest in sustainable, ecofriendly architecture. Tax breaks for new buildings that complied with the approach resulted in a high-tech corridor that resembled a utopian city. Gerald's company, Neurogen Bionics, was six stories of Neo-Organic architecture at its finest. Reed admired the brown concrete façade in the setting sun. It was warm. Natural. The lines of the building curved softly into bridges connecting sections of the structure or up into terraces draped with lush dangling vines. Other terraces held green walls of manicured bushes, still others supported small stands of maple and dogwood trees with leaves in explosions of red and yellow and orange. Too perfect to be natural, a sparkling brook meandered around the side of the building and into a stand of bamboo arches. It struck Reed as a modern Hanging Gardens of Babylon. A thing of beauty.

"I had a wasp nest in my backyard last summer," Nat said as they walked up the steps to the entrance. She pointed at the building. "Looked like this place."

A faint smile pulled at his lips. "It's all silver linings with you, isn't it?"

The lobby had a fountain made of a massive obsidian sphere spinning lazily on a layer of water. It spilled over the raised ledge into a shallow reflection pool. Soft music drifted throughout the open-floor design. Reed and Nat walked along the natural wood floors past two-story-high windows that washed the area in natural light. Couches and chairs were arranged in groups and wall display screens showed scenes from underneath the ocean, lending a rippling, blue tinge to the lobby. Reed navigated around a set of thigh-height spheres in stone, glass, and wood grouped together for conversation. The visitors and staff in the open-air workspace looked like they belonged in an art collective. Comfy sweaters, natural fabrics, beards, and long twisted hair. Neurogen Bionics seemed to fully embrace the granola co-op atmosphere. The aesthetic was more spa than high-tech company. Then again, Reed thought, that was probably the point.

A receptionist met them at the teakwood counter with a friendly smile. She was young, artificially tan, with long, glossy dark hair. She had a soft, soothing voice. "May I help you?"

"Detectives De La Cruz and Reed," Nat said, and flashed her badge. "We're here to see Mr. Price."

The receptionist's smile grew tense, and she glanced at the computer screen in front of her. "I'm sorry, do you have an appointment?"

"Tell him it's about the new investigation into his brother's death," Reed said.

"Oh, I didn't realize there was an investigation. He . . ." she glanced at a potted palm standing next to the reception counter. Then lowered her voice to a whisper. "I thought he died of an accidental overdose."

"You weren't told he committed suicide?" Reed asked. "Now that's interesting."

"Uh, did Mr. Price know you were coming?" She typed on her keyboard, faint frown lines stretching across her smooth forehead. "Otherwise, I'm not sure if he's available. He was about to leave for the day."

Reed spotted the camera hidden discreetly in the fronds of the tree. It was subtle. Expensive. He caught Nat's gaze; she'd seen it too.

"That's fine. We can start with interviewing Gerald Price's staff." He pointed to a bank of elevators, started moving toward them. "Is this the elevator to the research floor?"

"Detective, you need clearance to use those elevators. If you'd like to come back later, I'm sure I can find an appointment time for you to meet with Mr. Price."

Nat checked her watch. "Actually, it's dinner time. How much you wanna bet we can find everyone we need to talk to at the company cantina?"

"Good idea. Can you tell us where your cafeteria is?" Reed did a turn, pointed with his leather notebook to a group of businessmen at a conversation corner. "Or better yet, we can talk to the people here first. Can you point out who works here and who doesn't? I don't want to accidentally involve any business clients in this."

"Detective, I don't think that's appropriate—" Her headset trilled, and she touched her finger to the earpiece. "Yes, sir." She nodded, murmuring softly. She turned away from them. "Of course. Absolutely. Right away, sir." She turned back to them. "Very well. Your escort will be here in a few moments."

Nat and Reed thanked her and wandered over to the sitting spheres. Nat gave them a light kick with the toe of her shoe before settling on the marble one. He leaned against the window frame, watching.

"So, you just chose to piss them off first thing?" Nat whispered. "A head's up would have been nice."

Reed grinned. "These guys living up here in their ivory towers, making decisions that'll affect all of us; they need their cage rattled once in a while. Makes them slip up."

"What am I supposed to do?"

"Oh, you can just be yourself," Reed grinned. "Your commentary is distracting enough."

"Sure, I'm totally the odd one on this team." She glanced around the ceiling. "They keep a close watch. How many cameras you think are peppered around the lobby alone?"

Reed slid onto the polished wood sphere seat next to her and leaned in close. "It's the listening in on the receptionist that interests me. That's a special kind of paranoid. Not your typical in-house security."

The elevator doors opened and the two of them stood. A thin man, young, impeccably dressed in very expensive casual wear walked past the receptionist without bothering to look at her. Reed and Nat met him in the middle of the lobby.

"Detectives De La Cruz and Reed?" Pale with an impassive gaze, he smiled stiffly. They nodded and he motioned for them to follow. "I'm Corbin's assistant, Taylor. May I ask what this is about?"

"Is he listening in right now?" Reed craned his neck, searching the ceiling of the elevator for cameras. If they were there, they were well hidden.

"Of course not, sir."

"Then I'll wait until I see him to say why I'm here."

He saw Nat smirk out of the corner of his eye.

"Very well," Taylor said with a bit of huffiness and used a secure fob to start the elevator. He passed up the floor buttons and typed in a code on the keypad next to them. They rode up the rest of the way in silence.

The elevator doors opened onto a single massive space peppered with work areas and tables. Low hanging bowl chandeliers, massive pieces of carved out stone, lent a muted light to the floor below. A thick shag rug in deep brown and matching drapery muffled the sound of their approach. Floor-to-ceiling windows lined the south-facing wall. Their automatic tint letting in the soft light of the waning sun.

A sheet of frosted glass separated a section of the floor from the rest of the office. Behind it, two figures faced each other. Men, Reed imagined, given their height, bulk, and way they moved. They were talking, but with animation, large swinging arm movements, leaning into the other's space. He couldn't tell for sure, but it looked like an argument and the smaller man was the aggressor. Reed twitched his nose at the nearly imperceptible hum of a sound buffer. Whatever the conversation, they didn't want anyone to be able to hear. Taylor motioned for them to wait and then knocked on the frosted glass. A door lock clicked, and Taylor slipped inside. A second later, the frosted glass turned completely black, obscuring everything behind it.

"I'm gonna check out their website, poke around, see what I can see," Nat said and found a place at an empty work area to tap on her tablet.

Reed wandered the rest of the space and realized, though uniform in aesthetics like colors and fabrics, the result of a decorator, he guessed, the personal artifacts, the detritus of living, showed a polar opposite pair of brothers. One side of the vast room held the everyday supplies of business. Antique metal file cabinets, a long granite meeting table, a glass and metal desk. Welded pipe lamps with light bulb cages lent a cold, almost industrial feel to one side of the room. Mounted on the wall behind the desk were various trophies and plaques. Leadership awards, Chamber of Commerce accolades, golf tournament prizes.

The other side seemed more like the study of an absent-minded professor. A massive antique desk and lawyer's bookcases dominated the Persian carpet. Art Nouveau standing lamps with sinewy posts arched over a well-slept-in Victorian sofa. Tilt top tables held notebooks and pens, various white schematics rolled and shoved into a bronze umbrella stand. Most of the books and files that had been on the shelves were partially packed in open boxes set on the floor. Paintings sat stacked on one another against the side of the desk. Reed flipped through them and found mostly landscapes of the same place. A rocky beach. Gloomy. Some still life studies of flower arrangements. A few Rothkoesque abstracts of gray and black. An eclectic collection. He couldn't quite see what Gerald had been going for when he chose them for his office. They were so different in style and tone. Reed glanced around the space. Bubble wrap, tape, and more boxes sat on the couch cushions. They were packing up what was left of Gerald.

Reed spotted a lone photo mounted on the wall near a work area and walked over. The Price twins were not identical. Reed could see it in the way each stood. One, confident, arm around the other, direct gaze at the camera. Corbin. The other, soft, timid, pale. He bore the tug of his brother's arm with discomfort. As if he'd been pulled into the photo last minute. Gerald. Reed scratched at his scar with the pad of his thumb and wondered how such a dynamic difference in personalities got along.

The door opened behind him, and Reed turned to see Taylor exit the door.

"Mr. Price is finishing up his previous engagement. He'll be with you shortly," Taylor said.

He turned to leave, but Reed held his notebook out, stopping him. "Did Gerald and Corbin work well together?"

"Of course, they did. They were very close," Taylor said with a frown. "Everyone here is devastated."

"How long have you worked for the Price brothers?" Nat asked, wandering over.

"Please, you make them sound like a pizza joint," Taylor said with a look of disdain. "They were luminaries in the field."

"How well did you know him then?" Reed asked. "Did you know about Gerald's drug addiction?"

Taylor's ears went red. "We all knew, Detective. Gerry was very open about his journey to sobriety."

"What about his depression?" Nat asked. "Did you guys all talk about *that* around the water cooler?"

Taylor's face went red. "I really don't think that is any—"

"It's an espresso machine, actually," Corbin Price said from the door. Light brown hair like his brother, he had the rounded shoulders and lean muscle of a swimmer or a rower. "And yes, he talked about his struggles with mental illness. Gerry was an open book. My brother felt that the only way to beat adversity was to look it in the face."

"Do you share the same sentiment as your brother?" Reed asked, walking over. "Because we'd love for you to answer some questions about him for us."

Corbin gave him a stiff smile. "Of course."

He led them into the separate space and Reed realized it was a kind of showroom. Unlike the warmth of the outer office, this space was designed to elicit awe, particularly of technology. The windows were frosted, and glossy white walls curved instead of meeting at corners. Clear acrylic table and chairs stood in the center of the meeting place. Glass display sheets hung from thread-thin cables over the table and displayed computer animations of various devices. The looping presentations showed surgical insertion and activation of miniscule devices and filaments into the brain. The clip switched to patients first shaking uncontrollably, then, with rock steady hands, writing letters or feeding themselves. Another showed a woman who seemed confused by how to put on a windbreaker, suddenly walking and talking along a hiking path with friends. The promises of brain-computer technology.

The bigger man, the one Corbin had been arguing with, was standing against the window as they entered. Short hair in a near buzz cut, arms crossed, terse nod as they passed. Reed took in the watchful stillness, the coiled way he held himself, and thought, military. That and the black work boots he wore with his suit. The cut of the blazer, loose at the hip, to hide a belt clip holster, said private security. Another layer of paranoia. Reed wanted to know why. The man didn't introduce himself.

Corbin didn't ask them to sit. Instead, he stood at the edge of the table and crossed his arms. "Where's the other detective?"

"We're just cross checking your brother's case," Reed said.

"Well, I'd like to know what's going on with my brother's case. Why are you investigating his suicide?"

"Why *wouldn't* you want me to?" Reed asked. He looked at Corbin innocently.

"What?"

"According to Taylor out there, you guys were peas in a pod," Nat said.

Reed nodded. "Don't you want to know what happened to your brother?"

"I know what happened to him. He succumbed to his demons. Gerry was the genius behind everything you see here. He was a singular individual. Some say the greatest mind of his generation. But that kind of genius takes its toll. My brother struggled with mental illness our whole lives."

"And the drugs?" Reed asked. "When did those come into play?"

"I told all this to Detective Rossing. It started after a boating accident. Gerry hurt his back and our doctor gave him pain pills. After that, he would be fine for a few months, maybe even a year, but something would happen and then he'd disappear, and we'd track him down in some flop house or a shelter. This happened all through college. During our initial projects as well." Corbin shrugged, his expression sorrowful. "Detective Reed, though unfortunate, my brother's end wasn't a surprise. I'm just sorry I didn't see he was spiraling sooner. I might have been able to stop it."

"So, you thought he was doing fine?" Nat asked. "No signs at all of what he was going to do?"

"Gerry attempted before," Corbin said quietly. "During spring break senior year. He took a bottle of vodka and a bottle of some of his pills and walked into the woods behind our family home. The gardener barely found him in time."

"Mr. Price, doesn't it seem odd to you that your brother would choose such a dangerous and filthy place to die?" Reed asked.

"No." The bigger man pushed off from the wall. "Gerry used to go off on benders. And we'd find him in motels or rest stops. One time under a bridge."

"You must be head of security," Reed said.

"Michael Slater," he shook Reed's hand, and a strange look flashed on his face. "And yes, I've been with Neurogen Bionics for three years."

"You said, 'we'd' find him," Reed said. "Are you the one who would go find him?"

"Usually, yes." He nodded at Corbin. "Mr. Price deserved discretion. Some dignity."

"That's a unique skill set, isn't it? Tracking people?" Reed shot back. "Did the military train you in that?"

"Listen, Detective," Corbin said. "The point is Gerry chose these places to disappear. That's the whole point of drugs, right? To forget?"

"Ironic though, isn't it?" Nat piped up. "You guys work with memory augmentation and your brother was busy forgetting."

"I beg your pardon—"

"What my partner meant was that we understand your company worked with devices for neurological intervention, right? Deep-brain stimulators for disease?"

"Uh, yes. We do." Corbin said, his mouth turned down as he glared at Nat.

"Like the ones in Gerald's brain?" Reed asked. "The strange artifacts we found are why we're here."

Corbin startled, his face going stone still. "What are you talking about? What artifacts? No one said anything about that when they called to tell they'd found him."

"The x-rays told us, see?" Nat held up a copy on her tablet for Corbin.

"Oh." The tension left Corbin's body. "He overdosed five years ago and suffered terrible seizures afterward. Those stimulators saved his life. Literally. His heart once stopped during an attack."

Reed nodded. "And lucky for him you make them."

"Lucky for millions," Corbin corrected. "The research on those devices paved the way for our Alzheimer and dementia treatments."

"Worth millions, too," Nat said.

"That's my question," Reed said, ignoring Corbin's glare. "What happens now?"

Corbin looked at him, confused. "What do you mean?"

Reed stepped closer, getting in his space, keeping track of Slater. "You just said that everything, all the technology, was your brother's creation. What are you going to do now that he's gone?"

"Gerald worked with a team. And as you can see, everything is in the open. Under his leadership they've made great strides and there are a few promising researchers who've committed to stay. In fact, we're set to release a new memory aid for traumatic brain injury in the spring."

"So, losing your brother won't bring the company down?" Reed asked.

"No, thankfully my brother and I made sure that if one of us should want or need to leave, we could." Corbin said as he checked his watch. "Are we done now?"

As if on cue, Slater moved forward. "If there isn't anything else, Mr. Price has other things to attend to."

"We'd like to see where your brother lived," Reed said, refusing to move. "Will you give us permission to see his place?"

"I don't even know what you're looking for," Corbin snapped. "You never explained why you've opened an investigation. He had drugs in his system. I was told he left a note, though I haven't seen it despite my asking several times."

"Just a walkthrough of his place and we'll leave. I'm not talking about bringing in a forensics team or anything."

"It's already been packed up and cleaned," Corbin said. "It's empty."

"So soon?" Nat asked. "Why?"

"It was too painful to think of his place sitting empty and cold. Gerry always had music going and food cooking." Corbin let out an exasperated breath. "Anyway, I don't have to explain myself to you. We have family flying in. We're planning a funeral. And I see no reason for you to keep my brother's body any longer."

"The shotgun for one," Reed said.

"I'm sure Mr. Price, with all of his drug connections and money, could get one if he wanted," Slater said.

"From you, maybe?" Nat nodded to the bulge under Slater's blazer. "You seem to like weapons. Are you sure you didn't slip him one? Maybe for protection at all those sketchy places you said you found him?"

"I'm done here," Corbin said and turned to face the windows, dismissing them. He touched the glass and the frost disappeared, leaving a spectacular view of the distant lights in waters of Elliot Bay.

Reed pulled a photo print from his suit jacket pocket and held it up. "Do you recognize this mark? Have you seen it before?"

Corbin looked over his shoulder at the picture of the wound Reed had found on Maggie's scalp. He stilled and the muscles of his jaw clenched. He turned back to the window. "No."

Slater led them out of the office and walked them to the elevator doors. "Mr. Price just wants to put his brother to rest."

Reed showed Slater the picture again. "What about you? Ever notice any kind of injury like this on Gerald when you'd find him after a bender?"

"Yes. We'd usually have to hit the ER after I'd find him. Broken fingers, cuts that required stitches, sprained ankles. Addicts hurt themselves. In more ways than one."

"And no one thought to get him help?" Reed asked. "No one noticed he was that on the edge?"

"Gerry was stressed, sure. Did he seem suicidal? Maybe." Slater looked behind him at the now re-frosted office glass before continuing. "I didn't want to say anything in front of Mr. Price, but I saw Gerry coming out of his office restroom the other day and he was rolling his sleeve down. It could have been nothing, but . . ."

"You didn't have proof," Reed finished.

"No, and you don't go around accusing your boss of shooting up in the company toilet without it."

Slater stepped back as the elevator doors closed. Nat opened her mouth to speak, but Reed put his finger to his lips. He pointed to a small pinhole camera in the corner of the ceiling. They rode down in silence.

Once in the car, Nat let loose as she drove them out of the parking lot.

"That Corbin guy is a piece of work. He used his brother's genius to make millions and drove him to the ground with the pressure. He couldn't even squeeze out a tear for show."

"That's one way to look at it." Reed scrawled in his leather notebook.

"Okay, what do you see?"

He stopped writing and sank back into the car seat. "I lost my nephew a few years ago to suicide. My sister's kid. He was seventeen."

"Oh, man," Nat said, pulling into traffic. "That sucks, Reed. I'm sorry."

"It took her months to even go into his room."

"And yet Corbin has his brother's place on the market inside of two weeks. What do you think that's about?" She honked at someone, veering around them.

"People grieve differently," Reed murmured. He swiped through Nat's tablet. She'd opened it to the ME's files, and he stopped on Gerald's suicide note. He read it, confused. "It's just a poem? Three lines?"

"The note? Yeah, I saw that. You'd think a man as smart as he was could figure out something of his own to say."

"Yeah. Unless he didn't write it." Reed sketched the beach scene he'd seen in Gerald's paintings on his notepad. "Did you see how Corbin reacted at the mention of artifacts in the brain?"

"Yeah, it's like he forgot or something." She glanced at him when he didn't answer. "Reed?"

"Or something . . ." His phone pinged and he read the message. It was from Sanders at the ME's office. "You know that substance Sanders found under Gerald's fingernails? He thought it might be blood?"

"Yeah. What was it?"

"It was paint. High end oil paint, to be exact. Sanders thinks it's for art."

"Art? Like paintings?" Nat slowed to a stop at a light and looked over at Reed. "A lot of those stressed-out tech types have pieds-à-terre."

"Pied . . . ? You think he might have had a secret apartment or studio?"

"Why not? I'd have a hideaway if I shared every aspect of my work life with my brother. Especially one like that."

"Rossing didn't mention an art studio in his notes about his visit to Gerald's place during the initial investigation. Nothing in Rossing's file says anything about additional property, either."

"And we know how thorough that guy was." The light turned green, and she honked at the car in front of them to go. "I'm telling you; this guy was creative. Did you see his side of the office?" There was a stack of paintings over by his desk. Maybe they were his."

Reed was surprised. He hadn't seen her looking. "So, if there wasn't an art set up at his home . . ."

"Then he probably had one elsewhere. And that's kinda the point of having a place like that, right? It's supposed to be hidden . . . a hideaway. Makes sense Corbin wouldn't know about it. Or he didn't mention it. But I don't think so. He'd already have it for sale by now, too."

He looked at her for a few seconds, then sat up straight. "We should check and see if he does have something like that on the market. Also, let's get started on another search of Gerald's records, specifically finances. I'll ask Tig to get working on a warrant in case we find something."

"Okay, but first I have to eat or I'm gonna get grumpy."

"Tell you what, if it turns out you're right, your dinner is on me."

7

He glared at the detectives through the window as they walked across the Neurogen Bionics parking lot. Anger churned in his gut, and he slammed the side of his fist on the glass. Everything was going wrong. The detectives had made too much ground too quickly and that sent a shard of worry boring through him. This put everything in jeopardy. All the plans. All the sacrifice. He could not let that happen.

The big one especially was a problem. He was smarter than he looked. At the college earlier, he had taken apart the crime scene like it was nothing. And now he was at Neurogen already. What did he know? What had been missed? The detectives stopped at their car. The woman climbed into the driver's seat while the big cop stood and looked up at the building. He was taking notes in a notebook. Maybe even sketching. This Detective Reed was dangerous. It was in his eyes. The way he seemed immovable. He may hide in sheep's clothing, but the detective was a killer. A hunter. Like the men from before.

The detectives drove away, and a wave of frustration burned through him. That and the inklings of pure panic. The mission was on a razor's edge, and something must be done. Something bold. A move to clear the board of his enemies and light the way. It would be dangerous, but worth it.

Certainly unexpected. If he told no one, he could pull it off. One way or another, for the integrity of the mission, Detective Reed had to be stopped.

He pulled out his phone, dialed out the number from memory, and waited through the ring. Sepulcher picked up on the second.

"What is it?" His voice was low, gravelly. His words formed around the chew he always kept tucked in his lip.

"Tell me the venue is ours."

"I was in and out of there yesterday. No problem. No one will ever know I was there." There was a pause and then, "And the surprise?"

"I will deliver as promised." He watched as the detectives drove off and he caught a glimpse of Reed staring up at the building. "But there may be a problem."

8

Queen Anne District
9 p.m.

Reed swung at the heavy bag and the sound of his punch snapped throughout the garage. He hit again, and again, grunting as the burn of his deltoids intensified with every swing. Jab, right hook, retreat. Push in, lead hand, right cross, retreat. Over and over. Sweat flew with every impact, his breath coming in vapor against the chill. He worked the bag and flashed back to when he couldn't even make it move. Swinging at it with the spindly arms of a street kid. Nose still bloody from his father's backhand. Anger roiling beneath the surface. Always there. Always ready to flare out onto somebody.

The gym owner had let him be. Let him tire himself out. It was better than the fights he was getting into at school. On the street. Every day he'd attacked that bag. Every swing a silent scream of frustration. Of helplessness and anger. And every day he grew stronger. His chin harder. All he had to do was survive, he'd told himself. Just make it to the next day.

Reed had eventually started boxing, the owner, Morty Cobb, taking on his training himself. No charge. Just a kind act that had saved Reed's life. He was sure of it. Though he'd risen in the local bouts, Reed's heart hadn't been to gather belts. In the end, he'd left everything and everyone behind. Joined the army and disappeared. The gym was gone now. Morty, long dead. He wondered if that grizzled old man knew how much he'd changed the trajectory of Reed's life.

A creak from the anchor beam in the garage's rafters snapped Reed from his thoughts and he paused, bouncing on the balls of his feet, listening. Dust floated down in the harsh shop lights. He tugged at the laces of his gloves with his teeth and pushed his way into the kitchen of his condo.

Reed lived less than ten minutes from what had been the bad part of Belltown before gentrification, which was where he'd grown up. Though there was still a significant homeless population, which was why he'd found a great deal on a place in a building from the 1930s when he'd left the army. It was small and old, but well-kept with original fixtures. The real estate agent had called it a 'vintage charmer.' She'd been particularly enamored of the moldings, but Reed liked that it had built-in shelving for his books and vinyl, and that it was on the ground floor. That and it came with an attached garage. The only unit in the building with one, though it meant he had no parking space.

The gritty forlorn vocals of Nirvana's Cobain belting out Come As You Are drifted through the condo. He was about to hop in the shower, but the takeout guy rang his doorbell. It wasn't hot so Reed plated it and threw it in the microwave for a few minutes. His kitchen was small, and he grabbed a beer while he waited, cracked it open, and drank it while leaning against the counter. He could see into his room from there. Reed let his gaze travel the still made bed, the countless small pillows he never understood, Caitlyn's pink robe draped over a chair. He cleared his throat, shook his head, and headed to the couch. His blanket and pillow were pushed up against one side and he sat on the other. Leaning over his coffee table, he ate out of the take-out container, while reading his notes. They'd put in for county records to do a search for undiscovered properties associated with Gerald Price. He'd also put a query in for Tig to spin up a warrant to search the place, if they found one. Reed wouldn't hear back on either of those until morning. Nat's message about their head injury search query was merely an update. They still had too much information and not a lot of clues to help sort it.

Reed thought about his encounter with Corbin and Slater. Something was weird there. The dynamic wasn't quite CEO and head of security. It displayed different. Almost adversarial? Slater bugged him. He seemed out of place. And Corbin was definitely volatile. He slipped from helpful to hostile too quickly to not be hiding something. Caitlyn's file sat on a pile of books stacked against a fake fireplace mantle. *What did you step in, Caitlyn? Whose attention did you pull?*

A tap at his window made him smile. Reed grabbed some naan from his bag and walked over. He slid up the sash and out of the dark of night, a crow walked onto the windowsill. He stared up at Reed with a wet black eye.

"Hey there, Edgar." Reed fed him a piece. "I wondered if last night's storm blew you to Canada."

Reed leaned out of the window feeling the cold of November sting his face. Early Christmas lights flickered on balconies across the street. Someone had made fried chicken and the scent of it wafted along the brisk breeze. He ducked back in, went to shut the window, and froze at the crack of a twig in the bushes just outside. Edgar flew off in a fit of dirt and stray feathers, squawking with irritation.

Reed pivoted, flattened his back against the flanking wall. He hit the lamp switch, casting the living room into near darkness, and crawled to where he'd left his firearm on a side table. He crept back to the window and peered outside. A form backlit by the streetlight in the distance crouched just to the right of the building. Reed squinted but could only make out a silhouette. Then there was a flash. A glint of metal, maybe? Before he could register what it was, the figure darted from the side of the house.

"Hey!" Reed shouted and scrambled out of his window.

He took off, sliding on the wet grass with his boxing shoes as he chased the figure down the building's sloping lawn, but lost him in the bushes between his building and the next. A crash to his left snapped Reed's head toward the adjacent alley and a figure sprinted away from him. Dark hoodie, black bandana covering the bottom part of his face, gloves. Reed barreled toward him, running past folded lawn chairs, milk crates, rolling trash bins. Windows flashed in his periphery. A lady at a sink. A taped-up screen. The flicker of television light inside another.

The runner was fast, his stride long and steady, like he'd trained. Reed panted, his workout catching up to him as he jumped over a stack of toppled wood pallets to close the distance between them. He could almost touch him, felt the cotton slip between his taped fingers, and coiled to spring, when the runner turned mid-stride and threw something in the air. Reed ducked and veered to the right. He tracked the object, trying to avoid it landing on him. Only it didn't. In the downward arc of its fall, it froze and hovered above him, keeping pace as he ran.

A low hum made the hairs of Reed's arms stand and he dove into an alcove behind an air-conditioning unit. A flicker of movement flashed across his vision as something slammed into the metal of the AC unit. Shrapnel feathered away, slicing at his cheek and lip and neck. Another volley of hits sounded and then the hum changed as the small drone maneuvered for a better angle on Reed.

He threw himself back into the alley, hoping to outrun its tiny rotors, but it moved in quick jerks forward, homing in on Reed's location with a targeting laser. It fired another round of projectiles that exploded against the bricks, the asphalt, the chain-link fence. Thin slivers of metal fanning outward as the rounds disintegrated on impact. Reed slipped in the loose gravel, righted himself against a bin, and grabbed the lid. He sprinted, chest burning, for the end of the alley and slipped around the corner. As the vibration of the miniature engines approached, breached the street, Reed swung, baseball style and slammed the lid into it, sending the drone into an uncontrolled, frenetic spin. It crashed into the side of the opposite building, pieces flying everywhere.

Panting, Reed peered down the open street both ways. The runner was gone. The drone sparked and spit on the asphalt and as he squatted down to look at it, the main body of the device caught fire. The plastic melted, leaving a black puddle of burned nothing on the street. Reed rocked back on his heels and leaned his back against the alley wall. He wiped at the bloody cuts on his neck and face with his hand, thinking. Two things were crystal clear. Someone didn't like where the investigation was going. And they were watching him.

9

Pioneer Square Arts District, Seattle

The next morning, Nat yanked him from a dream about crows and lasers when she called to tell him that the County Clerk's Office had found a property listed under Gerald's mother's maiden name, an artist's loft in the Akira Arts Building. She wanted to head out with the forensic team, and he said he'd meet her there. It was on Yesler Way, an area Reed knew well so he took the unmarked department car he drove home most nights and stopped a few blocks from the loft so he could grab breakfast. He had a craving for one of those combination donut-croissants and he was in just the place that would have it.

Pioneer Square was Seattle's original downtown, but everyone knew it now as the historical arts district. Old brick and concrete buildings with grand entrances that housed bookstores and bistros. Reed favored the breathtaking Romanesque Revival buildings that had survived the "Great Fire" of 1889. He liked the rough-hewn stone, wide, rounded arches, and towers. They looked like small castles to Reed. Though he was pretty sure the tower on the building across the street was used as a yoga studio now. The Pioneer Square was a small area you could explore in less than a day, it attracted walking tourists who wanted to take pictures of their pastries from the artisan bakeries or stage elaborate picnics in the cobblestoned Occidental Park. The city's Partial Stay program that sheltered the homeless during the colder months had pretty much cleared them out save for a few exceptions. Tucked near the park's entrance, a tattered puff tent listed in the breeze. Two men sat near it on the curb sharing a can of beer and pointing at tourists.

Reed passed a favorite café and lifted his face to catch the scent of rich coffee and breakfast paninis. His mouth watered and he abandoned his search for the elusive Cronut and grabbed a couple of mozzarella, spinach, and egg sandwiches to go.

He thought about Gerald as he passed yarn bombed trees in vivid knit sleeves. Wondering if the delicate genius, as his brother had put it, found peace in this creative space. Metal wind sculptures wound in the breeze, their polished surfaces reflecting the unusually bright morning sun. The art walk crowd chatted outside one of the galleries on their monthly route. City ordinance kept most progress at bay, but the stray automated luncheonette or food delivery bot reared their anachronistic heads if you looked hard enough.

The artist's loft, according to Nat, had passed to Gerald when his mother died fifteen years ago. Something about the way it was set up in a private trust made it easy to miss on the first pass. It was in an old art nouveau building and on the top floor, which meant Reed had to climb into one of those service elevators where you pull the strap and the top and bottom gates snap shut like a mouth. It wheezed and trembled up to the fifth floor and he was sure he was about to plummet to his death in a cacophony of twisted metal and fiery elevator brakes, when it stopped. Nat yanked the guard gate to the side and frowned.

"What happened to your face?"

Reed held out a foil wrapped panini. "I owe you a good meal. You were right about Gerald having a hidden place."

"Oh, no. You said, 'dinner is on me' not some sorry breakfast burrito."

"It's a panini from Tomeo's," he said, and tossed it to her. "Eat it and feel ashamed you called it that."

She tore open the foil, sniffed it suspiciously, and took a bite. Then rolled her eyes with ecstasy. "Okay, tell Tomeo I'm sorry."

"You see?"

"I see you avoiding my question about your face," she said between bites.

Reed nodded, finished the last of his sandwich, and gingerly wiped his mouth around the cuts on his lip. "I caught some guy looking in my window last night."

"You have a Peeping Tom . . . Tina?" Nat couldn't hide her skepticism.

"More like a guy who looked like he was going to break in. So, I chased him down."

"As one does."

"The guy threw some kind of armed drone at me. I lost him in the hail of tiny daggers."

"Shut. Up!" She looked at him with wide eyes. "Did you report the attack?"

"And say what? It was dark. He had a mask." Reed bothered the cut on his lip with the tip of his tongue. "The weapon, the drone . . . vaporized itself. And the projectiles disintegrated on impact. I can show them the puddle of melted plastic on the asphalt. That's it. The guy didn't even make it into my house."

"What do you think it means?"

"It means we rattled someone's cage."

"According to the ME and Detective Rossing, Corbin can pull some important strings if he wants to. You think he has the cajones to stalk you? Maybe he had his own personal GI Joe do it."

"You clocked that, Slater's military training?"

"I could practically see the *Semper Fi* tattoo on his butt." She scrunched her nose, bothered. "You'd think he'd be smart enough not to hit your house hours after you question his boss though, right?"

"Not if I wasn't supposed to survive. Besides, homicide detectives have enemies. I have a few death threats too. It's conceivable it was someone else."

"Do you think it was?"

Reed shook his head and tossed his napkin in the trash. "I don't know. I have to think about it a little. Something about it is . . . weird."

Nat took a bite of the panini with one hand and held up her tablet with the other to show Reed "I'm going to finish this out here, but the electronic warrant came through ten minutes ago. So, we're good to go."

The forensic team had arrived before Reed, and they were already inside the loft dusting for prints, photographing the area, and cataloguing the contents. He grabbed some gloves and shoe covers at the door and slipped them on. Gerald's loft was surprisingly modest. A gift to his mother on her wedding day from her father. High ceilings, natural light from large, high windows, worn, wood floors, industrial piping running along the walls. A kitchenette took up one end with a small fridge, butcher block counter, and cooktop. A café table sat near a window overlooking the street below. The other end of the studio had a large easel set up on a drop cloth in the corner. A table stood next to it against the wall. It held containers with palette knives, expensive sable brushes, tubes, and cakes of paint. Sketches taped around the edges of the large canvas had curled with moisture.

Nat went over to a rolltop desk where another tech sat fiddling with a tablet. Nat stood next to her and waved him over. The woman was messing with the loft's home control system and the automatic tint on the windows darkened the room momentarily, like a cloud passing the sun. She adjusted the light again and then Reed heard an irritated murmur from the guy dusting the counter for prints.

"Reed, this is Imani Jones. She's a guru at getting into files."

Imani had her hair tied into a fluffy poof at the top of her head, white finger tattoos, and a septum piercing. She gave him a curt nod and pointed to an icon on the tablet screen. "I found a second calculator app."

"What does that mean?" Reed asked, peering at the open file list. "Hidden files?"

"Yeah, a lot of them. They're mostly financial stuff. We cracked the passwords for those in five minutes." Imani pointed to a file with numbers instead of letters for a name. "It's this one that has us interested."

"What is it?" Reed leaned in as if he knew what he was looking at.

"It's behind another login page, a more secure one, so we don't know. *This* one takes a six-digit alphanumeric code, not just a pin," Nat said with a huge grin. "But if he took the time to hide it—"

"Must be important." Reed finished.

"We're going to try some brute force attacks to see if we can get past the login page but if not, we have some tricks back at cybercrime we can hit it with," Nat said. She pointed to the other side of the room. "You see the painting?"

Reed walked over and peered at the light pencil lines on the large canvas. A work in progress. He unfurled the sketches. They were of the beach he'd seen in the paintings leaning against Gerald's desk at Neurogen, only this time with the outline of a woman standing on the rocky shore. He wandered to the storage shelves underneath the row of windows on the north wall of the room. Cubbies filled with sketchbooks, some dated as far back as ten years. Reed sat on the floor, whipped his tie back behind his shoulder, and grabbed a stack. He leafed through them half listening to the chatter between Nat and Imani. It sounded like they were getting close.

Gerald liked to sketch nature, specifically, the beaches surrounding his home near the Salmon Bay Bridge. But there was always the dark beach. The one from his paintings. Reed finished a sketchbook and picked up another. He could see the spiraling of Gerald's moods. His strokes got harsher, the colors ranging from deep purple to midnight to black, like a painful bruise on his mind. And then the dates would skip. Weeks. Sometimes months. And Gerald would sketch again. Filling the pages with hope and beauty before it grew cold again. The struggle with depression, a never-ending cycle.

Reed pulled the last art journal on the shelf. This one was leather bound. Bespoke, with an entangled G-P in gold foil script on the cover. Reed looked through it with growing fascination. Gerald had spent every page painting different views of the same beach. Various angles like he was studying it. On the sand looking down a shoreline that butted up against a metal railing. Craggy boulders and driftwood piled on the sand. Another from the shore looking at the arm of a peninsula jutting out into the sea. A third from a street angling down at the ocean. A row of small shacks on stilts at the edge of the water caught his eye.

They looked familiar. Reed took photos of interesting pages. They were watercolors mostly. Full of movement, the seascapes tumultuous with ominous churning skies. The swell of the wave underneath a small, rudderless boat, foreboding in its strength. The sea caverning like a hungry mouth beneath the rickety vessel. A sense of doom and inevitability. It reminded Reed of Winslow Homer's work. His mother's favorite. She'd said it felt like Homer could paint exactly how it felt in her head, sometimes.

Reed ran his thumb over the rough watercolor paper. He stared at the bleak drawings in Gerald's sketchbook. And always a lone figure standing on the shore, wrapped in a dark sweater, hair blowing across a delicate face or from the back, her shoulders hunched against the wind. Never her face. Until the last book. The last page. The one Gerald worked on the week he died, according to the date scrawled in the corner. She was beautiful, south Asian given the Bindi on her forehead. Her dark eyes were intense. Intelligent. Long hair whipping in the breeze. Gerald was a talent, Reed thought. And he longed for that place, that moment with the woman. He painted the scene, over and over, yearning for it.

The one that got away, maybe, Reed thought.

"Hey, we got something," Nat called him over and pointed to a glass cube the size of a basketball. Reed thought it was an award or a sculpture, but Nat pointed a remote at it and a holographic scene started playing within the cube. It was Gerald and Corbin, at a banquet or ceremony. The presenter handed a plaque to Gerald who opened his mouth to speak only for Corbin to step up to the podium microphone. He grabbed Gerald's hand and held it aloft with his own, a winning team. Whatever he said, made Gerald look away, his jaw grinding.

"Is there sound?"

"There should be, but I think the file is corrupted. This is an old holo-display. They made it smaller, cheaper. I bought myself one for Christmas." Nat tapped more buttons.

Another scene filled the cube. This one of Gerald and Corbin as young boys. They ran along the beach in a race trailing an older man. Reed guessed their father. They favored him with the same hair and noses. He looked back, gesturing with his arm for them to catch up. Corbin ran a close second, laughing and roughhousing his brother who was falling behind.

"Competitive," Reed muttered.

"Didn't their father die of Alzheimer's disease?" Nat asked. "I know I read that somewhere."

"Yes, in the company literature. It's what inspired them to research the field," Reed said, watching the race repeat as the scene looped within the cube.

"Imani strikes again," Imani said and high-fived Nat. "You're in, my dear." She rose out of the seat and started packing her toolkit.

Nat slid into the chair and squinted at the screen. "You gotta see this, Reed."

The file Imani opened was two images. Two sides of a postcard. The photograph depicted a house, distant and dark against a storming sky. Black sand led away to a foaming surf. A line of decrepit shacks on stilts in the foreground. Reed held up Gerald's journal. It was the same place.

"Can you tell where this is?"

Nat right clicked the photo, reading the information that popped up. "There's nothing printed on the postcard itself and the metadata doesn't have a location. I can try and do a reverse image search back at the station. Cybercrimes has a location match algorithm, but the normal consumer ones wouldn't be able to place this, I don't think. It looks too much like every other soggy place out here."

"Enjoying the weather, are we?" Reed said with a grin. "Buy a coat yet?"

"Of course, I have a coat. I've been here for years." She rolled her eyes, but she gave him a sheepish grin. "Ok, I lost it. And it's just my luck I sent out the new one for tailoring the week Seattle decides to go full fall. This cold is biting."

"Wait till it rains sleet," Reed said. He tapped on the screen. "What's on the back of the postcard?"

Nat swiped the screen and the back of the postcard slid into view. It had no address, just a couple of handwritten lines in sweeping feminine script. *Jaan, I wish we could go back to that time. I would do things so differently.* It was signed with a symbol. A triangle within a square within a circle.

"Well, that's weird." Reed studied the shapes. "I haven't seen that in any of Gerald's artwork."

"It looks . . . pagan or something," Nat said. She zoomed in on the symbol. "See how it looks like a photo of a carving?"

"Best guess?"

"Nothing off the top of my head but there're some guys in IT who might have something. A couple of them did internships with the FBI, so . . . real brainiacs. If I bribe them with something caffeinated, they might be able to point us in the right direction." Nat stood, stretched, and adjusted her blazer. "This is good though. We found something, right?"

"Yes, but you know what we *didn't* find? Drugs." Reed glanced around the loft, his brows knit. "This was a private place. His own twin didn't know about it. If he was doing drugs, he wouldn't need to hide them."

"The super said he never had guests. Like . . . not once."

"And we didn't find one sign of the drugs this apparently 'spiraling' man was doing?"

"More questions than answers," Nat murmured. "Which makes it more urgent I get cracking on this symbol with cybercrime."

Reed checked his smart watch. "I'll meet you back at the station."

"You have something? A lead?" She looked suspicious.

"No, just need to talk with someone. A guy I knew from before I joined the force."

"Oh yeah? Anyone interesting?"

"Well, he was interesting enough for me to arrest him."

"So . . . *not* a friend from the old neighborhood?"

"No, he was." Reed scrawled something in his leather notebook.

"Are all of your friends criminals?"

Reed chuckled. "Don't be ridiculous. Of course, not *all* of them."

"Okay, but what does your friend have to do with this mess," she said and gestured around the loft. "Is he some sort of art thief?"

"He's a thief, yes. Just not art." Reed shrugged. "He owes me a favor. A big one."

"What'd he do? Steal your car and you let him off with a warning?"

"He shot me, and I didn't kill him."

Nat looked at Reed for a beat, her expression just short of shock. "And you're going to see this guy who shot you? Now . . . with no backup?"

"Yeah, well, he also happens to be my best friend."

"Does *he* still think that?"

Reed let out a long, tired sigh. "I guess we'll see."

10

Apocalypse Cyber Café

Survival forged a different kind of relationship. The fires of fending for each other, the rages of loss, and the pressure of loyalty can mold friends into brothers. Or cast them as enemies. Reed and Coyote never could decide which they were. Sometimes they were both. Most times they were nothing to each other. And rarely, they were two forces coming together for a brother on the edge.

Reed sat in a purple velour wingchair by a fake fireplace filled with fake fire made out of an orange light, a fan, and cut up orange polyester 'flames.' The pine bough currently decorating the mantle had little Christmas lights in the shape of a drunk elf. He held tiny bottles of booze, and each bulb depicted him in various modes of drunken stupor. At the bottom of some tiny plastic stairs, teetering on a fence, with a lampshade on his head. Reed had picked out the innermost corner of the café and watched the clientele come and go from his place in the dark. He'd not seen that much black clothing outside of a funeral. Shocking pink and orange hair, piercings, and tattoos styled with argyle sweaters with brown leather oxfords. Like an English boarding school for goth kids. If dark academia was a place, it would be Apocalypse Café.

A needlessly ornate brass coffee system steamed and hissed on the far side of the counter. The fragrant brew filled the space with a warm scent that seemed to combat the cold pressing in on the windows from outside. Ceiling to floor bookshelves lined one wall, a salvage that had been a near impossible feat getting down the stairs of the decommissioned library. In hindsight they agreed they should've brought a dolly. A darkly patinaed electric candle chandelier that had come with its own cobwebs from being in an old barn for years hung over a grouping of newly covered and mismatched club chairs. Upholstering them had been hot and itchy, and one of the last times Reed remembers really laughing.

Stained glass from local artists covered most of the windows. The light streaming through the colored glass cast a rainbow of colors on the floor, the walls, the patron's faces. Not that they would notice. Their eyes were glued to the blue of their screens. They were data brokers, identity thieves, hackers and digital opportunists who came for the free encrypted data stream. But everyone knew it was a front for the speakeasy in back where Coyote took bets and moved 'evening soothers' to middle-aged tech bros.

Movement behind his right shoulder made him turn.

"Morgan Reed, as I live and breathe. Still sittin' with your back to walls and watching sightlines?" Coyote drawled. "We left Yemen years ago, my brother."

He was leaning against the side of a bookcase in the hallway leading to the bathroom. Coyote hadn't worn his jet black mohawk up and it fell over the shaved sides of his head. He wore ripped jeans held up with a spiked leather belt, pant cuffs folded up over combat boots, black long-sleeved shirt. He worked the silver ring pierced through his bottom lip as he regarded Reed with a stone face. Coyote was hidden from the café patrons by a curtain partially pulled back to hide the hallway. He held a Glock down at his thigh.

Reed rose, his gaze sliding casually from the gun. He strolled past Coyote into the hallway, yanked the curtains shut, and leaned his back on the opposite wall. "I see you heard I was looking for you."

"Didn't know which man was going to darken my doorstep. The terror of Belltown from our better days or *Detective* Reed. I figured this would work for either." Coyote shrugged. "Though I have to admit, I'm disappointed that it wasn't my rotten soldier. Those geeks out front could use a good scare."

"I'm still here," Reed murmured.

"Hence, the weapon."

Reed peered through the slit in the curtain to the café. "Someone told me you opened a while back."

"Yeah, four years ago, Morgan," Coyote said. "Thank you for stopping by in such a timely manner."

"Would you have pulled a gun then, too?"

"I didn't know what you wanted. For all I know you're settling old scores—"

"If I wanted you dead, Coyote, you'd already be missing," Reed murmured. "And I did stop by. The week you opened."

"Well, I must've been in the can because I didn't seen hide nor hair of you."

"Makes sense. You always were full of shit."

Coyote smirked and pointed his scruffy chin at Reed's scarred eye. "Butter told me he got you good, but damn. That's two Doucets now who've left their mark on your lumberjack-looking ass."

"The Doucets saved it too. More than once." Reed shoved his hands in the pockets of his suit pants. "Hence, your still beating heart."

Coyote eyed him for a moment, then slipped the gun into the back waistband of his jeans. "I heard you ran ahead of SWAT. Tried to give him a chance."

"He brought a knife to a war."

"And you didn't draw on him."

"I try not to shoot dumb kids. I don't like the nightmares."

"They know?"

Reed knew he meant outsiders. The law. Not them. He shook his head. "There's no connection between me and the Doucets anymore."

"You made sure of that."

Reed let the comment go. "Well, they won't find out about it from me."

Coyote leaned in. "And that, my old friend, is the only reason why I let you walk in here instead of hauling your ass out back for a beating."

"I'm sure you would have tried," Reed said, with a little steel in his voice. "Now, stop stirring up shit, Coyote. What's done is done, yeah?"

Coyote considered him for a few moments. Then, his face changed. The tension replaced with amusement. "Anyways, you sure cleaned up nice." He nodded with approval. "This is better for you than narcotics. Didn't recognize you toward the end of those days."

"Nineteen cases. Just as many convictions."

"Still nearly killed you." Coyote tapped his knuckle on the bookshelf behind him. "Can't let you in."

"I'm not interested in busting up bets."

"So, you're just strolling down memory lane coming here?"

Reed turned, watched the rain sliding down the window in the back exit door. "There's a bed for him. All he has to do is take it. They helped me kick."

"He's not made of the same stuff you are. Butter's weak. He likes the danger. Thinks he's a badass gangster."

"They're using him to mule."

"Morgan, you know my cousin's got a room temperature IQ. He thinks he's gonna rise in the ranks like some banger star employee." Coyote looked down at his boots, shaking his head. "Can't make him do anything. You know his mama tried. Besides, he's not here."

"I didn't come here to drag him to treatment," Reed said. "No one could help me when I didn't want it."

"I remember." Coyote tilted his head, looking at Reed with interest. "What *can* I do for you then, Detective Reed? That's what you're going with now, isn't it? And more importantly, do you have a warrant?"

"I just have a few questions."

"And I'll have my lawyer answer them."

"Oh, it's like that, now?"

"Hey, the law is the law. Even if he did date my sister."

"Stop screwing around. This is more important than your little side hustle."

Coyote crossed his arms over his chest. "Why'd you really come here, then?"

"I got a dead girl, a freshman. Maggie. She was eighteen years old and died in a suspiciously staged suicide. Her death is possibly connected to a murdered tech genius." Reed paused, thinking. "I can't prove they're connected. But I know they are. I can feel it in my bones, man. I can't let it go."

"Well, you were a lot of things back in the day, Morgan, but you were rarely wrong. You know that. But I fail to see what I can do about it."

"I have suspicions that I think you might be able to confirm."

Coyote thought about it for a moment and then made a come here motion with his index and middle finger. "Get in here. You look like you could use a meal. A real one. Not that take-out shit you probably eat every day."

He moved a book on the shelf, passed a security card over the reading eye, and a hydraulic lock released with a hiss. The bookshelf swung out revealing a doorway leading into a purple lit bar. Reed followed Coyote into the speakeasy, past the three-stool bar and five of the smallest booths he had ever seen. All that could fit in the small space the size of a train car. Though the boarding school vibe stayed true throughout with mounted deer heads, tacked up scrolls, and for some reason, Scottish tartans stapled to the wall. Music blared, Coltrane, Reed thought. One woman sat at the bar. Shoulder length red hair, fair and freckled skin, soft cat eye makeup. She was reading a book, sipping a chardonnay, and pretending they weren't there.

At the end of the room, Coyote slipped into the last booth. "Who're you huntin' then?"

Reed took the bench opposite and leaned on his forearms. "What do you know about Neurogen Bionics? The Price Twins, specifically?"

"That guy on the news streams? I wondered if you landed that case."

"Tech is your wheelhouse, isn't it? What do you know about them? Personally, bad habits, bad blood, bad decisions. I need to know what's not in their prospectus."

"I know they're hemorrhaging cash. Or were. Some kind of deal was in the works, but word is it hit a snag." Coyote's specialty was insider information. The tech bros he served, paid in more than crypto currency to hide their drug habits. He bought and sold for third parties like a hedge fund manager. A broker for criminals not big enough to buy a real one's silence. It was like gambling to him. "I heard the smart brother took himself out."

"Does that change things? Financially?"

"Can't y'all look that up on your own?" Coyote raised a brow. "Or is this another one of your side projects? Is that how you got your face hacked up?"

Reed rubbed at the scab on his neck. "I got a warning to back off last night."

"And, of course, you're doubling down." Coyote shook his head. "Is it a murder?"

"Like I said, it's a suicide right now. Someone with pull is trying to keep it that way. I can't get a warrant for the financial stuff."

"Are you saying it wasn't?"

"I'm looking into it. Let's leave it at that."

Coyote clicked his tongue. "The vagaries of the right side of the law."

"What'd you hear?" Reed sat back when the bartender set a bowl of crawfish étouffée and a lemonade in front of him. The stew was thick and rich, and he ate it while watching Coyote wrestle with himself internally.

Finally, he sighed and shook his head. "Alright, look. I heard the Price Twins were struggling. They suffered some sort of setback in research. I'm not lying when I tell you the whole ordeal sent my tracking algorithm into a frenzy. I think they were going to do an initial public offering soon."

"An IPO? The brother didn't mention that."

"Did he mention the fight they had?"

"No . . ."

"You know I have, uh, operatives, inside key player's homes."

Reed nodded. "You pay off maids and cooks."

"You make is sound so tawdry." Coyote looked genuinely insulted. "The familial home is where Corbin likes to entertain clients. And he's been doing it a lot lately. I hear he's been trolling for cash to stay afloat. And some say from the kind of partners where profit or perish is the only game. Dark money. Though I could not ascertain if it was foreign or domestic."

"So, they were in trouble. Was there a rift?"

"A helpful birdy told me contractors had to be called in before a dinner party to patch up holes in the walls, grind out some marble tiles, get blood out of a hallway carpet." Coyote sat back with shrug. "Then again, that's brothers for you."

Reed finished off the étouffée and pushed the bowl away. "I don't suppose you know what the fight was about."

"What do partners always fight about?"

"Cash, control, or corruption."

"Or all three."

Reed's brows shot up. "You're sure?"

"As sure as the dawn," Coyote said with a crooked smile. "Word is Neurogen is either set to go stratospheric or implode. Not sure what's happening now that the smart brother is gone. The weasely one is scrambling from what I hear. Their numbers are volatile right now, but it could go either way. You can buy brains to work for you. But, the surviving brother, Corbin, I think it is . . . he is definitely on a tightrope over lava."

"Not what he says."

"Would you expose your underbelly to a cop?"

Reed sipped the lemonade, thinking. "No. I guess I wouldn't." A text came in; Nat telling him they figured out what the symbol was from the postcard. "I need a favor."

"That's new. Morgan Reed asking for help?"

"It's not for me." He rapped his knuckles on the table, slid out, and looked down at the oldest friend he had. "I'll call you later with details. And you know I was never here, right?"

"Never heard of ya," Coyote said and then a shadow of worry darkened his eyes. "If someone is sending you warnings, maybe back off just this once? Some would say to let the rich eat their own."

"This isn't the old neighborhood anymore. I can't just turn my back."

"Well, at the very least, watch it. Especially with bodies dropping. One of these days those bullets aren't going to miss," Coyote called after him as Reed walked away.

He picked up Nat's call as he left the café heading to his car.

"Oh my god, Reed, where are you?" Nat blurted. "We found something."

"Good or bad?"

"It's straight up, weird."

"Weird, how?"

"I think we just fell down a very dark, very deep rabbit hole."

11

NW Precinct Station
8 p.m.

Reed hit the station on his way back from Coyote's. The homicide floor was slowing down for the day. A few guys had left to catch dinner. Another had a lead and was going to go home after. He looked for Nat and was just about to call her when a message popped up on his phone. She was on the sixth floor, Cybercrime Division.

Though not as secure as the Technology Tower, Reed still had to get a new identification card to walk around on the locked floor. Nat met him at the security counter, her face lit up with excitement.

"What do you know about alchemy?" She asked and led him down the hallway while swiping on her tablet. Several closed doors lined the corridor, all with metal mesh embedded windows. It looked like a high-tech psychiatric ward, and it gave Reed the creeps.

"It's an ancient philosophy, right? Greek or something? That's all I've got," he said.

"Yeah, no, you're basically right. They practiced philosophy but also protoscience, which is where we get the whole, 'changing lead into gold' thing. *But* they had a penchant for using this cryptic language." She tilted the tablet for him to see as they walked. "That symbol on the postcard we found in Gerald's art studio? The triangle within a square within a circle? We found it in an alchemic codex."

"You're kidding."

"Wild, right?" They stopped at the door and Nat typed an alphanumerical code on the embedded screen. She pushed on the door bar, looking up at him. "The symbol is called Petraeus. And get this, it means eternal life."

Reed furrowed his brows. "Eternal life?"

"Sorta ironic with all the bodies dropping, isn't it?"

He followed her into the bullpen of the Cybercrime Division. Set up markedly different from other department floors, this one looked more like a flight deck than an office space. In addition to the standard wall monitors, each workstation had a half circle monitor screen that nearly encompassed the person at the desk. A woman in a booth wore VR goggles and swung her arms from side to side like she was drawing or manipulating her virtual environment while dictating notes.

They stopped in front of a display wall that two other people were working on. Imani, the IT Tech he'd met earlier, and another detective from cybercrime whom he didn't know. They turned as Nat and Reed walked up.

"I heard you found something interesting, Detective," Reed said, shaking their hands. "We're veering into the occult now?"

"It's Alice Conroy," the detective said as she pulled down an image and zoomed in for Reed. She had crinkles at the corners of her eyes like she laughed a lot. Tall and lithe, her blonde hair had the faintest wash of green at the ends from too much chlorine. A swimmer, Reed thought. "You guys caught an interesting one."

The image compared a high-resolution image of the symbol on the postcard to the one from the codex. They were the same.

Reed rubbed his forehead. "So, Gerald takes the time to encrypt this postcard. Was it real? Is this a photo of an actual postcard?"

"Yeah, originally. In fact, I'm pretty sure this postcard was sitting on the surface of that rolltop desk in Gerald's loft." Nat ran her fingertips along the display screen. "I recognize the nick in the grain."

Reed peered at the photo. "The photo of the beach is nothing special, right? You checked it for, what is that . . . stegosaur—"

"I think you mean steganography," Alice said with a smirk. "And no, we didn't find any hidden data or information encoded in the image."

"I had a handwriting guy take a look while you were gone. The hand-written script is likely female writing. And I ran the two lines the sender wrote. No notable poems or lyrics match," Nat said.

Alice nodded in agreement. "We're also thinking that the sentiment isn't why he took such care to secure it."

"So, we're left with the symbol." Reed rubbed the scar in his eyebrow with his thumb. This was taking a left turn. "What'd you find out about it?"

Alice swiped the images away with her palm and pulled a file down from the edge of the display screen. Black text boxes flashed and disappeared, and then a three-dimensional spiderweb appeared. Its strands stretched out in all directions making a cocoon network of interconnected points on a 3D grid. "We ran the symbol and any mention of the name Petraeus, other references, etc. through our crawler."

"That's the AI that we use for deep dive information scraping. It goes through government sites, public domain, everything. It also hits the histor-ical archives, The Wayback Machine, digital archives, etc." Nat explained. "We also hit the Deep Web, so content not indexed by the standard search engines. Things behind paywalls, log in screens, web forums . . . stuff like that.

"Whatever we're authorized to do without a warrant, of course," Alice added.

Nat snapped her fingers. "Oh, and we ran specialized software, configu-rations, and authorizations to access the overlay networks, too."

"I knew some of that," Reed said.

"The Dark Web," Nat said.

"Tell me something popped."

"A little sliver of a crumb. But yes," Alice said with a smile. "So, Google Dorking is basically an advanced search strategy where we use specialized query techniques to look for specific things like file types, data ranges, and information not normally available with a standard search. You can find things like unsecure files, etc."

"Hacking," Reed shrugged. "You're hacking."

"We're exploiting gaps in coverage," Nat said. "You'd be amazed what people forget to secure. Lists of active firewalls, backup document files, restore points, texting logs. Tons of sensitive stuff."

"And it's just . . . there? Anyone can access it?"

"I mean, you have to be seeking these vulnerabilities out deliberately. And you gotta know how to phrase the query, but yes, these files are unsecured, likely forgotten, or the users don't realize they have to deal with them," Nat said. "Think of it like we're conducting a search of a house, and these are the things left open in a room long forgotten. They aren't secured papers. They're just lying around. The owner doesn't ever remember them. But, the law says, if we find the room and the files are in plain sight, we can look at them."

"Splitting hairs," Reed said, unsettled and wondering what his vulnerabilities were.

"Still legal," Nat said with a shrug. "Anyway, we ran a specialized search binding several key words associated with Petraeus, Seattle, Gerald Price, etc. We got a hit."

Reed was shocked. "In that roiling soup of the internet. You fished something out?"

Alice nodded. "We found a fragment of a document in a temporary file on an old forum. It looks like a user log for a digital message exchange board. Both Petraeus and Jaan are on the list."

"Jaan?" Reed flipped through his leather notebook. "Right, the postcard was addressed to Jaan."

"I looked it up," Nat said. "It's Hindu. It means, lover."

"Lover. The woman in Gerald's paintings of the beach." Reed muttered. "She wore a Bindi."

"Which I thought might make her Hindu, right?" Nat bounced on the balls of her feet. "It's them. I know it. All those paintings are of her."

"Wait, you said you found this user log on a message exchange site? You mean pre-internet bulletin boards?" Reed asked.

"Exactly," Nat said. "No one even remembers those days, let alone how people connected before websites and social media. It's a brilliant place to hide your activity. Even now."

"Petraeus was already hiding their identity and what they were up to decades ago. That can't be good." Reed said. "What was she into already in her late teens?"

"We traced the message board to a cache of backup data files, also unsecure, stored in a University of Washington archive server," Nat said. "Guess who also went there twenty-five years ago? And took classes together in the computer engineering lab?"

"I'm guessing Gerald Price . . . Jaan."

"The one and only," Nat said.

"And we also found some pieces of an exchange, though it's with someone else." Alice opened the documents and pointed to the text. "Looks like they were backups for individual conversations on that university forum. There's evidence of tampering, like someone was trying to corrupt or delete the data. But it is Petraeus. The same symbol. What we could restore was a back and forth with someone who keeps referring to a file and another set of numbers. We believe it's an encrypted transfer path to a secure account. It reads like a negotiation for a deal."

"You're saying Petraeus was running a digital storefront while in school?" Reed clarified. "For what? Test answers? Research papers?"

Alice shook her head. "That would've been the best-case scenario. This was a marketplace. Stolen data most likely. But, you know, there hasn't been any activity for years."

That caught his attention. "What do you mean stolen data? Company secrets?"

"Sure," Nat nodded. "Classified data for sure given the file type and end to end user encryption protocols. But this was a while ago."

Reed paced the room. He flipped through his leather notebook. To the quick line sketch he'd done of the Neurogen Bionics office. Two starkly different brothers. A struggle for control that might have come to blows. A house divided.

"I talked to someone who has his finger on the pulse of that industry. He says there was trouble between Gerald and Corbin." Reed told them what Coyote had said about the brothers' financial and personal trouble.

"Seems like the twins weren't as close as Corbin wants us to believe,"

Nat said. "You think Gerald was selling company secrets through this Petraeus woman?"

"I don't know what to think. I need more. I need a name." Reed let out a long breath. He stared at the graphic interface of the old bulletin board site. "Can we leave a message?"

Alice and Nat looked at each other and then back at him. "But they'll know we're looking for them. What if they go to ground?"

"If you're poking around, and they're that sophisticated, chances are they'll have a trigger on anything that gets close to them, right?"

"I mean, maybe. This is an old site. Like, older than me, old," Nat said.

"But they might get it?"

Alice shrugged, her gaze on the wall screen. "If she was already doing this as a college student, I'm sure she can watch her back much better by now."

"What do you want it to say?" Nat asked as she walked over to the terminal.

Reed looked around, found an empty seat, and started writing out a message. He looked up at Nat when he'd figured it out. "Say, 'Gerald is compromised. They know about what he gave you. We need to talk.'"

Nat looked at him strangely. "What are you talking about?"

"I've not seen that woman mentioned or photographed with Gerald at all. Not in the files, his social media, nothing that has come across my desk shows her anywhere in his sphere. You just said the last evidence you have of them connecting is decades ago. But he sketched her face the week he died. I'll bet a recent meeting with her dredged up old memories."

"Can I see the sketch?" Nat asked.

"I took a photo," Reed said and sent it to her tablet. He pointed out the date in the corner. "It's really stylized. You think you can do something with it?"

"Maybe," Nat said. She'd cast it to the wall screen and was already calling up filters.

Reed continued, pacing. "And if he reached out to her, it must've been for help. My source said that Neurogen Bionics was deep in trouble. The brothers were fighting, physically. Corbin was seeking funds, by any means necessary. Maybe Gerald was too. Maybe he reached out to his old friend in the data brokering business."

"That kind of desperation makes people do stupid things," Nat said, her gaze going to the cuts on Reed's face.

Alice looked from him to Nat and then yawned. "In any case, I'm going to continue with the queries. The AI is doing its thing, probably all night. I'll set it up and check in the morning."

Reed looked at Nat. "Are you staying?"

"Yeah, the break room has comfy couches. I pulled a lot of all-nighters in cybercrime so it's no problem. I'll sift through the information as it comes. If anything interesting drops, I'll call you." She looked over at him with dark circles under her eyes.

"You look exhausted."

"It's no problem. I stay here alone all the time." Nat tried to hide her fatigue with a smile.

"Yeah, that's not how partners work." Reed checked his watch. It was late. He hadn't noticed how long he'd been with Coyote. "Between the head injury query from the Virtual Depot and now this one, you'll have reams to sift through."

"Yeah, we don't really print out things on actual paper anymore—"

"I'm staying." Reed shrugged out of his suit jacket and took off his tie, tossing them on a nearby workstation. "I'll go grab us some coffee and snacks."

Reed sat up with a start, groggy. His head full of thoughts of his old neighborhood. Fighting shoulder to shoulder with Coyote in the dirt field behind the apartments. A brawl over angry words, likely Reed's. They'd walked away from the fight, but barely. Their classmates left writhing on the ground. Coyote had stolen an ice-cold soda for Reed's quickly forming black eye. It had been a hot summer evening and they'd sat on the train tracks daring each other to stay the longest when the vibrations of its approach started.

Reed watched, mesmerized, as the engine's headlight grew bigger, brighter, until it lit up his face like the sun. Louder and louder, the horn blaring through his chest. Coyote had yanked Reed off the tracks, his face full of incredulous terror. But Reed's pulse hadn't changed. Not with the rush of wind as the train passed, knocking them to the ground. Not when his friend screamed at him with wide, frightened eyes. Reed shook the sleep from his mind. He thought he'd stopped that dark dance long ago.

"Reed!" Nat waved at him from the terminal. She was sipping on a can of caffeinated juice and bouncing on the balls of her feet.

"I'm up," Reed said, pulling himself to his feet. He looked around the dimly lit cybercrime bullpen and rubbed his face with both hands, getting his bearings. He'd fallen asleep at a workstation while going over the transcript of the fragment they'd found on the university server. He checked his watch. It was three a.m. "What's going on?"

"I said she's talking to us! Get over here. At least it looks like she's going to . . ."

Reed hurried over to where she and Imani were standing near the wall display screen. A text box was open. With their message to Petraeus and cursor blinking below it. Finally, Petraeus answered.

Who is this?

Nat and Imani looked at Reed. He stared at the words, thinking. Then leaned forward and typed on the keyboard.

A friend.

How do you know Gerald?

"Are you going to tell her he's dead?" Nat asked. "If she finds out he's dead, she might disappear."

Reed blew out a long breath, then typed, *I found him. He'd shot himself.*

The indicator blinked. No incoming message. They watched it silently. Then . . .

He would never do that. He was afraid of guns. More silence and then, *I can't believe he's gone.*

Nat looked at Reed. "She didn't know."

"She must be off grid," Imani said. "Best way to hide."

Reed thought for a moment and then, *I am going to be honest with you. I'm a homicide detective. I think Gerald's suicide is suspicious and his death might possibly be linked to others. I think you're in danger too. Let me bring you in. We can protect you.*

I can take care of myself.

Reed shook his head, typing quickly. *If we found you. They can.*

The indicator blinked for almost two minutes; Reed barely breathed the whole time.

Then, a series of numbers popped up. Degrees and time. Then the connection terminated.

"I think those are coordinates," Nat said and typed them into her tablet. She cast the mapping program to the wall display and zeroed in on the location.

"I'll be damned," Reed muttered. The street view showed a dark sand beach. He tilted his head, taking in the rocky outcroppings, the arm of the peninsula. "I guess we're in it now."

12

Alki Point Peninsula, West Seattle
9 a.m.

They arrived an hour before the meet, taking measures to avoid being followed, and pulled into the parking lot of the public beach. Alki Point was far western Seattle, on the frigid Puget Sound. It had deep, almost black sand that stretched for nearly two miles. The sky was overcast with dark, low clouds that brooded over the water. Wind swept in from the tides bringing with it a frigid fog. It was the worst kind of cold. The kind that chilled to the bone. In the distance, the Seattle skyline and Olympic mountains peeked through the mist rolling onto shore. A barren, beautiful place. Somewhere to lose oneself.

Driftwood, seaweed, and other detritus from a recent storm piled up against the metal railing that separated the sand from the sidewalk and street. Reed and Nat walked along Sixty-Fifth Street past trendy condos and historical beach bungalows that overlooked the marina. Many of the buildings were in poor condition having been built in the 1860s and sporadically upgraded. But they were exquisite examples of the Arts and Crafts movement. He sketched one out as they walked past the cement grills and benches the city had peppered along the strand.

"Are you an artist or something?" Nat asked. "Because I've never seen anyone draw in their official notebook like you do."

"Me? No." A sad smile pulled at his damaged lip. "My mother was. Mostly pen and ink because it was cheap."

"And she taught you?"

"Sometimes, when it was too hard for her to talk, she'd sketch. And I could see it. Understand it."

"Her pain?" Nat asked.

"And how she loved." Reed snapped his notebook shut and put it in his pocket. "She was a complicated person."

Petraeus's coordinates led them to an old home that was further down the point than the other buildings. Past the sidewalk and street that separated the public area and marina from the private beach. The road was blocked with a single metal bar gate that looked like it hadn't been opened recently. The house itself, a once grand residence had been chopped up into four individual rental apartments. The owner had added balconies to both top floor units, but they blended well with the older design. The place was supposed to be empty according to the owner who'd spoken to them via a video call from his home in Sweden. The entire building was up for sale but kept hitting bureaucratic snags. The owner had cut power and water for the winter. But a light shone from behind the glass sliding door of one of the top units.

He nudged Nat with his elbow. "You see that?"

She nodded.

They walked up the double front door and tried the doorbell buzzer to be let in. They waited, heard nothing, and tried it again.

"This is the place, right?" Nat asked.

A thump up high pulled Reed's attention.

"Yeah, this is the place." Reed stepped back and stared straight up the façade of the building to the second floor. "Did you hear that?"

Another, louder thump. The flash of a woman's arm flailed over the balcony rail followed by a muffled scream. Reed pulled his weapon. "Something's wrong."

Nat followed suit, her face going tense. "Mitigating circumstances?"

"Call it in," Reed said and stepped back. He took a breath and rammed the door with his shoulder, crashing into the foyer, Nat behind him.

Weapons drawn; they ascended the narrow staircase leading to the second floor. The old wood planks creaked. Mold and sea air wafted to them as they moved down the corridor. Two doors on opposite sides of the hallway stood shut. Reed stilled, head tilted, listening. Nat's breathing, traffic outside, the scrape of a chair on a wood floor, an angry grunt. His head snapped to the right. There. Nat ran over, flanked the door, her back to the wall. Reed banged on the door with the side of his fist.

"Police, open up!"

Two shots slammed through the thin wood of the door. Splintered wood sliced past his face as he rolled left, to the wall on the other side of the door. He locked eyes with Nat.

"Ready?"

She nodded, her face weirdly calm. "Go."

Reed pivoted back in front of the door and kicked it open, stopping the swing back with his foot as Nat threaded into the room going left. Two people struggled on the balcony at the far end of the apartment. A tall man, masked, with a hoodie, his arms wrapped around a woman. She flailed wildly, inhuman moans ripping from her throat.

"Freeze!" Nat screamed. "Let her go!"

The man swung the woman back into the apartment by her hair, firing at Nat as the woman tumbled to the floor. Nat dove left as Reed fired back. He hit the glass sliding door, which exploded, then the man's shoulder jerked back, his gun flying over the balcony. He turned to look at Reed for a split second, before he grasped the railing with his other arm and swung himself over the top in one motion.

"What the hell?" They were two floors up. Reed ran through the shattered sliding door. The assailant dangled from the floor of the balcony, his feet a whole other story up from the ground. "Stop right there!"

"What is wrong with her?" Nat shouted.

Reed looked back into the apartment. The woman on the floor moaned with pain, eyes rolled back into her head, fingertips bloody from scratching at her own face. Her body spasmed.

"Call for a bus," Reed said, holstering his weapon. "Can you stay with her?"

Nat nodded and Reed grabbed the railing and leapt over. He dangled from the bottom of the balcony, walking hand over hand to the edge. There was a fence on the ground floor. Sturdy enough to use to get to the grass. He spotted the assailant to his right. He'd made it over to the piping attached to the wall of the house and was trying to make his way down. A bleeding arm slowed him, enough for Reed to gain ground. Reed dropped to the fence, steadied himself, and pulled his weapon, aiming up at the descending assailant.

"Don't move!"

The man dropped from the wall, firing at Reed as he fell. Reed jerked back, tumbling off the fence onto the dumpster behind it, and rolling off. He landed on his feet and scrambled back up and over the fence. The assailant was already running. Reed took off after him, tie flying in his face,

The assailant sprinted, slipping on the sandy surface, down the slanted sidewalk leading to the marina level on the other side. A group of families were gathered around sailboats, watching the owners decorate them for the annual holiday parade of boats. The assailant wasn't as fast on this terrain, Reed thought. Not like he'd been in the alley. He gained easily, cutting him off. The man veered right, jumped onto the nose of a small daysailer boat, then a rental canoe, then another. He leapt from vessel to vessel making his way across the marina. The noses dipping deep into the water and splashing back up. Reed ran parallel, keeping him in sight as he navigated the slips, angling to intercept. The man leapt back onto a floating dock and threw himself across the waterway to a parallel slip. His head swiveled, looking for Reed. But he was already flying at him from the side. Reed took him down like a linebacker and they tumbled, grappling as they rolled down the embankment onto the sand behind a cement wall. The man came up first, grabbed a hefty piece of driftwood and swung at Reed.

Reed's fists snapped up, his head ducking behind them as he rose and twisted. The blow glanced off his forearms and he cocked his arm back and punched through his shoulder, rocking the man's head back viciously. The assailant stumbled back, squared off and swung again. Reed ducked right, moving to the balls of his feet, he swung a haymaker with his left. But the assailant was ready, and he twisted, kicking with a roundhouse that sent Reed flying. Reed landed on his back; breath knocked out of him. The man leapt at him arms swinging, and landed one blow, two to Reed's face. Reed thrust with an uppercut, catching him underneath the ribs, and shot the heel of his hand up under the guy's chin. But he was faster and dodged the blow, landing another punch to Reed's gut. Growling, Reed grabbed the guy's sweatshirt with both hands and threw him up and over his shoulder, then rolled, coming up with his weapon drawn. Blood from his opened scar leaking into his eye.

"Don't!" Reed shouted. "Don't move."

The man stopped mid-lunge, hands going up, breathing hard. His gaze slid to the group of school children cresting the sidewalk ramp. They were walking toward them. The teacher chatted with the kids cheerily and they were pointing down at the boats, oblivious. Reed slipped the weapon down near his thigh, his eyes on the assailant who pulled something from his sweatshirt. The ting of metal sent the hairs on Reeds arms standing. A field knife glinted in the morning sun as the man stepped closer to the crowd of kids, his knife low, throat level. Reed glared at him, panting.

"I walk away, they walk away," the man breathed through the mask.

Reed ground his jaw but nodded. The kids walked between them. Some of the stragglers wandered the sloping sidewalk to stomp on dry leaves littering the ground. The assailant took a few steps backward, then turned and ran. Reed darted across the sidewalk, trailing the man as he ran onto the crossroad. He stopped an oncoming car.

"No!" Reed shouted, waving at the woman.

The assailant yanked her door open and threw her out. Reed aimed, his sights on the driver's side window, but a crowd ran toward the woman having seen the attack. The car did a screeching U-turn and sped away.

Reed walked back across the noise and chaos of the marina. The sound died down as he returned to the barren side of the street. With so few people around, he doubted anyone had heard the gunshots. He felt around in his mouth with his tongue. There were some rips from the punches, and he spit blood in the sand. When he got to the house, he searched underneath the balconies looking for the gun. He didn't find it in all the bushes and plants lining the area. It was thick, a small wildlife preserve area. They'd have to send in a guy with a metal detector to find anything.

The woman's unsettling shrieks made his skin crawl even from the first floor. By the time he got back to the apartment, her cries twisted his stomach. She was lashed to an oversized chair with a sweater and a belt. Her head rocked back and forth, drool extending in threads from her chin. Scratches burrowed deep red lines in her face and her gaze roved wildly. Her clothes were torn, buttons missing from her cardigan sweater, a rip in the seam of the T-shirt beneath it, yoga pants twisted on her body.

Nat stood out on the balcony talking on her phone, wind blowing her bangs all over. When she saw Reed, she ended it and walked back inside.

"Is it her?" She asked, her face pale.

Reed called up the photo of the painting from Gerald's loft on his phone. Whatever had happened to her contorted her features into a mask of insanity, but there was no mistake. The woman in the chair was Petraeus. "Yes. I think so."

"Bus is on the way." Nat crossed her arms. "Have you ever seen anything like this before?"

Reed nodded. "In narcotics, there was this guy sitting across from me at a club. He gave himself a hot shot. Fried his brain. He tried to rip off his own lips."

"Jesus, Reed," Nat said, looking at him horrified. "Next time say no."

Reed smiled at that. "You asked."

She tried to look mad, but her color was coming back. "You look like you got your ass kicked. What happened?"

"I literally got my ass kicked. Across the sand." A punch had opened up his scar and he wiped the blood out of his eye with his tie. "Something was wrong. I can't put my finger on it."

"Petraeus shouted, a low guttural sound that pulled Nat's gaze. "What did this guy do to her?"

Reed stared blankly out at the balcony. Through the shattered glass. It didn't make sense. Neither did the attack at his condo earlier.

"Why risk being seen? Why let her get to the balcony? She's a hundred pounds soaking wet. The guy I just fought would've had no trouble containing her." Reed shook his head, staring at Petraeus's spasming body.

He knelt down by the chair, peering at her scalp. She moved with awkward jerks, her head whipping as she fought with the restraints. He pulled a pen from a nearby table and used it to separate sections of her hair. "There," he motioned to Nat, who leaned in. "Do you see it?"

"A circular burn." Her eyes snapped to his. "Just like the one on Maggie and Gerald. That's proof. Gerald, Maggie, and now Petraeus all have the same injury."

"I'm going to call Tig and see what he can do to get a better look inside Gerald's head."

"You're ordering an autopsy?"

"I think it's warranted now. This whole investigation is just . . . going off the rails."

"Any idea what this guy is doing? Why kill Gerald with a gun, but not Maggie? And what was he doing with Petraeus?"

"I think . . ." Reed rubbed his face with both hands, trying to wash the nightmare away. "I think he was trying to get her over the railing. To damage the head."

"I can't even fathom . . . What the hell is going on?" Nat breathed. "I mean, is this guy some sort of serial killer?"

"That's not the worst scenario."

"What could be worse than that?"

"Crazy you can catch. It's a man with a mission who's the nightmare."

"Is that what's going on here?"

Reed wandered the living area, his mind churning. "I don't know what's going on here. Not yet."

Patrol arrived, they set up a search for the gun and then boots sounded from below when the paramedics arrived. A few minutes later, the forensics team showed up with their equipment. Reed pointed out some black scuff marks near the front door and some other things he wanted photographed. The sparse furnishings didn't help. The owner said the building was supposed to be empty, so Petraeus must have moved a few things in, but not much. Not enough to tell if they'd been disturbed.

The paramedics restrained, sedated, and carried Petraeus down to the ambulance with difficulty given her flailing. When Reed asked the paramedic what he thought her outcome was, the guy just shook his head. One of the EMT guys from the second bus, took a look at his eye.

"Uh, that BioBond stuff, once it splits, you can't glue the cut again. You need a plastic surgeon."

"And get kicked to light duty?" Reed shook his head. "I'm not letting go of this case. Not now."

"Can't you just throw on those super sticky tape thingies?" Nat asked, walking over. She cringed at his cut. "Clearly, he's not gonna go in and he can't be walking around with his forehead flapping in the wind."

Reed smirked. "Flapping in the wind?"

"Too deep," the paramedic said. "I can use the quick stitcher, though. It's not pretty, but it'll keep it closed. You'll have a more noticeable scar though."

"Do it," Reed said.

The EMT stitched him in the hallway outside the apartment. Skinny white tapes over his eyebrow covered the little black threads, but other than that, he looked decent.

A Critical Incident Supervisor arrived on scene and took Reed's statement, but it wasn't much. Baggy sweats hid the assailant's body type, the watch cap pulled down to his eyebrows and a loose neck gaiter mask obscured the rest of his face, the jawline and neck, everything. That and the blood in his eyes from the split scar had ruined a good look. He had brown eyes. That was all Reed could really say for sure.

The forensic team had set up in the room where Petraeus was attacked first. So, Reed wandered the parts of the apartment he hadn't had a chance to see after he initially cleared them. A cot and a sleeping bag. Duffel bag on the floor with clothes. Sparse toiletries. He bent down and looked through a stack of worn paperbacks she'd piled by the cot. A spartan life. A focused one.

Nat walked in and Reed pointed to the bag. "Looks like she was on the run."

"From this guy or the law? Because there's a lot of dangerous people in the world of stolen data. Connected. And the payout is enormous so to them, the stakes are worth it. Especially if she trafficked in stolen personal data. She could be mobbed up. Maybe even working for foreign actors."

"I think that's highly unlikely. I don't think she was in it for the money," Reed said.

"Why, because of this place?" Nat scoffed. "She could have an account in the Caymans for all we know."

"I doubt it." Reed stood with the books he'd found, held each one up. "I read this in college. It's about citizen's rights to monitor their government's clandestine activities." He held up another. "This one is a biography of a guy who took down his country's secret police because they were disappearing their own citizens, and this one has essays about the fight to hold countries accountable for human rights violations and protecting civil liberties. All of these are about transparency. They're about freedom of the press. And the fragment you guys pulled off the old message board. Have you read it?"

"The one on the university servers? They were negotiating safe path for transfer. That was about money."

"Yes, it was, but not a payment. The fragment mentioned a name. Champen. At first, I thought it was a company. One the guy Petraeus was talking to stole from, but it's not. It was a court case. And there were allegations of dark money influencing the judge's decisions. I think they were trying to expose or stop it."

Nat chewed the inside of her cheek, thinking. "She was a freedom fighter back in college?"

"I don't think she ever stopped. I don't think Petraeus sold corporate secrets. I think she was a whistleblower."

Nat looked around the room. "You think that's why he destroyed her equipment?"

Reed gave her a surprised look and she motioned for him to follow. In the part of the apartment that was supposed to be for a dining table, Petraeus had set up a multiple level workstation with glass monitors and other computer equipment. All of it looked damaged beyond saving. Monitors tipped over, their screens cracked, the table itself sat off kilter as if it had been shoved aside carelessly. The office chair was pushed against the far wall. Computer towers lay on the floor, the middle of the tetra cases sagged, the material melted. Inside, the hard drives were likely nothing but molten metal. All of it destroyed with something that looked like goopy acid. It still let off a haze of fumes and the forensic team had set a clear containment tent over it. The screen on the side flap displayed the collection and analyzing of the gaseous make up. Reed glanced at it but had no idea what he was looking at.

"The assailant did that? Why?"

"What do you mean, why?"

"Petraeus had something he wanted. My guess is Gerald gave it to her."

"He could have done it after he got what he wanted."

"Maybe. It just seems like there are easier ways to destroy hard drives, right?" A decorative night-light caught Reed's eye. "Why chance carrying around acid? And it wasn't a few drops. That's a lot of fluid to haul around."

"I mean, true," Nat said. "What would Gerald have on Neurogen that would interest Petraeus, then? Maybe tax evasion? Maybe their product doesn't work."

"It does. It saved Gerald from seizures, remember?" Reed stared at the night-light. It was something you'd buy for a kid. A laughing snowman with a hat and scarf. It was the only piece of décor in the apartment.

"Your informant said Corbin was looking anywhere for money to save the company, right? Maybe Gerald was too. Maybe he was selling the technology. They gotta have patents worth millions." Nat followed him. "I mean sure, she releases documents to expose corrupt governments, but maybe *this one time* she did her old boyfriend a solid. Maybe she reached out to the wrong people for him." She shook her head. "Wait . . . that doesn't explain how a college student like Maggie is involved. She didn't even go to the same school as Petraeus and Gerald. How is this guy finding them?"

"I'm not sure what brought that guy to her door, but I think we can find out." Reed stepped back from the snowman night-light and motioned for a forensic tech. When he walked over, Reed pointed to the eye. "Can you see what that is?"

"What's going on?" Nat asked.

"Does this look weird to you?"

She looked at it and shrugged. "Not really."

"Night-lights are for sleeping. You use them so you don't trip going to the bathroom in the middle of the night in a dark room."

"Well, kids do," Nat said.

"Then why is it out here?"

The tech ran an electronic reader over it. He looked at Reed. "That's a camera. A good one."

"She got him," Reed whispered. "The whole thing."

Nat stared at it, a smile forming on her lips. "Looks like Petraeus couldn't be silenced after all."

13

They had to wait for someone from digital forensics to arrive with their equipment, but there was a problem with the lidar scanner. The forensic lead argued it out over the phone with whomever was causing the problem while Reed sat brooding with a chemical ice pack to his face. Nat got impatient and made a call to Imani Jones, the tech from cybercrime, who showed up twenty minutes later.

She frowned at the Santa night-light, looked up something on her phone, then nodded. "This is definitely high-end, but it's consumer grade. Same guts as what we deal with back at the station. I can get into it."

Reed negotiated with the forensic lead and then the technicians dusted the night-light for prints, took pictures and video of the night-light in situ, and only then did they let Imani touch it. Imani had the file open on a portable screen inside fifteen minutes.

"You guys are so lucky I'm on your team," she said with a wink at Reed. "Make sure you stay on my good side."

"Absolutely," Reed said. He shot a look at Nat as Imani walked away. "She's kidding, right?"

"Yeah, no. She's not kidding," Nat said absently. Her eyes were on the screen Imani had set up on the kitchen counter. "You ready?"

Reed nodded and Nat started the recording. It was a wide view angle of the computer room. Petraeus sat at the desk facing her consoles. The blue light cast her petite form in silhouette. She was typing something on a black screen. Her white, green, and red text scrolled across the monitor. Petraeus wore headphones and she swayed as she worked, humming along to whatever was playing. She got up and walked past the camera. Green tracking squares appeared on the recording, following her as she moved, the camera software adjusting direction to keep her in frame.

"How far is the camera's range?" Reed asked.

"The snowman shape was genius," Nat said. "With the camera in one of its eyes, the head turning on a swivel was perfect for maximum coverage of the room and part of the entrance hallway."

Petraeus wandered out of range. From the angle, Reed guessed she'd gone to the kitchen. The sound of a bubbling electric kettle, pouring liquid, the ting of a metal spoon as she stirred. She reappeared in the frame and the night-light camera tracked her back to her desk.

"How far back is this?" he asked.

"Looks like a few hours before we arrived. Hold on . . ." Nat called up a navigation strip underneath the video and skipped ahead a few seconds at a time.

Petraeus swayed, got up, came back, typed, and drank all in the jerking motion of fast forward speed until something caught Reed's eye.

"Wait, what was that?"

Nat backed up the recording and played it. Petraeus had just sat down after refilling her mug, started up work again, when she stopped typing. She lifted one of the headphone speakers off her ear and stilled, listening. Then she rose and crept toward her front door. The camera followed her, green squares centering her, zooming in for distance. The wall separating the computer room from the living area and balcony contained a large archway. And when she walked to the door, the camera lost her behind the wall. A few seconds passed with the green squares centering on the chair Nat had lashed her to, then on the light switch on the wall, looking for her. She walked back from the doorway, appearing through the archway again. Petraeus seemed to relax, the tension in her shoulders letting go and she chuckled to herself, she ran her hands through her long hair.

"Come on, Prisha," she said to herself. "I think you need to take a breather—"

A figure pushed out from the other side of the arch. Dark sweat gear, tube of cloth pulled up over his neck, ears, and nose. A knit watch cap on his head. He closed the distance before she had time to scream. His gloved hand shot out and closed around Petraeus's throat pushing her back toward the front door. The camera lost them and then the assailant stumbled back into view. Petraeus screamed, angry, guttural, as she charged at him. He threw his hands up as she advanced, a curved dagger in her hand. She slashed at him, pushing him back on his heels, forcing him to defend himself. He lunged, but she ducked, and sliced at his throat from the side. He staggered, grabbing at his neck.

Petraeus ran into the computer room, lifted up a clear lid and slammed her palm down on a button. The computer screens lit up bright green and then went black. Smoke poured out from the vents of the towers, their innards glowing red hot. The assailant ran after her, but he was too late. He grabbed her by the throat again, knocking the knife from her hand, and lifting her off her feet. She clawed at his glove, gasping for air and then he threw her down onto the floor. Petraeus coughed, shaking as she glared up at him.

The man squatted down and grabbed her by her buttoned up sweater. He pulled her close, looking down at her. "You know what I'm here for."

"Good luck getting anything, asshole," she said and spit in his face.

He rose to his feet taking her small frame with him and then threw her at the console table. She went over the chair, her legs knocking it over as she hit the table full of monitors. They fell backward, onto the floor and shattered. Petraeus rolled off the table, her hand to her side. She cried out, wincing, but her face seethed with anger.

Nat sat next to Reed, her hands in fists as she glanced at the computers in disarray across from where they sat. "That bastard threw her like a ragdoll."

"At the computers," Reed muttered. "Why would he do that?"

"Because he's a violent psycho, obviously," Nat said shaking her head.

Reed's gaze flitted to the office chair pushed up against the wall. It was upright. "Why fix the chair and nothing else, though?"

Nat shrugged, her eyes on the recording.

The attacker walked to the prone woman and stood over her. "You know what I'm here for," he repeated.

Petraeus let out a crazed cackle and flipped him off. "Bite me, you jack-booted mercenary. All of you deserve what's coming to you. Everyone will know what you've been doing."

The attacker grabbed Petraeus by the sweater, cocked his arm back, and punched her. Her head snapped to the side and her body went limp. He walked her over to the overturned office chair, righted it with his other hand, and tossed her unconscious body onto it. The dagger sat in the fore-ground of the video and he walked to it, picked it up and pocketed it. He searched the floor for a couple of minutes.

"We need to tell forensics. They'll need to swab the floor where the dagger landed and the wall where she slashed him. We might get some-thing," Reed muttered.

The assailant left the computer room, walked back toward the balcony, and returned with a metal briefcase.

"That's how he got in. He climbed onto her terrace," Nat said. "Two floors up, she probably thought she was safe."

Reed looked back at the room. The attacker hadn't even tried to save anything on the hard drives. He didn't care about the computers. They're not what he was after.

The assailant opened the metal case. It released with a hiss and a vapor cloud floated out from inside. He pulled out something, a syringe and a glass ampoule full of a liquid. Petraeus moaned, her eyes fluttering open. The assailant reached back inside the case and pulled out duct tape. He used it to bind her arms to the office chair, but he pulled down her sleeve first, wrapping the tape over the material, not her skin.

Nat tugged on Reed's sleeve. "Gerald's shirt in the Virtual Depot, it had something on the sleeves near the wrist. I asked the ME to test it, but I'd bet my paycheck it's residue. Adhesive residue."

Reed nodded. "Another piece of evidence linking Gerald's death to this guy."

The assailant was talking to Petraeus, whispering. She shook her head vehemently.

"You won't get it from me," she spat.

"Who did you tell about Mercy?" He slipped something from the case. A thin piece of metal and held it in his hand like a crown. "Where will it publish?"

Petraeus laughed. "Everywhere. I have a dead man's switch. You kill me, you destroy everything."

"Think of the code to the dead man's switch," he said. "Where do you enter it? Where is the device?"

Petraeus shook her head. "I loved him with my whole heart.'

"Did he tell you that would work? Because it didn't stop me from getting what I wanted from him." He held up the syringe. "You can't hide what I want."

"He proposed," she cried, her voice hoarse. "Did you know that? But he was wealthy, privileged, a son of power. I-I wish I could go back to that time. I would have done things so differently."

"Last chance," the man said and held the syringe aloft over her thigh.

Petraeus met his gaze with defiance. "Go to hell."

He plunged the syringe into her leg, but she kicked and the metal piece went flying out of his hand. She writhed, screaming in pain, and then stopped, her body tightening into a single spasm as she arched off the chair. The assailant scrambled for the metal device, tried to get it on her head, but she convulsed, her legs, body, and head flailing uncontrollably. The awful moan turned Reed's stomach again. The man wrestled the device onto her twisting head, but his body blocked the view of the device. Petraeus keened, a long, shattering wail and then she slumped forward.

"Oh my god," Nat said and got up. "Oh my god."

Reed kept his eyes on the assailant. He removed the crown piece from Petraeus's head and then tugged on it. Reed couldn't tell what he was doing. The man discarded the device into the case but kept something in his hand. It was small. Reed tried to rewind and see it, but it wasn't visible from the camera's angle. Nat wandered back over, beads of sweat on the top of her lip.

"You okay?'

"I'm okay," she murmured. "What's he doing now?'

"It looks like he removed something from the main piece he put on her head."

The man squatted in front of the metal case, his hands working on something inside. Then he pulled out what looked like an injector pen. Like the kind used for epinephrine, only this time he drew not from a vial, but a metal disk. Three pinpoint indicator lights lined the metal rim around the base of the injector pen. They flickered white. Reed squinted at them. Then the assailant stood, paced a bit, leaned back against the wall, and shook his head.

"It's like he's trying to talk himself down or something," Nat said, her face a mask of disgust as she looked at the man.

"Or *into* something," Reed muttered.

The man looked up at the ceiling, took another breath, and jabbed the needle into his neck, the plunger depressing even as his own moan left his lips. He fell to his knees, his head in his hands, moaning, and then his head whipped back, eyes rolling until all you could see were the veiny whites. His body contorted, and he arched, his head almost touching the wall behind him. Reed watched with growing dread as the man rose and walked with wooden stiffness as if sleepwalking. He bumped into walls, grabbed at thin air, and then his hands went to his throat. He backed up as if pushed. Slamming his back against the wall. Then he swung with his hand, coughing, gasping as if released from a chokehold.

"What the hell is going on?" Nat asked.

Reed didn't answer. The man rocked back and forth on his feet, and then a low, mournful groan escaped his lips. He screamed, long and loud and full of anguish and then he stumbled back against the wall, slid down, and sat on the floor. The man panted, his nose bloody when he looked up and the camera caught his crystal-clear gaze. He got up, stumbled a bit but went back into Petraeus's room. He was gone for a moment, the camera losing him. And then he walked back into frame.

Petraeus, still in the chair, stirred. Her breath came in gasps. The man walked over, slit the duct tape with a folding knife, and tore the pieces from her sweater sleeve. He wadded them up and shoved them in his pocket. Then he used her dagger to cut a part of her cardigan away. He glanced at the ground next to her, bent down, and pointed or rubbed the surface with his finger. Satisfied, he stood and lifted Petraeus by her sweater. She growled, agitated, her hands clawing at her face, biting at him. He moved with her back to the front room, dragging her toward the sliding door to the balcony when he froze. His head whipped toward the door. He stretched for the metal case and came back with a gun.

Three loud bangs and then Reed's voice sounded from the recording. The man fired at the door. He grabbed the case, slammed it shut, and threw it over the balcony. A few seconds later, the door crashed open, and Nat slipped into the room, then Reed. The camera trying to track everyone with the green centering squares as the man threw Petraeus at Nat. Reed fired, and then ran toward the balcony and out of camera range.

Nat struggled to get Petraeus onto the chair and then used her sweater to tie her to the chair. Nat slipped off the belt from her own pants and used that too. Then a few minutes later, Reed returned.

"Who the hell is Mercy?" Nat stopped the recording. "You think she's another victim? Or his next one, maybe?"

"He didn't ask Petraeus *where* Mercy was, he asked *who she told* about Mercy." Reed scribbled the words in his notebook, thinking. "It doesn't sound like he's hunting for someone. It sounds like he's protecting them."

"That's all we need. More people tangled up in this mess," Nat said. "Whoever that guy is, he's a monster. I feel like I need to wash my eyes out with bleach after seeing that."

"He cut a piece of her sweater away, did you see that? I'm thinking it was a forensic countermeasure."

"Yeah, I saw it. Maybe his blood from when she sliced him?"

"That tracks. We should also check traffic cams. Just in case, but it's so secluded out here . . ." Reed muttered. "Did we find a case?"

"No, but we weren't looking for one. We didn't find the gun yet either."

"Let's update the scene supervisor. See if we can get some of our people looking for a metal briefcase as well."

Nat nodded and left him staring at the frozen recording.

Reed rewatched the recording, going over and over; the part where the assailant cut her sweater and then did something to the floor. Reed stood and went to the spot. It was discolored. A green liquid almost dried. Bending forward, he touched it with his gloved hand, brought the ends of his fingers to his nose. He pulled back at the pungent smell. A flood of memories rushed to him. Smoke drifting with the mountain wind, the roar of a transport vehicle, the red-hot rounds of a firefight slicing through the dark night. Reed looked at it for a moment, then he motioned for the tech again.

"Can I get this looked at, too?"

"Whatcha got?" Nat asked, walking back over. She took a shot of the stain with her tablet while the tech was positioning his camera.

"I used to investigate war crimes for the army," Reed said quietly, mouthing for her to follow him. They stood outside the one bedroom in the apartment, away from everyone else. "I was CID, and they had us tracking this rogue black ops team we believed were committing atrocities on civilians near the western shore of Yemen, in a city called, Al Kadhah."

"Okay . . ." Nat shifted on her feet, her brows knit. "What?"

"Stay with me," Reed said, holding up his hand and showing her the fluid on the tips of his fingers. "This smells like something called, PT7. It's an industrial grade solvent these guys were using to sanitize their kills. It degrades blood, prints, even eats through hair. And it smelled just like this. Ammonia with a weird earthy, mushroom scent. I've never come across that combo anywhere else."

"Maybe we can look up manufacturers."

"There's only one," Reed said, as he wadded up his glove and shoved it in an evidence baggie. "The US Government."

"You think the attacker was a soldier?"

"Or was trained to be one."

"There's a former military guy close to the case already. Slater." Nat wrinkled her nose. "On Corbin's orders?"

"Maybe," Reed mused. "Though what they're doing is beyond me. If they tried this on Petraeus, and Gerald has the same wound . . ."

"Then he had his own brother lobotomized?" Nat asked. "Why?"

"I think that's what Petraeus was hiding. The reason for all of this."

They wandered to Petraeus's room, and Reed stood in the center. He let his gaze travel the room. Over the surfaces, up at the light fixture, and then to the closet. Petraeus was petite, couldn't be more than five foot three. He looked around the room. There was no stepstool, no crate, nothing to stand on. She'd likely chosen a hiding place low to the ground so she could reach. Reed patted his pockets, found his mini flashlight in the interior pocket of his suit jacket, and pulled it out. He opened the closet door, shone the light along the floor, the sides, the ceiling. A pulled-up piece of the carpet near the back corner of the closet caught Reed's eye.

"See that?" He shone the light at the section of the rug and Nat, who'd come up behind him, nodded.

"I see it."

Reed leaned forward, pulled back the section of carpet and revealed a metal door the size of a safety deposit box. The door hinge was broken. The cubby it hid, empty. "She had something hidden in here."

Nat pointed to the door. "See how it's lined with mesh? That's a faraday cage. It's a shield to block electromagnetic fields. She wanted continuous coverage. Whatever was in here could send and receive signals."

"Could it be a dead-man's switch? Like Petraeus said?"

"I'd have to see it to be able to tell you. But she thought it was valuable."

"More valuable than what was on her computers." Reed stood, scratched at the scruff on his chin. "This is where she put what Gerald gave her. It was what the assailant was after. It's why he didn't care about trying to salvage her equipment."

"He turned her into a vegetable for it," Nat whispered next to him. "He fried her mind like it was nothing."

"Well, it's empty. The faraday cage. He got what he was looking for," he said and stood.

Maggie's pale face flashed behind Reed's eyes. Her blank stare as she looked unblinking up at the sky. She didn't know Petraeus or Gerald. She was too young. Yet the assailant had left the same mark on her scalp. Had done the same thing to her. Reed wondered if her mind was gone before the bastard threw her off the roof.

"If he got what he wanted, does that mean he'll stop?"

This was about more than they understood, Reed thought. He was sure of it.

"No," he said, his voice low, tired. "I think he's just getting started."

14

Reed sat on the roof of the building, boots dangling over the edge, gaze down at the asphalt below. The weather had cleared since the last time he'd been at Maggie's crime scene. Sun shards streamed down from breaks in the clouds, and he tilted his head toward the warmth as he sketched the view in his leather notebook, thinking. A stack of printed papers bound by an alligator clip sat next to him on the ledge and the sheets fluttered in the cold breeze. Students wandered to the last of their classes before Thanksgiving break, laughing, hurrying, oblivious they were walking over the spot where a classmate died. There was nothing left of Maggie's tragic end. She'd been washed away by rain.

Light footsteps on the stairs made him lift his legs up and over the ledge. He was facing the door when Nat walked onto the roof.

She spread her arms out, irritated. "What happened? I thought we were meeting back at the Virtual Depot, but they said you left before I got back. Then you text me to meet you here ASAP, but there's already an entire forensics team rolling up behind me. What is going on?"

"I had a hunch," Reed muttered. "I wanted to verify what I thought before I dragged you out here.

"Nuh-uh," Nat said walking over. "I'm your partner, right? *And* I'm supposed to be learning from you while I'm at it, too. How am I going to do that if you leave me out of your process—"

"It wasn't process. It was a gut feeling."

"Those count," Nat said, stopping in front of him. "I count those. I want to know about them."

Reed put his hands up in surrender. "Got it. To be fair, though, I did put 911 in my message . . ."

"So, what did you rile everyone up over?" Nat's gaze went to the stack of papers next to him and her expression tensed. "Oh . . . crap. You got the results of the head injury query."

"I did." Reed folded his arms. "Though the one you sent to my phone had something missing that was in the printout I requested earlier."

She took in a big sigh and blew it out of her lips, puffing out her cheeks. "I should've known you'd use actual paper."

"Why did you remove it?"

"I didn't take it out permanently. I just needed to think about it."

"What?" He shook his head, confused. "Why?"

"Because of what it would do to you. You already feel horrible for doubting her, now it turns out she may be—"

"Nope." Reed rose, walked over to her. "That's not why. At least that's not the only reason. I'm the one calling bullshit this time."

Nat chewed on her thumb nail. "Okay, look, you said Caitlyn was in a car accident. Not that she was impaled. Considering how all these other deaths are turning out to be staged, it seemed like you've been keeping secrets about this case from me since the get go."

"I didn't know."

"Yeah, uh-huh." She stared up at him with a stubborn jut to her chin. "You're trying to tell me that you, a detective first-grade, didn't know how your girlfriend died? Come on, man. I was born at night, but not *last* night."

"I didn't know . . . by choice." Reed let his head fall back and watched the puffy clouds cling to the azure sky. Then he turned and walked back to the ledge and looked out over the school, arms crossed. Nat followed and stood at the ledge next to him. Neither of them looking at each other. "I was on duty when she died. I heard it over the radio," Reed said quietly.

The flashing lights of the police cruisers at the scene when he pulled up burned behind his eyes. Rain poured, that night, muffling the light of the halogens the first responders had set up for the extraction. The roar of the jaws of life as they tore at metal rattled down Reed's spine and he shook off the memory. "When I got there, they wouldn't let me close. Tig and the others held me back. They kept saying, 'you don't want to see her like that.' They said I was in the way, so I gave them room to, you know . . . to save her. Because *of course* they were going to save her—" Reed cleared his throat. "And then she was bundled up and in the ambulance. When Tig and I got to the hospital, there'd been some sort of miscommunication because we were told she was in surgery. I wasted time going up to that floor, arguing about next of kin with the nurse, waiting for them to figure out what they could tell me, but . . ."

"She never made it to surgery." Nat nodded. "No one ever told you about her injuries?"

Reed shook his head. "Caitlyn's sister, Tabitha, she'd been in and out of jail since she was a teenager. She hates cops. She hated that her sister was one. Always said things to let her know. She certainly didn't want her to date one. When Caitlyn was pronounced, in the ER, they called her. Sanders said she showed up, almost passed out, and said she didn't want anyone to see her sister that way and barred visitors. Then she arranged for her body to be transported almost immediately. Tabitha had her cremated and had a private ceremony to which I was not invited."

"I'm sorry, Reed," Nat muttered. "I didn't know. You just seemed to glom onto this case as part of Caitlyn's conspiracy really fast. I know you're this 'case breaker' and all, but still. And then I see that she was impaled through the head—"

"I was told a piece of rebar went *through* her . . . not where. I didn't ask. Tig was right. I didn't want to think about her that way. It was obviously an accident. At the time, anyway. The report said that she hydroplaned in the rain, skidded off the road, and crashed into a construction site. Caitlyn never wore her seatbelt. A patrol cop habit, I guess. I was told she died of massive blunt force injuries. I didn't know about her . . . uh," Reed shook his head, breathing through the ache in his throat. Picked up the stack of papers, shaking it between him and Nat. "I didn't know. I'm not hiding some secret knowledge about this case. I really and truly just learned about it from this query."

Nat didn't say anything. The bun at the nape of her neck had let out long strands of wavy hair and they whirled in the wind. She stared out at the campus, her jaw working. "Your approach to investigation makes me nervous. You're so smart it makes you weird." He glanced at her with a raised brow, and she put her hand up. "You know what I mean. It's not bad. You just, throw me off balance. I pulled the file on Caitlyn from the query results because I was going to talk to Tig first, okay?"

"I'm really not that complicated, Nat. You have an issue with me, you talk to me," Reed said. "We clear?"

Nat nodded. "Yeah. We're clear." Then her face changed. "Are you okay, though. For reals?"

"I will be once I get this guy." Reed swallowed hard, looking back out at the fiery colors of the leaves below. "He did that to her, Nat. He burned her away."

"We'll hunt him down," Nat said, pulling on his sleeve and making him look at her. "He'll pay—for all of them."

"I'm glad you're so sure but," Reed shook his head. "I'm flailing in the dark. The guy's a ghost."

"We'll find him. They always slip up." She frowned at his silence and sat up on the ledge. "You gonna tell me why you're here? Why you called a forensic crew? If you need to go over the scene again, we have the Virtual Depot."

"I came here for this." Reed slipped his hand into his suit jacket pocket and pulled out an evidence baggie. He held it out in front of Nat. "I found Maggie's shoe."

She snatched it from his hand with a look of shock. "Shut up! Where?"

"After losing Petraeus's attacker and then finding Caitlyn's accident report at the station I decided to start over. I wanted to look at everything again. With all we've learned, our first impressions of everything, including Maggie's initial crime scene were wrong. We haven't known what's happening since the get go. So, I came back to the beginning. Maggie's parents are set to pack up her things soon. I wanted to walk through her dorm room one more time. Just sift through everything. Junk drawers, pockets, everything. I thought, maybe Maggie saw something she shouldn't have. Maybe she saw this Mercy the assailant was asking about do something illegal."

"And did you?" Nat asked. "Find anything?"

Reed shook his head. "No, but I found this." He took another baggie out; this one had a card on a lanyard.

"A gym pass?" Nat took the baggie, squinted at the contents. "The student athletic lounge. I don't remember seeing a gym bag with her stuff."

"There wasn't one. I thought maybe she kept her stuff in a locker there, like a rental. The manager said they didn't do that. Students brought their bags with them to shower and change. Just in case, I stopped by the lost and found."

"And found the shoe." Nat handed the baggies back. "You think she was initially attacked in the gym?"

"I think so. I called her roommate, Cara, after I found the lanyard. She said Maggie went every night almost. Usually around nine or so, when it was empty. She liked having the pool to herself."

"So, that's why you called forensics," Nat said.

"Not sure it'll do any good. I talked with the head of cleaning services. That gym is sanitized nearly every day to keep viruses down in the student population. The perfect place to compromise evidence. Like I said, the guy is good."

"Ok, but what are you thinking?" Nat pushed. "You think she was attacked either going into the pool locker room or coming out?"

Reed thought for a second. "I didn't smell chlorine on her when we found her, so I'd say before."

"The assailant attacks her in the empty gym, does the brain thingy . . ." Nat rubbed her forehead with the pads of her fingers, working it out. "And then drags her to the roof?"

"Yes. I think that's exactly what he did. If she was like Petraeus, she wouldn't be able to stand. He'd have bound her. Put her on the ground . . ." He knelt on the roof, grabbed a handful of the gray pebbles and let them fall from his hand. "The assailant would've looked to make sure no one was around first, and then tossed her over."

"The gravel . . . it got in her hair when she was on the ground up here."

Reed stood and watched a pair of students set up a picnic blanket in the one patch of sun on the grass. He went to the ledge, arms out as if carrying a tray, then pivoted toward the edge. "I think when he went to throw her over, that's when he noticed her shoe was gone. When he swung her feet over."

"So the other one had to go," Nat said, repeating Reed's words from their first meeting.

"And he couldn't find the other one or was interrupted in his search by a student or cleaning staff, so he had to get out of there."

"Where'd they find it?"

"It was behind a changing bench in the swim locker room. A student turned it in."

Nat kicked lightly at the ledge with the toe of her shoe, her brows knit. "What does this young girl have to do with a tech genius and a dark web hacker, though? I don't even think she had a single computer class. Wasn't she a political science major?"

"I was hoping you'd help with that." Reed said. "Between Caitlyn's notes, the head injury query, and the current victims, I'm missing something."

"We can grab a study room here," Nat said, hopping down and whipping the tablet out of her blazer pocket. "That way you can be on scene in case forensics finds anything and you don't have to go back to the dreaded Virtual Depot."

Reed smiled a little at that. "My brain thanks you."

They grabbed a room easily. The study hall monitor was a little miffed about them not having reserved one in advance until Nat bullied him into submission by pointing out no one studied the day they leave on vacation.

When they got there, she frowned. "They charge how much to go here and then turn around and give you a rabbit hutch to work in?"

Reed thought they were cozy. There was always a beat-up overstuffed chair in the corner, a decent sized table for books, and one time he even found that someone had left a box of free granola bars. He used to rent the rooms for finals, preferring the silence to the din of a café for studying. Reed had wrestled with philosophy like his life depended on it, even graduated with a degree. Though, he never did find any of the answers he'd been looking for.

When they were settled, Reed grabbed his stuff from the car and spread Caitlyn's papers out on the long table as well as notes he'd made. Nat fired up the wall screen and cast photos and files onto it from her tablet. They worked mostly in silence for a few hours. Reed got a call from the forensics lead and was told what he suspected. Not a lot of evidence to collect, but they'd process what they could get. He and Nat weeded through dozens of deaths, a lot of them strange, but not suspicious. Do-it-yourself tool mishaps, vehicle repair accidents, backyard stunts gone wrong. They broke for lunch, ate some vending machine sandwiches with ice-cold sodas, and started up again.

Reed went back to his notes from the Virtual Depot. He'd written down a few names during that first session with Gerald's crime scene walk-through. Flipping through his leather notebook, he tapped the page. "Remember when we first looked at the head injury results, and I pulled a few that sounded weird?" Reed asked as he stood, stretched, and tossed his napkin in the dented metal trashcan. "What was the deal with the light rail train guy? The one who got dragged?"

"Oh, yeah," Nat said, calling up the public transit system's routes on the wall screen. "Gross."

Nat's query from the Virtual Depot for head injuries had spit out Alastair Kuntz. A homeless man. Reed pulled up the report. The autopsy photos showed a middle-aged man, slightly pudgy, laid out on a metal table. He was mangled from the impact and subsequent dragging. Reed went to the written report. Alastair had thrown himself onto the tracks of the One Line just as the ten o'clock train was pulling into the Angel Lake Station. He'd not left a note and the only witness was another domestically challenged man, who gave a statement about Alastair's erratic behavior before he jumped. Patrol could not locate the witness again. The report went on to say that though Alastair was previously thought homeless, given his appearance, smell, and apparent drug use, but when they ran his prints, Alastair popped as a Canadian citizen in the US on a current travel visa.

"What did the security cameras pick up?" Reed asked.

"Nothing," Nat said, calling up photos of the site. "The extension south was delayed with bond issues so there's still a lot of construction going on there and further south. Angel Lake station is in use, but the cameras have been down for weeks. Not that it would catch anything with all the scaffolding and tarp. Notes here on a work order say the cameras were vandalized."

"Convenient find or premeditated attack point?" Reed murmured as he went back to the report. The homeless witness was described as tall, lithe, with brown eyes and covered head to toe in a watch cap, scarf over his face, and a filthy coat. When the ME ran the victim's prints, he was apparently not homeless. He lived on his boat and was a citizen of Canada down on a trip visa. Reed showed Nat Alastair's ID photo. Long greasy hair, 70s mustache, glazed look in his eyes.

She wrinkled her nose at it. "You think this guy was a victim?"

"Can you get any more information on him?"

"Why, what do you see?"

"He looked so unkept and unhealthy the first responders thought he was homeless, but the guy came over on a recent travel visa? And he wasn't emaciated. Long-term homelessness brings health issues like malnutrition and skin problems. This man has decent skin, quite a gut, and he just paid for a recent travel visa. The body doesn't fit the narrative."

"Yeah, okay. That's . . . really good." Nat nodded, her fingers flying over the virtual keys. "I'll see if Imani can find him on the lesser-known databases. Maybe call up to Canada and Interpol." She frowned, then leaned over and pointed at what Reed was looking at. It was a list of names Caitlyn had suspected were victims. "Hey, I've seen that name before, Abernathy."

Reed's eyes snapped to hers. "Where?"

"Uh," She swiped through her tablet files. "Here . . . not Iris like on Caitlyn's list, but close. Professor Rand Abernathy. Maggie took a class with him. He teaches world politics here at Seattle City College."

A student had stopped to gawk via the small door window and Reed stood, pulled down the privacy shade, and then flipped through his leather notebook. "I don't have anything on an Iris Abernathy."

"No, I saw it when I was going over Maggie's grades with the provost. Lemme look." She did a search of the usual databases, DMV, NCIC, Insurance clearinghouses, and public aggregator sites. A few minutes later, she shot a data packet over to the screen and Iris Abernathy's accident report spread across the wall display.

Reed walked over, reading aloud. "Iris Abernathy, forty-nine, victim of a hit and run."

"Oh," Nat said, pointing to her tablet. "She was married to Professor Rand Abernathy. Address on file is close to campus. The accident report says she jogged every morning around here, up in the back trails, down in the dirt roads. It's where she was killed."

Iris Abernathy had been hit by an unknown vehicle, possibly a truck or jeep from the bumper height, and her body had tumbled over the ravine to the rocky bed of a dried-out stream. Reed went over the report with a tightening knot in his gut. There had been no cameras, no witnesses, no evidence other than her body collected, and no arrests. The ME's report stated the damage to her head and body was severe. The detective investigating had suggested in his notes that she'd been run over more than once. They had to use her belongings to identify her. She was still being housed at the morgue.

"Iris had her head bashed in by a bumper," Nat said. "How much you wanna bet that was to cover up what really happened?"

"Her being married to a professor that works here could be a coincidence," Reed said, though he didn't really buy it.

"And her hubby just happens to teach another one of our victims?" Nat shook her head. "I don't think so."

"Is he still here?" He checked his phone. It was still early. "Last day of classes, he could be gone."

"But he's not," Nat said and flipped her tablet to show Reed. "He has one more class, it's going on right now."

Gathering his things, he shot her a hopeful grin. "What do you say we crash the good professor's class?"

15

Political Science Building

Reed and Nat stopped by the gym while they waited for the professor's class to end. He handed in the evidence he'd found to forensics and sent over the photographs he'd taken with his phone while waiting for them to arrive. He talked to the forensics lead, Marisol Pena, the straight-laced right hand of the ME, who explained how her team had scoured the place, but the school had suffered a series of rampant flu strains moving through the student population. The board voted to hire extra help with cleaning. She pointed to the mist-spray sanitizing bot in the corner. That and a few of the little shoe-box sized floor scrubbers had effectively decimated any evidence the killer might have left behind.

There was an update on the swabs of the floor and wall at Petraeus's place. The lab had been able to confirm the presence of the PT7 solvent and because it was used, the samples they'd taken of the walls and floor were too degraded to be usable. Still no metal case and gun, though patrol reported crushed vegetation around the side of the building when they searched. They figured the assailant might have already doubled back. Disappointed but not surprised, Reed and Nat headed to the Political Science Building.

They found Professor Abernathy in the large amphitheater lecture hall as his students were leaving. He stood on a raised dais centered at the bottom of tiered rows of seats. A large projection screen behind him displayed scenes from a rally.

"Detectives, right?" He called up to them as they descended the stairs between the rows toward him. "I thought you were here to tell me you'd found the guy, but that's not what your faces are saying."

Abernathy was short, soft around the middle, and had a friar tuck halo of hair that was gray. He wore a sweater with actual elbow patches and brown slacks. Metal spectacles sat on the edge of his veiny nose, and he looked over them at Nat and Reed as they approached. Abernathy leaned on the lecture podium and frowned. "How can she be run down in broad daylight, and no one gets arrested? There're tons of joggers out there usually. I even paid for a phone bank, but no useable tips came in." He looked from Nat to Reed. "Has no one come forward?"

Reed shook his head. "I went over the accident scene and the surrounding areas. No cameras, undeveloped land that's pretty rough. Did Iris usually run there alone?"

"Yes, she loved the terrain. She did cross-country in college and said navigating the natural landscape helped her clear her head of stress." Abernathy pushed his glasses up on his nose, looked at Reed earnestly. "Did you find something out there? Is that why you're here?"

"That's what we wanted to talk to you about." Reed dug through his phone for a photo. "We think your wife's accident may be linked to others."

Abernathy straightened up. "Oh? I haven't heard from the other detective in over two weeks. Now there's a conspiracy?"

Nat held up her tablet and showed him a photo of Petraeus. She'd had the nurses send it to her from the hospital. "Have you seen this person before, professor?"

"Oh my god, what happened to her face?" Abernathy reared back dramatically, then squinted at the picture. "Wait a second. Is she dead?"

"No," Reed said. "And the scratches . . . she did that."

"Jesus." Abernathy shivered like a ghost had walked through him.

"You're sure you've never seen her before?" Nat asked.

"No, I mean, I don't think so."

Reed showed him a photo of Maggie. One taken from her college ID. "How about this student?"

"That's the student who just . . ." Abernathy trailed off. "I looked her name up when I heard. It sounded familiar. Apparently, she took one of my classes last semester."

"Did you know her?" Nat asked.

"I wracked my mind trying to remember any kind of interaction with her, but I don't think we ever spoke." Abernathy gestured at the hundreds of empty seats. "Thousands of students every year attend my lectures. I don't interact with students on a personal level enough to know if they're in trouble. Especially if they don't sign up for office hours."

"We're not ruling Maggie's death a suicide just yet," Reed said. "She's one of the possible victims who may be connected to your wife."

"Really? How bizarre," Abernathy pursed his lips. "What do you think these women have to do with Iris?"

"We're not sure," Reed said. "I'm going back, talking to witnesses and family, seeing if anything occurred to you since you were last questioned."

"I suppose that's thorough." Abernathy pulled on his earlobe. "Unless it means you have no leads at all."

Reed smiled, the professor was smart. "Was your wife upset at all before her death? Did she seem troubled?"

Abernathy sighed heavily. "No, in fact things were looking up."

"What about any weird calls or threats," Nat asked.

"Uh, I don't think so—"

"Wait, what do you mean?" Reed pushed. "What was going on before things 'started looking up?'"

Abernathy stood back, crossed his arms. "Nothing serious. She'd been an adjunct professor in this department for a few years, but she wasn't happy."

"Why?" Reed asked. "What happened?"

"Nothing, she just wasn't—"

"Your house is here. You work here. She jogged here . . . had friends," Reed ticked off with his fingers. "But she left for no reason? Come on, professor."

"What, did she mess around with someone?" Nat asked. "Was she getting sexually harassed?"

"No, nothing like that!"

"Then tell us why she left, professor," Reed pressed. "Don't you want to know what happened to your wife?"

"Too much controversy, alright?" he snapped. "Her lectures drew criticism."

"Over what?" Nat asked. "Office politics?"

"No, no. Iris was diplomatic, social. She got along with everyone here." Abernathy looked out at the seats, up to the open doors at the top of the auditorium that students used to enter from the upper campus. "Her field was more suited to less . . . idealistic minds."

"What were her lectures about?" Reed asked.

Abernathy gathered his folders from the podium and motioned for them to follow him out of the door behind the dais. It led into a hallway, and they walked with him to his office. Anemic attempts at holiday decoration were taped to the walls. A paper turkey dressed as a pilgrim, some fall leaves in a windblown pattern, ears of corn. Someone had left mini pumpkin muffins on a snack table in an alcove, and they smelled sickly sweet. Reed plucked one from the tray, peeled it, and popped it in his mouth. It tasted like it smelled. He ate it anyway.

Abernathy unlocked his door and let them in. It was a small office, but smartly appointed. His shelves were filled with books, piles of papers, and mementos from around the world. Reed's gaze traveled the wooden masks, ceramic bowls, and woven baskets. They were all labeled with the place, people, or site associated with them.

The professor waved his hand at the one chair in front of his desk. Neither Reed nor Nat took the seat. "A few years ago, Iris started doing some work for a think-tank out in King's County, Briar Ridge Solutions. She holds . . . uh, held a masters in geology and did some research and analysis for them on one of their mineral rights projects. They offered her a job last year and she took it."

"You're saying she left for a paycheck?" Nat asked.

"No, not really," Abernathy murmured. He fiddled with a paperweight of a beetle trapped in resin. "She had a lot of student activists, environmental types, writing the dean and demanding her resignation over some controversial papers she wrote."

"A controversial geologist?" Nat asked, her brow raised. "How'd she manage that?"

"Her papers were about rare earth metals and how they're the silk of the next millennia. She encouraged, among other things, mining for Lithium and other rare earth metals in other countries and our own. I told her to tone it down," Abernathy said. He sighed heavily. "But Iris wasn't one to back down. Eventually, a student environmental group discovered her ties to Briar Ridge, which was apparently on some list of companies most dangerous to the environment. There was a protest outside her office. A sit-in. Her car was vandalized multiple times with pig's blood. She tried to shrug it off, but then someone followed her to her car one night. That terrified her, though she said it didn't. She took the job at Briar Ridge a couple of weeks later."

"And that was . . . ?" Nat asked.

"A year ago, in December. She left at the end of her semester contract."

Reed wrote the dates in his notebook to check later. "After she left, were there any more incidents of people threatening her?"

"No one ever threatened her directly. No letters or messages. Just general anger. It's why I was reluctant to tell you. A group of kids with painted poster boards and a megaphone caused a ruckus. Nothing more." His gaze slid from Reed's at that last part. He was lying.

Reed took a tusk or horn off its stand on a nearby shelf and looked into the hollow end. "If I talk to security. Are they going to tell me the same thing?"

Abernathy watched him play with the piece, his face tense, but didn't protest. Instead, he said, "Look, she was gone almost a year when the other thing happened." Abernathy paused, realizing he'd said too much.

"The other thing?"

"No, I . . ." Abernathy blanched. "I misspoke."

Reed just stared silently.

Abernathy chewed his inner cheek for a few moments, then sighed.

"Ok, a semester ago, my guest lecturer got the flu and cancelled at the last minute. Since it was a world policy symposium, I asked Iris to do a guest lecture on the nexus of minerals and technology. One of the attendees stood up in his seat and burst out into a tirade about the environment and the earth, or something. He had to be escorted out."

"Was he arrested?" Nat asked, pulling her tablet from her blazer. "You know his name?"

"No, he wasn't. The security guard said he'd calmed down quickly so they let him go. And no, I don't know his name. Those symposiums are open invite. Anyone, even nonstudents can attend." Abernathy took off his glasses and used his sweater to clean them. "Nothing personal happened there either. The man was angry at policy not Iris, really. It's not relevant."

Reed took a turn around the professor's office. Framed photos of him with students at a display booth, cleaning up a highway, at a protest when Abernathy still had hair. *Groups, clubs, the social strata of college*, Reed thought. He slid into the chair in front of the desk and looked up at the professor.

"This young man, the one who interrupted your wife's lecture, was he associated with any particular environmental group? Did he say a slogan or have a T-shirt with a logo on it?"

Abernathy shook his head. "I don't think so."

"What about Restoration Republic?" Reed asked. "Have you heard of them?"

The professor's face tensed. "What do they have to do with anything?"

"You've heard of them?" Nat asked from the window. She was typing on her tablet. "Because I can't find anything about them on the school website."

"They're not an officially sanctioned club, but that doesn't seem to stop them from meeting here. It's small, started by students, I believe, but growing. I hear it's becoming a local grassroots movement. I think they're conservationists or something. Maybe political? They've gotten into some shoving matches with other gatherings around campus. They love to counter-protest and cause problems, especially for faculty they don't like. They shut down the Mars Project festival over at the science pavilion with their antics. Space . . . they protested space!" Abernathy's brow wrinkled as he spoke, he gestured with his hands as if lecturing. "They launch targeted attacks to email servers, excoriate teachers via social media, one professor was doxed. His address given out and *that night*, his house was vandalized. They sit in the hallways blocking students from getting to class. Horrible. Which is why I asked the FBI Agent investigating them to keep my name out of his report."

Reed looked at Nat. She was as confused as he was.

"You spoke to the FBI recently?" Nat asked. "When?"

"I don't know. Before Iris's death. He said he was investigating that group, the Restoration Republic, because they'd called in some bomb threats during a campus meeting or something. It ended up being a prank. He wanted to know if they'd given me any trouble. I said no, thank god. No one wants to be targeted by organized teenagers with time and laptops."

"That's it? That's all he asked?" Nat asked, a doubtful look on her face. "Not really an 'investigation', per se."

"Well, yeah," Abernathy looked puzzled. "I guess I was the one who did most of the talking to be honest."

"That's a good interrogator," Reed said. "What did you tell him?"

"It was weird. We somehow got into my years in Afghanistan. I worked as a contractor for the Department of Defense a few years before the pull-out. What was that, almost fifteen years ago? Maybe more?" Abernathy pulled out his chair and sank into it. "I worked with interpreters there. Terrible what happened to our allies when we left."

"Did the agent say why he thought talking about your time there was important?" Reed asked.

"No, I think he was listening out of courtesy," Abernathy mused, chewing on the arm of his glasses, thinking back. "He'd mentioned the student who called in the prank bomb threat might have attended my classes and lectures in the past, but he wasn't quite sure of the name. Farad or Firash, maybe." Abernathy snapped his fingers. "I remember now. The name launched me into my time in Afghanistan because it reminded me of a student I had a few years ago. Now, Firash is a common name in the middle east, but *two* young men, causing issues in the same department?"

"What did the Firash who was your student do?" Nat asked. "And do you remember his last name?"

"Mmm, I don't know about a last name, I'll have to look that up." Abernathy bent over, pulled out a desk drawer, and rifled through some files at the very back. "No . . . three to four years ago would be in storage at my house."

"We'd appreciate it if you could look," Reed said. "What did this student do, specifically?"

"He was a smart kid. I think he was a STEM major. He didn't need help understanding the material and he wasn't behind, so I was surprised to see his name on my appointment list. But he didn't want help. Firash showed up already upset. All he would talk about was the US pullout from Afghanistan. How it went sideways." Abernathy shrugged. "I understood. He said his family was there during that time. I thought he just wanted to vent. But then he started trying to get me to go into detail about my time there. I don't know how he found out about my work, but I told him details of my job there was not for public consumption. A lot of what we did there was and remains classified."

Nat looked up from her tablet. "And the agent seemed interested in this former student from a few years ago?"

Abernathy nodded. "He seemed to be. I think it's because I told him the student got more and more vocal about his displeasure with how the situation was handled. Other students started to snap back, tell him to be quiet . . . I thought I was going to have to speak to administration and have him removed from my roster, but he stopped attending."

"Firash?" Reed asked. "Do you think you could sift through your files at home in storage, maybe look for his last name?"

Abernathy frowned. "I don't understand. This student attended my course a few years ago, which I told the agent as well. What does any of this have to do with Iris's case now?"

"With the school administrative offices out for the holiday, we'd have to wait at least until Monday, and we need this name now. Even if just to rule him out," Reed hedged. "This man, the one who protested during your wife's lecture recently, could he be this former student? If it was three years ago, couldn't he be senior here?"

"Maybe you didn't recognize him after three years," Nat said.

"Possibly. These kids change so much in four years." Abernathy looked past Reed's shoulder to his bookshelf, thinking. "My student was angry with the US for our middle eastern politics, from almost two decades ago. The man heckling my wife, was angry about the environment, if I recall. He yelled some vulgar terms about how we're treating the planet. Do you think they're connected?"

"The agent certainly seemed to think so," Nat murmured.

Reed caught her gaze. He agreed.

"So, you do think they're connected?" Abernathy asked them.

"We just need the name for now, professor," Reed said.

Abernathy was smart, knew he and Nat were keeping information from him. A flush crept its way up the man's neck, his cheeks. He was getting upset.

"Please, detectives, do you think this student, this man hurt my Iris?"

"We're still investigating," Nat said evenly.

"Are you? Because your whole purpose for being here seems to be about everyone *but* Iris. What is going on? I demand you tell me something other than these evasive answers! I can't—" He stood at his desk, his chest heaving, eyes going wet. "What do I tell her family? It's the holidays . . ."

"Being in the dark about someone you love is torture. I-I know this." Reed's voice sounded gravely, and he stood and faced the grieving professor. "All we can do is our best to understand what happened and make those responsible answer for what they did. We need your insights, Professor. So, please try to answer our questions the best you can, alright?"

Abernathy nodded, he pulled a wadded-up handkerchief from his sweater pocket and wiped his eyes. "No, of course. I get that. I do."

"I know you've not had answers for weeks. But we're here now. And even though they don't make sense at first, asking you these questions *will help*. I don't know how, but they will. It's how these things always seem to go," Reed said.

Abernathy tugged on the hem of his sweater, getting himself back together. "I don't know, if this Firash individual the agent was asking about is the same person as my student from years ago. That would be like you showing up looking for a guy named John. And there happens to be another guy named John who also got upset here, but years ago. The odds are . . . well, a lot that they aren't."

"But hypothetically, say . . ." Nat urged Abernathy.

"It is possible, timewise. He would've been a freshman in my class at the time. World Politics is a required undergraduate course for that grade. Iris had her encounter with the heckler at her lecture a few months ago. Last semester. With three years in between. I'd say he could be maybe twenty-three or twenty-four. Older if he didn't enroll immediately after high school, which I sort of get the sense my Firash was. A little delayed."

"Some people take a gap year," Nat offered.

"No, this young man did not have money. He had one of those food assistance cards they give to kids on scholarship here. I saw it dangling from his bag on a lanyard. It keeps them from eating instant ramen noodles for four years. If he started late, it wasn't because he was traipsing around Europe finding himself."

Reed looked at the professor, thinking. He was *almost* catching a wisp of something but, it kept eluding him. His gaze settled on Nat. He gave her a look. Anything? She shook her head.

"Alright. Thank you for your time, professor," Reed said. "And I'm sorry for your loss." They rose and headed for the door, but Reed turned back. "Do you remember the agent's name? Did he leave a card?"

"No, he didn't, but . . ." Abernathy rooted around his desk. "I wrote down his name. Along with his number"

"Can I have it?" Nat said, already walking back in and activating her tablet's camera.

Abernathy set the note on the desk for her to photograph. He looked at Reed. "The number doesn't work. I called it to tell him that Iris . . ." he shook his head. "Anyway, it is out of order. I called the main office and asked for them to look him up, but Johnson is apparently a very common name for agents in the FBI."

"Do you happen to remember what he looked like?" Reed asked?

"Just, average. Brown hair, brown eyes, tall," Abernathy said with a shrug.

They thanked him. Talking as they walked across the parking lot to the car. Nat swung the car fob in her hand. "An older guy. Didn't Maggie's roommate say she was seeing an older man?"

"She hid it," Reed said. "She was eighteen, from a small town, close family, given the interview I had with them earlier. That's an age gap of six years, possibly more. Maybe she was afraid her parents wouldn't like her seeing someone so much older."

Nat's face twisted into a frown. "Or maybe her mystery man was trouble. That'd be a good reason to hide the relationship and his name even from her roommate."

Reed fought with the chilly wind as he tried to jot down his thoughts in his notebook. Cheery Christmas lights flickered from the tree in the quad. "What do you mean?"

"I was following up on information about Maggie's activities that we got from our interviews with her parents, the provost, and Cara. She was in the Madrigals, a school singing group. I found that. She was also in the drama club. I found her in the official club photo. But, I couldn't find the student group the provost mentioned she was in because it's not an official campus club. I was scouring the college website when it was just a Google search away. What a rookie mistake."

She tilted her tablet to show Reed the Restoration Republic website. It was a cheap build done on a free hosting site. There was one page, and it was all climate crisis and extreme solutions. Photos of flooded cities in India and Pakistan, dried out lake beds with dead fish on the shore, fires eating up the forests. Garish banners with catchy slogans touted taking back the planet by any means necessary.

"Ah, shit," Reed muttered. "Maggie was an eco-warrior?"

"Yeah, and not tree-huggers, either. These guys favor violence and vandalism to make their point."

"Her mother had said she was nervous about something. A project. I'm thinking it wouldn't be a school issue. Not during Thanksgiving break, right? She might've been planning something with this group."

Nat nodded. "Another prank? They've already done a bomb threat according to the mystery agent."

"That bothers me too. We should call the local field office and see if they sent an 'Agent Johnson' out to talk to professors."

"I'm betting he was lying. What agent doesn't hand out cards? They practically pee all over themselves showing off that shiny FBI seal. And the number was disconnected?" She clicked her tongue. "Sketchy.

Reed's stomach growled. The mini muffin had only made him hungrier. The setting sun cast a peach tint to the horizon making the hour seem later than it was. It was only five thirty but fall got darker earlier every day.

"We need to find out more about this Restoration Republic," he said. "Who runs it. What their goals are . . . If it's more than just students like Maggie. I'll put in a call to a guy I know at the ATF. If this group was implicated in a bomb threat, they might have some information on them."

"I'll see about getting a warrant for membership to the website. Maybe we'll get lucky with a last name on Firash if he's a member," Nat said. "I also shot a message over to that think tank, Briar Ridge Solutions, that hired Iris. Maybe she had a coworker or assistant we can talk to."

Her phone rang and she answered. After a few uh-huhs and some nodding, she ended the call. "That was Imani. They've been going over the night-light recording. Apparently, Petraeus spoke to herself on it, she said, 'Prisha.' Cybercrime thinks they're getting close on name for our hacker. Prisha Kapoor . . . they're pulling stuff up on her now, but she's done years of sanitizing. Since college. Also, the warrant for her files came through for the equipment they were able to save from that acid stuff. Imani thinks they may have uncovered something interesting." She looked at him, expectantly. "They could use some help."

"You want to go do your techy thing, don't you?"

"Yes."

"Okay, I'll talk with Tig about the warrants, then." Reed checked his watch. "We can hit Briar Ridge in the morning."

"Oh," she smacked his shoulder with the back of her hand. "While I'm at cybercrime, I'll start a query through our AI crawler to scrape through social media, forums, etc. for anything having to do with Restoration Republic and other activist groups active in the area around the college. I'm hoping this guy who disrupted Iris's lecture pops up, but I doubt we'd have anything useful until morning."

They got in the car and sat staring out of the windshield while Reed finished his notes. She sighed heavily, pulling his attention to her.

"Something wrong?"

"This case just keeps getting more and more convoluted. And Petraeus . . . what that guy did to her was something out of a horror show. What did all these seemingly random people get tangled up with?"

"A web," he said. "Someone out there is pulling strings and tying off loose ones. And I'd bet my right eye Maggie was caught right in the middle of it."

16

_____

He stood motionless just inside her back door, listening to the quiet of the house, slowing his mind to focus. The creak of the big tree in the backyard as the wind moved through its old branches soothed his nerves. A pink vintage refrigerator hummed in the corner. Closing the door to avoid notice by the neighbors, he locked it for good measure. He was in a small kitchen, antique aqua tile from the sixties lined the counter, wallpaper with faint outlines of roosters holding coffee cups, a white iron stove. The room smelled like lemons and ginger, he thought. Like tea or cake.

She was not home. He had watched her leave, talking loudly on her phone to her friend as she hopped into her car. There was time to search. And he needed it. The detectives, already too close, had made even more ground. Detective Reed was more formidable than he had feared. He could feel the man gaining, chewing up the space between them, bringing him to bay like a relentless hunter cornering a deer. After, it would not matter. But he had to make sure the plan was put in motion.

The living room was decorated also in the retro style. A lava lamp glowed on a small table shaped like an amoeba. Over her couch was a sunburst clock with white and blue glass fanning out from the center. Crocheted Afghan blankets stretched across the back of wingback chairs. They looked handmade, soft. Like he used to own. Pushing the thought from his mind, he moved down the hall to her room and stood at the foot of her bed, letting his eyes adjust to the dark. A bed with pillows and more blankets. A closet filled with suits, blazers, and slacks. She had mostly sensible shoes, except for a few spiked heels shoved in the back. She had framed photos of herself and what looked like her sister on a small work desk. They looked alike, anyway, the women. Same smile. His mood soured at the sight of her laughing.

He scolded himself for becoming distracted. For softening with nostalgia. He had reasons for coming here. For risking detection. Information. He looked around, let his eyes adjust to the soft light provided by the sunset outside her window. This room is where he would hide a tablet. Pulling out the drawers, he paused when he heard a sound. He listened for a few seconds, and decided it was branches scraping along her roof. Going back to work, he rifled through a basket on her dresser. There was old mail, some folders, and a few takeout receipts. No tablet.

Where would she put it? The woman detective seemed to always have it with her, she would need to charge it after work. He stepped back, checked the outlets. He found a cable that snaked from behind the desk, through a hole in the surface, to a charging stand. It was empty. Frustration burned through his chest. He must know what they knew. How close were they to guessing the plan? Had they found the others? The man paced, opening and clenching his fists, fighting the panic.

Think.

He went back out to the living area. People liked to work on couches. Shoving his hands between the cushions, he checked the sofa, the big chairs, on the bookshelves filled with photos and, for some reason, jars of sand. She had a large aquarium built into one of the shelving nooks and it bubbled and churned the water for a couple of black Angelfish and guppies. He tapped on the glass, making them scatter.

She opened the door without warning. Walked in, still on her phone, keys in her hand. He froze, finger still touching the glass of the fish tank. Quietly, his hand slipped to his backpack, to the device in the outside pocket.

Detective De La Cruz tossed her keys onto a glass bowl on a table near the front door, turned, and locked her bolt and chain. Her purse slid from her shoulder, down her arm, to the floor where she left it near the couch. "No worries. Really. Sitters fall through. It happens. Besides, we'll catch up at Friendsgiving. I promised Imani I'd bring some tamales from the lady who sells them out of her trunk. They are to die for—"

He tossed the drone, its oval body tore toward her, the laser guidance slicing through the dark of the room. She moved quicker than he expected, diving behind her couch just as the drone stopped midair and hovered quietly above her, scanning the terrain on nearly silent rotors. It bobbed up and down, seeking a firing angle.

"If you think I didn't know you'd show up here, then you're even stupider than I thought," her voice floated out behind the couch.

This was not fear, he thought. And then the ratchet of a gun slide sounded. A shot rang out. The lava lamp exploded next to him spewing sizzling slime in all directions and cloaking the house in pitch dark. He shouted with pain, the hot liquid burning through his sweatshirt. The drone locked on her, spitting the projectiles at rapid speed. They slammed into her books, shattered photo frames, dug into the couch and sent up tufts of stuffing.

He soldier crawled, slithering along the glass and slime toward her kitchen as he reached back for another drone. Rising to throw it, she popped up from behind the wingback and fired, the bullet grazing his arm. He yelped, and the drone went wild. It bounced off her shelf and wobbled midair, trying to right itself. She shot at it.

"You throw worse than my abuelita," she shouted, further now. Almost to the kitchen. "What's the matter? Still hurt from Petraeus kicking your ass, you coward?"

He scrambled on his hands and knees past the fridge when she peeked around the corner of the kitchen door. Running for the back door, he yanked on it, fumbling with the lock when she fired. The door window shattered outward, and he reared back almost going down. Glass flew at his hand, slicing at it.

"Freeze, asshole," she shouted, stepping into the room.

The lines of the laser guidance system slipped across her forehead a second before the drone fired. Dozens of flat, dagger-like projectiles fanned out from the device that had followed them into the kitchen. She screamed, covering her head with her arms as she ran back down the hallway. He should leave. He should save himself, but he turned and chased her, the shameful words she'd uttered ringing in his head. *Coward.*

She ran to her bedroom, the door slamming just as he got to it. He banged on it with both fists, turned and rammed his shoulder, cracking the frame. She fired through it, the rounds searing past his cheek. He stepped back, unable to breathe with the fury crowding his throat. This woman and her partner were hunting him and had to be stopped. Throwing himself against the door again, he growled, an angry animal shriek as his body jarred with every kick of his boot, the frame giving way. He slipped on something and looked down. A smile pulled at his lips when he saw what it was. Blood seeped out from under the doorway. He would get her. He would make her pay.

17

NW Precinct Station

Reed sat on the stairs with Tig in the south stairwell. He was drinking his seventh cup of coffee and eating a dinner of vending machine chips and a mystery meat sandwich. It was an old habit of theirs, something about the weird echoes and isolation always helped Reed think.

Tig was supposed to be eating gluten-free according to his wife, so he scraped the filling of a sandwich cookie off with his teeth, tossing the actual cookie in the metal trashcan on the landing below. "When is your witness showing up?"

"Nat said she agreed to meet with me after her niece's party. She's helping her sister at the ice rink." Reed checked his watch. "Kids don't party that long, right?"

"My six-year-old melts down after forty-five minutes on a good day," Tig said. "Then again, so do I at kids' parties. How's De la Cruz working out?"

"She's good. Wicked smart." Reed frowned "Trusts me about as far as she can throw me."

"De la Cruz has reason," Tig said. "Give her time."

Reed waited for more, but Tig left it at that. "Hell of a first case for her though."

Tig leaned his forearms on his knees, fiddling with the cookie package. "Tell me."

Reed caught him up on what they knew so far. That Maggie, Gerald, and Petraeus all seemed to be attacked by the same device, possibly the same person. Now Iris seems to be involved somehow via her husband and Maggie crossing paths at school. Tig was doubtful about the whole student coming back and protesting angle Firash had brought up. But the mystery agent . . . that caught his attention.

"Something's going on in the background we can't see. The local FBI office is supposed to call me back, but I think Nat's right. It sounds like a cover to question the professor." Tig shook his head. "The balls on this one."

"Yeah," Reed said, thinking about the guy he'd chased from his condo. He didn't get the impression he'd wanted to talk. "We might have uncovered a couple more bodies tied to this, but it's all held together with spit and desperation right now. I need a solid, actionable lead . . . soon."

"This guy going around digitally lobotomizing people, is he a psycho or is there a purpose to all of this?"

"Oh, he's unhinged, no one can do that to another human and not be nuts. But he's not compromised in the way that would make him impulsive or reckless." Reed shook his head. "He watches them. Plans where to attack. It's why he keeps getting away with it. Every hit, and I think that's what they are, was executed perfectly. No witnesses, no forensic evidence, nothing. Hell, I couldn't even prove these people *weren't* killing themselves, until Petraeus's video."

"How did he find her?" Tig asked. "You guys tracked her via the postcard, right?"

"Another way, I guess. He might be part of her world, the data brokering." Reed pulled out his leather notebook and flipped to the drawings he'd done at Gerald's art studio. "Or maybe he knows her from somewhere else. Somewhere close."

"I'm looking at the head of security over at Neurogen. He works for the brother of Rossing's victim."

"Why're you looking at him?"

"Just that he's probably former military and he's got a weird vibe. He looked . . . rattled, I want to say, when we met in Corbin's office."

"Speaking of Corbin Price, he complained to the mayor about your antics in his office and the unnecessary delay in his brother's case. The mayor complained to the chief, who dressed down the Chief of Ds." Tig hooked his thumb at his chest. "Guess who got the next call?"

"This is coming to a head. The guy's been killing for at least three weeks and leaving almost no forensic evidence. But he's starting to make small mistakes. Maggie's shoe. Petraeus's video. The residue from the PT7. All of it will start piling up."

"I've got some warrants on the way. We can use them when we need them, but we're running out of time. The evidence linking these cases is thin at best, and Rossing's grumbling about closing out the case on Monday." Tig took apart another cookie. "What does this asshole want, anyway? You get a read on him yet?"

"I don't know. I'm getting close, but something's weird about him." Reed stared down into his chips bag as he reached for something just at the edge of his mind. "It's like he's . . . conflicted?"

"What do you mean?"

Reed's phone buzzed and he answered. It was the desk sergeant telling him someone was looking for him. "I think that's my witness. I'll be right down." He stood up, tossed his trash.

Tig got up with him, walked with him back up the stairs. "You've gotta stop this guy, Reed. Hunt him down, fast."

"I'll get him," Reed said as he split off from Tig and headed out to the front desk.

⸻

Mika Lee was young, early twenties, jet black angular bob, polished professional clothing. She followed him back into the bullpen, eyes wide.

"I've never been in a police department before," she said. "I've never even gotten a traffic ticket. Of course, I don't drive. Not that I would get tickets if I did. Oh, my god, I'm rambling," she said and might have hiccupped.

Reed smiled reassuringly and led her to an interview room. Designed to be inviting, it had a small conference table and four chairs. He motioned to one and sat opposite her across the table. "I'll be brief, Ms. Lee. I only have a few questions."

"Please," she said, warming up. Reed thought he caught a flush rising up her throat. "Call me Mika."

She pronounced it *mee-kah* and when they shook, she held onto his hand a second or two more than she needed to.

"Okay, Mika. Thank you for coming in."

She nodded. "I mean, you almost missed me. Iris had a lot of things to wrap up and hand off, but I start a new job after the holiday. Today was my last day."

"Then I'm happy I lucked out," Reed said and smiled. He pulled out his leather notebook and a pen. "Tell me something. Did Iris seem bothered at all before her death? Did she have any run ins or phone calls that seemed to upset her?"

Mika pressed her lips together, brows knit. "Her job was stressful, sure, but she got along with everyone there. They were so stoked they snagged her from the college."

"What about home life?"

"Oh . . ." Mika's mouth tensed. "I don't want to gossip."

"It's not gossip if it's true," Reed said. "And it might help me find who did this to her."

"Yeah, okay, you're right, but I promised I wouldn't mention this." Reed waited out her hesitation quietly. Mika took a breath. "She was getting letters. On her car window at work. Iris didn't want her husband to know because she said they'd just fight about it."

Reed stopped writing. "Did she say why?"

"Only that he was worried for her safety. She said he took things like that more seriously than he needed to." Mika smiled sadly. "Iris was fearless."

"Did you ever see who left the letters?"

"No, the parking area is patrolled but there's no cameras. It's a privacy thing for our clients." Mika wavered, biting her lip, then, "But they *did* scare her. I could tell. I arrived at the same time as she did one morning, and she looked absolutely shaken after she read it. I asked her what it was, and she just blew off the question. Changed the subject."

"Did you ever read one?"

"No, she shredded them."

Reed leaned in. "Really? Did she ever say who it was?"

"No, they stopped. But then she started to get phone calls. A guy was all upset and demanding to speak to her. He was an activist, I think because he used that jargon, you know? Irreparable global damage, corporate corruption causing a climate crisis, like that."

"Was it one guy or more than one?"

"Oh, definitely the same one," Mika said.

"How do you know? Was there something about his voice? Did he have an accent?"

"Nope, no accent. But he did sound . . . old-timey?" Mika shook her head. "No, that's not right. More like he was too formal."

"Formal how?" Reed prompted. "Elevated vocabulary, weird references, maybe a lack of contractions?"

"You know, it was the contractions thing. He didn't use them."

"Did he ever speak to Iris?"

"Oh, no, I would never put him through, obviously, but just hearing about them seemed to upset her. I think she had issues with harassment at the college and was hoping to leave it behind. I guess controversy followed her to Briar Ridge after all."

Reed pulled a printed photo out of his suit jacket pocket. He held it up. It was a snapshot of Petraeus that Nat had cleaned up. She'd removed the long red scrapes from her face. "Do you recognize this woman? Maybe she came into your offices recently?"

Mika tilted her head, looking at it. "No. We don't really get visitors. We got a reporter, but not like . . . people who want to visit anyone who works there. It's a pretty secure building. If staff wants to have lunch with someone, like a spouse or client, they meet at a restaurant."

Reed stopped her. "A reporter? What were they investigating?"

Mika hesitated. "I'm . . . not sure how much I'm supposed to tell you."

"Tell me as much as you can. I'll see about getting the DA involved past that."

"Ok, that seems fine." Mika squirmed in her seat. "Iris was a geologist who specialized in rare earth metals—"

"Let me ask you this," Reed said, holding up his pen. "How exactly are rocks big money? I get diamonds . . ."

"Gotcha," Mika smiled. "Rare earth metals are used in technology. Uh, you've heard of Cobalt, right? We make rechargeable batteries with that. And Promethium is used in guided missiles. This stuff is super valuable. And because of what it's used for, really controversial. Especially because of where we have to mine it from. Places like China. It's a complicated issue."

"Then it fits that the caller would be an environmentalist," Reed said. "And Iris 'advised' companies about mining these metals?"

"Yes, she offered analysis on viability of certain areas, helped to navigate local and foreign entities with the client to keep the program on track, that kind of thing."

That sounded rehearsed, Reed thought. "She brokered deals, didn't she?"

"Look, I signed an NDA when I was hired and they very kindly and clearly reminded me of it when I turned in my resignation. I don't want to get sued here."

"I can get the DA in here," Reed glanced at the wall clock. "It'll take couple of hours though. The holiday—"

"I'm treading a fine line here, Detective."

"We think this guy, the one who hurt Iris, may have hurt at least two other women." Reed leaned forward on the table, held her gaze with his. "Please, Mika, help me stop him."

She bit at her thumbnail, and then sighed. "Okay, yes. And that was what the reporter was asking about too, only he was specific. He asked about Ghanzi Provence."

"Okay, now I'm asking," Reed said. "Is this a deal?"

"This is where we get into some sticky territory. I can tell you about the project generally because I've heard Iris talk about it at symposiums and stuff. But names, dates, anything specific, and I need to call legal over at Briar Ridge."

"I'll take what you can give me."

"Okay, then," Mika said. "The Ghanzi Provence is two things, a place in southeastern Afghanistan. A dried lake, I think. But secondly, and more importantly, it's a project to mine that ground for Lithium. That stake is rumored to harbor trillions of dollars' worth of product but given its location, untouchable."

"Ah," Reed said, understanding. "But not for Iris."

"She had connections there, I heard. From years ago. I think she might have even worked over there, but yeah, she claimed she had an in. That this deal was going to happen. It just had to get through some sort of hurdle."

"What does that mean, hurdle?"

"I really don't know. That's above my paygrade. And I'm at the limit of what I can tell you without permission."

"Do you know if she talked to anyone about it? A boss or human resources?"

"No one at Briar Ridge. I know that. She asked me to leave it to her. I think she didn't want to cause waves." Mika sat up straight. "But she did tell someone named Joshy, I think."

Reed wrote the name down in his notebook. "Joshy? Did you ever put someone with that name through to her before?"

"No. This call didn't go through the network. It was on her cell. I had just gotten back from the cafeteria and saw her in her office, pacing back and forth. She was pretty riled up. When I opened her door to see if she needed anything, I heard her say, 'Joshy.' Then, 'I'm getting worried.' She shooed me away, finished the call, and then went to a meeting like nothing." Mika shrugged. "A week later, she was run over."

Reed sat back and looked at Mika, wracking his brain for more questions, something that would help him pry loose a clue. "Do you remember anything else about this call? Did Iris ever bring it up?"

Mika shook her head. "That's all I got."

He checked his watch. It was six thirty. "When this reporter came in, did you get surveillance on him?"

"Yeah, the lobby has a surveillance camera aimed at the reception desk since we take packages and have petty cash."

"You think I can get a look?"

"Oh, sure," Mika nodded and stood. She gathered up her purse and coat. "I'm sure we can get someone to print it out for you if get the okay from legal. Marty's there all night."

"Okay, let me make a call." He got up and opened the door for her, already thinking about getting the photo of the reporter in front of Abernathy. "We'll get an electronic warrant and I'll follow you back to the offices—"

A chorus of phone rings started up. First his, then a few out in the hall, then another. He turned, looking into the picture window of Tig's office. Saw him on the phone. Rossing, stood up at his desk, worried eyes locking with his. Everyone in the room was looking at Reed. Tig's door opened.

"It's De La Cruz," Tig breathed. "She's on her way to the hospital right now. Someone attacked her in her home."

"Is she—" Reed's hand went to his head and Petraeus's awful, crazed eyes seared behind his lids. "Did the bastard burn her?"

Tig looked at him, tense. "Situation is muddy as we get reports coming in. But, uh, patrol says she was . . . she's coming in with a head injury."

Reed shook his head, his breath ragged, chest tight. "Did they say how she's doing? Is she talking?"

Tig shook his head. "That's all I know."

"I have to—" Reed wandered in a circle behind his desk. "I have to get down there."

"I'll drive him," Rossing said, grabbing his keys.

"Go," Tig said. "Lights and sirens."

18

Seattle Haven Hospital

Bar lights on the squad cars lit the falling rain in strobes of blue and red. Large puddles in the asphalt reflected the bright lights of the hospital. Reed jogged with Rossing across the parking lot, his face tucked behind his trench collar. The tiny drops stung like cold needles on his cheeks and forehead. Everything was the same as with Caitlyn. All of it. The automatic doors opening in slow motion as fellow cops from the station turn to watch him walk through. They huddled in groups, hands in their pockets, murmuring as he passed. Reed texted Nat again, staring at his screen, willing her to answer. A Smart-arch positioned just inside the doorway sprayed them with antiviral mist as they pushed into the lobby.

"Come on, Nat," he muttered, knot in his gut. "Not like this."

He and Rossing went up to the reception desk, and Reed fought with the information kiosk, practically piercing the touchscreen with his finger until Rossing took over. It directed them to the surgery floor. They rode up the elevator in silence, Reed's gut tied in knots.

"Did someone call her family?" he asked.

"I heard she doesn't have any." Rossing pulled out some gum from his suit jacket and offered it to Reed.

"Wait, what?"

"Yeah, lost them in a fire or something."

"How is it you know this, exactly?" Reed asked, a little irritated that he didn't. "She's been on the job all of five minutes."

"Hey, you were the ones who ambushed me during my lunch. And she was so annoying, I pulled her file."

"That sounds completely ethical."

Rossing shoved the stick of gum in his mouth. "Do you wanna know or what?"

The elevator stopped and they scooted over to let an orderly and the oldest woman Reed had ever seen, roll in. She glared at him with rheumy, wet eyes. The distinct scent of vapor rub assaulted his nostrils. "Yes, I want to know."

"They died down in San Diego, I think her dad was a sheriff there."

"She mentioned that."

"When her family passed, she moved up to Seattle to live with her grandmother for her last year of high school. She ended up going to UW for her criminology degree."

"She lost everyone?"

"Parents, sister . . . everyone. Poof. Up in a literal cloud of smoke."

"That's . . . terrible." Reed watched the floor numbers over the door. "She didn't say anything."

"How would that even come up?" Rossing said as the elevator dinged, and the doors slid open on the surgery floor. "Nice to meet you, I'm an orphan of a suspicious fire."

"Now it's suspicious?"

Rossing snapped his gum. "I don't know the details, man. Ask her. Just . . . maybe not *right* now."

They walked to the circular counter in the center of the floor. Several screens displayed information, directions to common places like the cafeteria, and prompts to call for person-to-person. A medical aid robot rolled along the hallway carrying medicine in its locked belly, its soft, androgynous voice asking visitors to watch their step. A nurse sat in the center of the circle at a smaller, square desk, working on a screen. Reed got his attention by knocking on the counter loudly.

He looked up, sighed, and wandered over. His lanyard card said his name was RN Sturgeon. Like the fish.

"Are you Detective Reed?" he asked as they walked up.

"Yes. I'm here for—"

"She's in observation," he said and pointed to a room in the far corner. "The trauma surgeon is just finishing."

"Trauma? Is she alright?"

"Back. Room," the nurse repeated, and walked back to the desk, dismissing them.

Reed strode down the hallway ahead of Rossing, stopping when the door to the observation room swung open. A doctor pushed through and ripped off his mask. He tapped furiously on a medical tablet.

"De La Cruz?" Reed asked, jogging up to him. "You're the trauma surgeon treating Detective De La—"

"Trouble," the surgeon said.

Reed stopped cold in his tracks. "She's in trouble?"

"No, she *is* trouble." The surgeon waved his hand over a biowaste receptacle, and the lid popped up. He tossed his mask in. "She wants her BioBond done in the room instead of the lab like a normal patient. And, she's refusing to be admitted."

"Does she need to be?"

The doctor's eyes narrowed at Reed. "Are you the partner?"

"Yes," Reed nodded, glancing into the small window in the door. The curtain was drawn to hide the bed. "How bad is she? Can she . . . can she talk?"

"Oh, talking isn't a challenge for her, no. She's talking a million miles a minute. Kept asking for you. Reed, right?"

The steel band squeezing his chest loosened just a little. "She's okay?"

"No, she looks like she got caught in a tornado made of razors, but she'll live." The doctor shook his head. "See if you can convince her to reconsider staying for observation, will you?"

He didn't wait for Reed to answer, walking away quickly he was already on his phone. Reed reached for the door but froze. He stared at his hand wrapped around the handle. She's ok. He slowed his breaths. It's not the same.

Behind him, Rossing called. "Tig just got here. I'm gonna go get him."

Reed nodded and walked in. Her voice sounded from behind the curtain. "That better be Detective Reed."

She yanked the material back and she looked pissed. The orderly standing next to her bed jumped, his hand holding the BioBond tube over her forehead frozen in midair.

"Hey, Nat—"

"Who was it?" She asked, wiggling off the bed with effort. The orderly tried to stop her, and she slapped at his hand. "Who'd you send?"

"I can explain." Her forehead, neck and hands had nicks on the skin. A long, bonded cut sliced cleanly from just beneath her hairline at her temple to her widow's peak.

They both looked at the orderly who put up his hands and left without a word. When he had, Nat's gaze snapped to Reed's.

She glared up at him, her hands on her hips. "Not only did I have to fend off the most spectacularly bizarre attack I have ever experienced, but I had to then tap dance around questions from the Incident Supervisor about who the second assailant was who kicked open my back door and blasted a shotgun into my kitchen. I've been acting confused, and shell shocked just to keep from saying that I have no idea what you did or why!"

"Listen, I know I should—"

Her finger shot up between them and she held it just underneath his chin as she spoke. "What did I say about keeping me out of the loop? Are we partners or not?"

"You're going to rip open your face glue if you don't settle down," Reed said evenly, though the relief soaring through his chest would have made anything she said sound like music to his ears. "Look, I opted not to report my own attack. But I knew that would put you in danger with no extra patrol past your house or extra security. So, I asked a . . . friend, to keep an eye out. Just until we catch this guy. He must've heard the attack and fired at the guy. Must've scared him off."

"Who was it?"

"I can't, Nat. But I'd trust him with my life. So I trusted him with yours."

Nat crossed her arms, but her face softened. "Well, I mean, I'm not going to *say* that keeping me in the dark was a dick move, but I'm going to strongly imply it."

"Point taken," Reed said, amused. He looked at her for a moment. Her dark eyes were alert. Hands steady. Her anger burned through, she looked . . . fine. "What did you end up saying?"

"I was in my room, against the door," she held up her left hand, it had the telltale thread-thin blue lines of the BioBond adhesive. "Bleeding like a stuck pig, I might add. And, I did hear the blast, but through the door. I told them I had no idea who it was because I honestly didn't."

"You're okay though?" Reed shoved his hands in his pockets and leaned back against the wall. "For reals?"

"I'm more than okay." Nat smiled and grabbed her tablet from the overbed table. "Check this out."

On the screen were photos of a small, oval device with rotors. A bullet hole pierced its fuselage. "You killed it?"

"I shot the little bastard out of the air. This one we can process. Maybe the guy who threw it wasn't wearing gloves."

Reed manipulated the image, enlarging it. "They don't sell weaponized drones on the consumer market. This looks like it could be military grade."

"Yeah. And we know a possible soldier for hire. Corbin's head of security."

"The confirmation of the PT7 solvent at the Petraeus scene does make it likely the assailant is ex-special forces."

"Like Slater probably is," Nat said. "Shouldn't we be watching him? See if he's involved in his boss's death."

"Some hunches and little cleaning solution won't get us a warrant to track him."

She slapped her palm on the tablet. "Then let's get something on him. How can we find out what he did in the military?"

Reed shoved his hands in his suit pants. "I still have hooks in with army CID. I'll find out if Slater served and where."

"If he is involved, do you think Corbin knows? You think he's involved, too?"

"I don't know what Corbin's angle is," Reed said and told her about his conversation with Mika "We need to get a photo of Slater and one of the guy who posed as a reporter at Briar Ridge in front of the professor. See if he recognizes either of them."

She checked her smartwatch. "It's late and I still have to talk Tig into letting me stay on the case."

"You'll stay. With the mayor and a billionaire tech guru in play, he wants this case cleared as soon as possible. This is going to take both of us to pull it off. I'll tell Tig I need my partner."

Nat looked at him for a beat, a whisper of a smile on her lips. "I mean, that'd be cool if you did."

"I'd be dumb if I didn't." He grabbed her blazer from the chair in the corner and held it out to her. "Let's get back to the station. I want to take a look at the killer drone you captured."

"That guy, the one in my house. He was looking for something. I was supposed to be gone most of the night with a friend. Dinner and a movie, but her sitter cancelled. He wasn't there to attack me." Nat winced when she shrugged into her blazer. "If he was, he would've seen I was gone and come back. Not let himself in and rifle through my stuff. From what I could tell, nothing was stolen."

"He could have broken in to lay in wait for you."

"When I walked in, he was tapping on my aquarium like a dumb kid. The most lit up area in the whole, dark house. How is *that* lying in wait?"

"He was tapping on your fish tank?" Reed shook his head. "I sort of figured you for a dog person, honestly."

"Listen, don't start with me," Nat said with a smile. "The bubbles are soothing and stuff."

Reed chuckled. "You're thinking he wanted information on the case."

"Yeah. I think he's been following us for a while. Like maybe from the beginning."

Reed nodded, he'd thought the same. "Breaking into a detective's home is ballsy at best, absolutely unhinged at worst. Let alone *two* detectives. The guy's desperate."

"Desperate's bad. Unpredictable." She pushed through the door ahead of him, and they walked past the grumpy nurse. Reed spotted Tig over by reception and pointed. They headed in that direction. She turned to him. "This guy is panicking. He thinks we're closing in."

"That's because we are," Reed said. "His days are numbered."

"Oh, one more thing. The recovery guys at cybercrime came through with something. A transfer packet on Petraeus's computer was salvageable. Seems like she encrypted and then transferred a copy of a file to a foreign device three weeks before she was attacked. It's a huge amount of information. The device's memory would have to be in the terabytes to accommodate it. Everything else we could salvage was just bits of code and encrypted messages on different servers. This is the only file she offloaded recently."

"You think this is what she transferred to the kill switch?"

"Yeah, the Faraday cage in her closet was jimmied, the attacker uninterested in the computer system itself. So, this has to be what he was after, right?"

Reed accidentally rubbed his stitches and winced. "Makes sense. Any way to see what the information actually was?"

"Not yet. It's all encrypted, of course. Now, Imani said she knows a guy at the FBI, but it'll take a while. We *do* know the file is full of docs, images, video files, etc. But get this . . . the file name wasn't encrypted." She swiped her tablet screen and then handed it to him as they walked. "You ever heard of something called Spectre?"

Reed shook his head, but a dark dread settled in his chest. "No, but something tells me there's more to all of this than just one guy running around lobotomizing people."

"Maybe he works for them?" Nat asked.

Tig waved her over and she left Reed staring at the file name. *Spectre.* What kind of entity had access to a weapon that could obliterate someone's mind? Why are they doing it? He watched Nat argue with Tig, a stubborn jut to her chin. More importantly, who was next?

Nat went to sign herself out and gather her things. While she was doing that, Reed walked down the back hallway of the hospital, through a pneumatic exit, and out onto the asphalt near the refrigeration units. A whistle sounded. Quick bursts, familiar. Reed answered back with his own pattern. Then he listened. Mercury vapor streetlights glowed sickly blue against the dark sky. Satellite constellations blinked in the firmament. A distant ambulance approached, its siren echoing in the night. Reed heard the crunch of gravel and then a form walked out from the long shadows cast by the hospital.

"Your partner is one hell of a fighter," Coyote's drawl sounded from the edge of the blacktop. He had on a sailor's peacoat, dark cargo pants, and his Doc Marten's. A black knit cap covered his head. Bright orange flared bright at his lips and then his smoky breath drifted upward. "I was nearly redundant."

"Did you see him?"

Coyote shook his head. "He walked in, I think. No one saw a car at the corners, and I had four guys out there freezing their nuts off watching your partner's place."

"What'd you think?"

"Of him?" Coyote chuckled and hot vapor from his breath tumbled out into the air. "You want me to score the guy?"

"Yeah."

He thought for a minute. Dragging on his cigarette. "I suppose he didn't really seem like he had his head screwed on right, to be honest. When I kicked in the back door, he was yelling and throwing himself against the bedroom door like he'd lost his mind. Slipping and sliding all over the hallway. He didn't even try to shoot the door lock."

"You're sure he didn't have a gun?" That surprised Reed.

"Not that I saw, no. Your partner though, she was shooting up the place like she was trying to win a carnival prize. And ooh, she was mad. I think I learned some new Spanish curse words tonight."

"The thing is, I think I've fought with this guy before, and I could barely hold my own."

"Someone gave *you* trouble?" Coyote chuckled. "Sounds like someone I need to meet."

"He knew what he was doing. Especially with a gun." Reed blew out a frustrated breath. "This doesn't make sense."

"You could've hurt him when you fought before."

"I might've shot him, actually." The assailant twisting on Petraeus's terrace slipped through his mind.

"Now that does sound like you," Coyote said. "Pain forces mistakes. Clouds thinking."

Reed shrugged. "Maybe."

"Sorry I couldn't see more, man. I kicked the door in, blasted a round, and he took off out the front door. It was either give chase or check on your partner and see if she was still breathing. When I heard her on the phone with 911 through the door—I popped smoke got out of there."

"Wasn't for nothing. I owe you one."

"Not quite," Coyote took a final drag and flicked the butt at the dumpster. "I might've shaved a little off my tab though."

Reed looked at his friend. A man who'd been through hell and back with him. "You showed up ready to waste a stranger on my word. That's more than even."

"Hell, I'd do that for free." Coyote stepped forward, his look intense. "You know what you did for me, Morgan. My debt is done when it feels done. Besides, I got to check out your girl."

"She'd tear you a new one if she heard you say that," Reed said with a grin.

"She's a hurricane, that one. A singular kind of woman." He bobbed his brows at Reed.

"Dude, don't even go there—"

"She seeing anyone?"

"Get the hell out of here," Reed laughed. "You wouldn't survive an hour."

19

Reed called the professor after leaving the hospital the night before and arranged to meet with him at the college in the morning. Abernathy was cranky about it, saying he was just popping in to grab his plants and then he was gone for the holiday week traveling. Reed promised it would be quick. The professor said he was leaving at eight on the dot because the bug sprayers were coming after, and he didn't want a migraine for his whole vacation. Reed assured him he'd get there on time.

First thing in the morning, he hurried over to Briar Ridge Solutions. Mika, Iris's Assistant, had agreed to meet him there with someone from the legal department and Marty the night security guy, who seemed put out he had to stay and wait for Reed. After mucking about with in-house counsel for twenty minutes and having to get a digital warrant for the images to cover their corporate asses, they got him some good stills off the surveillance video of the 'reporter' who showed up demanding to speak to Iris.

Nat was already at the station. She'd gone in early to plead her case to

Tig about staying on the investigation. Reed had put in his two cents via phone call the night before. The lieutenant didn't need convincing. Pressure from the mayor to stop the attacks trumped procedure.

When Reed hurried into the station, she met him at the duty desk. She was holding a steaming Styrofoam cup of coffee with both hands and blew across the surface with ruby red lips. She smiled when she saw him, the minute slices peppering her face already healing.

"What's the verdict?" Reed asked, taking the disposable cup of coffee she held out to him. "Did they fire you from homicide already?"

"You wish," she shot back. "No, as long as I don't shoot anyone or get shot, I'm good."

Nat seemed to view coffee as a sugar and milk delivery system and had made Reed's the same way. He sipped the sugary, lukewarm drink as they walked back to the bullpen. It was early, roll call was going. The gloom of the morning pressing against the windows.

She nodded at the manilla envelope in his hand. "Did ya get it?"

Reed slipped the surveillance video still out of the envelope and she took it, squinting at it.

"Huh, I have to show you something in a minute." She pointed at the other photo in his hand. "Is that Slater's?"

Reed handed that one to her too as they rode the elevator up to homicide. "My guy, Stucky, over at Army Intelligence could only get me a bare minimum on Slater's military service. His file's behind a security wall."

"That's not sketchy at all." She sighed, hugging the tablet to her chest. "What'd you get?"

"Service Photo. His name, rank, and that he served eight years ago in the marines."

"That's it?" She looked disappointed. "That's something though, right? I mean normal everyday soldiers don't have redacted files."

"Stucky'll keep digging into Slater's military records. If something's there, he'll find it." Reed checked his watch. "I just have to put together a picture array with Slater and five other similar looking guys, another array for Firash, and we can go meet Abernathy."

"OR . . ." Nat put one photo face down on the screen of her tablet and scanned it. Then the other. Finally, she called up a program. "I can do that with PIXIS."

"I don't trust that AI."

"It makes random arrays of mugshots and SPD personnel for a totally unbiassed selection. What's not to like?"

"I'm just used to doing it by hand."

"So were the people who used to crank their cars to start them, but they adapted," Nat said with a grin. "You'll live."

She finished putting together the first array and Reed eyed it with suspicion, but agreed it was good. He took another sip of his coffee and realized he hadn't eaten breakfast yet. "Let's hit the road, get the identification from Abernathy, and get something to eat."

While she worked on the second array, Reed called the ME, Sanders. Who gave him an update on Maggie's autopsy. He was chewing something crunchy on the other end and Reed listened to him eat happily while his own stomach growled.

"Her tox screen came back. No drugs or alcohol. She did have a partially digested pill in her stomach. It came back as the antidepressant you found in the dorm."

"So, she *was* taking them," Reed muttered. He hadn't thought so and that threw him for a loop.

"Well, hold on," Sanders said, his mouth full. "Standard specimen collection for a suicide includes vitreous humor. The fluid in the eyeball. Hers was negative for Tricyclics, which was the kind of antidepressant she ingested."

Reed took down notes in his leather pad. "Other than the one pill in her stomach and a medicine bottle with no label, there's no other evidence she was on antidepressants?"

"Not that I can see. As for her injuries, she didn't appear to have any kind of trauma inconsistent with the fall from the roof, but you can hide a lot of damage with a four-story impact. I called for her medical records from her family doctor. We'll see what he says about the antidepressants, but the holidays are really slowing things down."

"This guy is just—" Reed bothered the stitches over his eye, thinking. "Anything new on Gerald?"

"Some new complaints. His brother tried to stop the autopsy with an injunction. I just got a call this morning. It was quashed but still. He's probably reaching out to the governor next."

"How far did you get?"

"Toxicology finally came back on him, too. He had a LOT of heroin in his system. Enough to kill him for sure."

"Would he have been incapacitated? Could he have aimed and shot himself with a shotgun if he was that drugged up?"

"He'd been an addict for a long time. They have a lot of tolerance." Sanders made a humming noise. "I honestly don't know. It's not impossible to think he shot up and then shot the weapon. A few seconds is all he'd need."

"I'm looking for something conclusive, Doc."

"Well, he only had two recent needle marks."

"Two?"

"The one in his arm that delivered the heroin and one on his thigh that had an unidentifiable substance on it. The second injection site was obscured with what looked like rat predation. I'm running it through some paces. I'll tell you what I find. The other needle marks were very old. Scarred over. I did get his brain out of his skull. What I could, anyway. I'm going to do some slices here in a few minutes. I'll have more to tell you after that."

Reed thanked Sanders and hung up, no longer hungry as he thought of sliced brains on a metal table. He told Nat about the call while they headed to the college to talk with Abernathy.

Nat drove while Reed sketched in his notepad. His phone pinged.

"Stucky sent me an update." Reed read the file on Slater with a growing sense of dread. "This is bad news."

"Something interesting in Slater's military file?" Nat asked as she turned wide out of the station sending Reed against the passenger side door. "What's it say?"

"What my guy could get is almost completely redacted." Though it wasn't raining, a heavy mist moved over the grounds, not yet burned off by the morning sun. She didn't seem to notice and barreled through a stale green light at an intersection. Reed kept his eyes on the file for his own sanity. "He was special forces, MARSOC, from what I can tell. Honorable discharge."

"Marines?" Nat shook her head. "Figures. They're crazier than SEALs."

"The file says he served abroad and in the middle east, nothing specific. Looks like he was a marine raider, master sergeant. That would've made him team leader."

"He's a special forces operator?" Nat asked. "You think he might've worked with the PT7 solvent you found at Petraeus's?"

"It makes it more likely," Reed muttered.

"Enough to get a warrant to track him?" Nat asked.

"We'll see. It'd be easier if Abernathy identifies Slater as impersonating an FBI agent."

"Here's the thing. I think . . . no, I *know*, that I'm pretty badass, but I doubt I would've survived an attack by a special forces marine. Not this unscathed."

"You surprised him. He wasn't there for you."

"Come on, Reed. Be real. He kicked you across the sand and you're what . . . six-two, six-three? And he chooses drones instead of hand-to-hand? Why didn't he do that at Petraeus's apartment? Send one after us, escape in the melee . . ."

"That's been bothering me too. Sometimes he uses them, sometimes he doesn't." Reed looked out the window. "He runs when I see him one time, then tries to kill me with his bare hands the next. There's a duality to him I can't wrap my mind around."

"He must've been holding back for some reason. Maybe we're not just looking at one perp here." Nat chewed on her pinkie nail while they waited for the light to turn green. "Also, I keep going back to Maggie. What does a college freshman have to do with these kinds of people? A dark web hacker, an evil tech genius, and now . . . a trained killer? Do you think she saw something she shouldn't have?"

"I can't fathom where." Reed's scar itched and he pushed on the bandage. "How did their path's cross? Did we dump her phone location files?"

"We should have. I'll call Imani," Nat said, slowing for the onramp. "Oh, that reminds me. Grab my tablet. I have something for you to watch."

Reed pulled her tablet from the center console and flicked it on. "What am I looking at?"

"Abernathy sent over the lectures that were archived. The ones from the time this Firash student might've taken his class. Me and a couple of guys from cybercrime went through them last night."

"I take it you didn't go home and rest like you were supposed to," Reed said, with a wry smile. "Shocking."

She waved away his comment with a flick of her wrist. "Hey, listen. I did go home and rest. I just also had pizza and beer delivered and some of my work friends came over to watch videos."

"Of three-year-old World Politics lectures. Possibly on fast forward."

"Oh, they definitely were," Nat said. "Anyways, we might've found something. The video is cued up, just press play."

Reed did while she pulled onto Jasper on the way to the college. The video was taken by someone at Abernathy's lecture. They were seated halfway down the amphitheater's seating midway between the doors at the top of the stairs and Abernathy who stood down at his podium. The student had begun recording after an initial disruption because Reed could see entire swaths of students moving to look behind them. The camera swung from Abernathy, up to a man standing on his seat, back partially turned to the camera, who was holding up a sign and yelling down at the professor. Brown hair. Clean cut. No accent. Reed squinted at the video. The young man was yelling about a conspiracy to rape his homeland and poison the earth.

We cannot stand by as the west rapes the land, brutalizes innocent people, and poisons their water for what? More riches? More power? More means to destroy? We must put a stop to this avarice. To this unquenchable lust for—"

Someone threw a water bottle. Others yelled for him to shut up, hurled insults, or simply booed. Security arrived. The burly men yanked him from his chair by his hoodie and ripped the sign from him. The young man threw a punch, and the security team pounced, taking him to the ground and escorting him away in cuffs to cheers from the rest of the students.

"College educated. Articulate. Smart," Reed said closing the video.

"With a temper," Nat said as she wove in and out of traffic. She tapped her horn at someone and then passed them. "Now look at the other video."

Reed fought with the tablet until he was able to open a second video file on her desktop. "What's this one?"

"I asked the college archives for a video of Iris's encounter with the heckler when she guest lectured for Abernathy. Unfortunately, since her location was the open-air amphitheater across campus, they didn't record it live because of wind. An audio reading of the lecture by Iris done before-hand was offered instead."

"What about—"

"Howevah," Nat said, exaggerating her own slight New York accent. "I had the AI crawl around social media and blogs posting with hashtags like Iris's name, the subject she talked about, the school, 'lecturer gets heckled,' stuff like that."

"You got something?" Reed was impressed.

"Who doesn't like to post meltdowns and troublemakers?" Nat stopped at another light, reached over, and hit play.

The second video was also taken by an attendee of the lecture. This crowd was a mix of students and older people. Iris stood on the dais; the shade cloth stretched over the podium area cast her in shadow. Blue skies floated over the edges of the rows of seats. Again, the recording started after an initial disturbance because the man was already yelling down at Iris. He was in profile to the camera this time. His jaw more angular, he was taller, but the hair was the same. He also moved the same as the student in the previous video.

He started the recording again and Reed leaned in to listen to the tirade. The young man, spoke to the crowd, his gestures grand, full of emotion. Though he started out speaking against Big Oil, the agribusiness cabal, and other contributors to climate change, his focus took a turn.

And finally, I condemn the voracious appetite for destruction of the US, which has not ceased to brutalize the innocent and violate the land for more ways to wage war.

Reed looked at Nat. "That sounds familiar."

"Same spiel, better vocabulary," she said. "He tacks it on at the end, but this guy's spouting the same thing as the kid in Abernathy's class."

"A lot of protestors, the truly committed, they cultivate phrases to yell when the news drones are around. Catch phrases. This guy is doing that. He's couching it in environmental arguments, but there's directed anger here, specifically at the US." Reed held up the photo he'd gotten from Briar Ridge against the tablet. Reed looked from the photo to the video still and back. Though he'd posed as a reporter to get close to Iris, hiding under a ballcap and raised collar, it was the same guy. Reed would bet his house on it. But there was something else. It pulled at his attention. "No contractions."

"What?" Nat asked, pulling up to the college. Trash collector bots wandered aimlessly along the empty parking lot.

"Mika, Iris's assistant over at Briar Ridge mentioned that both the crank caller and the guy posing as a reporter to see Iris spoke in an 'old-timey' way."

"What, like a Larper?" She wrinkled her nose. "Those guys who pretend they're medieval knights and go around saying, m'lady this and m'lady that?"

"No, but this sheds light on your dating life." Reed chuckled. "When I was growing up. I lived in an area with a lot of people who were second language learners. Polish, Mexican, people from Africa and Asia. A lot of the time, contractions are hard to get right if you didn't grow up with them. Without them you'd sound formal . . . or old-timey. Both videos, the guy sounds like that."

Nat stared at the video in Reed's hand. "That really looks like the same kid, just a little older to me. This is Firash, right? Is that your take?"

"I'm as sure as I can be with amateur phone camera recordings." Reed handed back the tablet and got out of the car. "We need to get his, and Slater's photo in front of Abernathy. And who knows, maybe searching through his old student files jogged Abernathy's memory and he'll be able to tell us Firash's last name. Then we can pull his files."

"If it was Slater pretending to be an FBI agent," Nat said as she slammed her door, and they walked side by side toward the building entrance. "That means he's been looking for Firash. Why? What could this kid know? Are Neurogen and Briar Ridge connected somehow?"

"Let's get these arrays in front of the professor, see what he says, and go from there," Reed said as they headed toward the building. "I can get warrants on them both once we have positive ID's."

"How long does it take to grab some plants, anyway? You see his car?" Nat looked around. "And by the way, shouldn't he leave the stupid plants if he's traveling? What's he gonna do, take them with him on the plane?"

"I don't think he's flying anywhere." Reed pointed to a brand-new RV parked off to the right a little, halfway between them and the building. It was shiny new and fully packed. Automatic awning, nearly silent electric motor, towing package. Expensive. "He said he was traveling for the holiday. I think he meant on the road."

"That looks brand new." She whistled. "What is that, like a hundred grand to start?"

"Mika said Iris made a lot of money brokering deals. With her gone, Abernathy seems to have been living it up."

Nat whistled her approval. "Maybe we shouldn't have eliminated him as a suspect."

"Who said we did?"

Up ahead, the door to the building pushed outward and Abernathy walked out carrying boxes. They headed in his direction together. The wind blew Abernathy's sparse hair upward as he struggled with two boxes each holding multiple large plants. He smiled when he saw them.

Reed jogged to meet him, passed the nose of the RV, and opened his mouth to say something when a bullet tore through Abernathy's chest blowing the plants right out of his arms. Soil, blood, and shredded leaves blew outward, flying into Reed's face as Abernathy stumbled forward, landing on his face in the pavement.

"Get down!" Nat screamed, her hand at Reed's elbow, yanking him toward the RV. Reed's weapon was already out, jumping in his hand, his eyes locked on the slip of light in a top window. And then the ground spit up chunks of asphalt, churning in a line toward Abernathy's prone body.

Reed dove with her, the RV windows spraying glass over their heads, rounds slamming into the metal siding. A tire hissed in front of him, and the RV listed with the loss of balance.

"Central this is De La Cruz. Shots fired, shots fired," Nat screamed into her phone. "Send backup to my location. Seattle City College—"

"Abernathy!" Reed shouted.

Dragging himself on the ground, the professor's terrified gaze locked with Reed's, mouth opening and closing, bloody hand reaching out. His strangled voice pled, "H-Help me!"

20

Reed lunged for the professor, his hand nearly to him when a round blasted asphalt into his face. He reared back and another bullet tore through the back of Abernathy's thigh. The professor screamed, shaking with pain.

Reed called over his shoulder, "Nat!"

"I got you," she shouted as she scrambled on her hands and knees to the rear of the RV. She fired two shots at the window, then, "Go!"

Reed lunged again, Abernathy flailing, his bloody hands slippery. Another volley of rounds from the assailant blasted into the side of the RV, Nat answered back. Reed grabbed for the professor's arm and dragged him behind the RV. He was bleeding from a wound in the upper right of his chest, and more spread out from underneath Abernathy's shoulder. Reed undid his tie, slipped it from his neck, and used it to push on the wound in the front. Warm crimson seeped out from between his fingers.

"Through and through, I think it tore up his shoulder blade," Reed said as she crawled back.

She nodded, looking up at the shattered windows of the RV. "You think he's reloading?"

"Or running down the stairs to finish the job."

"Oh, man," she said, her eyes wide. "I really don't want to deal with another one of those killer drones."

"Really? They're kind of growing on me." Reed got to his feet and chanced a peek through the RV to the building. "Either way we have to move."

"Backup will be here in a few minutes."

Abernathy coughed, pink foam bubbling out of his lips.

"Ah, no," Reed breathed. "He might've taken a hit to his lung. He won't last without an ER."

Nat glanced behind them. At the patrol car. "I can run for it."

"I should go. I'd be faster."

"Okay, first of all, Bigfoot . . . no, you wouldn't. I was in track. All State."

"Speed aside, you'd be running across an open field of sight. You wouldn't last two steps." He tried the door to the RV. It opened. "Help me get him inside."

Reed went in first, crouch walked to the button on the wall of the RV and used it to lower the blinds over the shattered windows facing the building. A few rounds rammed into the side of the vehicle, but Reed was already back outside, helping Nat drag Abernathy into the RV. They struggled with the professor. He'd fallen unconscious, and his head lolled as they maneuvered him. They put him on the floor of the small galley and Nat leaned on the wound with both palms while Reed crept up to the front, stopping behind the driver's seat.

"What's the plan? Hide out or drive out?" Nat looked up at him, face flushed. Another round slammed into the metal siding making her flinch.

"Get to the patrol car. We have vests to cover Abernathy, a shotgun. It's a faster car. We can go lights and sirens to the hospital with him." Reed leaned around the seat, eyeing the dashboard. It was advanced. All digital. It looked more like a spaceship console than a camper. "Nat you have to get up here. I don't even know what I'm looking at."

Nat peered up from Abernathy. "It's a digital key. We gotta get the professor in the driver's seat to start it."

"What?" Reed spotted the facial recognition lock near the steering wheel. "Why can't we just use keys? What is wrong with keys?"

"Just . . . give me a second." She patted Abernathy's body. His sweater, his pants. "Hah!" She pulled out a phone, then held it over Abernathy's face. "Hey! Professor." She smacked his face a couple of times with her palm and his eyes fluttered open. The phone lock chimed, and she tossed it to Reed. "You can start it with that."

Reed found the RV's remote-control app and pressed the ignition icon. The RV started, not a roar, but a subtle vibration. "Is it on?"

"Yes, it's on. Let's go!" Nat's hands were covered in blood. "Like, now!"

Reed peeked over the bottom of the driver's side window, reached up and switched gears. The brake released. He crouched low, keeping his head beneath the window, and pressed on the accelerator with one hand, the other one on the steering wheel. They started to move, and then bullets smashed through the side of the RV. Nat threw herself over Abernathy, shouting obscenities as Reed leaned on the accelerator. The RV lurched forward, the blown tire throwing off the level, turning slowly but surely out of firing range. Sliding into the driver's seat, Reed steered away from the building, heading toward the patrol car, picking up speed. A blast from the building behind them shattered the rear windows and then nothing. He looked back at Nat. She was still trying to keep Abernathy's blood inside his chest.

"You okay?"

She shook her head. "Too quiet too quick. You don't suppose he gave up?"

"I doubt it. He's got us against the ropes—"

The roar of an engine made the hairs on Reed's arms stand on end. Craning his neck, he spotted a motorcycle shoot out from behind the building toward them.

"Is he actually chasing us?" Nat's voice turned hard. Angry. She crawled to the rear window, popped up to look, and ducked when he fired. She shot back. He veered right, flanking the RV and gaining.

Reed kept him in his peripheral. The RV was nearing top speed as he barreled past the patrol car and out of the school parking lot. "Change of plans. Not enough time to get Abernathy into the patrol car safely."

"What about backup?" The RV jolted back and forth, the flat tires slowing them down.

"Find out where they're coming from. We'll head in their direction.

Maybe lead the shooter to them." Reed fought to keep the RV stable as he sped up. "Give them a heads up."

She tapped frantically on her phone and held it to her ear. "On it."

The motorcycle pulled along the driver's side. Black helmet, mirrored visor, head to toe leather riding suit. A sniper rifle strapped to his back. The driver raised a handgun, leveling it at the window. Reed yanked the wheel to the left, the tires screaming as the force of that much shifting weight sent a shudder through the RV. The rider pulled away in an arch and lined up again for another run at Reed.

Again, the motorcycle closed in, but Reed was ready. He swung his weapon over his chest and shot at the driver with his right hand, steering the swerving behemoth with his left. The RV hit and the motorcycle careened away sharply, the driver fighting for control, nearly laying it down. Reed glanced at the side view mirror as the rider sped through the smoke of the tires, angling for a better shot.

"Nat!"

She was at his shoulder in seconds, her hair whipping in his face. She steadied herself against the dashboard, gaze locked on the shooter.

"I'm going to bait him. Veer away like we're going to go right. He'll follow. Be ready."

"Got it." She slipped away from him and took a position at the window behind his seat. She tapped his shoulder with her hand. "Go."

Reed took a breath and using both arms, swung the RV in a sharp arc away from the oncoming motorcycle. The rider sped up, exposing himself broadside as they turned, his arm coming up, the front tire of the bike wobbling with speed. And then Nat fired. Three quick bursts dead on. A round pinged off the rider's helmet, one shattered the headlight, and another blew the engine as he was trying to turn away. The shooter fired wildly at the RV as he fought to right the bike.

Nat, at Reed's side again, pointed to lights flashing between the trees lining the road. "Cavalry's coming from the north."

They pulled onto the road, and roared up the hill, the RV shuddering with the effort. Something was missing. The sound of the bike. Reed's head whipped to the side, he couldn't find the shooter. "Do you see him?"

She shook her head. "I think he took off."

Reed slowed to a stop along the main road. He scanned the exit and flanking paths coming from the school, but the shooter was gone. Patrol cars skidded to a stop on the road up ahead, the drivers shouting into their shoulder radios as they scrambled out. Reed watched the dust churning in the air, listened to the whir of the air conditioning, the ragged tires giving off a sharp, burnt scent. This was wrong, he thought. This wasn't supposed to happen. He'd not seen it coming and that pissed him off.

"You ok?" he called to Nat. He looked back. She'd slipped back toward Abernathy and was talking to him. Reed left the driver's seat and joined her on the floor. She was holding up her tablet, whispering to the professor softly.

"Just point if you see the student from your class or the man who heckled Iris."

Pink foam bubbled at the corners of his mouth, and he raised a shaking hand, touching the surveillance photo with his index finger. "H-him."

"That's good, Professor Abernathy," she looked at Reed, her face pale.

"The FBI agent was looking for him." Abernathy let his hand fall to the carpet, a sigh leaving him. "Firash Nuri . . ."

"One more, okay?" Nat's hands trembled as she tried to navigate her tablet. "Just a second . . ." She cursed angrily at herself, her fingers unable to work the pad. "I have it right here—" She held it over Abernathy. He didn't move. He didn't blink. "Professor?"

"Nat." Reed put his palm on her knee. "He's gone."

She stilled, her eyes clenching closed. "He didn't . . . I couldn't get Slater's face in front of him fast enough—"

"We did what we could." Reed sat back on his heels. Patrol cops swarmed past the RV into the parking lot and building. Securing the area. He heard someone put out a BOLO on the bike and rider. They set a perimeter. All the right moves. None of them would work. Reed held out his hand. A bullet had skimmed past his chest and seared a trail across the skin of his wrist on its way out the passenger door of the RV. He never even felt it. "There was no stopping that guy."

Paramedics checked him and Nat out. They'd both needed basic wound care for cuts from the flying shards of window glass. He had some cuts on his scalp. Nat's arms looked like she got attacked by a gang of angry cats.

She sat on the bumper of an ambulance, one of their thin shock blankets over her shoulders, and silently watched the ME and his team extricate Abernathy. They zipped him up in a yellow bag. Reed couldn't sit still. He paced, walked the path of the RV. His head throbbing. The sun was peeking through the clouds overhead and his eye caught a glimmer on the asphalt. He walked to it, tilting his head with confusion as he peered down at the pavement. Lying in a pothole was a metal half-circle, like a crown or halo. It was the headpiece he'd seen in Petraeus's recording. The one that wiped her mind. The rider must have dropped it when he nearly went down.

Reed squatted near it, and something tickled his nose. He looked back at the forensics team by the RV, and then at the crown. When he touched the back of his fingers to it, a wave of vibration murmured from the metal through the bones of his hand. Reed yanked it away, his heart pacing up. Had this been around Caitlyn's head? Tangled in her soft hair, burning her to nothing?

The photos of Caitlyn's body in the accident file had seared into his brain. All the guilt for not believing her, for letting her get wrapped up in this alone, slammed into him and he couldn't breathe. He stared at the metal half circle. It was the key to everything, he thought. Figure it out and he'd find the killer. No question.

His phone rang and he pulled it out of his suit jacket and looked at the screen. It was an unknown number. Reed answered it.

"This is Detective Reed."

"Detective," Slater said, the noise cancelling hum in the background softening the edges of his voice. "This is Michael Slater. Neurogen's head of security. I'm making this call on behalf of Mr. Price. He's desperate to learn when he can bury his brother. The whole family is on edge."

Reed listened to him, his gut tightening at the artificially cordial voice. The weird timing. Something was off. Abernathy was the only one who could identify the fake FBI agent and Firash. Was Slater involved? And if he was, did he attack to protect himself or the former student? How were they connected?

Slater's voice came over the phone again. "Detective Reed?"

"He can't have the body."

"May I ask why?"

Reed debated for a second, then took a gamble. "We found something that needs further investigation."

"Something . . . on Gerald's body? At the motel?" Slater's voice changed; the tension in it subtle, but there. "Can I tell his brother what you found?" A few moments went by and then, "Is this no longer a suicide?"

"I'm not at liberty to say, Mr. Slater, but we have reason to believe things aren't what they seem. We've just secured a possible witness," Reed lied. He debated for a second and then, "Has either Corbin or Gerald ever mentioned a young man named, Firash?"

Silence on the other end, churned his gut.

"I don't think so, but I'll ask Mr. Price."

"Do that," Reed said evenly.

"You'll most likely be hearing from his lawyers."

"He'll need them," Reed murmured, his voice low, edged with steel. "Tell your boss we're closing in. He won't have to wait long."

Slater waited a few moments before ending the call without another word. Reed let out a long breath, his anger roiling just under the surface.

"That'll shake something loose." He looked over at the ruined RV, his injured partner, the shocked gawkers on the grassy field. A shell casing lay just a few feet over, glimmering in the sun. "Your move."

21

_____

NW Precinct Station Morgue

Things were ramping up. Tig showed up with the Critical Incident Supervisor, the Chief of Ds, and the mayor's aid, a smarmy, skinny guy with slicked back hair and suits that were too shiny. Lenny Roubideaux spoke in sound bytes and his pale blue eyes were constantly roving, especially when he was standing next to the mayor. Reed thought he had the same vibe as the gators he'd seen off Coyote's pontoon when they'd slick down the bayou during summers. Watchful. Ready to strike.

All four bigwigs squabbled among themselves at the edge of the crime scene, eventually deciding to take Reed and Nat's statements, but let them stay on the case. For now. Things were moving quickly and the mayor, Roubideaux had said, didn't want to lose momentum. His orders were to stay the course. Which Reed found charming, given that the mayor had never been in law enforcement or served in the military. In fact, the only service the mayor had ever given was his tennis swing. But he took the win. He didn't want to be sidelined. Not now.

The sniper's hide was an empty classroom on the third floor of the Political Science Building. No casings. Reed stood where the shooter would have been. He leaned out the window, staring down at the asphalt, the milling cops and forensics techs walking the lot looking for evidence, the paramedic leaning a little too close to Nat as she laughed at something he said. Reed borrowed a scope from one of the techs and measured out the distance. The shot to take out Abernathy would have been a difficult one. The wind, the light, the trees blocking the field of vision. It was beautifully executed, Reed thought, by a stone-cold killer.

He and Nat were released from the crime scene and spent a couple of hours talking to their reps and filling out paperwork. Reed showered and threw some civilian clothes on, black jeans and a dark gray sweater he'd had in his gym bag. Nat had kept a spare pair of slacks and cardigan in her locker. She showered, changed, and then met Reed at his desk when she was done. Damp hair, flushed skin, and crossed arms. She looked mad.

"We'll get him," he assured her. "For all of them."

All she could do in the moment was nod.

Finally free, they walked the metal half-circle first, through evidence and then, to Detective Conroy in cybercrimes. She and Imani scanned it, x-rayed it, and waved devices Reed suspected were from the future over it. He watched the results pop up on the wall displays and listened to Nat, Imani, and Conroy argue over what they were looking at. Conroy wanted to take it apart right then but agreed to wait until more tests came back on the metallurgy.

Reed wanted to walk it down to Sanders at the morgue in the meanwhile to see if it matched up with the wounds on Gerald and Maggie's scalps. It was past breakfast and Nat munched on a humongous apple fritter and some startlingly pale coffee as they rode the elevator. She looked up at Reed mid-chew and shrugged.

"Sugar helps me think," she said with a tired smile. Her phone rang and she handed him her donut, wiped her hands on her pants, and answered it. Reed broke a piece off the bottom, popped it in his mouth, and suffered her wrathful stare while she listened. Nat ended the call and took her donut back. "The reverse engineering techs took apart the drone I shot. Turns out it wasn't military grade. It's a kit. You can buy it online."

"A mail order weaponized drone? How, the Dark Web?"

"Nothing that complicated. These are just cheap hobby drone kits you can buy anywhere online. They're made to look like they're authentic military surplus with paint and texture. People use them to stream their hiking trips, take fly throughs of homes for sale, stuff like that. But you can download schematics to convert it from a surveillance drone to a weaponized version."

"You're kidding."

"It's scary how easy it is. Of course, you have to know where to look, but there're free, open-source 3D print plans for just about anything. The reason it was so rickety was the cheap build material the guy chose to make it out of." She nibbled on the fritter again. "Oh, and the daggers . . . they're made from a metal alloy solution used in machine shops and hobby spaces. You mix the separate components, pour it into a silicon mold, and presto. You've got deadly, paper-thin daggers, brittle enough to disintegrate on impact."

"A simple kit like this would be child's play to a trained operator like Slater. Easy to get in the field."

"Yeah, and cheap, too. You'd just need some simple tools. Explains why he seems to have a lot of them."

"Then why didn't he use them?" Reed muttered, shaking his head. "He took a shot from a building that was what . . . six hundred meters away? And he had a handgun that he used almost too well, while on a motorcycle."

"You sound impressed," Nat said, a frown marring her forehead.

"Just confused." The elevator doors opened, and they walked down the white tiled hallway toward the morgue. "Passive, then aggressive, then passive at your place—"

"I wouldn't call him passive. He tried to ram himself through my bedroom door."

"But he didn't shoot out the lock." Reed gestured at the double doors. "He obviously has access to weapons. Why make a goofy kit that, let's be honest, didn't really do a good job of hurting anyone?"

"The more I go over what happened. It was like he used the drones as a kind of distraction."

"To get away." Reed tapped his leather notebook on his open palm. "The guy at your place used a remote weapon to escape confrontation.

Same at my condo. He ran, used the drone. Keeping his distance. But then, at the college, he took a bullet to the helmet and kept chasing us?

"Two different objectives?"

Reed thought about it for a second, working it out. "You're saying Slater's attacks on us were to throw off the investigation. Hurt, but not kill. That would bring the full force of the SPD down on the city. But injured, we would have been put on light duty, the case passed to someone else who has to start over."

"I think so, yeah, that could explain why he attacked so differently, right?"

"That should have worked." Reed twirled the pen in his hand. "But that would mean he's also working through people for some *other* reason."

"Maybe they're able to connect him to something or someone he wants to stay hidden. This Mercy chick, probably," Nat offered.

"Then what is this guy doing? Protecting this Mercy by taking witnesses out in the most unreliable and inconvenient way possible? Why not just kill them like he did Abernathy?"

"I have no idea. I'm just spit balling here," Nat said with a shrug. "That or he's got multiple personalities."

"Wouldn't shock me at this point." Reed let out long breath. He opened his notebook and wrote out names, circled them, and connected them with lines. "Look, what we do know is Gerald, Petraeus, and Maggie, all had the same mark on their scalp. Now, Maggie connects them to Iris and Abernathy via the school." He circled all five names and drew a line from *that* group to two other names: Corbin and Slater. "Gerald connects everyone to Neurogen, which happens to be on the cutting edge of neurology."

"Yeah, but they cure epilepsy and PTSD. They're working on Alzheimer's, not turning people into produce."

"Okay set that aside." He drew another arm off the group of five names. From Iris and Abernathy to Firash. Everyone connected to everyone. "What do you see, Nat? What's missing?"

She ran her finger over the notebook paper in his hand. To the one name in the center of all of it. "Everyone on here has a personal connection to someone else. Gerald and Petraeus were lovers. He gave her something to hide from this assailant, presumably. Gerald and Corbin are brothers,

and they have a relationship with Slater. A personal one. Iris and Abernathy . . . married, they both had close encounters with Firash. But Maggie .
. . she's an outlier."

"Yes! She's the linchpin and I think I know how." He tapped his pen on
the cover of his notebook, relieved she saw it too.

"Uh . . . walk me through it," Nat said. "For clarity."

"Other than being enrolled in Abernathy's class, and remember, he
didn't even remember her, Maggie doesn't seem connected to anything
anyone is doing."

Nat nodded. "Not involved with hacking, or brain implants, or stalking
Iris."

Reed's hand went up. "Remember, though, she is." He opened his notebook and flipped back to his interview with the provost. "Sort of. Firash was
upset about environmental issues and Maggie was in that club. The one
Abernathy mentioned the FBI guy was interested in."

"Right, right . . . Restoration Republic," Nat grabbed her tablet from her
blazer pocket. "We're still waiting on a subpoena for their member list."

"If this fake FBI guy was looking for Firash and thought he'd find him
via Restoration Republic, then that's where he must have crossed paths
with Maggie."

"That tracks. He must have thought she knew something, or he
wouldn't have gone after her. But what's a college freshman gonna know
that's worth killing her over? She was just a kid."

"Just a kid . . ." Reed drew lines under the words he'd written down from
Cara's statement. *An older man.* "Maggie had been hiding her older
boyfriend. Hundred percent it's Firash. I think that's where they're
connected. They could have met at this club. She understands his anger at
Iris. Maybe even helped him stalk her."

"You think she and Firash knew or saw something they weren't
supposed to?"

"Iris had shady connections. I looked up this Ghanzi Province deal. It's
controversial. A lot of human rights and environmental groups are up in
arms. Briar Ridge and the people they represent are negotiating with
members of the Afghan government who were known leaders in the
Taliban."

"That's both messed up and stupid," Nat said, her brow furrowing. "Who does Briar Ridge represent?"

"I don't know. I couldn't find out by conventional means." Reed looked at Nat.

"Gotcha," she smiled. "I'll see what we can get the AI crawler to dig up on it. I've got some friends in forensic accounting who can help."

"This project is set to pull trillions out of that country. And Firash was definitely watching Iris. It's not a leap to think Maggie might help his cause. So yeah, if they were following her around, they might have been noticed by the wrong people."

Nat smacked Reed's bicep with the back of her hand. "You think he's next on Slater's list of loose ends to tie up?"

"This kid is tangled up with this somehow. I just can't see it yet." Reed stopped just in front of the morgue doors. "You were able to get a positive ID from Abernathy. That was smart, tough to do, but smart. Let's see what we can find out about this Firash Nuri."

"Already running a search. Photo and name. I'll find him."

Reed led the way through the morgue, past the scanners and cleaning bots, to the tables with the disembodied robotic arms ceaselessly working. Sanders took the device over to a metal table and stood hunched over looking at the crown through a giant lens on an extendable arm. He straightened up, pushing the lens away.

"This is . . ." Sanders held the metal half-circle in his gloved hands, inspecting it with awe. "It looks positively alien."

"At this point I wouldn't be surprised," Nat said.

"We're hoping it's something that leaves hard evidence on the brains it was used on," Reed said. "But I'd settle for blood, fingerprints, anything."

"Let me get my cameras."

Sanders hurried around the lab pulling equipment, messing with lenses, doing something with the display screens. Nat jumped in to help, arguing over cord management and filters. They set up a smart table and took 360-degree pics with the gyroscope arm extending down from the ceiling. He was adjusting the halo when he pulled back, startled.

"What is it?" Nat asked, leaning over.

"Well, it's nearly undetectable, but I could swear this thing is vibrating."

"It is," Reed said. "I felt it too. In the field."

Nat took a step back. "Why do you think that is? You think it's still on?"

Sanders squinted at one of the protruding nodes on the headband. "Hold on." He pulled back the lens, then looked at the row of minute tools on the shelf over the table, selecting one as he put the device on the examination table. "I think there's some damage . . ."

The crown vibrated on the metal table and Sanders went to grab it when something shot out of the middle node. A spray of threadlike filaments thrust outward from the center of the crown, their razor-sharp ends slicing through Sanders's finger. He yelped as Reed yanked him back by his lab coat. Sanders stared at his hand for a half-second and then rushed to a wash station. The automatic first aid kiosk scanned and sanitized his wound, and he came back looking a little rattled.

"Should've seen that coming," Sanders held up a bandaged finger.

"What are those things?" Reed leaned in and pushed the long strands around on the table with a pen. "Wires?"

"I think they're filaments," Sanders said. "I've seen something like it in surgical videos used for teaching. They're used in brain surgery."

"To what, harpoon tumors?" Nat asked. She crossed her arms frowning at the table. "This is what happened to Petraeus?"

Sanders nodded, "Yes, and sadly, there was no need for such destruction. These filaments are usually placed along specific areas for focal stimulation. But *proper* insertion is done with robot assist instruments because the surgical AI has vessel avoidance programmed in to minimize damage. This is just . . ." Sanders shook his head, walking over to his display monitor. He called up the light keyboard, which shone on the table in bright red. He started typing, calling up something. "Whoever built this didn't care what was destroyed. Only that the path be true."

"Well, clearly this isn't a medical device. What do you think it does then—"

"What path?" Reed interrupted her. "You're saying these filaments were directed? How?"

"By something like this," Sanders pointed to his screen. Two lines traced across a graph. They were joined in one section and then split apart. He pointed to the top line. "This is Fluorine 18. It's a radioisotope that's used as a tracer for brain imaging. Remember I found traces of an unknown substance in the tissue surrounding the needle mark in Mr. Price's thigh? The results came back inconclusive, but I think it could be an altered version of a tracer isotope like Fluorine 18." Sanders pointed to the second line. "You see here. Where Fluorine 18 is perfect for uptake in specific cells. Malignancies for example, this other version is designed to be a tracer for something else entirely. And with protein folding models available even in consumer grade programs, you could design it to target just about anything."

Reed regarded the graph, wrapping his mind around the science. "Tell me if I'm getting this right. The injected isotope traces a specific path along the brain, and the halo device somehow directs the filaments to follow the chemical trail?"

"Yes, I believe that's what it was designed to do." Sanders said.

"Does it go to a specific, uh, area?" Reed fought for a foothold on the motive. "Aren't there certain parts of the brain assigned to different functions?"

"Yes and no," Sanders tilted his head side to side. "Some functions like eyesight have a specific focal area, but other brain functions use several different parts of the brain all at once. Dreaming, for example. The brains of people dreaming light up like Christmas trees in PET scans. Being in love and eating chocolate also light up various areas."

"What is the actual point though?" Reed tapped his notebook cover on the table, thinking. "I thought what happened to Petraeus . . . her brain damage, was because the device wasn't used right. He was interrupted. But you're saying it is designed to shred the mind of whoever it's used on? What's the point of that? Why not just a bullet to the head?"

"This is pretty close," Sanders said. "The rate of acceleration with which the charge propels the filaments through the brain is considerable."

Reed stared at the filaments on the table. "What happens to them? Do they just stay there? Because you didn't find any in Gerald, right?"

"I didn't. But I think I know why. I think they dissolve," Sanders said. "Like internal stitches. Some only take a matter of hours for the body to absorb them."

"No wonder Petraeus was so messed up. That guy set off a mini explosion in her head," Nat said with disgust. She looked at Reed. "You think we can get a scan of her brain? She has the only evidence not damaged by a fake suicide."

"She's alive so you'd have to go through her family." Reed scratched at his sideburns. "But we should try. Tig'll know how to get it. Maybe it'll help us figure out what the device is designed to do. It can't be just to scramble people's minds."

"This might help." Sanders positioned the lens over the halo again and then pointed to one of the nodes. It was broken. Snapped in half. "I think there's a piece missing. Possibly during your reenactment of OK Corral. Whatever it was might explain what the halo does."

Reed nodded to the door of the holding freezer. "And you have proof this was definitely used on Maggie and Gerald?"

"Absolutely," Sanders said with a smile. "You remember Gerald's brain that I sliced. He tapped on his keyboard and a display screen on the wall lit up with high-res images. "These are photos of a cross section. See those pinholes?"

Reed nodded. "Yeah."

"Okay this is another view of his brain." Sanders touched the display glass and a different kind of image emerged. A 3D render of Gerald's damaged brain. It was incomplete, marred at the back, but recognizable. The image spun lazily in the black of the screen. Sanders manipulated it to give them a profile view. "I found what looked like tunnels in these sections. I thought it might be prions. But when I compiled the MRI slices into one image. I got this . . ."

On the side view of the 3D brain, hair-thin lines traced from the top of the brain stem upward, threading through tissue like tendrils reaching toward the forehead.

"A specific path," Reed said quietly. He regarded the thread-like tunnels through the pale tissue, a wisp of a theory floating just beyond his reach. "Did you find this in Maggie too?"

"As soon as I saw it in Gerald, I checked Maggie's brain. It's there. They were both definitely attacked by the same device." Sanders rotated the 3D rendering of Gerald's brain on the display screen with his index finger. "These tunnels span areas across the entire brain . . . at least what I could salvage given the shotgun's damage. The same with Maggie. Extensive damage hid most of the tunneling, but I did find evidence in her frontal lobe."

Reed took in a deep breath, pushing the thought of wires spiking through his brain out of his head. He turned to Nat.

She stared at the screen, and bit at her pinkie nail. "Well, that's confirmation at least. We're not wrong about the victims or what's happening to them. We just don't know why."

Reed's gaze went to the dissecting lines on Sanders's graph of Fluorine 18. Different paths. Both true . . . "Were they the same?"

Sanders frowned. "What?"

"The filament trails through Gerald and Maggie? Did they take the same path?"

"I'm not sure." Sanders regarded the images of the sliced brain on the wall. "Like I said, the damage . . ."

"If you had to guess, though," Reed pushed. "Did the halo send the filaments in the same *exact* path for both victims?"

"If I were a betting man, I'd say no."

Nat bumped Reed's elbow with hers. She pointed to her own head. "Hey, what's churning up there?"

"I don't know yet, but . . ." Reed shrugged. "I don't know yet."

"Something you might find interesting," Sanders said as he walked across the lab to retrieve a small specimen jar with liquid from the back table. A square piece of metal rested at the bottom of the solution. Sanders opened the jar and retrieved the metal with a pair of alligator clamps, walked over to the table with the halo and the filaments, and looked at them under the lens. He turned, typed on the keyboard again and the view blinked onto the display screen. "This is a deep brain stimulator for epilepsy. I took it from Gerald's brain."

Reed looked at the two pieces of metal side by side, digitally enhanced to a high magnification. He wouldn't have seen it with the naked eye, but on the screen, it was clear as crystal. The strange, oil slick pattern etched on the surface of the filaments was also on the stimulator.

"Cured in the same matrix." Reed touched the screen, running his fingertips along the pattern. He glanced at Sanders. "It was a proprietary method created by Gerald, correct?"

"Yes, in a lab. They're too small, too delicate to be extruded by conventional machinery."

Sanders tipped his chin at Reed. "Very good, Detective. How did you become an expert on devices for neurological intervention?"

"I watched the online versions of the demonstration videos that were playing in the Neurogen office. They had archives on their website."

Nat smiled. "Nice work for a guy who hates tech."

"Well, it was interesting reading. This material, the stimulators, were next level innovation at the time. The technology put them on the map." He turned to Nat. "And the last of the patents just ran out last year."

"Your 'friend' said they were desperate for cash." Nat put her hand to her forehead and looked at Reed. "I can't believe Gerald was killed by his own product . . . that is seven kinds of messed up."

"This isn't one of their devices, though, Detective. Not according to anything they offer on the market. I had my assistant look up patents that either Neurogen Bionics or Gerald Price hold as well as anything pending. Nothing. This is . . ." Sanders nodded down at the halo and tangled filaments on the table. "No way this would get approved past the schematic stage. Look at what it does."

"I don't think this design was ever supposed to be made public," Reed said. He caught Nat's gaze. "This must be what Gerald found out. What he gave to Petraeus."

"Gerald was the whistle blower," Nat said. "On his own brother?"

"Yes. And Corbin's been running us around since the beginning." Reed turned and strode for the door, his stomach churning. "I think it's time to ask Corbin Price if saving his own ass was worth having his brother killed."

22

Neurogen Bionics

Corbin's arm twisting had pissed off a lot of powerful people. He'd gotten progressively aggressive and, Tig heard, had moved on to threats to get his brother's case closed. Fortunately for Reed and Nat, one of those people was Judge Stojanovic. The son of Serbian immigrants, he'd clawed himself up the judicial ladder with grit, brains, and ruthlessness. He hated soft, rich men who used their money to influence what he called, the 'Purity of Law.' Reed pushed that angle during the meeting in chambers.

The PT7 solvent used by special forces found at Petraeus's apartment, the official though heavily redacted military file Tig was able to get, and Reed's account of the high-speed firefight at the college, all convinced Judge Stojanovic to grant narrow warrants for Slater's apartment and his office at Neurogen Bionics. Stressing that he believed another victim was in the killer's sights, Reed got any common areas of the Neurogen building thrown in. He hoped that was enough.

Tig and Reed wanted to hit both places at once. Nat and a SWAT team went to Slater's apartment and Reed drove with a couple of patrol cars following to Neurogen Bionics. Reed needed something that would get him closer to Corbin. That kind of technology didn't happen under the radar.

Someone at Neurogen had to design that device, those wires, and whatever was in that injection. He doubted it was a jarhead like Slater, however well-trained he was to kill. Reed's phone rang and Nat's voice came through his earbud.

"The address to the apartment was fake," she said, disappointment thick in her voice. He could hear people talking in the background. "A nice old couple just made me eat cookies I swear were as old as they were while they told me they've lived there for nearly a decade. It was never a valid address. And get this, Imani just sent me a peek at Slater's financials. Slater hasn't spent money in Seattle for three years. His employment records show him leaving Neurogen Bionics at the same time."

"I guess I should ask him how he just happened to be right next to Corbin when we showed up."

A car door slammed on her end. "You think he'll be there?"

"I just got off the phone with the receptionist. According to her, Slater walked out the door after we left that first meeting and hasn't been back." Reed turned into the parking area near Neurogen Bionics. "I'll take another run at Corbin. Maybe scare him a little. He's either involved or he knows something."

Nat shouted something but it was muffled. The car horn honked and then she was back. "I'm on my way to you with an evidence team. I'll be there in twenty if traffic holds."

As he drove closer to the building to park, he had to navigate around two heavy-duty work trucks, an excavator, and a bulldozer. Giant wood spools of cable sat atop a flatbed truck in front of the entrance. He scanned the parking lot. It was empty save for a few cars at the far end and a blue and white security car. Reed strode to the glass doors and peered in while he waited for the patrol officers to catch up. The lobby was dark, but he could see a light coming from the security office door a few yards down. He'd grabbed a radio and comm earbud at the station and used them to call the patrol officers.

"Looks like it's closed. See if you can find any of the workers that go with that equipment. Ask them what their work orders are. I'm heading in to speak with security. Detective De La Cruz is on her way. Keep an ear open for screeching tires."

"I literally heard that," Nat's amused voice came back in his ear.

Reed pushed through the security office's glass door and the guy at the desk looked up from his handheld gaming console with a suspicious gaze. He was young, barely growing peach fuzz on his chubby cheeks, his dirty blonde hair gelled back within an inch of its life.

"Uh, Neurogen Bionics is closed for maintenance, sir."

Reed held up his badge. "What kind of maintenance?"

The kid shrugged and went back to his game. "Think they tell me anything?"

"Is anyone inside?" Reed leaned on the interactive counter between them and scrolled through the options that lit up underneath the glass. "Can I get in contact with Mr. Price or Mr. Slater through this?"

"Nah, just that snooty secretary in the lobby. She's gone too though. And I don't know anyone named Slater, but Mr. Corbin was here earlier. I'm not sure if he's at lunch or not."

A patrol officer walked past the door and the security guard's eyes went wide. He puffed out his chest to compensate and asked, "Something happening I should know about?"

Reed glanced at the guard's scraggly mustache and said, "Do me a favor, man. Stay here, direct my backup when they get here. I'm going inside."

He tried to look disappointed, but the relief came through. "Yeah, no prob. I'll be on the lookout."

Reed left the office and met up with the ranking officer in front of the main entrance.

Officer Dutton looked like she broke horses or won rodeos. She had short dark hair, like an aggressive mom cut, but spiky, a tough jut to her chin, and weathered skin. She read from her notepad. "Crew boss says their work order was for a maintenance on the network cables, but there was a problem with the permissions. They're waiting on instructions from their boss. He did say the order was rush, came in late last evening."

"I'm going to do a walk around to see if I can find anyone to let me in." He pointed with his notebook at the security office. "The guy inside says Corbin Price was here earlier. If you come across the guy, hold him and give me a call."

"What's he look like?"

"You know that social media guy, comes off like he's a robot?"

"Yeah."

"The same but this one looks like he'd sell his mother for a piece of gum."

Dutton managed a smirk. "Got it."

They split up and Reed walked along the outside length of the building on the grass. He wove in and out of the gardens, trying grates and maintenance doors. Everything was locked. The building curved back behind a retaining wall, and he followed the access path downhill to some nondescript structures hidden behind the main building. They were functional. Storage and electrical most likely. He headed that way. Reed got about five steps before a man's voice floated across the pavement to him. It was a groan of pain like he'd heard at Petraeus's. Faint at first. It was coming from further down the access path. He followed the sound to a brick building set back from the rest, a metal security door sat slightly ajar. Louder now, another moan made him move. He depressed his communications earbud to speak.

"Nat, I've got a possible distress call in the rear of the main Neurogen building. The brick one, way in back."

"I'm still ten minutes out."

"I think it's Slater. He's got someone in there—"

A bloodcurdling scream rattled through Reed from behind the door. He pulled his weapon, and yanked open the door, sweeping with the flashlight. It was a corridor, dark, and cement lined. Frost encrusted the upper wall and ceiling. Safety strips on the floor glowed on with his movement. He heard static in his ear, the connection gone. Low, anguished cries warbled out of the darkened corridor. Reed moved, weapon close to his chest, along the wall silently. Listening. The floor lit up as he walked, a little in front of him, going dark behind. It was cold, more than it had been outside, and getting colder. Frigid, even. His breath came in cloudy puffs.

The floor angled down, Reed felt it in his knees. Rumbling in the walls and below his boots felt mechanical. Probably the refrigeration units. Banging, like a hammer on metal sounded deep in the dark and Reed walked that way. He was lower than the ground now, the muffled silence of the deep earth almost deafening. More static in his ear made him pause. He pressed his earbud twice and waited for an answering bleep. Still nothing.

A blue glow on the floor, then the walls and ceiling as Reed walked was coming from an open doorway at the end of the corridor. Intense vibrations seemed to flow in waves out of the doorway making his teeth feel soft and his skin tingle. He slowed, sliding along the wall to the side of the pneumatic metal doors. A placard on the wall next to the door read, *Archives*. He peeked in quickly. Rows of servers stood floor to ceiling down the center of the narrow room. Blue and green lights twinkled from within their dark, wired bowels.

Reed slipped into the room, walking along the edge in the dark. Soft yellow lights illuminated the space, and the steady hum of equipment drew him to an area with storage shelving that stood butted up against the far wall. Crates and metal containers sat on the shelves and on the floor, someone having gone through them. Files and tapes were tossed in a metal trashcan. Wood shavings littered the floor. Two industrial shredders ground through the stacks of papers and what looked like data strips shoved into the feed chutes. Reed shone his light on the crates. They all had the same label, 'MER-C System. Classified.'

He tapped the wording with his index finger, and the assailant's question to Petraeus ran through his head. *Who did you tell about Mercy?* "Not a person. A project."

Crying on the other side of the server room pulled his attention. He walked over. Metal stools fastened to the ground with bolts sat in front of two workstations on the other wall. Bright lights illuminated a keyboard built into the surface of the desk. A smart screen with several open windows ran through scrolling lists of file names. None of them readable. They were numbers and symbols with a few letters peppered in. Reed touched the back of his hand to the stool. It was still warm.

Voices sounded from the display screens hanging over the desks. It was a recording of a small hospital room. Time stamp put it four years ago. The room was brightly lit, sterile. A patient lay strapped on a bed, their head rocking from side to side as they cried out unintelligible sounds. Gerald sat in front of the patient, talking straight into the camera. A sterile tray on a table next to him held surgical equipment. Reed recognized some of the clamps, he'd seen them in the ER. Vials with purple fluid and syringes shared space on the tray with the long, finger-like appendages of a surgical assist robot. In the pinchers of the robot hand was a single metallic thread, barely visible in the overhead fluorescent lights of the room.

Gerald let out a defeated breath. "Subject twelve has taken a turn. I just . . ." he rubbed his eyes underneath his glasses. "Although there is definite evidence of the augmentation taking effect. I believe the damaging effects of the serum is insurmountable—" the recording froze. A pop-up warning appeared over the image that read, 'deletion scheduled for section 1r*t7, press any key to save.'

Before Reed could act, the recording fast-forwarded to another section. This time with Gerald sitting at his desk, his feet up, a glass tumbler in his hands. The paintings of Alki Beach and Petraeus had hung together on the wall behind him. He was drunk, slurring as he spoke to the camera.

"I initially sought to extract key executive functions and enhance them —chemically, hormonally, and yes . . . electrically, minimally so. There's a bit of Mary Shelly for you." He chuckled. "The augmentation serum should make a deeper impression. Help them retain core abilities, personality traits, and motor functions longer but the serum . . . it burns them—"

The video deleted again. Moving forward further still. Skipping as the timestamp counted through the hours, days, and months. It stopped again. But it wasn't Gerald this time. The resemblance was uncanny, but it was Corbin. He stood at a worktable, one of the crates open in front of him. Over it, he held a small, round object. Like a chocolate coin but as thick as a stack of cards. Holding it up, he admired it, displaying it to the camera.

"This is the containment pod. It's self-sustaining for up to two hours, then the cooling system in the case maintains stasis and slows decay." He pulled a halo from the crate. This one was shiny chrome, and the nodes were much larger than the one Reed had found. "We're taking the weight and the circumference down in the next iteration, but this is the device. Capable of firing three complete filament clusters before needing to be reloaded." He attached the containment pod, snapping it into place. Corbin then held it up to the camera, showing it off, a sly grin on his lips. He turned and spoke to someone off camera. "And fully portable for the field. As requested."

Reed noticed movement at the edge of the video frame. A leg as someone sitting next to Corbin just off camera, adjusted in their seat before answering. "I'll inform Danzig."

It was a male voice, clipped, rough. Reed had heard it on the phone just hours earlier. And then, he heard it behind him.

"I wondered how a city detective was gaining on me," Slater said as he moved out from behind a server tower, gun at his thigh. He was sweating despite the cold, gloved hands shaking. His T-shirt stained with blood. Ragged skin on his knee showed through his torn field pants. "And then I read your file. You took out Fourth Quadrant."

Reed glanced over his shoulder. "They were out of control."

"The army made you a hunter, didn't they, Detective Reed? Or did they just hone one from what was already there?"

"We all have our aptitudes," Reed said, turning to face him.

"Relentless!" Slater half laughed, half shouted as he shifted on his feet. He wiped his brow with his forearm. "When did you figure it out?"

Slater looked both injured and unhinged. Reed saw signs of a concussion, uneven pupils, the imbalance, blood in the ear canal. He glanced at his watch. He didn't know how long he'd been down in there.

"She recorded you," Reed said. "Petraeus did. She caught all of it.

"She recorded me?" Slater's hand went to the cut on his neck. To the slash from her dagger as she fought for her life. He swayed back on his heels as if drunk.

"We saw the halo and how you dosed her with what I'm guessing is that augmentation serum, Gerald was just talking about. And I heard the questions." Reed slid his leading foot forward, gauging distance. "You were looking for something specific, weren't you? Using the questions like breadcrumbs on a trail. But I couldn't figure out what you were doing. Not until we took Gerald's brain apart, saw the paths the filaments took when they shredded his mind."

Slater nodded, his face pulling into an anguished frown only to morph into rage. He grabbed a containment pod from one of the crates and shook it at Reed. "You don't know what I'm trying to stop! There was no time for lies. I had to know who she'd told."

"Those are memories, aren't they?" Reed pointed at the device in

Slater's hand. "That's what all of this is? Corbin took Gerald's research and turned it into this . . . atrocity?" Reed's blood raced in his head. "You're ripping people's memories right out of their heads. Stealing the very core of who they are from them."

Slater grinned crazily and raised his weapon. "The best heist you'll never remember."

Reed licked his lips. "For who? For Spectre . . . or is it Danzig?"

Slater froze. "What did you say?"

"Reed!" Nat's voice reverberated down the corridor and Reed dove for Slater the millisecond he was distracted.

They hit the floor, Reed's head banging on the edge of a work desk, stars flashing behind his eyes.

Slater scrambled to his feet, aiming for the door. "Detective De La Cruz! Hurry, Detective Reed is hurt!"

"Nat," Reed croaked, fighting to stay conscious. Her flashlight beam slashed the dark of the corridor, footsteps, light and fast, hurried toward them.

Reed rose as her footfalls sped toward them. Something tumbled across the floor. He leveled his weapon at Slater. "I won't wait for you to shoot first."

"*There's* the Terror of Belltown," Slater growled, looking over at Reed. A metal ring dangled from his index finger. Nat's form filled the doorway just as a blast rocketed through the room.

23

The train was coming for him again. Its headlight an angry eye in the dark tunnel. A furious wind rattled through him, and he choked in the smoke. The train horn blared, loud and piercing and, somehow . . . wrong. It morphed from the shrill cry of a whistle to the clang of a klaxon alarm. Reed coughed himself awake, heart racing, and blinked in the semidarkness. Thick smoke drifted in the yellow emergency lights. He shook his head, his ears ringing so loud he thought his skull might fracture. Stumbling in the debris, he picked up his mini flashlight and found his gun, holstering it. Reed let his eyes adjust, the blurriness fading as he steadied himself. The bulk of the damage from the explosion was by the door, but the shockwave had knocked over the closest floor-to-ceiling servers, which fell like dominos. The twisted metal and wires blocked the exit.

Fire suppression systems in the server vault tried repeatedly to close the damaged pneumatic doors to quell the flames that engulfed the storage shelves, but they were blocked by something. They would close almost completely only to bounce back a few inches and try again. The hiss and grind of the mechanism echoed through the room just beneath the alarm. He climbed over the fallen tower closest to the doors and pushed back the debris, but one of the doors had warped in the blast. He tried to pry them open with his hands but couldn't get enough leverage before they slammed back together. In the moment they pulled apart, he saw movement in the dark of the tunnel. A flash of Nat midway down the corridor. Her hair awry, soot on her chin, dark eyes intense as her gaze locked with his the moment before the doors snapped back. Another glimpse of patrol cops running back out toward the light of day, going for help.

She appeared at the small gap as the doors reopened, relief flooding her face. "Oh my god, I thought you were vaporized!" The doors snapped closed. When they opened, she was pointing up, "The ceiling is unsteady —" the doors slammed together. They pulled apart, "Stay away from the door—"

Reed nodded and backed away. Something landed on his shoulder, and he looked up at the suppressant powder drifting down from the fractured ceiling pipes like snow. The fire in the corner spread steadily atop one of the overturned shredders. A busted crate caught alight, its wood shavings igniting and sending smoke swirling to the ceiling. Reed coughed, looking for an extinguisher when the alarm stopped, and the sudden silence pierced through him.

Slater moaned from behind a fallen server. He was sitting on the floor leaning against the wall. Fury roared through Reed, and he scrambled over one of the towers to Slater, grabbed him by the shirt, and shook him.

"The Terror of Belltown?" Reed shouted. "How do you know that name? Only *one* person outside of my past knows what I was. Caitlyn."

Slater's eyes swam. "Caitlyn? Who's Caitlyn?"

Reed pushed him back against the wall in disgust. He stood pacing, fury roiling in his chest, stealing his breath. He pulled his weapon, training it on Slater, hand steady. "You don't even remember her!"

Slater moaned, his head lolling against the wall. He looked up at Reed at an angle. A wound under his eye made him look like he was crying blood. "Too many are me now, to remember . . ."

"What?" Reed stepped back and shone his flashlight beam along Slater's body. He was trapped, his legs pinned beneath a fallen server. Holstering his weapon, Reed bent down, assessing the damage. It was bad. The server tower was heavy with metal and electronic structural support inside, and when he tried to lift it, Slater yelled with pain despite it barely budging.

Reed squatted beside Slater, looking at his uneven pupils. "You're in bad shape, man."

"What is it saying?" Slater pulled his T-shirt up to reveal a Vitals Vest. SPD SWAT teams wore something like them. Bullet proof, the vest relayed the wearer's telemetry to a central platform.

Reed squinted at the flexible readout window. Multiple red alerts scrolled across the mini screen. "It says, uh . . . tachycardia, elevated blood pressure, and elevated potassium. The vest thinks you might have a crush injury."

Slater let out a wry chuckle. "Of course, it does. Always misses the most important problem . . ." he tapped his head with a finger. "The real threat."

Reed moved to answer, and froze, realization slamming into him. Slater's T-shirt exposed his arms and Reed didn't see any burns on either of them. Nat's lava lamp had exploded all over her attacker in her house. She'd said he screamed.

"You didn't come after me and my partner, did you?"

"And pull your attention to Neurogen?" Slater looked at him, his gaze lucid, sharp. "Why would I do that?"

"And the drones?"

Slater half-coughed, half-laughed. "What the hell are you talking about?"

"That wasn't you." Reed sat back on his heels, rubbing his face with both hands, trying to push through the headache storming at his temple. "Two assailants. Two different goals. Dammit, how did I miss that?"

"Firash," Slater said almost wistfully. "Harder to catch than I thought."

"You were sent after him?"

Slater turned away, his lips pressed together.

"Look, we already know you went to Abernathy. He told us you were asking about this Firash. He identified you as the fake FBI agent," Reed lied. "Why were you tracking him?"

"The kid worked for us, under a different name, we found out. He'd changed it years ago, and our background team didn't flag it." Slater wheezed, his brow sweaty. "That's what happens when you hire hackers to infiltrate your competition. They tend to wander."

"Okay, so he was snooping." Reed nodded. It was a worry with their own cybercrime force. The kind of mind that seeks out threat assessments can also bypass the security to stop them. "Firash found out about the Ghanzi Project and wants to stop it."

"How the hell do you know all of this already?" Slater snapped, frustration on his face.

"Iris Abernathy worked for your boss, didn't she? What, did Firash see a file with her name and recognize it? Made the connection between Briar Ridge and whoever you work for? Who is her connection? How did she plan to push through the deal?"

"I warned them about you. I told them what you did before. Even with their turncoat's help, you were always gaining."

Reed froze. "You're saying there's a mole in the Seattle PD?"

"I'm saying you're screwed. If I died here, I wouldn't even make it to your morgue. Danzig's reach is vast, and he wants everything tied off . . ." Slater faded, his head lolling back as if falling asleep.

The fire in the far corner licked up the walls. Reed was running out of time. He slammed his fist on the metal side of the server. Slater woke up with a start. "Is that why you killed the professor, too? To shut him up?"

A jag of coughing gripped Slater and when he looked at Reed, his eyes swam again. "It was time to clean house. Iris can be traced to us . . ."

"What is Spectre?" Reed cut across him, but Slater shook his head, squeezing his eyes shut.

"N-No."

Reed pushed again. "Your skill set, your background, I'm guessing private military. You're a mercenary, aren't you, Slater?" Reed grabbed Slater's chin, forcing him to look at him. "This is what I think. Three years ago, you were sent to Neurogen Bionics by whoever Corbin approached with this . . . device, his idea for it, anyway. Probably to oversee the new design. What'd you do? Get him a team to help make the changes to Gerald's therapeutic device? But mostly you were sent to keep an eye on Corbin, am I right? The little weasel couldn't be trusted. So, you posed as their head of security until the sale went through. But that was three years ago. Why are you back? Was it to kill Gerald? To protect MER-C?"

"Gerald wasn't even on our radar! At least not until he started sticking his nose where it didn't belong." Slater yanked away from Reed's grip, his eyes wild with anger. "And you have no idea what's going on. I wasn't even here for them. If Gerald hadn't noticed the wounds on the body, he never would've guessed I was back. He brought it on himself. Never should've looked into what we were doing. So, in effect, he killed himself—" he stopped himself.

Reed stilled. "That's how you see it? Sounds more like you're trying to justify murder to me."

Slater coughed and Reed didn't know if it was genuine or to buy thinking time, but the room was getting heavier with smoke. The readout on Slater's vest had a lot more red alerts than before.

"Say it! Speak the words, so I can hear it out of your own mouth." Reed pressed. "Gerald found out, didn't he? He found out what you guys did with his technology and who Corbin sold it to. That's what he gave Petraeus. Gerald was going to blow up his own company to stop you two."

"So many people are going to die," Slater's laugh devolved into a hacking cough. Blood coated his lips. "You're in the deep water now, hunter."

Slater's words sent doubt crashing through Reed. "Who is going to die?"

"All of them." His head did the toilet bowl swirl, his face going pale. "One of them . . ."

A slow dawning crept through him. "Oh, my god, I've been blind!" Panic knifed through Reed's gut. He'd read this wrong. He'd read this completely wrong. "How did I miss it?" Reed breathed, both hands covering his mouth. He slid back down to Slater's level and tapped his face lightly to keep him conscious. "Hey! Wake up! What did you mean? Gerald was a side quest from what? Why were you *really here* in Seattle?"

Slaters eyes fluttered open. "If Gerry hadn't gone back to the drawing board none of this would have happened. He wanted to fix the serum and try reviving the memory augmentation project. He thought he could make it work and dug into the archives, the hidden files, everything."

It took Reed a moment to realize. "The poor bastard happened upon Corbin's side project with you?"

"Those brothers beat the shit out of each other, but Corbin thought he'd convinced him it was just a prototype. That it hadn't been sold, but Gerry found out anyway. It was the frozen skin that tipped him off that I was in Seattle again. He must have seen the videos. I think he went to see the bodies. Several MEs around Washington were asked about scalp wounds. I think Gerry was working off the information he'd dug up on the MER-C project and knew I was using the device, looking for something." Slater laughed suddenly. "And then he went and involved Petraeus. She was going to expose everything."

"So, you killed them to keep the MER-C device a secret. And then just continued your mission to find Firash?" Reed rubbed his scar with his thumb, revulsion turning his gut. "This whole thing with Neurogen was just a pit stop to you, with two bodies?"

"I was sent to stop Firash. Gerald and Petraeus just got in the way."

"What is Firash going to do, Slater? What do you have to stop?"

"I—I was on the roof earlier. Scoping out Abernathy going in and out of his RV with the plants and this memory of last Christmas kept coming back to me." Slater banged his head with the heel of his hand. "It was my dad's last, and we were sitting near this huge fireplace drinking out of snowman mugs. The tree behind him had ornaments I had made in grammar school. And he was telling me how proud he was of me but . . ." Slater started crying. "He called me someone else's name. And then I remembered my father died when I was two. I don't know—I don't know who I was in that memory, but in that moment, it felt so real—" He wiped his face with his bloodstained palm leaving streaks on his pale cheek. "They take over, man. They aren't supposed to be there, and they just won't go away."

Reed turned at the sound of scraping on the metal doors. The fire had spread despite the suppression powder, its flames eating up the display screens and work desks, melting the panels. Heat lashed at his face making his skin feel tight. He turned back to Slater. "Your main mission was Firash? Why are you looking for him? Did he steal something? Information on the Ghanzi Project? Were you trying to silence him?"

"Not silence. Stop. He wants her dead, dead, dead . . ." Slater sing-songed, and fell into a wracking cough. He sat there wheezing, and then he looked at Reed. "You can't stop it either. He's already so far ahead of all of us."

"I don't—" Reed fought for understanding. "Who does Firash want dead? And how will he stop a project half a world away?" He leaned down, trying to catch Slater's gaze. "Hey, you have to help me find this kid."

"Kid!" Slater yelled, his arms flailing at his sides. "He is no kid. He's built a weapon. You have to stop him. He's going to massacre—"

"Tell me how, dammit. What is he doing?"

"No one can know. It'll blow back on us—" The Vitals Vest blared alarms as Slater's eyelids fluttered and his body shook.

Reed fell backward, his eyes on Slater's seizing body. *Massacre*. He had no more time. No choices. Rising to his feet, he turned and climbed back over the server to the metal case where it had landed after the blast. The containment system inside was damaged, vapor leaking from the bottom with a steady hiss. He searched the floor for the halo, the syringe with a dose of the serum, and the metal and glass injector pen, pawing through the debris. Reed found them under a section of storage shelving and tossed them into the case, closing it. As he climbed back over the server, pounding at the door and voices made him pause. It was a fireman from the look of the yellow coat sleeve on the arm trying to force a fire extinguisher between the doors. It wouldn't fit.

"He's seizing! We need an ambulance!" Reed yelled when a loud bang rocked the wall and then the safety doors slammed shut. He stared at them, wondering if he'd just been sealed in to burn to death.

Reed went back to the toppled servers, slid down the back of the tower nearest Slater, and set the case down. Slater was still, his eyes wide open and empty. The Vitals Vest displayed a chaotic blip on the echocardiogram. Reed lifted the halo from the interior and held it in his hand. The subtle hum moved through the bones of his fingers and wrist, tickling his nose. In the video, he'd seen Corbin attach the coin-shaped pod, so he took one from the case and clicked it into place. The halo turned ice cold and Reed leaned over Slater's head, speaking clearly.

"Who do you work for? Who have you killed in Seattle?" He reached for the syringe with the serum, palming it. "What is Firash planning to do? What is the weapon he built?"

Slater didn't move, he didn't blink. Reed tried to push on Slater's chest, the man's sitting position against the wall, the server protruding over his abdomen, made CPR impossible. The vest continued to blare a flatline. The image of Petraeus's anguished face flashing back to him, making him nauseous. He shook his head, his hand steady on the syringe. Then the vest went silent. The readout going black.

Reed's voice shook as he leaned over Slater's body. "Think about Caitlyn Reece!"

He plunged the injector needle into Slater's thigh with one hand, while pushing the halo onto Slater's head with the other. Slater's body didn't arch with pain like Petraeus. He didn't scream like she had. Instead, his body trembled and then his head jerked forward as the filaments shot into his head. Slater's pupils pulled suddenly to pinpoints before blowing out completely. Reed reeled back with horror. He ran a few feet from Slater's body, and nearly vomited. He walked off the nausea, trying to catch his breath. What was he doing? Was he mad?

A soft hiss startled him, and he looked over at the body. The circular pod attached to the halo made a loud click and dropped from the halo onto Slater's shoulder and then bounced to the floor. It rolled away and Reed rushed to grab it, but something wasn't right.

The ones he'd seen before didn't look dented. They also didn't feel wet. Reed shone his flashlight on the surface of the pod. There was a tear in the metal surface and mist leaked out in a wispy rivulet. A loud clang at the safety door made him glance over. The corner of the metal glowed orange and he wondered how long it would take to melt their way through to him. An hour, given the security precautions on the door, maybe more?

Two hours in the pod before decay, he remembered from Corbin's demonstration video. That was for a working one. Reed tilted the containment pod in his hand, this one was not. Slater had said there was a weapon. He'd said a massacre was coming. He'd also said they had someone in the SPD. Even if the information in the containment pod survived . . . what would happen to it? Stored in evidence, the secrets within locked away while a weapon is in play?

Reed took in a deep breath and reached back into the case and pulled out the metal and glass injector he'd seen Slater use in the Petraeus recording. He found the inlet port on the containment pod and tried to insert the needle but kept missing. Taking a breath, he steadied his hand and inserted it. The plunger pulled back automatically, and purple fluid pooled into the vial.

Reed held it up in front of his face, his pulse pounding in his ears. The glass of the injector showed fractures and the row of three lights lining the metal rim around the base flickered red, not white like in the Petraeus video.

"That seems bad," Reed muttered to himself.

He leaned back against the server next to Slater. A rumble beneath him, like the thunder of a train, shook him to his core. The doors to the server room slammed in their tracks as the fire crew tried to force their way in. Hand shaking, he positioned the needle against his neck, his heart racing in his throat. He took in a quick breath and pushed the point into his flesh. The injector bucked in his palm. It's plunger thrusting all the way down, shooting the serum into his artery. A rush of cold soared through his head. Reed gasped, his chest seizing tight. A groan escaped his lips as his mind exploded with light.

24

A wave of images and sounds slammed into Reed, crushing the shout of pain from his throat. Like a shot of epinephrine to the brain everything moved in a frantic, frenetic pace. Voices flew out of the darkness, over-lapped, echoed, and then faded only to blare incoherently from far away. And he knew. He knew everything. Every moment had meaning. The noise of a ship engine while he crept deep within its bowels toward a target. That last step before a night jump, adrenaline spiking through his veins. The scream of a missile overhead, the smell of piss and fear suffocating in a foxhole.

Reed gasped, panic coursing through him as he fought for sense of time or place. Flashes of rooms, people talking to him, running from him down dark streets, flared bright and detailed before him. The smell of gunfire, blood spraying warm and wet across his face, his hands wrapped around a screaming throat. An eruption of scenes that burned bright and real and detailed only to collapse into themselves, sucking the color and light from around him.

And then he had a dirty coat in his hands, the fabric scratchy against his palms, as he propelled the man wearing it in front of him. Alastair Kuntz's limp body stood swaying in front of him at the edge of the platform as the sound of an oncoming train squealed in the tunnel. The weapons dealer had been hard to find, but his sailboat had served as a great place to rip his memory. The smell of burning skin floated through Reed's mind and he gagged. Through Slater's eyes, a sign overhead said, 1 Line – Angel Lake Station. Reed caught sight of Alastair's profile, saw the drool streaming from his chin. A rush moved through him as he shoved the defenseless man in front of the barreling train engine. Reed twisted away, and a whirl-wind of noise forced him forward.

The moon peeked through the pylons of a bridge. He stood against the railing and looked down at the water, to the falling body of Georgia Henry, her financial information on Firash safe in the containment pod in his hand. He waited for the splash and then walked back down the bridge road, leaving her car and the note he'd made her write behind. Someone's fireplace sent the smell of pine floating through the night.

Claustrophobia gripped Reed, he couldn't look away, couldn't look around. He was trapped in the memory as Slater mused about where to eat after he washed the blood from his hands. Checking in a gas station mirror for splatter on his sweatshirt. A cold numbness spread through Reed's mind, severing any self. Any other. There was only the reality of the memo-ries and the knowledge that moved within them. Georgia had mentioned a Professor Abernathy, and Slater decided to pay him a visit.

The force of the impact slammed Reed into the steering wheel of the stolen SUV. Iris's body bouncing up over his hood, her head crashing against the windshield. He tried to pull away, to stop himself from backing up like Slater had done then. The sickening thump underneath the tires as he ran her over again threaded horror through Reed's mind.

Then, he was carrying someone. A body in his arms that was already cold and stiff from where he'd hid her on the roof. The student. Gravel crunched beneath his boots as he walked with her to the ledge. Rain whipped icy drops at his face, down his coat. Her shoe glowed in the moon-light and a shard of worry spiked through him. One was missing. He lay the student on the flat of the ledge, wiggled off her other shoe, and then sat her up. Jumping up onto the ledge, he pulled her up, positioned her with her back facing over the drop. And pushed. The storm snatched away the sound of her body hitting the ground. Sorrow and anger burned through Reed, he tried to shout, to back away. But the memory held fast. Forcing him to peer down at her limbs akimbo, pale face exposed to the falling rain.

Reed fought for consciousness, locked in the flurry of sights. Gerald screaming in a dirty motel, his brilliant mind charred. The name Petraeus floating across his mind.

Then he was in Corbin's office, his face still hot from arguing. The fear palpable on Corbin as they turned to see Detectives De La Cruz and Reed walking through the office. A jolt of recognition pierced Slater when he saw Reed, a man he'd known only from Caitlyn's memories.

Confusion mottled Reed's thoughts. Slater's point of view merging and separating from his own consciousness, only to merge once more. And then he saw Petraeus.

Her face, her apartment in Alki beach, her wide eyes as she saw him step onto the balcony. A sense of forward movement propelled him faster through time, flashes of her struggle, her attack with her dagger, her final scream. And then banging. Reed's heart throbbed frantically as he saw himself burst through the door firing. Detective De La Cruz running to his right, diving from his bullets. A round seared past his cheek, exploding the sliding glass window behind him. Another blew the gun from his hand. Unsettling déjà vu roared through him as Slater vaulted off the terrace. He looked up, saw Reed . . . himself, climbing fast, gaining as Slater had jumped from vessel to vessel. Unable to shake him. Pressure to escape building in his chest.

They fought on the beach. Reed's memory of the fight blending with Slater's. The tell he gave with his shoulder before he punched, the impact of kicking Reed across the sand. The smell of the kids as they walked between them. Cold hard steel in his hand with the flick of the knife.

Reed concentrated on a name. *Danzig*. He fought to keep it in focus. The memories washed over and through him, fast forward scenes of firing on an RV. Reed's arm jerked, fighting to right the motorcycle as he fired at himself in the driver's seat.

Spectre . . . Danzig. Reed struggled to see through the hurricane of thoughts and images. To hear through the cacophony of voices shouting all at once.

"Slater!" Everett Danzig turned to him, as the world ground to a halt, a vast hangar forming around him. A Gulfstream strobed into view behind the billionaire, bathed in the overhead lights. Jet fuel and grease assaulted Reed's nostrils. The man's piercing blue eyes locked onto his, searching. "Protect the asset. Find out who this Farad or . . . what was it?"

"His real name is Firash."

"The Ghanzi Project *will* go forward. On Time. Am I clear?"

"Sir. We know he means to make contact with her."

"He's an amateur. He'll either make a public scene, blackmail her directly, or give what he has to the press. All we need to do when you find him is discredit, disappear, and dump his body a few weeks later." Danzig shrugged, unconcerned. "You see? Contained. Like I asked you to do weeks ago."

Dread rushed through Reed as Gerald's threats to stop him echoed through Slater's thoughts. If Danzig knew that it was Slater's mistakes with the bodies that had almost exposed MER-C and the entire mission to stop Firash, he'd be dead himself.

Slater shifted on his feet. "Unfortunately, sir, I think Firash's plan may be worse than we thought. The weapons dealer confessed to selling him Ferrin."

"Dammit!" Danzig's salt and pepper hair fell onto his forehead as he turned to pace. "Did he say what form? How it will be used?"

"He didn't last that long. But it's the quantity that's the real problem. Enough to take out an entire stadium if he wanted."

Danzig pinched his nose with a manicured index finger and thumb. "Neutralize him. If there's blowback, we can arrange for you to be out of reach."

"There's a cop," Slater's voice left Reed's mouth and an image of Caitlyn in uniform walking into the station flitted across his vision unbidden. "She's getting close."

"Take her out," Danzig said. "But find out what she knows first. And who she told."

The scene started fading, to feather at the edges and Reed reached for more, tried to see past the moment to understand, but it was distorted, distant, and melted away like old film when he looked at it. He flew forward, through days and weeks, and then he was staring at Caitlyn's anguished face. Her soft hazel eyes alight with pain. She cried out for him. For her mother, her voice cracking with the intensity of her scream. He felt the pierce of a needle at his throat and then a flood of memories poured into Reed. How he'd looked down at her, his face full of skepticism. The cold weight of abandonment pushing through her as he told her there was no 'suicide pattern,' that she was imagining things.

Reed moved with her, walking around her bedroom, peeling back the covers of the bed, a song in her head, the Christmas jingle that had been there all day, coming out in a half-hum. She froze, a surge of shock rattling through her at the sight of a figure just inside her hallway.

Reed couldn't breathe, he couldn't move. He tried to reach for her, to warn her, but instead he grabbed her, shoving the halo on her head. His heart roared in his ears. Dread and anger pushed through his consciousness. He couldn't see this. He couldn't do this to her. The scene dissolved into flashes of being tied to her own kitchen chair, the sight of the needle in her exposed thigh, and then the deep, frigid fear that howled through her mind.

The scene billowed into itself, the walls morphing, blowing out to become the construction site. Her car crumpled against the newly built retaining wall. Rebar and cement blocks pierced the windows and littered the ground. Smoke drifted in the wind from her hood. His hand reached out, picked up a rebar from the bound bunch on the gravel. The engine ticked away heat in the driving cold of the rain.

No, no, no, Reed thought.

He walked around to the driver's side, opened the door, and pushed her slumped body away from the steering wheel. It was a classic car and the roll down the hill had gained enough inertia that the impact had split the skin of her forehead open. No airbag to stop the hit. Reed's stomach slithered, cold sweat sliding down his spine.

I'm sorry ...

Reed slammed the car door closed and then walked up toward the fender. He leaned over the hood to peer at her through the cracked windshield. Her eyes stared up at nothing, her mouth hanging open. Bringing his arm with the rebar back he swung it toward her face—"

A scream tore out of him, "I'll kill you!"

He flailed, fighting the forward motion. Something pulled on his arms, dragging him to the ground. He fought with everything he had, yelling her name. He reached for his weapon, yanking it from the holster, aware of his body once more. A hand caught him by the wrist. Bright lights flashed outside of his lids. And then a burst of cold blew in his face, over his chest and arms, acrid powder filling his mouth.

"Reed!" Nat's voice pierced the veil. "Reed, snap out of it!"

He moved toward it. Clawing his way out of the dark. Another burst of ice and he gasped, the server room slamming down around him. The smoke and heat of the fire pushing in on him once more. Two patrolmen held him down. Nat stood over him with a fire extinguisher in her hands and horror on her face. She leaned down, locking eyes with him, and he realized he was sweating and covered in white powder.

"Let him go," she said to the patrol cops. They hesitated, looking at each other. She waved them away. "He's back. He's okay. Let him breathe, already, dammit."

They let him go. Two guys he'd had beers with before at Rampart now looked at him like he was a drug addict on a wild binge. They stepped away, giving him room. Other personnel had wandered in pretending not to gawk at his shaking form on the floor. Firemen quelled the fire over by the storage shelves and shredders. Paramedics had pulled Slater over to a clear area of the room to work on him. Patrol cops sifted through debris in between fallen server towers.

"What happened?" Her palm settled on his forehead as if she were checking for fever. "Where did you go in there?"

Reed touched his neck, felt the raised welt of the injector needle. "Slater—"

"He must've died after he attacked you," Nat said a little too loudly as she looked behind her. She leaned in and nodded toward the injector pen on the floor next to his hand. "Right, Reed? He dosed you and then you pulled it out of your neck and dropped it on the floor." She held his gaze. "That's what happened, right?"

She knew what he'd done. Was trying to protect him. Giving him a reason for his fingerprints to be on the injector.

He reached for her hand, his breath still coming in ragged jags of panic. "It's worse than we thought, Nat. Slater was trying to stop an attack."

"What?"

He grasped her wrist, pulling her close. Helplessness bleeding into his every word. "Hundreds are going to die, and I have no—I have no idea how to stop it."

25

Firash

He watched the paramedics carry out Slater, or at least he hoped it was him, in a yellow body bag on a stretcher. The big detective, Reed, walked among the other officers at Neurogen. It was the second time Firash had seen him and the woman partner, De La Cruz, at the building. The first time, he had watched them through the window of his car while he sat in the parking lot spying on Slater. Firash wanted to follow Danzig's security man, to see what he was doing at this Neurogen place, but the detectives showing up had frightened Firash. They were not unfamiliar to him. He had seen them before. At the scene of Maggie's death.

The hollow sorrow of her passing weighed on him. And his abandoned faith offered no solace. He had turned from it years ago. When the men who hunted down his father did so in the name of their god. Firash's breath caught at the thought of that time. The smoke and sand and awful fear. His world had gone down around him in flames that night. And he had never been the same. Until he'd met Maggie.

He had gone to the campus to warn her. To tell her everything. Only he had been too late. Slater, the man Danzig had sent after him got to her first, looking for him. It was his fault. He should have known that he would lose everything to achieve his goal. The future did not belong to him. It belonged to those who would benefit from the legacy of what he vowed to do. He knew that now and it hardened his heart for what was to come.

Detective Reed spoke with someone. A man who wrote down his words on a tablet asked questions. Something official, Firash guessed, about the incident. Their voices floated across the parking lot to him, too far to understand. Firash wished he had one of those parabolic microphones he had seen the soldiers use. Perhaps he could rig a microphone to one of his drones. His gaze went to the battered backpack on the passenger seat. He still had a few left.

Pain from the burns on his arm and side bothered him and he adjusted the bandages he had wrapped around his wounds after fleeing from the woman detective's home. That had been stupid. He thought he knew what Slater was doing, until he had seen him speaking with the big detective. Firash knew of Danzig's reach. His influence within the halls of power. He had seen it in the network's hidden connections and files. And a homicide detective would be a useful asset to have. He was almost sure this man worked for Danzig. How else would he have figured out what Slater was doing? Firash raised his phone above the dashboard of the car and snapped a photo of Reed. He opened it and zoomed in on the detective.

He would have to be careful. This man was formidable. One he barely escaped. Exactly the kind of man Danzig liked to have around. Detective Reed looked both battle-hardened and smart, a combination Firash knew well from his childhood in Kabul. On all sides of the conflict. Men with hard faces and sharp eyes who moved through his memories like the creatures that prowled the darkness beyond the firelight. Soldiers.

He tensed, thinking about the night he first realized Slater was after him. Firash had been late to meet up with Alastair at Angel Lake Station. He had missed his bus and had to walk. Terrified the man would not be there, he checked the locker they rented for their exchange and heard him screaming. Firash tensed at the memory of what he saw when he crept toward the platform that night. Slater, using a terrible device on the weapons dealer, was asking questions about him. Stalking him. For trying to stop another atrocity on his people. On *his* land. Firash gripped the steering wheel until it made a creaking sound beneath his white knuckles. Running. He was forever running.

Firash steadied himself, like he had done since he was a child. He could do this. He did not know what Slater's death meant. He knew only that he would not fail this time in finding out what the detective knew about his plans.

26

Everything happened in slow motion as Reed sat on the bumper of the ambulance and held an oxygen mask to his face. His hearing still seemed muffled, but it was clearing up. He worked his jaw as if trying to pop his eardrums after a dive. He'd given his recount of the events and then Nat gave her statement to the Critical Incident Supervisor and Tig. They stood over by some patrol cars to his right. She talked with her hands and kept glancing over at him. Something wasn't right. He could tell when Tig was mad. He held his spine stick straight and barely moved when talking. Right now, he was doing a good impression of a statue.

Reed tensed when a couple of firetrucks rambled into the parking lot, their lights going, horn pushing gawkers from the other buildings back. News crews showed up quicker than Reed expected and set up on the steps of the Neurogen Building, some wandering close to the crime scene tape for B-Roll footage beforehand. Everyone was at the scene, and more were coming.

Additional patrol and paramedics arrived to cordon off the area. Sanders, and his forensics team came a few minutes after. Chase Kennedy, the Chief of Police, a stalwart, graying man Reed had never met personally, but always thought reminded him of a grizzled sea captain, arrived within the hour. Lenny Roubideaux, the mayor's minion, arrived with him. He was practically gleeful about the news conference he was setting up for the mayor on the front steps of Neurogen.

Tig broke from the group and walked over to the ambulance. Reed had been watching them huddle outside the crime scene tape perimeter and stood when he walked over.

"Good talk?" Reed asked nodding toward Nat.

"What're you doing, man?" Tig said, his face tense. "Your partner is telling me some wild things."

Reed tried to look over at her, but Tig stepped in the way. "Did she complain?"

"Complain?" Tig scoffed. "No. She's done everything to try and justify all the shit you've been doing. Like not reporting an attack in your own home. Not reporting you believed it was connected to the case."

"I couldn't prove it, alright? None of my security cameras caught him and even if they did, he was covered from head to toe." Reed snapped, irritated with the pain behind his left eye. He scratched at the scar over it.

"She was attacked by the same guy, *in her home*, days later!" Tig pointed at Reed, his hand shaking with anger. "You talked with me in that stairwell knowing full well your partner was at risk."

"She wasn't unprotected."

"Oh, was it your 'friends' from the old days? Are you back in touch with them?" Tig shook his head when Reed didn't deny it. "You brought criminals into an investigation on top of it, didn't you."

"Things were moving fast, Tig. We always played things close to the vest."

"Not from me, Reed! Not from me!" Tig spat. He gestured at Reed's face. "That scar didn't teach you anything, did it? You were reckless then and you were reckless just now. You ran into that server room without backup."

"I heard someone screaming," Reed said, his patience dwindling. "It was exigent circumstances."

Tig stepped forward, his face inches from Reed's "The ME found wounds on Slater. His scalp had the same burn marks as his victim's. You're telling me he did that to himself?"

"He said that there was a weapon in play. That this kid he's been tracking was planning—"

"Stop, Reed . . . just . . ." Tig put his hand up. Stress lined his eyes making him look exhausted. "Slater was nuts, okay? We just heard from his former employer, High Rock Holdings. They already had a police report out on him. And the rest of his army records came in. He was medically discharged from the marines."

"That's not right." Reed didn't understand. The redacted records his contact at CID had sent him showed Slater honorably discharged.

"He worked personal security for the founder of High Rock Holdings, and was let go for erratic, paranoid behavior. They sent us his disciplinary records. They date back two months. That's right before the murders started. They believe he stole information from them with the help of one of their data analysts, Firash Nuri."

"Firash is the kid who attacked Nat and me. He's the one making the weapon."

"No, he's not. Slater was having a paranoid break. High Rock's in-house counsellor confirmed he had delusions of grandeur, believed a vast conspiracy was gathering around that only he could stop."

"And the device? The halo and serums?"

"None of those trace back to High Rock. All of it is here at Neurogen where he worked temporarily before leaving for personal reasons. He came back, broke in, and stole equipment. Three weeks ago, security noted a break in of that same server to the local precinct."

You think the one you stole was the only one? A flash of Slater's interrogation of Gerald in the motel flashed behind Reed's eyes. "No, that was Gerald," Reed corrected.

"Right, they reported a burglary by their own CEO," Tig shot back. "Slater was loose in Seattle on some self-assigned fantasy mission. That's why he hit the college where he stalked Maggie and the Professor and Iris Abernathy."

"No, he was . . . trying to stop a murder," Reed said, stepping back, not believing. "A woman. Firash wants her dead."

"Slater is the only one who's been murdering people!" Tig counted his arguments off on his fingers. "Slater made the weapon. Slater did the killings for his own insane reasons. Slater had access to the murder weapon. He wasn't 'ripping' memories from people. He was overdosing them with something and then shooting their brains full of wires. That's Dahmer type shit. And you think he was telling the truth about why?"

Reed's palms flew to his temples, his mind reeling. It wasn't a drug trip. What he'd seen was real. It had to be. "No, the memory serum works."

"Are you hearing yourself?" Tig shouted. "He mixed up some drugs he found in a place that makes brain altering drugs and ranted about memories! Neurogen has no patents for anything like this! No one does. We would've heard about it, but we haven't because it's *fiction!*"

"But I saw—"

"What did you see, really, huh? After an explosion and getting dosed with Slater's special cocktail?" Tig paced in a circle. "The fire was eating up the oxygen. You could've been delirious, hypoxic. Not to mention, Slater was trapped under a server when you assaulted him with an unknown device. Assaulted, Reed!"

"What I did to Slater was after he was gone. And I didn't get 'dosed.' I took the memory that was in the containment pod because I was trying to stop a massacre," Reed tried to sound reasonable.

"For the love of god, stop talking!" Tig glanced around at the officers who looked away suddenly. He leaned in, his voice a harsh whisper. "You assaulted a corpse, then. Does it even register with you how messed up that is? And now you just admitted to destroying evidence by taking whatever was in that injector? On a case involving multiple bodies, you're destroying evidence. Really? You're out of control!" Tig paced, his chest heaving. "I shouldn't have called you back. I knew you were lost. I saw you were grieving—"

"That has nothing to do with any of this!" Reed shouted, his face burning hot.

"That's *all* this is about!" Tig stepped to Reed. "And you have no right to play out your guilt over her death on my watch!"

Reed's head filled with the muffled pounding of his pulse, he lunged for Tig before thinking, grabbing his suit lapels. Tig flailed, hitting Reed in the mouth in their struggle. Patrol officers and firefighters swarmed them, pulling them apart. Shouting for them to back off each other. Reed yanked away, pacing as he wiped the blood on his lip.

"Let go! He's done," Tig shouted, backing them off. He pointed at Reed. "This is your official notice. You're suspended. Get out of here!"

Reed looked at everyone staring at him, with a mix of confusion and outright alarm. Nat stood just outside the melee, shock and betrayal on her face. He turned and limped away.

27

Hours later, Reed slouched on his couch, his head leaning back, while he stared at the ceiling and listened to the haunting vocals of Mazzy Star's Hope Sandoval. Caitlyn would play their music when she was melancholy The haunting vocals in Fade Into You, filled Reed's head, crowding out the flashes of faces that kept invading his thoughts. The familiar songs felt good. Grounding. He concentrated on that in an attempt to ignore the deep body aches from the explosion creeping up on him. His lungs still felt heavy, and his throat burned from the smoke. He'd been screaming, Nat had told him, and she'd looked spooked.

After taking an app car service home he'd collapsed and slept for a few hours. His dreams were garbled, fear-filled trips and he woke in a cold sweat. The dinner he ordered arrived hot and perfect in the little take-out delivery bot, but it had no taste. Usually his favorite, something was wrong with the texture, so he'd thrown it out. His phone blinked on the coffee table with missed calls and messages. When he moved to get it, he winced at the sharp ache in his joints. Giving up, he tossed back the rest of his fourth beer and set the empty bottle on the table. Frost crept from the edges of the living room window, the flurries landing on the bushes just outside. A sprinkling of snow for the Thanksgiving holiday coming soon. Reed rose and walked over to turn on the fake fireplace space heater near the kitchen, and the hologram fire sent flickering firelight dancing across his walls.

A gust of wind forced itself through the cracks of the old building, howling softly and then he was looking down at Maggie's broken body from the rooftop, her eyes staring up at him through driving rain. Reed sucked in his breath, heart thrumming in his throat. He staggered on his feet, for a second, blinking it away. He'd decided another beer was a good idea when his front door security screen lit up. There was motion on his driveway. The small screen focused on the visitor. It was Nat standing in a huge puffy jacket and a scarf probably taller than she was.

Muttering, he strode over, yanking open the door.

She froze, fist raised to knock. "Hey."

"Get out of here, De La Cruz. You're risking your career coming here." Reed moved to close the door, but she stopped it with an outstretched palm.

"De La Cruz? It's like that, now?" She pushed on the door a little. "Don't make me stand out here, it's cold." Reed regarded her for a moment, and then turned and walked back into his apartment leaving the door open. She followed him in, shutting it behind her, then hung her scarf on the wall hooks next to his coat. "Thank you."

"What do you want, Nat?" Reed sank back onto his couch, his head throbbing.

She paced his living room, restless. Stopping to look at the photos he'd taken on a hike up by his cabin, fiddled with a piece of driftwood art on the built-in shelves, and pulled out a couple of his albums. Finally, she ended up behind the wing chair that came with the sofa. "The Feds showed up right after you left. They cleared everyone out."

Reed nodded. "Who called them?"

"No idea. Tig and the brass looked surprised though. They took over jurisdiction so all the evidence, the bodies, we're cut out of any access. I swear, it didn't even take them an hour to box everything up."

"And Corbin? The body they found in the supply closet down in the archives, that was him?"

"Yeah, it was. Shot once in the back of the head, execution style. And before you ask, that's all I know. Like I said, the Feds are taking everything.

They even cleaned out the evidence at the ME's office. The halo you found at the RV chase, all of it. Sanders was way pissed." Nat slipped around the chair and sat down gingerly as if she expected him to yell at her. "Listen, Reed, I wasn't trying to get you in trouble. I was . . . you were delirious. You tried to pull on me."

He vaguely remembered that.

"I wasn't delirious. Not in the medical sense, anyway."

She leaned forward, held his gaze with hers. "What happened in there? I heard you and Slater talking and then all hell broke loose. We had to wrestle you to the ground before you pounced on the paramedics."

Reed slumped back into the couch and rubbed his face with both hands. "I'm not sure anyone would believe what happened. I'm still struggling to believe it, myself."

"I need to know what's going on. I'm meeting with the Office of Professional Conduct tomorrow with my rep and I don't know what to tell them."

"The truth." Reed shrugged.

"I don't know what that is!" Nat snapped, frustration tensing her mouth. "You're saying one thing, this vast and impossible conspiracy, and Tig is saying something else entirely. He's saying Slater was crazy. That he pulled us into his delusion."

"Well, Tig is wrong. He doesn't have the truth. He has what Danzig wants him to have."

"The founder of High Rock Holdings?" Nat made a face, doubtful. "He's in on this?"

Reed nodded. "He's the man pulling the strings."

"He's the man helping us. Danzig voluntarily sent over proof he'd been trying to locate Slater. With dates from weeks ago. Missing person's reports, internal memos, all without a subpoena."

"You couldn't pull something like that off? If you really had to?"

"Why would a man like Everett Danzig even need to?"

Reed shrugged. "To cover his ass. Slater got his orders from somewhere because he was just muscle. They were trying to stop something. I just can't . . . remember what."

"*Remember*?" Nat murmured, her gaze meeting his with desperation. "What happened to you in that server room, Reed? Please, tell me. Because otherwise I have to believe that this brilliant detective I heard about . . . who I got to work with and learn from . . . has lost his mind and taken me with him. You told me to trust you. Give me a reason why."

She deserved the truth. Even if it pushed her away. Hell, Reed thought. That might be the best thing for her at this point. Reed was now radioactive to anyone's career, and he knew it.

"Alright," he said and let his head fall onto the back of the couch. He stared at the ceiling while he told her about the confrontation with Slater after finding the archives he was trying to destroy. He explained that the 'Mercy' Slater asked Petraeus about wasn't a person. It was the name of the memory retrieval system they'd seen him use on her. He told Nat about finding the boxes with the MER-C System on the storage shelves and Gerald's video explanations of what it was and what it did. She made a disgusted face when Reed recounted Corbin's glee as he showed it off to a buyer. Reed explained that Slater had said he'd tell Danzig.

"That's why you suspect him," Nat murmured. "He was in the memory?"

"Yes." Slater had insisted, Reed explained, that he hadn't attacked either of them at all. That the kid, Firash, the one they thought was Slater's next victim, was planning a terrible attack. He told her everything Slater had said about how Firash had hacked the system of his employer and stumbled onto something that set him off. Reed told her about Slater's warning about a weapon, the possible SPD mole, and Firash's wish for someone . . . a woman, to die to stop something in Afghanistan. Even as he spoke, Reed knew he sounded insane, but he told her all of it, well, nearly all of it. He couldn't talk about Caitlyn and what he'd seen. Nat sat silently, taking it in as he rambled for nearly an hour about what he'd experienced in the memory. The trapped, chaos of it.

"It was so real, Nat. The smells, the taste. It was more vivid than us right now. Like an undercurrent of pure, unfiltered emotion, flowed through every moment. I *knew* that hangar. The feel of the steering wheel in my hand. The horror that moved through their minds."

When Reed was done, he felt no closer to understanding what was coming or how to stop it.

"Okay, first of all, that sounds completely traumatic. Second . . ." Nat got up, walked to his kitchen, and got herself a glass of water. She took a long drink before setting it down and wiping her mouth with her palm. When she returned to the chair, her face was pale. "You're saying Slater was ripping their memories with this serum, and you took it? We have no idea what he was even dosing them with!"

"It wasn't the serum. It was the fluid from the containment pod."

"The effing brain juice?" Nat's hands flew to her temples. "What is *wrong* with you?"

"The containment pod was damaged in the explosion. There was no telling if the memory was already decaying, and I had no idea how long it would take you guys to get to me. On top of that, I told you that Slater said there was someone working with him on the inside—"

"So you just injected a crazed murderer's memory? Do you even know what that does to someone?"

Reed stood, anger flaring at her words. "Were you listening about the weapon Firash built? You heard me say massacre, right?"

Nat jumped to her feet. "Mmhm. Mmhm." She bobbed her head at him, unfazed at his looming figure. "Look at my face. Does it look like I care about that right now?"

Reed pointed out of his window. "All the evidence is gone. Slater told me, his body would never make it to the morgue either and look what happened!"

"I just can't . . ." Nat sank back into the chair and buried her face in her palms. "How is what Slater said even possible?"

"Okay, you need evidence. A reason to believe I'm not nuts. Understandable." Reed grabbed his notebook, leafed to a specific section, and sat on the coffee table across from Nat. "We've been on the cusp of brain-computer melding for years according to what I looked up. And Gerald was already working on enhancing that connection to help his Alzheimer's patients retain their executive function." He slipped the notebook onto her lap where she caught it. He pointed to his notes. "These are from Gerald's own paper from the Journal of Neuro-Technology. In it, he said that memories are essentially waves of hormonal, chemical, and electrical signals that blaze across various paths in the brain. But he said they need an anchor point. A trigger. Because for most people a smell or a song, maybe an image, will spark a memory. But they aren't focal. Memories involve sight, smell, sounds, everything so the path would be different for each one. That's what Slater was doing in the Petraeus recording. His questions were making her think of what he wanted to know."

"That's why you asked Sanders about the path of the filaments? You knew back then?"

"Knew? No, I had a theory. One I didn't think was possible. Not until I saw the recordings in the server room. Then it was real. Then I saw how." Reed told her about the patient strapped to the bed, moaning like Petraeus. He looked off into the distance. Not seeing. "The serum, I think, was the key. Gerald was trying to improve it. Slater mentioned that he'd 'gone back to the drawing board' on the serum. It was one of the reasons Gerald was killed. He'd been trying to reformulate it to work with the tech they now had, I think. But Corbin had already bastardized it and sold it."

"Yeah, I think I heard Gerald had terrible claustrophobia. It would have been easy to hide what they were doing down in that tunnel. He would've avoided it like the plague."

She was coming around, he could see it in her eyes. Reed tried to remember the recordings. "In Gerald's version and in the demonstration clips in the office, the process is slow, deliberate. Artificial intelligence guided surgical robots with 3D maps of the exact path to place the electrodes, right? You remember that? Brain surgery, essentially. So, it would be long and arduous and very precise."

"Yeah, but that tech was nothing compared to the halo and filaments we saw in the ME's office. I mean, this stuff was down and dirty with no thought for the 'patient' at all."

"In one of the recordings, Corbin said that the MER-C System was portable. For the field. *As requested.*"

Nat's eyes went wide. "He made someone an infallible method of interrogation. Can you imagine who would pay for that? Cartels could root out undercover DEA Agents. Entire NOC lists would be compromised."

Reed nodded. "Corbin shopped around the idea of memory enhancement for soldiers to several branches of the government. But it was Slater who moved on the information, even though he's not military. He's private security. I think that's what Spectre is. They offered him astronomical money for it, along with exclusivity, and Corbin bit."

Nat tilted her head, her gaze narrowed. "What are you talking about?"

"It was in the files Corbin sent Slater through a mutual acquaintance, remember? The former aide to the US Ambassador to Germany that both of them had worked with before—" Reed stopped, blinking. "Wait."

"Yeah, how do you know that, Reed?"

"I saw the file." Reed looked at his palms. "I held it."

She looked at him, her face twisted with worry. "Reed . . ."

"No, I know. That was probably something Slater saw." Reed kept talking, trying to move her past what had just happened. "I keep trying to make sense of everything. I can't seem to figure out how Slater waded through it all and found what he was looking for. I even tried the questions thing, but none of it makes sense. It's a big soup of images and sounds I don't understand or remember the context of."

She looked at him for a beat, deciding something. Then, "I think you got a triple dose." Nat pulled her tablet from the coffee table and showed him some photos she'd taken. She pointed to the injector pen. "See that? The one we saw Slater use at Petraeus only depressed one third of the way. Yours was empty."

"The indicator lights on the rim were red, too. I thought that might be bad."

"You took in three times the amount of a normal dose."

"Yeah, but what's a normal dose of memories?"

"Well, it was designed that way for a reason," Nat said, incredulously. "That's one thing."

"And the other?"

Points of light flashed in his peripheral. The notebook in his hand flickered out of place for a moment, switching from the leather cover to a bloody field knife, and back again in an instant. Reed jerked, his face growing hot. But it didn't happen again.

"Did you just wig out?"

"No," he lied.

She mimicked his startle response. "Then what was that?"

"Nothing, I just had a flash of something cross my mind."

"Yeah, no. That's not what happened." She got up, her hands wringing. "Oh, this is bad. So, so bad."

"What is it?"

"Slater used that halo thing on Petraeus and Gerald, probably Maggie, right?"

"Yeah, and who knows how many other people. Like I said, he wasn't just trying to keep Gerald from exposing the MER-C system. His real mission was to stop Firash."

She bit her pinky nail. "Here's the thing. You didn't actually do the same thing Slater did to his victims, though. You know that, right?"

"Come again?"

"Each one of those people Slater 'ripped' let's call it, were clean. That had never been done to them before."

"Okay, yeah. Where are you going with this?"

"But you ripped *Slater*. A guy with other people's memories already in there. And you said he looked like he had a possible concussion."

Reed didn't like the sound of what she was saying. "Yes. His pupils were wrong."

"Yeah, and you waited until after he flatlined."

"I wasn't going to just off the guy, Nat."

"Yeah, but that means you ripped a dying, injured mind. Who knows what happens to the brain under those circumstances. It can't be like, 'firing' right. On top of that, you didn't just get *his* memories. You got his victims' too, didn't you?" She gasped and her gaze held his, worry lining her eyes. "Oh, Reed. Did you see what he did to her?"

Reed staggered back a step. His stomach dropping at the flash of Caitlyn's lifeless eyes staring up at him. The ice in his veins as he watched her die. "I killed her."

"No, you didn't." Nat reached out, touched his forearm. "Don't think that."

"I didn't believe her and I . . ." Reed took in a jagged breath. "I broke her heart Nat. I saw it in her face and I f-felt what I did to her." He sank back onto the couch, trying to push the memory from his mind. A band of guilt squeezed his chest and he shut down. His gaze traveled Nat's throat, the curve of her chin, riddled with scratches from the drone fire. People close to this died, horribly.

"You didn't kill her. You were dosed." She put her hand up at his protest. "Maybe it *was* a memory. And maybe Slater told you what he did, and the power of suggestion is doing the rest. Tig said the forensic tech that came with the FBI told him they believed that Slater was using a hallucinogen. Maybe . . . these aren't memories, Reed. Maybe they're flashbacks."

"The power of suggestion?" Reed took in a long slow breath, her earnest face making his heart sink.

"Whichever it is, you need to tell Tig what's going on with you, Reed. Tell him you're seeing things." She leaned forward. "Let me drive you to the hospital. We'll get your blood checked. Maybe an MRI because you literally just blew up."

"I didn't get blackout drunk. It wasn't a 'bad trip,'" Reed murmured. "I may have gotten knocked around, but I've been hurt worse and then humped it across the desert at night."

"This isn't war, Reed."

"Not one out in the open," he murmured as he glanced back outside his window, at the building blanket of snow on the grass. She didn't believe him. Danzig's misinformation about Slater had done its job. And if she didn't believe this was real, she wouldn't see them coming. Reed rubbed his face with both hands and stood. He walked to the door and held it open for her. His expression hard, unreadable. "Like I said, you really shouldn't be here. In fact, don't come back. We're done."

"What?" Nat rose from the chair, shock on her face. "What's done?"

"This case. Us. It's over, Nat. Your friends were right. You should've steered clear of me."

Her face turned red as she walked over, her lips pursed. "Just like that?"

"Just like that. Tig is right. You're right. Clearly, I'm messed up. I'll call him in the morning and tell him I'm taking a sabbatical. I don't think he'll object."

"Wait, you said there was a weapon. A massacre."

"And you just said I was having drug flashbacks. I can't prove to you what I saw."

"But, what if it's true?" Nat pushed. "You're just walking away?"

"You can't have it both ways. I'm crazy or I'm right. Looks like you'd made your choice before you even walked up." Reed nodded out the door. "Get as far away from me as possible. If they say I'm nuts, agree and move on. Save your career."

"And just screw whoever Firash was allegedly going to attack. Is that it?"

Reed shook his head. *Allegedly.* "Look, if something really is going on, the Feds can handle it. It's what they're built for. And I'm sure you and your cyber geeks can help them if they need it."

Her dark gaze searched his, disappointment pulling her lips into a frown. "So that's it?"

"I'm sorry, Nat." Reed stepped aside. "I'm done."

She brushed past him without another word, pulling the unmarked patrol car out of his driveway with a screech. He watched the taillights disappear down his street hoping he'd pushed her far enough away from him in time.

28

Reed stood underneath the towers of the Fremont Drawbridge in the wooded area just past the railing. An abandoned homeless camp underneath the thickest brush left food, torn tents, and other detritus littered all over the mud down to the water. He wondered how they stood the noise of the bridge rising and lowering all day. The bridge itself connected Fremont to Queen Anne and was notorious for long wait times whenever it was up. Which was often.

Reed stepped back further underneath the small overhang protecting the cement walkway beneath street level. An artist had drawn an entire fairyland with chalk on the path and he watched the rain splash away at it, fading the world to nothing. He checked his watch then glanced up at the soldier blue bridge that loomed dark against the sky. Outside lamps hooked out of the side of the structure illuminating the sidewalks set along the side for pedestrians. One of the most active drawbridges in North America, or so a sign said up where tourists went to go take pictures of the neon figures in the control tower windows. Reed favored the Rapunzel one.

A storm was brewing and the trashed tents on the ground tapped out the rhythm of the worsening rain. Overhanging branches bobbed in the rainwater pouring off the bridge. They cast frantic shadows on the metal walls of the towers. A flickering movement that pulled at Reed. Fronds slapped and brushed against each other. The sound of wind whipping through the leaves sounded like the roar of a shop fan. It appeared in front of him, flickering into existence like an old movie reel. Beyond it, a cavernous workshop bled into the surrounding area. He wasn't underneath the drawbridge anymore. He wasn't Reed . . .

Slater crept further into the space. The storm outside and the rock music echoing throughout the structure drowned out his footfalls. A containment tent reinforced with scaffolding hastily connected with wire stood against the south wall of the corrugated building. Opaque from top to bottom, he could still make out the form of his mark moving within. Caesar Gomez wore a yellow hazmat suit he'd bought online, which is how Slater had found him and this address. It wasn't even graded for what he was doing. Slater held his silenced pistol at his thigh as he approached. The heads-up display on his field goggles offering a vibrant temperature gradient reading on Gomez via infrared.

Gomez moved awkwardly, dragging a hose with him as he sprayed a car with banana yellow paint. He wore goggles and a respirator mask, and orange foam earplugs stuck out of his ears. Reed tried to change positions, to look around, but the moment held him fast to Slater's steps. Noises echoed in the memory, garbling the music, fading in and out. The hiss of paint spray, the chug of the fan, the buzzing of the overhead fluorescent lights. The song ended and the next one started and Gomez moved slowly around the car, his back to Slater who slipped into the tent in a low crouch. The respirator he wore leaked in the scent of aerosol. No matter, he intended to take him quickly, but he hesitated. Something was off with Gomez's body language. He bent suddenly whirling on Slater with a shotgun he must've had hidden near the wall. Reed reared back, his weapon already swinging out. The roar of the machines growing to a deafening cacophony as a muzzle flash blinded him.

"Whoa, whoa, whoa!" Coyote's voice ripped through the scene, and it broke apart like ashes in the wind. "What the hell are you doing?"

Reed blinked at him, tasting the bitter adrenaline in the back of his mouth, breath coming in ragged pants. The drawbridge rattled and ground overhead. Coyote stared at him, his startled face lit up with the cigarette at his lips. He had one hand outstretched toward Reed, the other on the gun at his back waistband.

"I'm cool, I'm cool." Reed holstered his weapon slowly, wiping the rain from his face as he stepped back under the overhang. "I thought I saw something."

He tried to hold onto what he'd seen, reaching for his notebook. There was something in the tent with them. Something he recognized but it was at the edge of his mind, unreachable. Like a word on the tip of your tongue. He held the pen over the page. Nothing.

"What'd you see, a ghost?"

Reed rubbed his eye and felt the dissolving stitches shift a little. "What?"

"You look like you just looked death in its cold, black eyes," Coyote relaxed, adjusting his leather jacket back over his gun. He regarded Reed silently, his jaw working. "You look awful, Morgan. Are you back using again?"

"I said I'd never touch the stuff again and I meant it," Reed said as he tried to shake the image of that shotgun barrel swinging up at him. "Were you able to find anything out?"

He'd told Coyote some of what was going on when he'd called for help three days before. He didn't have a choice. Reed had gone for a painful jog the morning after getting suspended to clear his head. It was early, the sun hadn't fully risen on a foggy morning. Dark and gray, it had taken him too long to clock the pair of male joggers about a block back who stayed with him, turn for turn, his entire route. When he got home, he checked his outside security cameras. A silver sedan parked down the street almost thirty minutes after he left the Neurogen crime scene. When Reed fast forwarded the recording, neither one of the figures inside ever left the car. He was being watched. By more than one team, he realized.

The next call he made was to Coyote with a favor. He'd need a car, some surveillance equipment, and a burner phone. Reed had turned his weapon in to Tig a couple days before along with his badge for his suspension, but he had his spare. That night, he slipped out on foot, jumped the neighboring fence, and met Coyote. He hadn't been back to his condo since.

"Yeah, I found some things out. But I'm not waiting out here next to a pile of iron in a lightning storm. We should get inside. Where're you parked this time?" Coyote handed Reed a tablet in a plastic shopping bag.

They walked together to the car Reed had parked down past the bridge. A small lot mostly used by maintenance and city trucks. The car, courtesy of one of Coyote's contacts, was one of the most invisible cars on the road. A beige, four door, decade, or so older sedan. The car could probably mow down a row of puppies in broad daylight and no one would remember it.

Reed fought with his coat as they settled into the sedan and caught Coyote watching him. "What?"

"You're on edge, brother." He motioned out the window. "Pulling all this cloak and dagger shit. Acting like you're back undercover and death's stepping on your shadow."

"I just need to know the players." Reed unwrapped the tablet from the bag and turned it on. He flipped through the documents, pausing to crack the passenger window down when Coyote lit another cigarette. "You know I'm suspended so this isn't exactly a sanctioned investigation."

"Clearly."

"I know . . . I *know*, Coyote, that something is going down and I need proof to get any kind of movement from the SPD."

His friend nodded. "Okay."

"That's it?"

"Morgan, you have one very annoying quality. Whatever state you were in, however drunk, sleep deprived, or otherwise screwed up condition you happened to be in at the time, you were almost never wrong." Coyote stopped his reply with an upheld palm. "That don't mean what you're fixing to do won't kill you. You'll just be right about it."

Reed had to smile at that, however exhausted he was. "I've been sleeping in the car. I guess it's time to get a room."

"How long are you planning on laying low? I'm told that three different people dropped by your place in the days you've been gone. Two looked very uptight in their suits."

"They want a statement."

"And you don't want to give them one?"

"What I have to say requires evidence or I'll end up in a very secure hospital room."

"I would imagine your absence is drawing the wrong kind of attention. You best make your move, Morgan."

"I'm working on it." Reed yawned, the lack of sleep catching up to him. "Tell me what you got on Danzig."

Coyote took a long draw on his cigarette, exhaling through the window slit before speaking. "My guys in the financial sector were helpful, but it was a special friend of mine who happens to work transfer protocols within a certain foreign banking system that truly paints a picture."

Reed swiped through the tablet, stopping on a photo of the man. Danzig. He was tall, lanky, with dark auburn hair, a patrician nose, and a broad forehead, tanned from the outdoors. An industry newsletter had posted pictures of a charity polo tournament in which Danzig had played. He looked tough, athletic, the kind of guy who'd drink whiskey on a wooden yacht he'd restored himself. When the video showed Danzig turn and face the camera, a flash of Slater's conversation blazed across his mind. Danzig had ordered Slater to kill Caitlyn. He ordered the deaths of countless others. That couldn't go unanswered. Coyote's voice came back into sharp focus.

"Anyway, enough about my little hidden asset. This is what she got. Everett Danzig is one of those billionaires we never hear about because he wants it that way. He comes from a family of rich assholes. His father was indicted for insider trading, but it didn't stick. He lived in Portugal with his third wife until he died in a boating accident. Danzig is the oldest of three kids. A brother and a younger sister. Both lawyers who work for Danzig. His company, High Rock Holdings, is a global conglomerate so he owns companies and significant share blocks in a huge array of fields. They're diversified in almost every sector from emerging technology startups, energy companies, exploration contractors, private satellite developers, shipping, *and* a personal security firm named Spectre Group. You were right about them. They pull mostly vets. Operators, special forces, from all services. I believe half of his contracts are with former soldiers from across the globe. That's some heavy-duty resumes for personal security."

"Spectre," Reed muttered. "They're not security. They're mercenaries for hire. Slater did some work out in Serbia. Wasn't for the government or its enemy. It was for a mafia family."

Coyote looked surprised. "Did he just spill his entire life story to you?"

"I thought we were going to die in that fire. Maybe he did too," Reed hedged.

"You really need to stop dancing with death, Morgan. It may decide to keep you close next time." Reed made a 'keep it going' gesture with his index finger and Coyote continued. "On paper, Spectre Group provides personal security for dignitaries, politicians, wealthy businessmen, what not. No stars, unfortunately. I would've loved to see some of those files," Coyote said with a grin. "But no. Just ordinary, boring rich people. Suspiciously enough, only a few of the clients are based in the United States. Spectre Group operates mostly out of Eastern Europe and the Middle East. High Rock Holdings has two satellite offices in the US. One here in Washington, but way up north. The other one is in Minnesota, of all places." Coyote shook his head. "One should never live anywhere that the weather can kill you."

"Doesn't Louisiana have hurricanes?" Reed said, swiping through the financial information.

"I know you didn't just besmirch my beloved bayou."

"Why would I? I just nearly died my first visit. Sucked up in a F5 or whatever."

"Those are tornados, Morgan. What you 'survived' was a summer storm," Coyote laughed. "No one even lost their roof."

"That's the bar? Structural damage or it's just a drizzle . . ." Reed paused. "Did you say 'exploration contractors' before? In the list of High Rock Holding's business ventures? That means what . . . mining?"

"Could be, or development and production of natural gas. Crude oil too, would fall under that."

Reed jotted down some notes in a new leather notebook. It was red. A personal one. "Can you find out if High Rock was involved in any kind of mining projects? Rare Earth metals specifically."

"Where am I looking?"

"All over but concentrate on countries of concern. Particularly Afghanistan."

"The Sand Pit?" Coyote flicked his butt out of the cracked window. "There's a hellhole I tried to forget."

"I think Danzig wants to mine there. I just don't know how he'd pull it off. The US won't do business with the Taliban. But there's something in play. According to Mika, the assistant, Iris was all but promising the deal was a sure thing. This Ghanzi Project Firash was upset about is at the center of all this death. I need to find out exactly what it is and who stands to benefit. Can you do that?"

"I can get you everything from what Danzig spends on his mistress to the color of his boxer shorts but it's going to trip some wires. That man most definitely has defensive security. You have to these days. I start making any kind of inquiries past what I've done, and he'll know someone's looking."

Reed stared out the rainy window at the low, angry clouds hovering just over the trees. He hunted pheasants with his dad on trips as a kid. Sometimes it was the only hot meal they had that week. You didn't just wait for them to take to the skies. You forced them to.

"Beat the bushes," he said to Coyote. "See what flies out."

29

Westfalia, WA

Reed sat in the borrowed sedan a block down the country road from Gloria Alvarez's home. The dry leaves still clinging to the bare, gnarled branches quivered in the buffeting wind. Westfalia's rural setting with all its brambles and gnarled trees along the roads gave excellent cover for his stake out. Forty-five minutes outside of Seattle, it had a population hovering around twenty thousand, give or take. Which made for almost no foot traffic along the outlier roads. It was a small town with historically preserved buildings and huge trees lining the main road. But Reed didn't want to have an old-fashioned milkshake at the smartly appointed soda shop. He wanted to find Firash and to do that, he needed Gloria.

For the last few days, he'd sat on her house, watching who came and who went, looking for a sign. It was a small home, but well kept. Newish paint and potted plants on the screened in porch. A bright wreath of yellow and orange fall leaves hung on the door. Gloria had gone out with the kids again, four of them. They'd come back with groceries. She took them on walks, watched them show her cartwheels and jumps on the lawn, her laugh floating out of the open kitchen window as they danced around in the kitchen. Normal stuff. Nice stuff. But as time ticked away on whatever

Firash was planning, Reed decided he couldn't wait anymore to see if he'd show up.

They'd gone out again, Gloria and the kids, and Reed waited ten minutes to let them get settled before he drove the car from his hiding spot to just in front of the little cottage house. He sat for a moment, feeling the eyes of the kids staring at him from behind the lace curtains in the front window. Pulling down his sun visor, he took in the stitches over his left eye, the slices from the drone daggers, and the bruises from the fight with Slater and frowned. Getting through the door was going to be rough. Especially without a warrant or a badge.

He walked through the screened in porch entrance, and was about to knock on the main door, but she pulled it open.

Looking him up and down, she frowned. "Police?"

"Afraid so. My name is Detective Morgan Reed. I'd like to ask you a few questions."

She wiggled her fingers at him. "What happened to your face?"

Reed smiled. "Killer drone."

Her eyes went wide. "What?"

"It's a long story." Reed shifted on his feet. He nodded toward the kids behind her in the living room. They stared at him with rapt curiosity. "And I don't mean to disturb you, but I need to speak with you about a former ward of yours. Firash Nuri."

Her face tensed. "I don't want any trouble here. These are good kids."

Interesting reaction, Reed thought. Not surprise at a name from the past. Not confusion. She knew something.

"You didn't ask why, you skipped right to trouble. Is that because Firash was a troubled kid?"

"No, but you're a detective on my doorstep. That's never *not* trouble."

Reed smiled, hoping it sold his sincerity "Just a few questions and I'll leave you to your lunch. Promise."

Gloria took in a deep breath and stepped backward, letting him through. "Is he hurt?"

"Not that I know of." Reed took out his leather notebook. "Why do you ask?"

"Just a question," Gloria said, crossing her arms as she turned to face him in the living room. "What do you want to know?"

"Have you seen him, lately?"

"No," she shook her head. "I have no idea where he is. Why would I? He aged out of the system years ago."

"We believe he's still here in Seattle and he's involved in something dangerous. I need to speak with him."

"What makes you think I can help you with that?" She shrugged. "The last time he was in this house was years ago."

"Do you mind if I take a look, then?" Reed asked, stepping around her. She jumped in his way, cutting him off.

"I mind. Get a warrant."

Reed looked past her shoulder at the children sitting at the table watching them. All of them were elementary school aged. Seven, maybe nine years old. Too young. They'd picked up her tone and gone silent. The wisdom of trauma. "Mrs. Alvarez, I'm not here to rile you up or scare the kids. I'm trying to find Firash to stop him from doing something we'll all regret."

"That doesn't even sound like him. He was a good boy." Gloria raised a single brow. "How did you find out he was placed with me, anyway?"

"I have friends in the system."

"In?"

"And within, yes."

"Oh, I see. You were a foster kid."

"For a time," Reed said.

"Is that supposed to soften me up?"

"You don't seem to need any softening up at all."

"Come again?"

"Firash was here the longest of all his placements. Three years until he turned eighteen. That's a long time for a foster family, especially an emergency placement. You'd have to request it."

"So, he was here when he was in high school, big deal." She waved her hand dismissively. "What makes you think he'd keep in touch with me? That was years ago."

Reed glanced at the warm bowls of soup on the table in front of the kids, the crusty bread. Handmade quilts, a little worn, but colorful sat across the back of the couch. Kid art, hand-shaped turkeys and pilgrims displayed proudly on the walls. He tilted his nose up to the ceiling, the vanilla candle took him back to that time. Standing in a strange living room once again, his things in a garbage bag, trying not to shake in his ratty shoes. It wasn't the first time. And then Eustace walked over, her smile soft, eyes warm. Different from the others. Reed had never felt safe like that. Not ever again.

"You don't forget a safe haven," he muttered and held Gloria's gaze with his. "And I know one when I see one. I'd like to help you keep it that way."

"And what's that supposed to mean?"

"It means you were the longest relationship he'd ever had. If he's in trouble, he might reach out. Kids don't forget the grownups who helped them. We're fiercely loyal of such angels."

Gloria looked away, her lip pulling down. "He was scared. He said someone was after him and he needed a place to crash, a place no one would know about. I told him he couldn't stay here. I wasn't putting the children in danger from whatever he had done, but . . ."

"But you couldn't turn him away." Reed nodded.

She wiped at her cheek with her palm, smearing tears and mascara across her skin. "I told him he could use the storage place I have in town."

"Which one?"

"I don't know, the one by the highway. It was my late husband's. Firash took the key."

Reed considered her for a moment. Something wasn't right. "Listen, if you have knowledge of where he is or what he is up to and fail to tell us, then you'll be just as responsible for what he does. And who he kills."

"Kills?" She turned to face him. The tears replaced with the flush of shock. "No, no. Firash was the one in danger. He was terrified."

"Of whom?" Reed started to dig in his leather notebook. "Did he give you a name?"

"No, he wouldn't say. Just that he needed a place to stay for a little." Gloria wrung her hands. "I thought I was helping him stay off the street."

"You said he hadn't been here in years," Reed said. "So how did he contact you?"

"Uh," Gloria sniffled, thinking. "Two months ago, he called out of the blue. I've had the same number for fifteen years so, you know, the kids will always have it when they leave."

"And that's when he asked you for help," Reed prompted. "Did you talk to him more than once?"

"Yes, once more. He texted me to say that he'd picked up the key I left for him." She pointed out to the porch swing. "I left some money and a key to the storage locker in an envelope outside. He said he could only come at night, and I have early mornings. Plus . . . he seemed edgy. I was worried about the kids."

"Do you remember the locker number?"

"No, I don't. Sorry. But he has the key."

"Mrs. Alvarez, Firash attacked two detectives with a drone and that was after breaking into their homes. Do you really want to keep protecting him?"

"Your face. It was you?" She looked away at nothing, her head shaking slowly. "I can't believe . . ."

"He's in a dark place. And he means to hurt, possibly kill a lot of people if I don't stop him."

"This isn't him, though." Gloria covered her mouth with her fingers, shaking her head. "He wouldn't do this."

Reed told her about his outbursts at the college, his harassment of Iris Abernathy, and his possible connection to a radical group called Restoration Republic via another victim named Maggie.

"My source says that Firash was angry about a deal going on in Afghanistan and that he has built a weapon."

"No, that's not possible!"

"He has a degree in engineering, right? Taught himself to hack well enough to get a job doing it. Has somehow managed to evade police and a trained mercenary, all while putting a plan into place. From what I've read about his behavior at college, his posing as a reporter to get close to Iris Abernathy, Firash sounds perfectly capable of doing this."

"No, but . . ." Gloria bit her inner cheek, her brows knit. "He was such a good kid."

"Tell me about him, then. Help me stop him from doing something terrible."

She crossed her arms, shivering and then reached back into the doorway, pulled out a coat from the hooks just inside the entry, and slipped it on. She leaned against the house, staring across the street at the Christmas lights dangling haphazardly on her neighbor's porch. Reed thought they looked better that way. Like a kid's storybook. The roof even had a few thin icicles from the light snow earlier.

"He was so small. So skinny when they brought him to me. He slept under the bed for the first couple of days. Every time there was a loud noise outside, he flinched. The counselor said he had PTSD from the war. He was just a kid." She sniffled, wiping her eyes.

"Afghanistan?"

"Yeah, that whole disaster when we left," Gloria said. "I was part of this nonprofit organization who raised money to sponsor orphans from refugee camps and other situations like that. There was a program that helped get them into homes as soon as possible. They thought it would help." She shrugged, impotent anger marring her face. "They killed his father. He'd been an interpreter for the US. Firash said his father had believed he was helping to save Afghanistan. During the pull out, Firash and his family tried to get out on the transport planes that were promised to the allies and their families because it was dangerous for them to stay, but something happened. Only Firash was able to get out. He got separated from his mother and sister and put on a plane out to California."

"Does he have family back there?"

She shook her head sadly. "He believes he does."

"But you don't?"

"We inquired when he was in high school. I helped him write to our congressman, who tried to get us information via a watchdog group. His mother was killed during a gunfight between the Taliban and soldiers helping people escape onto the planes. Her body was recovered by the Afghan military. But his sister, Kivah, we couldn't confirm. We think she might have ended up with a large group of people who crossed over into Pakistan on foot. The records at the refugee camps are terrible. That's the last anyone heard of her. Several children her age, she was six at the time,

Firash said, died of dysentery, but the photo of her that they sent us was bad."

"He didn't believe it was her?"

"No," Gloria took in a shaking breath. "He felt tied to his homeland because of the possibility she was alive. He wanted to return. I think that's where he went after he left here, but I can't be sure. He could never really leave that place, you know? He carried that day he lost everything with him all the time."

"What about a place of worship or a community center?"

Gloria scoffed. "We're in the boonies out here, Detective Reed. There's nothing like that this far out from the city. Besides, Firash wasn't interested in anything like that. He wasn't spiritual at all. He loved science. I really thought he was going to make it."

"Does he have any friends? Maybe another child in your care during the time he was here?"

"Firash didn't have friends. He tried so hard to fit in. But he was just so quiet. So wary. He didn't get picked on, just ignored. It's like he wasn't there. Somehow, I think that was worse for him. Firash was smart, brilliant even, but broken. That's why I tried to help him when he called. I thought he was back because he'd finally let go of trying to find his sister."

Or he found out what happened to her, and it set him off, Reed thought.

"I'll need permission to go into the storage locker," Reed said. "Do I have it?"

Gloria nodded. "Is he really planning on hurting people?"

"Do you think he's capable?" Reed asked.

"I don't know anymore. When he left, he was so angry and lost." Gloria swallowed hard, her eyes filling up. "Detective Reed, he's a damaged kid. Barely in his twenties. Please try to remember that."

Reed nodded, though he wasn't sure that would make any difference in the outcome. He turned to leave, then stopped. "One more thing, has anyone else come around here asking for Firash?" He flipped through his leather notebook, found the printed DA photo of Slater from his military days, and showed it to her. "Maybe this guy?"

"No." Gloria smiled sadly. "You're the only one who's ever asked about him. Even when he was in my home. No one cared."

Reed made it back to his car, drove around the block, and stopped at his surveillance spot under a huge old maple tree. The midday sun peeked through the clouds in large, bright sheets. Reed sat there watching the breeze ruffle the bushes, debating about what to do next. He could either sit on the house and see if his visit prompted a visit by Firash or he could check out the storage places.

He pulled up the map application on his phone and typed in storage facilities. There were only two in a small town like this. None by the freeway. Reed looked out over the hood, thinking. She hadn't wanted to betray Firash, but she also had to give Reed something. So, she'd been vague, but knew she'd get in trouble for lying.

Reed glanced back down at the map and typed in Gloria Alvarez's address. He clicked around in the settings until he got a terrain map overlay and then zoomed out. The property line ran back from the street to just beyond a small copse of trees. Squinting at the vegetation, he zoomed in on a dark shape jutting out from under the branches. Angular, it was definitely man-made. It had to be a roof.

"Gotcha," Reed whispered. So, she had let Firash use a storage facility, only it was hidden on the property. Gloria would know it wouldn't take him long to figure out she'd sent him on a wild goose chase. "Fierce mama. Still trying to give him a chance."

She'd given him permission to enter a fictional commercial storage unit, not a shack in her backyard. The legality was murky at best. He adjusted the view of the small building on his phone, thinking. To get to the small building, he'd have to walk past a large picture window in the living room and a kitchen window he'd spotted during his interview with Gloria. Afternoon sun angled lower in the sky. Sunset was in a couple hours. It would be better to wait for dark to go and check out the shack. That way he could steal in without the risk of being seen from the windows.

Steal . . .

The stench of sweat and stale beer hit Reed first. Then the texture of the wallpaper as Reed stood in Slater's footsteps in the Battery Hotel staring down at Gerald tied to the chair. Adrenaline pumped through his veins as he gripped the injector pen in his hand.

It really was a waste of a great mind. Slater's voice raked through Reed's skull. *You think what you stole was the only one?*

Reed gasped, his sweaty hands clutching the steering wheel as he blinked, back in the car. Of course, Gerald had stolen something more than the evidence of his brother's device and deal with a mercenary group. He'd stolen proof. The prototype in the video. It would be right there in the server room. But Gerald would be too smart to keep both pieces of evidence together. Reed guessed he gave one piece, the data files, to Petraeus. And hid the other. But where? The motel? Reed flipped back to his notebook pages he'd written after that initial walk-through in the Virtual Depot. With the turnover and cleaning crew, what there was of one, leaving anything in a room at the Battery would be too risky. Gerald would know that.

The case and its contents would be enough to get people moving on the investigation again, maybe get reinstated. At the very least he could prove that the fluid he injected into his neck wasn't a hallucinogen. That he hadn't lost his mind.

Tapping his pen on the paper, Reed worked the problem. Gerald would need a safe place. With his life and business so entangled with his brother Corbin's, it wouldn't be at his home or at the shared workspace at Neurogen. It would be someplace no one would expect. What better hiding place than one no one knew existed? *The loft.*

Reed checked his watch. A round trip would be an hour and a half. Throw in search time, he was looking at three, maybe three and a half hours before night. Then he could head back to Gloria's and search the shack. It was worth a check at the very least. He just hoped there was something left to find.

30

Firash

She called him on the burner he had left for her on the porch. His message urged her to only contact him in an emergency. As it rang on the worktable, a sheen of sweat formed on his upper lip. Could something have happened to them? He answered it, listening silently to the open line.

"Hello? Firi?" Gloria's voice came to him, and the ache of regret crowded his throat. "If you're listening, a detective came looking for you. He said . . . such terrible things about what they think you have planned."

"Was it Detective Reed?" Firash asked evenly.

"Yes, that's him. What is happening? Is it true, what he says?"

"You know that police are allowed to lie," Firash hedged. The pressure of being hunted weighed on his shoulders. "What did you tell him?"

"What could I?" she cried. "You won't tell me where you are." She told him about the conversation with the detective. How he'd found Firash and how she'd misled him about the storage locker. "I think he was watching our house, too. One of the kids said she thinks she saw him sitting in his car the other day when she was riding her bike."

Reed was stalking him and those he cared about. A dark coal of anger burned in his chest.

"I am grateful that you tried to cover for me," Firash said and meant it. She was one of the few who had ever had his back.

"After he left, I hiked out to the shed. It doesn't look like you've been there in weeks. Instead, there are crates and metal parts." Her voice broke. "I thought it was just your clothes and books, Firi. What did you bring to my home, hmm? What about the children?"

"There is nothing there but handyman supplies. It is nothing to be worried about, but I will remove everything." Firash rubbed his eyelids with his thumb and index finger. How was this man able to find Gloria? After so many years, he had hoped it would still be a place of refuge for him. "Is the detective still there? Did he park down the way to watch again? They do that. Sometimes in pairs."

"No, he left. I saw him drive away in the other direction. And I don't see any other strange cars around."

Firash glanced down at the tablet Maggie had given him. It was old, and she had set it to be untraceable except to fellow RR members. He had location turned off and used it only with Wi-Fi, usually on public transportation networks that offered encrypted connectivity for businesspeople. A subscription code bought under a fake name was all it had taken to disappear digitally. Firash used the tablet to take photos of the detectives as he followed them, trying to gain information. So, he knew that the detective's car still sat in the driveway of his condo. Again, this man had outsmarted him. He'd switched vehicles and left Firash to watch the detective's home like a fool. Shame burned his face. "What was he driving?"

"What does it matter what he was driving?"

"Please, Mrs. G," Firash begged. "It is important."

"I have no idea—" A young voice sounded muffled in the background and then she was back. "Taylor says it was one of those businesspeople cars, like a sedan. It looked light brown or champagne colored."

"Take the children and go," Firash said softly. "I apologize, but you must leave for a while. Perhaps go visit your uncle up north in his cabin. Remember we went there one time, for the Fourth of July?"

The crack of fireworks as they sliced across the dark sky, their strands of light reflected in the glassy surface of the lake, appeared unbidden in his mind's eye. It had been a good celebration. He had never been at a cabin or even to a lake before and the surrounding nature had felt like home to him. Firash used to dream about fishing out on the water, maybe even learning to swim to the floating dock. The edges of the phone dug into the underside of his fingers as he clenched it with a steel grip. He had wanted a place like that for his home. Back when he still believed he could make one for himself.

"Leave?" Gloria cried. "Why? Do you think he'll come back?"

"He will figure out that you lied about the storage place. This man is smart, and driven, so I believe he will return. Perhaps he is waiting for a warrant."

"A warrant? Firi, what are you doing?" Her voice changed, like she was whispering into a cupped hand to hide what she was saying. "Detective Reed said you wanted to h-hurt people. I can't believe that. This is not who you are. Please come home. We'll face this together, okay? Whatever you planned, you can still change your mind. You haven't done anything yet, right?"

"What you do, Mrs. G, is a gift," Firash murmured, his eyes stinging. "You are a haven for the lost."

"Then come back," the quiver in her voice pierced his heart. "Please . . ."

"There is no going back. And I am not lost. Not anymore. I know exactly what I must do," Firash said as he disconnected.

Standing in the cavernous warehouse, he pulled off his rubber gloves, lifted the goggles off his eyes and pushed the respirator down below his chin until it dangled around his neck on the strap. Vaporized paint from the spray gun drifted in the air over his workspace, falling like bright mist onto the concrete floor. The wooden pallets butted up against the wall. Scaffolding held crates wrapped in plastic film, ready for transit. He was so close.

Firash walked to the unfinished window of the abandoned building, his protective suit squeaking with each step. He stood looking down at the drainage ravine below. Recent heavy rains had flooded the streets and pushed Seattle's water collection system to its breaking point. Since the storms hit, a wild, churning river of rainwater had swept down the cement channel just behind the building. The water rose higher toward the lip of the concrete embankment each day. Firash had worried about flooding, but he was nearly done now. Wind pushed its way through the unsealed seams between the window glass and the wall creating a melancholy howl that echoed through the vast, empty space.

He was a mere step ahead of this Detective Reed, but it was enough. Sometimes it was but a moment's breath between success and failure. Firash believed that was all it would take. The span of one breath, and then everything would be decided.

31

Pioneer Square Arts District

Pioneer Square's nightlife experienced a revival after nearly a decade of being known as a slightly seedy meat market. Over several years, the flashy clubs and bars featuring local bands doing covers became posh speakeasys made to look like English drawing rooms and high-end arcades that served alcohol. You could relax on sumptuous chairs at a luxurious hukkah lounge with amazing food instead of yelling over pounding music in a dark nightclub. Not a bad direction, in Reed's opinion.

Last time he'd been in Pioneer Square, it was morning. The scent of breakfast pastries and piping hot coffee had given way to the spicy aromas of grilling meats, brick oven pizza, and bubbling hot pot broths in the restaurants lining the sidewalk. A fragrant whiff of pie, pumpkin, maybe, moved through the trees as he walked toward the Akira Arts Building once more.

It was later than he'd anticipated, having hit traffic back into Seattle, and the setting sun sent spires of warm peach light across the darkening sky. The wind had picked up and the smell of petrichor drifted with him as he walked. Another storm was coming down the pike. One in a series of cells predicted over the holiday weekend. He tucked his chin into his trench coat's collar against the damp chill.

Old buildings looked different at dusk. Their gables and porticos jutted out in angles to the growing night. Shadows from the ornate streetlamps lining the sidewalks made menacing shapes out of the once whimsical metal wind sculptures. Their slowly spinning blades whipping across the grass like scythes. A small community garden to his left had erected a fountain, a fat cherub happily peeing onto a water lily. In the waning light, its eyes seemed to follow Reed as he walked by.

Up ahead, laughter sounded in the dark of Occidental Park. Teenagers having a smoke or a sip of something they stole. Already the little security bot rumbled across the wet pavement toward them like an angry shoebox, its facial rec camera flashing. If it got them, their parents would be automatically fined, and it wasn't cheap. Glass shattered in the distance, and they ran, shouting curses at the machine as they pulled their hoodies down. And then the whine of the rental scooters came up behind Reed. He stepped out of the way as four of the sightseeing motor bikes rolled across the grass together, returning to their charging ports for tomorrow's tourists. The metal herd self-navigated through the streets, flashing their headlights cheekily at pedestrians not moving quickly enough out of their way. The silent, hidden lives robots led after their humans have gone to sleep always creeped Reed out.

Back at Gerald's art nouveau building, Reed took the stairs to the top floor rather than chance the janky basket-and-pulley-system they called an elevator in the dark. He pushed through the stairwell door into the hallway. The forensics team had sealed Gerald's door with crime scene stickers across the threshold. Again, legally murky territory. The investigation was over, according to everyone but Reed. The killer dumping bodies all over Seattle had died in that server room as far as the Seattle Police Department was concerned. Tig had made that clear. Slater's sins were accounted for with no need to look further, apparently. And yet, when he tried to fall asleep, Danzig's face as he ordered Caitlyn's death came back to Reed. Cold evil. Pure and simple. This wasn't over.

Reed pulled an electronic lock scraper from his jeans pocket. Affixing the small device to the doorknob, he punched in a few specs and waited.

The whir of the small motor seemed to echo down the hallway as it inserted motorized picks, and he looked both ways. The pins inside the lock clicked and then the device went silent. He tried the knob and it opened. Pulling a pocketknife from his trench pocket, he flicked it open with his thumb, sliced the sticker down the edge of the door, and walked in.

The forensics team had left the curtains closed on the high windows as was their policy, which helped hide the beam of Reed's mini flashlight as he panned the loft. He remembered the panel for the loft's control system was over by the kitchenette. He used the flashlight beam to help navigate past the café table to the wall next to the small stove. Reed popped open the panel and poked around in the control system until he found the lights. They glowed on, illuminating the loft.

Dark fingerprint powder marred the walls, outlets, counters, and anywhere else they thought might yield a print other than Gerald's. According to the report, the super, a house keeper, and Gerald were the only ones found. The personal effects, furniture, artwork, and supplies hadn't been packed up and the loft looked much like it did when Reed first entered it and probably would for a while. With Corbin dead, Reed wasn't sure who this loft would go to. So far, the Price family was already squabbling among themselves over the brothers' holdings, according to Coyote, who was following the meltdown of Neurogen with glee. As were his clients. Everyone wanted the whole ordeal to be over.

Reed wandered over to where he'd gone through the sketchbooks earlier. They were still piled on the floor where he left them. Where could the metal MER-C case be hidden that wasn't already searched by the crime scene techs? His eyes wandered the walls looking for vents or cubbies to hide something that big. High shelving held books, boxes, tools, and other detritus from a workshop, but nothing big enough. Reed toyed with the idea that Gerald had taken the device and the injectors out of the case, but decided it was unlikely. The containment pods needed the coolant system in the case after two hours if he remembered correctly. They couldn't be separated for long. And he had no idea if the serums needed cooling too, that hadn't been in Corbin's recording. So, it was more likely than not that Gerald would keep the device and injectors with the case.

Walking to the café table in the kitchenette, Reed sank onto the rickety chair. He looked at the loft as Gerald would have, maybe over coffee. He let his eyes wander. Something that precious, you'd keep it in your sightlines. An unconscious way to sooth the doubt that comes from concealing contraband. But Gerald was smart, he knew someone might find the loft, so he would've taken measures to assure that it wasn't easily discovered. Reed stood, walked to the center of the loft, and did a slow three-hundred-and-sixty-degree turn around the room, thinking.

Where would a genius hide a secret?

Gerald liked to play games. He and Petraeus sent encrypted digital postcards to each other. They had code names. Their interactions were on deep web message boards. Reed glanced at the paintings on the walls, leaning in piles. The dark sand beach, Petraeus's figure in the foreground, the peninsula and lighthouse. All recognizable as Alki Beach now that he'd been there. Their secret meeting place in plain sight, yet invisible to those who didn't know. An inside joke at the expense of others.

Reed spent more than an hour walking every inch of the loft, pulling out drawers, looking under tabletops, knocking on walls listening for a hollow sound, everywhere he could think of. But he'd been there too long. Nosey neighbors or someone watching the loft from the outside would get curious. Light was surely leaking out from between the curtains now that it was so dark outside.

Deciding to take one last pass around the space, Reed walked along the storage cabinets. Some were only waist high, their tops used as counter space for more clay figures, ceramic bowls, some abstract shapes done in painted papier-mâché. His eyes landed on a sculpture, and he stilled. In the corner where the wall of windows intersected with the north wall of the loft, a wood block pedestal sat atop a low table. It held a sculpture chest high, and Reed eyed the piece as he approached. In a sea of ceramics and canvases, it was the only glass sculpture in the room.

Reed touched the back of his fingers to the smooth surface. Nothing in Gerald's notebooks ever mentioned glassworks. None of the myriad design sketches he'd leafed through were of glass. He knew he hadn't seen anything that resembled the wave of cobalt and seafoam green that gleamed beneath the studio lights.

It had been dusted for prints and there were none. Not surprising given you generally wipe off the sculpture after it's placed and periodically for dust. Reed considered it for a moment. It was truly a stunning piece. A single sheet of molded glass rose in a wave of ombre blues and aquas before it arched down over the stand into pale green seafoam. The colors were not the dark steel and grays of Alki beach. They were vibrant, aggressive, the design lofty in its technical need to balance the weight of the glass against gravity. Reed looked back at the other pieces in the room. They were somber in color and composition. Gerald's sculptures were of dark clay or concrete. His sketches melancholy, full of barren landscapes or dying still life displays. This piece didn't fit.

Reed walked around it, taking in the art piece. Both sides of the arched glass wave were closed off with added hand-blown pieces resembling kelp and seafoam. He paused, imagining the dimensions of the sculpture. Sealing off both ends of the wave could conceivably create an open space within the barrel of the wave. There was only one way Reed could know for sure whether the hidden space within the sculpture was big enough to contain the metal case. Shaking his head, Reed reached out and toppled the sculpture over. It crashed onto the cement floor of the loft, shattering into dozens of glass pieces. And then Reed's heart sank. There was nothing there. He moved some of the larger pieces with his toe, but no, nothing.

Growling with frustration, Reed kicked the wooden stand viciously against the wall. Sinking down, he sat on his heels, his head tilted back, and stared at the pipes in the ceiling. Exhausted after days of surveillance and almost no sleep, he was running on fumes and still no closer to Firash or what he was doing. He needed sleep. He needed to eat. He'd circle back to Gloria's in the morning. Maybe get a hotel halfway between to sleep. Reed rose with a yawn, already thinking about the closest takeout, when something occurred to him.

There'd been something off with the stand when he kicked it, the feel of it hadn't been solid wood. Reed walked over to where it landed. It was made to look like a block of wood, but the corners of the 'bark' had pulled back. Reed knelt and rubbed his thumb on a patch of metal that peeked out from beneath the wood surface of the stand and realized the wood itself was fake. A veneer. It tore away in his hands like wrapping paper revealing the metal case. Gerald had beaten all the high-tech scanners at the crime scene with papier-mâché and some excellent painting skills.

Reed took a breath and opened the case. It held the prototype from Corbin's recording in the server room. He recognized the silver metal, more oblong shape, and larger nodes. The injector pen looked relatively similar to what he'd used but had no lights on the metal base. The serum vial and syringe were the same. And best of all, full. The lab could test the serum and prove it wasn't a hallucinogen, and more importantly, prove what it really was . . . a terrible weapon against anyone in clandestine work, anyone with a secret.

He stared at the case. Wondering what to do about it. With a possible mole or at least a reliable leaker at the SPD, he couldn't chance taking it in. Not yet. He couldn't keep it at his house, not for long anyway. He needed a place to hide it until he could figure out who to trust. Plus, he still needed to go back to Firash's storage shack in case he tried to clean it out.

Grabbing his phone, he pulled up Nat's number, and typed out a message.

I found something— Reed hesitated, thinking for a moment. He just broke into a sealed crime scene. Was most definitely going to leave with evidence. And he planned on doing worse at Gloria's property. Breaking and entering was something Nat didn't deserve to get dragged into. If he contacted her, it needed to be after he was done committing felonies. Finally, he typed, *Meet me at my place tonight at midnight.*

He hit send wondering if she would come alone or bring the entire station after him. Guess he'd find out in a few hours. Driving back, he thought about Firash's life with Gloria at the foster home. The cool, tree-shrouded spaces, the lonely paths through meadows, places in a small town where you could disappear. He wondered if a young Firash had sat and listened to the sounds of birds in the trees or dipped his toes in the creeks that ran through that whole area. Had he been happy there or just not in constant danger. Did he know the difference between exhaustion and peace? Or was he like Reed? Who never could tell the two apart.

Nat answered his text with a call, which he ignored. She followed up with several texts with choice words about ignoring her after a message like that. Reed turned the phone face down and stared out at the inky sky salted with jagged stars. He thought about fate and past misdeeds and maybe a little about karma. He mused about what Heraclites said about destiny and how a man's character shaped his fate. But mostly he thought of Caitlyn's laugh when she watched him play air guitar in the kitchen while he grilled burgers at the stove. It was that giggly, joyous sound of possibility that had been cut brutally short that pushed him further into the night.

32

Gloria Alvarez's Home, Westfalia, Washington

Reed parked on the other side of the house than earlier because it was closer on the map to the shed. He was glad for the waning light. It would help mask his movements. Gloria's property on the west side was hilly and she had left the rougher terrain to its own devices. Towering Douglas Firs, Ponderosa Pines, and scraggly bushes obscured the view of the house from the street and hid a thin dirt path leading behind the house. Reed had seen it earlier when he'd come up to the screen door. Where the front walk was flush with the street, the entrance to the side yard of the property was via a waist-high retaining wall accessible by four cracked cement steps.

It was nearly seven in the evening, well past winter sunset, and the kitchen was usually lit and full of kids and Gloria making dinner about now. Yet the house had been silent and dark since he'd arrived. They could be away at a relative's home for Thanksgiving, at the movies, out to dinner, maybe. But Reed knew that she always left the under-cabinet lights on when she went out with the kids. He'd watched her do it these past few days during his surveillance. Reed pondered the pitch-dark house for a moment.

Something teased at the edges of Reed's consciousness as he parked on the opposite side of the house, just before the cement steps. His headlights were off, and the overgrown trees blotted out the lights from the sparse streetlamps. There was no dark like the woods, Reed thought. In his own cabin, he had to memorize wood piles and equipment just to keep from walking into things when he arrived on moonless nights. Despite the frosty air, Reed took off his trench coat and threw it into the backseat of the car. A gust of wind rushed through the overhanging maple tree branches chilling him and sending dead leaves somersaulting to the sidewalk. They scratched at his arm as they fell and crunched underneath his feet as he climbed the steps.

Reed moved through the shrubs and dried grasses smelling the Winter Jasmine and waning Primrose as they succumbed to autumn's ravages. His boots trampled the rich damp earth beneath fallen pine needles. He felt his way along the vegetation until the soft ground gave way to hard packed dirt. The footpath led up an incline and Reed navigated via gnarled shadows and luck until he felt he was far enough into the property that his flashlight wouldn't be seen. He'd taped off most of the lens with duct tape so that only a thin beam shone through, enough to illuminate a few feet in front of him. The path widened to a dirt clearing where a small shack, a shed really, sat butted up against a stand of old pines. The edge of the roof jutted out into the clearing and that's what Reed had seen on the map program earlier.

He crept along the edge of the structure, trying to get to the windows on the side rather than go for the front door. It appeared more than empty. It looked abandoned. Hope of finding Firash's base of operations dwindled as he approached. The shack was a prefabricated work shed one might get at a home improvement store. People used them for gardening, storage, and man caves. They had power and you could hook it to water, but it was half the size of a one-car garage with wood siding and a shingle roof. Not really fit for living.

Disappointed, Reed wiped away the grime on one of the windows and peered through the single square pane. He peeled the tape from his flashlight and shone the beam into the shack. His beam crossed something bright orange, but he couldn't tell what it was. It was shiny, like new plastic, and cylindrical. Maybe a tube or barrel from what he could see but it was partially obscured by material, a drop cloth or sheet. He ran the light along the floor and saw some old work boots, the kind used for construction, a part of a piece of furniture, something like a stand, and some empty plastic milk crates.

Frustrated, he tried the window further down. More shrouded from the elements, it was less dirty and easier to see into. Furniture shapes emerged from the darkness, a shelf with books, a corkboard with photos of places Reed couldn't make out. Buildings, maybe a hallway or corridor painted gray, and a grassy field. Someone had sketched tent shapes in the field with marker. There was a portrait, a professional headshot of some sort tacked up as well. Reed pulled his phone out, turned the flashlight on, and started recording. Maybe Nat could fix the images so they could see enough for a warrant.

He crept toward the rear of the shack, looking for more windows, and found a large one in the back. It was rectangular and, unlike the others, slid open. Probably for ventilation. Reed tried it, and it opened for him. Only his eyes and nose could clear the bottom of the windowsill, but his flashlight afforded him a better view. The shelves housed tattered books, mostly repair manuals, do-it-yourself home projects, a gardening journal. There was a rusty tray with nails and screws. But it was the desk that was the most interesting. There were marks on the surface, burn marks and beads of metal. Like someone had soldered there. On the floor, little pieces of stripped wire littered the area near the chair. Firash was building something.

Reed debated whether to climb in or take what he had to Nat. The wind picked up, bringing with it the scent of fireplaces and pine. A sudden gust shook the trees, rattling the dry leaves, building in strength until it became a roaring wind that tore through the woods, whipping dirt and grass and twigs against the shed and him. He squeezed his eyes against the onslaught, riding it out. When the breeze died, he tried to get to the windows on the other side of the shed, but a rotted log and some rusty bikes blocked his way.

Deciding to come back with Nat, Reed took one last turn around the shed to the front door where he tried the handle. He caught movement out of the corner of his vision a millisecond too late. A figure burst out of the bushes next to the door, the bright yellow of a stun gun registering as the barbs flared out and slammed into Reed's torso. Paralyzing current crackled through Reed's body, the clicking sound of it cycling like a jackhammer in his head. He seized, going rigid, a shout of pain caught in his frozen throat. He couldn't let go, couldn't move, his muscles contracting endlessly. The five second cycle cut, and he staggered on wobbly legs, falling on his back. Firash leaned over Reed, his young face tense with anger as he pulled the trigger once more. The current seared through him again, his muscles going rigid. Unable to move as Firash leaned over him.

"You should not have come here," Firash whispered, his breath fresh with mint. "You should not have told her those things about me."

Reed couldn't speak, couldn't react when Firash lowered a wet cloth over his face. A sickly-sweet smell burned up his nose and the world fell away. He tried to stay awake, but his limbs were so heavy, his eyes refusing to focus. Firash grabbed Reed's ankles, the stun gun barbs still attached to Reed, tucked the stun gun under his armpit, and dragged him along the ground back toward the retaining wall. The dirt and leaves pushed up into the back of his sweater and scraped against his neck. His head bumped over roots and rocks, the pain sending shards of light flaring across Reed's vision. Nearly losing consciousness, he tried to catch the bushes and roots of the trees with his hands, but he couldn't work his fingers right.

Firash stopped, pulled the stun gun from under his arm and pulled the trigger. A new wave of pain tore through Reed, and he groaned, riding out the cycle, his gaze locked on the dark branches swaying in the wind overhead. Firash picked up Reed's ankles again and dragged him the rest of the way to the retaining wall, and then left him lying in the dirt. Disoriented, Reed tried to right himself, to sit up, but he only managed to roll to his side. Woozy from whatever he breathed in, he couldn't get his bearings. The trunk lid rose and then Firash yanked him to his feet. Dizzy, Reed fought with the kid, his knees giving way like melted wax. And again, the cloth was forced over his mouth and nose. His chest burned, and overwhelming fatigue pulled him down. They staggered to the car and then he was falling, tumbling down into something.

Reed looked up from inside the trunk, the corners of his vision going gray with the second dose. He flailed, reaching for Firash. "Y-You're under arrest—" and then the lid slammed down, plunging him into total darkness.

33

Reed woke to the sound of rain drumming on a metal roof. Not a bad storm, just a light drizzle but the steady thrum snagged him and brought him out of the dark. The back of his head hurt, and he vaguely remembered being dragged across the ground. His scalp burned, probably cut. He cracked his eyes open and realized he was duct-taped to a chair set in the center of an abandoned industrial space. Firash had looped the tape a couple of times around Reed's chest and around his wrists, but his legs were free. A few fluorescent lights directly above his chair buzzed and flickered weakly. What meager light there was did little to illuminate the vast space and the dark of night seemed to engulf the ends of the room. But underneath the rain, the rush of wind moving through the cavernous space, the buzz of the lights, was the sound of rushing water.

Reed tried to move, but his arms felt leaden. He yanked against the tape binding his wrists to the arms of the chair, pulling until the hairs on his forearms ripped away, the skin going slick with sweat. He struggled aimlessly, his thoughts sluggish.

A crash near the window made him still and he listened, straining to hear. It was cold, his breath visible when he exhaled. Broken out windows near the roof let in rain that dribbled down the peeling paint on the walls. His mouth was dry, and his throat felt raw, but he forced himself to take in deep breaths, trying to get as much oxygen to his addled brain as possible. The nausea subsided, but a headache grew at his temples and Reed wasn't sure if that was a good sign or a bad one.

His focus slowly returned, and he surveyed the space with a clearer mind. It must have been a mechanic's garage or chop shop. He recognized the metal pylons of a hydraulic car lift. An old compressor was plugged into the wall, its hose snaking through brown and orange overspray on the concrete. A worktable a few yards away sat empty and bent, listing to the right as if ready to fall over. Lengths of torn tape flapped down from the top. Rusted lengths of pipe littered the floor, along with old welding nozzles, empty wire spools, and spray cans. Overhead, shop lights, their once white hoods now rusted, dangled from the ceiling on thin chains. Of the six in a row, only one and half seemed to work. The far wall of the garage, where the sound of rushing water was coming from, had a gaping hole where a door should be. As if someone had pulled too hard and ripped it right out of the wall like in a cartoon. Graffiti and evidence of squatters looked old, at least a few months. Reed wracked his brain trying to place where he was. Industrial, abandoned buildings, secluded enough for Firash's purposes . . . water.

Reed scanned the room. What *was* Firash doing there? The compressor kicked on, cycling in more pressure. Reed focused on the rushing water outside. It sounded weird. He wasn't sure if it was because he was hearing it through the rain or his brain was still messed up, but it didn't sound like the ocean. He didn't smell the sea either. So maybe he was inland.

A door slammed nearby and Firash walked out of a small office built into the wall of the garage. He held the metal case in his hand and stopped a few feet from Reed, staring down at him from underneath his sweatshirt hoodie. He looked so young, and Reed watched him warily. Amateurs were unpredictable and rash.

"You're awake," Firash said, and Reed was surprised at the calmness of his voice. Something about it set off alarm bells. "I thought I would have to go and get water to splash on you."

Reed cleared his throat. "What drug—"

"Chloroform. Not difficult to make. Only two household chemicals."

"I chased you down the alley." Reed coughed, his throat scratchy. "You're the one with the drones."

Firash nodded. He held up the case. "In your trunk. You know, I thought it was money at first. When I watched Slater with this. He carried it with him wherever he went. Guarded it like a miser. I thought he had robbed a bank."

"A memory bank," Reed murmured. The kid was acting off. He went from gleefully electrocuting him to cordial conversation. The hairs on the back of Reed's neck stood on end, but he kept him talking. "Do you know what it is, now?"

"Yes. Slater used it on a man named Alastair. Then he threw that man in front of a train. I knew what it was at once. You have no idea the secrets Danzig keeps in his Special Projects files."

"Was Alastair a friend of yours?" Reed pushed with his forearms into the bands of duct tape at his wrists slowly, forcing them to stretch. He just needed a little give.

Firash set the case down, knelt next to it and opened the lid. "No."

"He traveled down from Canada to meet you, didn't he?" Reed asked, his mouth growing dry as Firash lifted the halo from the case. He talked fast, trying to stall Firash long enough to form a plan. "Alastair traveled back and forth from Canada a lot. More than the average person would for vacation. That set off red flags. I figured he was moving drugs, weapons, maybe even people. And we know his most recent trip was three weeks ago. And Slater found out he was meeting with you and killed him. Who was he? A contact? Are you working with someone? Restoration Republic?"

Firash tried to hide the look of triumph. It was fleeting, but there. Reed saw it and then the realization hit. "No. You're not working with them at all, are you?"

"You are as good as I have heard," Firash said evenly and reached back into the case, retrieving the syringe full of serum. "Though what I was told of your time in Yemen is hard to believe."

A torrent of wind rattled through the metal building and sent rain sputtering through the cracked windows overhead. The storm blew rain sideways through the hole in the garage's wall to the outside.

"Yeah, well, the years can add layers of shine to tales." Reed kept his eyes on Firash who reached back into the case and pulled out a containment pod and attached it to the halo. The hiss when it locked sent Reed's stomach squirming.

Firash rose, walked behind Reed, and held the halo over his head like he was going to crown him king. The hum of the device moved through the bones of Reed's jaw and Petraeus's wild eyes came back to him.

"Tell me what Slater told you," Firash said. "Think about who you told about my plans."

"Wait—" Firash shoved the halo down onto Reed's head. Frigid pain moved through his mind, the metal gripping the lower part of his skull like an icy vice. Pulsing vibrations rattled through his eye sockets, his nose, his teeth, growing stronger. Tendrils of panic tightened around Reed's chest and he fought for control. *Closer. He needed Firash closer.* "You're just going to abandon Kivah again? Leave her for dead like before?"

Firash froze, he moved back around, his furious gaze boring through Reed. "What did you say?"

"Gloria said you made up an entire fantasy about your dead sister. She said you couldn't accept she was gone." Reed pushed himself back in to the chair with his arms, raising his head as high as it would go. "What is that? Guilt over leaving her behind? Guilt that you saved yourself and never looked back?"

Firash's eyes went cold and he backhanded Reed, sending his head rocking to the side. "I was nine! How dare you—I went back despite the danger and looked for her. I never forgot her!"

Just a little bit more.

Reed tasted blood. "Bullshit, you forgot everything! You stayed in that safe little house with Gloria, playing in those flower meadows, pampered, and protected. You went to that cushy school, harassed middle-aged professors, and went to your safe little protests with college girls, and you left your sister . . . your *little* sister behind in that hellhole!"

"Shut up! Just shut up!" Firash shouted, his hands going to his head, the syringe pressed flat against his cheek.

"And now you think stopping some business deal in Afghanistan is going to erase all of that? Your cause isn't noble. It's nothing but a selfish means to appease your guilt!"

Firash pointed out the hole in the wall at the city beyond. "They promised we'd be safe if we helped. Instead, they abandoned my father! He was an ally and they left him behind to be beaten and murdered!"

Reed's gut twisted at Firash's real anguish, at the horror he'd endured as a child, at their profound and costly mistakes, but still he pushed him. Throwing him off balance. "Sounds like a family tradition."

"You bastard!" Firash screamed and dropped the syringe, lunging for Reed.

In one motion Reed snapped his body forward, the downward force ripping the tape as his forehead connected with Firash's nose. The kid stumbled back, his hands going to his face, blood running down his chin to his hoodie. Reed yanked his fists in an angle as if punching his opposite shoulder and the tape at his wrists broke.

A feral howl escaped Firash who ran at him again with wild eyes. Rising from the chair, he kicked Firash in the chest, sending him sprawling back onto the cement floor.

Reed ripped the halo from his head, tossed it at the case, and spit blood on the floor. "Where're you going?" He strode toward Firash who crawled on his hands and knees toward a backpack set against the wall. Bending down, Reed grabbed a metal pipe from the floor, he raised it over his head and then slammed it down on the portable table sending a resounding crash through the garage. Firash flinched, his eyes going wide as he glanced back. "No more games, Firash. You're going in, you're going to talk, and no one is going to die, alright? You see where this is going?"

"You cannot stop it. I made sure." Firash scrambled to his feet, backing up. "And I know you are working for Danzig. I will never get to a police station."

"Not everyone is in his pocket. He's not all powerful."

Firash let out a scornful laugh. "I saw who he owns in the files. What he knows. You are all corrupt!" Grabbing the backpack from the floor, he spun and ran for the hole in the wall, but he was limping, slower.

"No, you don't." Reed ran after him, closing the distance in seconds.

Firash struggled with the backpack as he ran and then he turned, trying to pull something out of it, the object snagging on the material. Reed crouched and then hurled the pipe at Firash like a hatchet, hitting him square in the chest and taking him down in cacophony of clanging metal. He was on him in an instant, yanking Firash's arms behind him, and holding him down. Reed grabbed the backpack next to Firash and dug through it with one hand. He found a gun, a revolver, loaded. Some more duct tape, and a lanyard with an empty plastic identification card holder. Reed used duct tape to bind Firash's wrists. And then he helped him to his feet. A square section of the concrete was dry. Like a large box or pallet had been there. On the floor next to the dry spot, an empty roll of shipping cellophane.

"What did you do?" Tapping his pants pockets Reed looked for his phone to call it in. "Did you ship something? Is that what you're doing?" Firash had gone suddenly docile. His eyes glazed. He didn't try to get away. He didn't try to run. "Tell me what you sent. To whom?"

"My mother begged for help in Kabul. When they came for American allies. She begged for help. But everyone was s-shooting and the fires . . . the smoke from the fires blacked out the sky." His voice broke.

"Hey, I didn't mean what I said, kid. I was just trying to rile you up."

But he didn't listen, like he was in a trance, just spilling his guts as Reed walked him toward the back entrance where he guessed the car was.

"And *after* surviving that, I get here, and I am hated. For being poor. For being foreign. For being broken," Firash's voice rose as they walked, his face contorting with grief. "They protested our numbers. They came in their air-conditioned vans and matching shirts, and they screamed at us for needing help!"

"You'll get a chance to tell everyone what happened, when we get to the station." Reed said, his head pounding. He had to call Nat. He had to fill her in.

They were passing one of the support pylons holding up the garage roof when Firash started to tremble and hyperventilate. He did it so fast, swinging his body and slamming his own head against the corner of the cement pylon with a sickening thud.

"Holy hell!" The impact yanked Firash's arm from Reed's and the kid stumbled back, blood pouring from the gash in his head. "What are you doing?"

"I will not let you use the device on me! Y-You will not stop what is fair, what is just!" His eyes swam and Reed reached for him, but the blood from Firash's head made his upper arm slick and he slipped from his grip.

Before he could stop him, Firash darted for the hole in the wall. Reed ran after him, the rain driving into his face, stinging his eyes. In the dark, lit by the glow of the streetlamps, Firash stumbled along the edge of the embankment, his arms still bound behind his back.

"Stop!" Reed yelled. He slid on the wet pavement, trying to catch up. "The ravine!"

Firash stopped at the edge, his heels hanging over. "Do you know what it was like? People turning on each other. Friends trampled one another just to get away. Terrified, willing to kill to save themselves!"

"No, I don't . . . you're right," Reed shouted back, extending his hand, offering it to Firash. Blinking away the rain, he edged closer. "There is no excuse. For any of this to happen."

"Well, you *will* know," Firash screamed. "You will know that fear, that pain, now."

Reed saw Firash's body teeter, listing back and he froze. "Don't do this."

Lightning spiderwebbed across the sky. A blinding claw that lit up the ravine, flashing into view the churning river rushing past their feet, lapping at the lip of the embankment.

Firash's face went serene, his eyes blank. "It is already done."

"No!" Reed fought the wind and the mud to get to him, his hand clutching onto his shoulder. Thunder roared over them, the sky strobing alight again, blinding them. Firash lurched in his grip, his legs pushing off the ground and then they were falling. The roar of the water raced up toward them, swallowing them both.

34

The cold cut through Reed, crushing the breath out of him as he tumbled into the frigid water, still clutching Firash's arm. The swell of the rain in the ravine moved like a river, the roar of it deafening. Rain pummeled the surface, splashing dirty gutter water into Reed's face, his nose, his mouth. Firash gagged and coughed, going under as Reed fought the chill to keep them both afloat.

A surge smashed them against the side of the channel, and stars flash behind Reed's lids. His breath came in tight gasps as he tried to get to the side, dragging the kid with him as he grasped at debris and the smooth sides of the cement embankment. Pushed by the water, the garage's façade faded into the encroaching dark. Reed flailed his free arm, unable to fight the icy flow that pulled them in a torrent down the ravine.

He felt in the water for Firash's wrists and ripped the duct tape apart, freeing his hands. The kid wouldn't help. Wouldn't try to stay above water, letting the rain bury him in the mud and trash washing down from the city and Reed grew too heavy and too numb to stop it by the second.

"Swim, dammit," Reed shouted through chattering teeth. "You're drowning!"

Firash seemed to snap back. He yanked himself from Reed's grasp.

"Let me go!" He screamed, pure panic in his eyes. "I will never—" Firash's words were snatched away by another volley of thunder.

"Get to the side!" Reed pointed to the debris pile. "Over there!"

But Firash didn't swim or flail, he leaned back and drifted out toward the whirling center of the river barreling down the cement channel, spinning in a lazy circle, his face flashing in and out of shadows as he passed the streetlamps lining the embankment.

"What are you doing?" Reed struggled to get to him, his boots and jeans weighing him down. Aching numbness enveloped his body, slowing his movements. Up ahead, large debris and trash washed away by the river had snagged against a maintenance railing leading down from ground level. A conglomerate of wood pallets, shopping carts, and a ratty couch sat tangled up against the wall with branches and parts of bushes, clogging the water's path. Reed felt himself drift further into the center as the water redirected around the blockage. The pile of debris jutted out to the middle of the channel and Firash was drifting straight into it.

"Firash!" Reed swam with the current, groaning as his muscles seized with cramps, gaining on Firash, then passing him. Too cold. They needed to get out of the water before they died of exposure. He tried to angle toward the outcropping of debris. He floated fast, nearly missing, but managed to snag a piece of trash, a wood slat, and clawed his way up until his chest was out of the water. He reached out, yelling for Firash. "Grab onto me!"

He heard his name on the wind, and then spotted Firash in a pool of light from the streetlamps just before his head slipped underneath the water. Thrashing underneath the surface, Reed felt material and grabbed it, hoping it wasn't trash. His fingers closed around Firash's arm. He was limp, floating freely, and Reed dragged him to the trash pile, but his arms were leaden, his fingers too stiff. Panting he pushed Firash upward, feeling his own strength fade. He couldn't hold them on the barrier anymore, and started to slip, his chest tight with failure.

"Firash," he called, but the kid just slumped forward onto his shoulder. They were falling backward, the rush of the water pulling Reed down. "I can't . . . I can't hold on—"

"Reed!" Backlit by the streetlamps, Nat picked her way out onto the debris, her voice piercing through the rain. Hair plastered to her wet face, she looked at him with utter irritation. "What the hell are you doing out here? It's raining!"

"I know it's raining!" Reed shouted, barely holding on. "H-Help me get him up!"

"What's wrong with him?" She leaned down and they worked together to get Firash as far up onto the pile of debris as possible. Nat strained, leaning back as she pulled on Firash's shirt, hauling him until only his lower legs were in the water. Firash's head flopped to the side, the gash on his head a gaping maw. She reared back, horrified. "What'd you whack him with an ax?"

"He smashed his own head. He just . . . smashed his own head." Reed slumped against the blockage, panting, wondering vaguely how long he could be that cold without his heart stopping. "I just need a minute to catch my breath."

"Reed, wake up!" Nat's voice scratched through the fog of hypothermia. "You're slipping!"

But it was too late. He slid down into the water and back out to the surging river, his hands grasping lazily for hold. He felt himself slip into shock. Felt the numbness, heavy and full, drag him down. And then something bounced off his head. Then another. It was trash and Nat was throwing it, trying to hit him. She threw another piece of garbage, a deflated basketball, he thought, and it smacked him full in the face, snapping him back.

"What are you doing?" She screamed, motioning for him. "Do I need to go find a rope or something? Come on, Reed!"

"This woman . . ." Reed murmured to himself but swam. Slowly, painfully, almost passing out. But he swam. "I'm good. Get him warm!"

Reed fought the current, the fatigue, his gaze locked on her. Something was wrong. She was leaning down, pushing on Firash. CPR. Then she ran back toward the ground level and disappeared. Confused, Reed wondered if his mind was playing tricks. If she'd been there at all. A surge spun him, pushed him toward the other side, and he was almost out of fight. She reappeared and leaned back over Firash.

Reed made it back and pulled himself along the side of the trash pile.

Rounding the edge and then back around to where he'd been swept away. Nat knelt over Firash, her hair dripping water into empty eyes. She stroked his hair as if he were a child. When she saw Reed, she scrambled over, helping him up. He lay on a bundle of cardboard strapped together. The rain had slowed to a mist, and he noticed the lack of shivering, which struck him as problematic, but he was too tired to care. He heard Nat moving, her footsteps retreat, and then she was back. His trench coat landed on his chest, and he opened his eyes.

"Get into that coat before you freeze to death," Nat said next to him. "I started your car, and the heater is going. We gotta get you to it, now."

Reed pushed himself to sit up, and Nat helped him to his feet, sliding the coat over his stiff arms. He hugged himself, his legs weak or numb. He couldn't tell. The streetlamps lit her face with a wash of warm yellow. She looked scared, unsettled.

"Is he gone?"

She nodded, her lips pressed tight. "Yeah."

"How did you find me?"

Nat reached up, yanked something from under his trench coat collar, and held it up. A circular piece of material with embedded wires.

"You tagged me? When?"

"At your condo." Nat zipped up her own coat and sniffed at the cold. "I figured you'd ditch your phone and your car, but never the jacket. You think it looks too cool."

He wasn't even mad. That was impressive. "That's a gross violation of my privacy."

"You ex-plo-ded!" she said, clapping her palms with each syllable. "And I *thought* you were talking like a crazy person after refusing help. I was worried you'd do something stupid." She gestured at the water and trash pile. "You're welcome!"

Nat turned and picked her way back to the embankment and Reed followed the best he could on wooden legs.

"Wait, you said you *thought* I was talking crazy . . . not now?"

"Wow, the cold really slowed that brain of yours down, didn't it?" She turned and looked at him suspiciously. "What's that smell?"

"I just took a swim in all of Seattle's street grime. I probably need antibiotics, to be honest. Now what changed your mind?"

"Imani and I got suspicious, and we ghost called the local FBI field office posing as a journalist, so it was untraceable. No agents were sent to Neurogen. Let alone a whole cleaning team."

"Interesting," he said and followed her along the side of the garage to where Firash had left Reed's car. He slipped into the passenger seat next to Nat who sat behind the wheel. The hot air blasted them, and Reed felt the pinpricks of thawing skin. He'd started shivering again, which he assumed was a good sign.

"You think that's interesting, wait till you hear what happened to Slater's body . . . and the ME's files," Nat said and shook her head. "You were wrong, by the way. Apparently, you can be both crazy *and* right."

His head lolled to the side to look at her. "What happened?"

"First a call came into the ME, like, immediately after Slater was transported. It was his mom, saying she saw the news and that she wanted to file a religious injunction against an autopsy."

"You're kidding."

"So, it slows us down for two days while they figure out what to do and to *me*, it all feels super suspect, right? I decide to track down Slater's mom. And turns out she's in a retirement home in Oklahoma. They said she's not conscious. In decline for a few weeks now."

"So, it wasn't her." Reed stared out the windshield, at the tiny flecks of mist reflecting the garage's outside light. The skin on his face tightening with the hot air blasting into it. "And the ME's files?"

"The office got hit. They made it look like junkies looking for drugs or something, but who hits a basement morgue for party favors? The theory is they set the fires to cover their tracks but *where* they set the fires was . . . telling."

"Let me guess, all the evidence?"

"The computer system was scorched. Literally set on fire. And because we were waiting on the judge to rule on the injunction, all the preliminary files on Slater were locally cached in the secure on-site drives. Turns out they weren't so secure. Cybercrime is on it, but we were hacked. Well. And whatever they didn't steal, they destroyed. Sanders lost everything in the fire. Cameras, computers, hard copy files, even the MRI models he had of Gerald's brain."

"And Slater's body?"

"We thought it got barbequed during the fire along with a couple others that were still on open tables. But it was missing." She looked at him, incredulous. "You were right. About all of it."

Reed rubbed his face with both hands. His skin felt gritty, clammy. "Danzig doesn't want anything connecting him to Slater, Firash, or whatever is about to go down."

"Yeah, and while he's destroying evidence leading back to him, he's covering up any way for us to figure out what's happening," Nat spat, frustrated. "And our best chance at stopping people from dying just drowned."

"We'll think of something. Danzig isn't untouchable." He motioned toward Firash. "We need to get him away from the edge. Call it in." She didn't answer and stared out the window instead. The look on her face set off alarm bells in Reed's head. "Nat?"

"I don't think it would be a good idea—" She pulled something out from inside her puffy jacket. She held up the halo with a containment pod and a syringe.

She hadn't been stroking Firash's hair. She'd been removing the halo. Reed's hand went over his mouth. "You didn't . . ."

"The tracker was just in case there was an emergency. I didn't check your whereabouts until I got that cryptic message from you. And I went to your house first because that's where I thought you had called from. There were people sitting on it. Watching for you. Were they your 'friends' from before?"

"No one I know is watching my house."

"Yeah," she took in a ragged breath. "I had a feeling. And then I got here. I saw the car with the trunk open. I smelled the chloroform. I thought you were inside, but when I got there the garage was empty but there was blood on the floor and then I saw the case. I thought . . . I thought you'd been . . ."

"Yeah," Reed said, remembering he'd thought the same thing about her not a week earlier. "I know the feeling."

She let out a half cry-half laugh and nodded. "So, I grabbed the metal case to keep him from coming back for it and I went to find you. I heard you yelling. And I helped you with Firash and then you got swept away and I didn't know what to do." She said, her voice cracking. "He was dead. I made sure, but what he knew . . ." she shook her head. "We had to save what he knew, right?"

"Yes, but . . ." Reed wiped the wet hair from his eyes, thinking. Worry crept into his thoughts. She didn't get the gravity of what she'd done. Nat, no one can know what you did to him."

"You did it!" she shouted. "What's the difference?"

"They don't know what I did! Not really. As far as they're concerned, I was zonked out on hallucinogens and tried to fight a dead body. They don't have any evidence."

"Reed, Firash knew about something that could kill a lot of people. You said Slater used the word 'massacre.' I had no choice."

"Aw, Nat. This will kill your career. You saw how Tig reacted."

"I was trying to do the right thing!" She looked at him with panic.

The rain grew harder, thumping on the roof of the car and Reed's gaze locked with hers. "You need to go."

"What?"

Reed pushed out of the car, walked around to the driver's side, and pulled the door open. "Get out of here. Get seen somewhere. Rampart or someplace like that. Buy a round of drinks. Make people there remember you."

"But what about, Firash?"

"You were never here."

"Reed, I can't just leave you to take the heat for a body."

"There's no body. You weren't here to see it."

She held his gaze, her eyes going watery, but she nodded. Pushing out from the car, she faced him. "What are you going to do?"

Reed looked back at the embankment. At the still, cold form of Firash. "Get out of here, Nat."

35

South Lake Union, Seattle

Reed cleaned up after Nat left and then called Coyote for a favor. Thirty minutes later he was at Holden House, a two story, six-unit building just off Dexter in Downtown that had once been a steam plant for dry cleaning equipment. An investor had bought it and turned it into residential units with the hope of riding the wave of incoming expensive condos going up at the time. Unfortunately, the community veered toward small business, storage, and other manufacturing spaces and the apartments fell into real estate hell until Coyote won the property three years later in a high-stakes underground poker tournament. The fact that it was sandwiched between a custom fabrication business and long-term storage was a bonus. No tourists.

His sister, Camile, turned the apartments into a stripped down, minimalist-style hotel with woven seagrass rugs, bamboo furniture, and sage burning at the front desk. As South Lake Union became a hub for life-science organizations and medical buildings over the years, the place developed a reputation for being a discreet place to lay low, especially if injured. Plenty of poor interns and research techs around to bribe for medical attention. And the kind of clientele that needed that sort of service, followed. No one saw or heard anything at Holden House. And they kept their mouths shut about it.

Reed stood in the hot shower for nearly a half hour and still hadn't managed to get warm. He'd scrubbed at his skin, trying to scrape the horror of the night off his body, but Firash's anguished face flashing in and out of the streetlights kept forcing its way into Reed's vision. He got out and listened absently to a wind chime that tinkled somewhere outside as he slipped on the gray sweatpants and black T-shirt he'd had in his go-bag. It sounded far away, carried on the wind, the ting-ting-ting of metal on metal pulling him into the moment and then he was on the deck of a sailboat, the wire rigging clanging against the mast...

Slater crept along the port side toward the stern, using the fog brooding over the marina as cover. The target moved along the guardrail, tipsy with a tumbler of brandy in his hand as predicted. The man froze in his tracks, spotting Slater on the boat in the early morning, waiting. He knew he was going to die, and he smiled scornfully, the anger twisting his expression. "I wondered if he would send you. That evil bastard couldn't even do it himself."

Slater didn't answer. He didn't move except to slide a field knife from his tactical vest. His gaze rested on the cobalt eyes of his victim for a moment, a sense of nostalgia creeping in, and then he lunged. Reed jerked, back in the bathroom he blinked at his reflection in the mirror. His teeth bared, a grimace on his face, and didn't recognize the hate in his own eyes. Bloodlust still pumping in his veins, he sat down on the toilet seat cover for a moment, catching his breath. The man, the old man seemed familiar somehow, important, but at the moment, Reed couldn't separate his own memories from Slater's enough to figure it out. Even as he struggled to retain the images in his head, they faded. Voices outside the bathroom broke his concentration and he gave up.

Coyote had called earlier as Reed was arriving at the apartment, and said he was stopping by with supplies and to expect a visit from a 'colleague.' The colleague, who had arrived five minutes after Reed did, was a man in his late fifties, early sixties, who introduced himself as Doctor John Doe. He was wearing aviator shaped glasses that slid down his long, aquiline nose and frizzy blond hair in a cut that would've been cool in the seventies. Doe wanted to examine Reed as is, muck from the ravine and all, and spent ten minutes muttering about Reed's injuries and staff infections before declaring him likely to live and dismissing him to take a shower.

The doctor was still in the hotel room when Reed left the bathroom, and he suspected that Doe had been told to stick around to make sure Reed didn't take a header in the bathtub. Doe stood near the front door talking with Coyote in a soft whisper.

"This gets me straight with you, right? We're solid? Because my ex-wife is ragging me for my kid's tuition."

Coyote clapped him on the back and smiled. "Hundred percent. You coming out at this hour, no questions asked . . . that doesn't go unnoticed. Your slate is clean, my friend."

Dr. Doe relaxed his shoulders, even smiled. "Your man looks like he's been through a wood shredder. He needs to take the antibiotics I left for him, and he needs to rest."

"He's been worse off," Coyote said, but his face didn't match his words and Reed caught it.

"I haven't even been shot yet," Reed said and smiled as if his whole body didn't hurt. He dug in his go-bag and pulled out some duct tape. He set it on the table while Coyote walked Doe to the door.

"For the meds and transportation," Coyote said and handed Doe a roll of cash. Doe said something and they both looked back at Reed. Then Doe left.

"What was that about?" Reed asked.

"He said you're lucky you didn't die of exposure." Coyote walked over to the kitchen. "I tend to agree."

Reed noticed he was still wearing his jacket and a few grocery bags sat on the kitchen counter though he'd left more than an hour ago. "Did you just get here?"

"The damn horses are making all the traffic worse." Coyote muttered, pulling the food out of the bags.

"Come again?"

"The police horses and the electric bike cops are out harassing pedestrians and confusing drivers as per holiday tradition."

"Oh, the traffic." Reed sat back, pulling on his socks. Letting Coyote rant on his favorite subject, Seattle and how he'd run it better.

"Every year, this city decides on the most convoluted detours to reroute traffic and it's never the same, mind you. Different every year and yet just as infuriating. I heard a fight already broke out between two moms over at the 5K Turkey Trot this morning. That is stress over parking, right there. Plain as day. Who schedules that on a Wednesday morning? As if people aren't already bogged down with family visiting and what not." He checked his watch, reached into the fridge, and then tossed Reed a soda. "It's almost eleven, you still want dinner?"

"I could eat." Reed said, the syrupy sweet drink never tasted so good. He wandered to the kitchen and started opening the frozen pizza boxes while Coyote fought with the oven controls.

"And then, we have the Thanksgiving Parade coming up tomorrow. Why do it *on* the actual holiday, I ask you? Add to that, people shopping last minute for food or heading out on holiday travel . . . why, it's no wonder it took me half my youth to go to the grocer's and back." Coyote stopped ranting and looked at the duct tape on the table. He raised a brow. "Are you abducting someone you didn't tell me about?"

"It's for you." Reed walked over to the kitchen table and grabbed a chair. He dragged it to the small living room. "To tape me to this."

Coyote looked at Reed from underneath furrowed brows. "Well, this took a turn. What the hell is going on, Morgan?"

Reed had thought about it all the way to Holden House, all during the shower, and as he watched his oldest friend speak with a man who owed him something. Despite all their static over the years, Coyote was not someone to keep out of the loop. Not on something like this. And he could keep a secret. No question.

Reed told him about the MER-C system. What it does. And what he'd done with Slater's dying memories. He told him about Firash, and Reed's fear that something bad was coming and how he intended to find out what it was. Lives were at stake. And time was short. Then he walked out to the car he'd been kidnapped in and brought the metal MER-C case into the room and opened it for Coyote.

"This is eyes only. No one hears about this from you. Ever."

"Man, I was happier when I didn't know this kind of thing was possible." Coyote stared at the halo, the injectors, and shook his head. "And there's no other way?"

"Not in the time I think we have left, no." Reed shook his head. "The way the kid was talking, and with how close it is to the holidays, my gut says this is the best option."

"Okay, Morgan. We do it your way."

"Just like that?"

"If you think this is the play, then it's the play. We've charged toward worse with less." Coyote shrugged. He picked up the duct tape, tossed it once. "Tell me what you need."

The tension in Reed's chest eased a little. "I need you to bring me back."

"I hope that sounded worse than it means."

"I don't know what to call it," Reed said, struggling for words. "The last time I 'took' a memory, I didn't know how to get out of it. I was stuck, like in a nightmare, thinking it's real, and glimpsing it's not—I was trapped. Nat pulled me from the chaos by blasting me with a fire extinguisher."

"See, this is why I should meet her. I feel like we're soulmates."

"You're not meeting her," Reed said, but it did pull a smile from him. "Get serious, man."

"I am. We need something similar in effect, then. Shocking enough to snap you out of a fugue-like state, essentially."

"Exactly."

Coyote shook his head. "Why is this sounding more and more familiar?"

Reed explained the procedure, showed him the equipment, and that he needed to jam the injector into Reed's artery. They double checked the coolants and then Reed drew the fluid from the containment pod that held Firash's memories. He placed it on the coffee table by the chair and called Nat. She picked up on the first ring.

"I was worried you'd turned into a copsicle out there." She sounded nervous, artificially cheerful. "Everything okay? Because I'm obsessively listening to chatter."

"You're good. Nothing's coming back to bite you."

"I was asking about you, actually." Worry leaked into her voice. "Where are you? Did you go to the hospital? Because hypothermia is nothing to sneeze at."

The fact that she's said that unironically wasn't lost on him. "I'm fine. I made it to a warm place," Reed said, lowering his voice. "A safe one. Everything will be okay."

She was silent for a moment and then, "Please don't do what I think you're going to do."

"Tell me another way."

"We process the garage where he took you. Find out what he was building or storing there. Maybe there's residue."

"Process what, Nat?" Reed whispered harshly. "He'd already moved whatever he built and the rain was busy destroying the rest. I took pics of the marks on the floor, but who knows if they're even related to Firash's stay. I saw evidence of squatters. Besides, how are you going to explain that you want to send a forensics team to an abandoned building, off what info? We don't even have Firash anymore as an excuse."

"They don't know that!" Nat shot back. "Maybe blood evidence can lead us to a partner or—"

"Who else do you think shed blood there, huh? Think about it." Reed waited out her silence. Letting her wrap her head around the situation. "It has to be this way. I'm not bringing in this MER-C case when I don't know who to trust at SPD. Besides, this is faster, unhindered by red tape, and I don't think we have much time left."

"If you think it's coming soon, imminently even, then that's even more of a reason we should tell someone."

"Again, what are you going to say? Your partner, who was suspended for going off the rails, by the way, told you some nebulous danger was coming?"

"You use fifty-cent words when you get defensive and it's sorta pompous," Nat said evenly. "And it's not some *amorphous threat* . . . Firash most definitely made a weapon."

Reed stilled. "You know this for sure?"

"Well as sure as I can be without warrants. I heard back on my inquiry to Canada. Alastair Kuntz, Slater's first victim. You know, the guy who got hit by the train?"

"The guy with the boat," Reed answered. "Yes, I remember."

"Turns out he's on one of Canada's watch-lists as a suspected weapons smuggler. He is tentatively linked to some real bad people, Reed. Cartels, rebels, militias, the kind of groups massacres tend to happen around."

"Tracking ties between Firash and Canada will take time we don't have. This way will get us actionable information. Something to take to Tig right away. Then we tell them. When we can prove something is happening and stop it."

"Don't take the memory, Reed," Nat whispered.

"It'll be fine."

"That's super optimistic of you considering how everything connected to this case has gone wrong every chance it got." The metal clang of a heavy door sounded and then Nat's voice came back echoey, like she'd gone into a hallway. "What if it scrambles your brain or something, huh? You were already twitchy after the first time."

"I wasn't—"

"Don't even try to lie to me, that's insulting. And to top it off, *this* memory retrieval didn't exactly go down like in the textbooks either. You don't know what that'll do to you."

The fear in her voice, the strain of what was coming grabbed ahold, squeezing his throat till it ached. "I saw how she died, Nat. I s-saw how he . . ." Reed cleared his throat. "If I don't do this for her, follow what she started to its end . . . I'll never stop feeling like I failed her because it'll always be true if I do nothing."

She breathed quietly on the phone for a few moments, then. "At least let me be there."

"I need someone on the force who has my back. Someone not tangled up with what I'm about to do. Especially if things go south."

"Not tangled up?" She let out a wry laugh. "Are you kidding me right now? And you can't do what you're going to do alone. You almost shot up the paramedics last time."

"I'm taking precautions," Reed said, his gaze flashing to Coyote who was leaving the room with an ice bucket.

He listened to her breathe for a few seconds and when she spoke all the fight had gone out of her voice. "But you . . . you promised not to shut me out of this investigation."

Come on, Nat. You know this isn't an official anything. Not anymore. I'm trying to mitigate the damage this whole thing has already done."

"Just . . . tell me where you are. I could bring you my tablet with an identi-kit or a way for you to sketch. You said it helped after Slater." Her voice was raspy, hurt. "Don't do this."

"I'm sorry." Reed squeezed his eyes shut, feeling like an ass. "I'll call you when I'm done."

He ended the call before she could argue and looked up as Coyote came back with ice and a bottle of apple juice from the vending machine.

"This what you wanted?"

"Throw some water in there too." Reed shut the door, locked it, and then walked around the front room yanking the curtains closed. He stared at the chair and bounced on the balls of his feet. He shrugged out the stress, rubbing his palms together to focus in. Coyote gave him a doubtful look and Reed forced a smile. "It'll be fine."

"Yeah, I ain't buying it any more than she did."

Reed slipped onto the armed dining chair and taped his own ankles and his right hand, then tossed the roll to his friend. Coyote wrapped Reed's wrist and then picked up the injector. He shook his head.

"Are you sure you want to do this thing? I've seen werewolves take less precautions."

Reed nodded, already collapsing into that three-foot space. "It'll be a piece of cake. In and out."

"Dammit, Morgan. You know things always go awry when you talk like that."

"Quit being a chicken," Reed said with a grin, his breath already pacing up with adrenaline. "Pull the trigger."

"Alright, then. It's your call." Coyote held the injector to Reed's neck. "Come back safe, brother."

The needle thrust out and cold threaded through Reed's mind like lightning, arching his body and tearing a gasp from his throat, as the world flamed bright and hot and full of fire.

36

A dark whirlwind engulfed Reed, yanking him through time, the loss of it, the backward momentum dropping his stomach. Flashes of scenes flew past, bright, but blurred. A home with music, a little old dog yapping at his feet, the dry skin of his aunt as she kissed his forehead. The scene dissolving into smoky tendrils.

Echoes whipped around him, snapping loud and sharp at his ears, making the hairs on his neck stand on end, only to fade away into low murmurs. Kivah's laughter as he made funny faces at her across their breakfast. Her eyes wrinkled at the corners as she copied him. Wind and the lift of momentum in his chest startled Reed as the metal squeak of swings sounded overhead, a park dropping down around him, the low rumble of military trucks down the street as kids ran to the fence to stare at them passing.

The park evaporated, replaced by his room, the line of light at the bottom of his door drawing his sleepy eyes as he listened to the happy conversations from the adults in the kitchen. His belly still full of the meal welcoming his uncle and his new bride. He smiled and the soft blanket brushed his cheek.

Then the voices shifted, became louder, angry, and fear grew in Reed's gut as the din of chatter focused to a crisp, clear voice. His mother and father appeared in the empty firmament in front of Firash, the black of nothing surrounding their argument in the small kitchen. Walls rose around them, jagged at the top, ending as emptiness. The table between he and his parents waning in and out of existence as they fought. The memory weak, faded, his mother and father nearly translucent. Their words felt strange as they moved through Reed's mind, yet he knew their meaning.

"Please, tell them no. This will put us all in danger." His mother's pleas pierced a thorn of fear through Firash's heart. Her face drawn in worry, eyes wet.

Firash's gaze rested on his father. On the soft way he touched her cheek, the brave tilt of his chin. "I cannot say no. I believe this is the only way to save us."

The dark storm propelled Reed forward, a sense of place and time snapping into his consciousness, and then the garage where he'd been held materializing around him. The rain beat against the roof, wind howled outside the hole in the wall, all of it like it would be. And a weird, displaced feeling snaked through his mind.

Stifling heat hit him. His own hot breath doubling back as he panted with panic, encased in the suffocating plastic of a protective suit. Firash squinted through the clear face shield of the hood, fighting with the malfunctioning paint gun. A nozzle bucked in his hand. He was spraying something, and material, thin like a tent was draped over a table just out of his vision. A whirly design, like fancy drapes, worked its way across the lower half. Worry squirmed through Firash's thoughts. Doubt. Ambivalence. Anger.

In the corner, where Reed had seen the dry outline, sat a pallet stacked with crates. They were already wrapped with plastic, ready for shipping and Reed tried to turn his head, to see it better but Firash had struggled with the nozzle and his gaze stayed rapt on the device. Reed fought to remember where the shipment was going, and he flailed in the memory, battling the hold of it, but the edges were faded, and he couldn't see past the moment. Firash wasn't thinking about the crates or even the nozzle. The buzzing of the overhead shop lights rattled through him, the ground seeming to quake and then a gust blew past Firash, throwing sand across the concrete floor, the cloying stench of smoke hit him, and fear clutched his heart. Dark plumes crawled along the ceiling. And when Firash looked up, the overhead bulbs grew intense, blinding, the light melting into molten fire falling from the sky.

The blast hit Reed first. It roared through his body, and he gasped, staring up at the dark night suddenly ablaze with patches of fiery debris plunging down onto the tarmac. An American helicopter, hit with a blast from the ground, rained wreckage as the rush of screams and gunfire hit him, shaking the air around him, and stealing his breath. He was in a crowd, and everyone flinched, hunched over as they ran with all that they had in their hands and on their backs. Darkness to his right shimmered and then a chain-link fence strobed into existence. Behind the fence, huge airplanes, the kind he'd only seen on television roared as crowds of people fought with each other to get on. Soldiers pushed back the crowd, shouting, and trying to help those who fell.

Then the screams slammed into Reed, the smoke and sand blowing into his face as he ran, clutching onto his mother's blouse, so scared he couldn't even speak. She was carrying his sister, Kivah, in her arms and she cried, clutching her stuffed animal, calling for their father who had not shown up. His mother was afraid. He could feel her hand shaking as she grabbed for his, her words promising that all would be fine drowned out by the fear in them.

Another gust of hot wind flew through the crowd blasting dirt into their faces. You couldn't see it in the dark of the night, but it floated up by the lamps of the air strip. Like dark clouds by a dying sun. It lingered in the air, coating his mouth, his nose, making his eyes burn. Another series of explosions pushed the people to panic. They huddled near the gates, banging on the metal fence, begging for help. US soldiers on the other side caught babies and kids that their parents tried to force over the top. Reed heard Firash's mother talking quickly, the grief in her voice making him look over. And then the crushing weight of panic hit him as the man standing next to them picked Firash up, forcing him up the fence, pushing him toward the top.

"No!" Firash yelled, his throat raw with the force of his scream. He struggled in the man's hands. Fought the marine who tried to stop his fall. "I don't want to go! I want to stay with you!"

The last image of his mother burned behind his lids, her lip trembling as she said she loved him, her hand reaching out, covered in soot. "Be brave, Firi."

Guilt sliced through Reed at the things he'd said to Firash in the garage. Anger and fear burning through his mind as his thoughts mixed with Firash's anguish, the helplessness and confusion of a child in desperate danger. His frightened cries for his mom ached in his throat, making it hard to breathe. Reed tried to turn from the scene, to pull away from the pain and terror. And then gunfire erupted nearby.

The Taliban fought with the Afghan soldiers. They were shooting at the planes, the families, trying to stop them from escaping. Bullets slammed into the military trucks and the metal siding of the airport buildings. A trail of them spitting up asphalt as they blasted in a line toward a transport full of scrambling, screaming people. Firash's heart rammed in his throat. And then the moment slowed, the panicked crowd moving at a glacial pace, flying debris suspended in the air, falling at an achingly slow pace, the staccato snap of gunfire growing lighter as it mutated into the steady tapping of a rickety fan blade. The hot, dark confines of the shed behind Gloria's house enveloped Reed and his mind stilled.

Firash leaned over the parts of a drone as he fiddled with the inner workings of an actuator. He checked the motor's rotation of the propellers, inspected the fins, wondering at the flight stability. Doing the math in his head as he squinted through a dark visor at the wires lighting up in the welding arc. Frozen in the memory, Reed couldn't look around, and the peripheral images were too blurry to make out. Thoughts blazed through Firash's head like tracers. Lighting up the darkness to reveal a moment in time, only to fade to black just as quickly.

The ride on the cargo plane where the rattle and rumble shook him to his bones as the scratchy green blanket did little to keep him warm. How the barred gates looked as he passed between them, their metal hot to the touch all the other lost and crying children clung to each other as strangers waved them forward. Speaking to them in a frightening, warbly language. A wave of sights and sounds rushed through Reed, cutting him.

The room spun like a top, tables skidding into view, kids walked out of nothing to fill the cafeteria. Reed was there, alone at the back table, staring down at his untouched tray of food. Laughter and talk all around him. Lonely in a crowd of peers. And then he'd see hair the color of Kivah's in a group of girls and he'd run over only to have her disappear. Gloria's face shimmied like rippling water before Firash, she was smiling and saying it would be okay. That there were no worries. And he had tried to believe her.

But then her voice changed. It lowered and took on a drawl as her kind features contorted into the pug-nosed, beady-eyed visage of another person. The decrepit warehouse flickered into view surrounding them. A man stood in front of a plastic wrapped pallet on the stained asphalt of a warehouse. He was smirking, malevolence in his eyes as he patted the package. He was a man who Firash knew only by a code name, Sepulcher. Hatred licked through Reed as the man approached, felt himself suppressing it, plastering on a pleasant face.

For the plan, Firash repeated to himself. *He is but a tool.*

"This is genius," Sepulcher said. "They'll never know what hit 'em."

"Do your part and I will do mine," Firash said, but his attention was behind Sepulcher. At a student he recognized from the Restoration Republic meetings. Maggie.

Time shifted forward and Reed watched her through Firash's eyes as she talked animatedly outside the campus café. Coffee and the scent of toasted croissants filled his lungs. The sun dappled through the trees and danced on their table. He had told her of Iris's plan to do business in Afghanistan and with whom.

"This will fund the Taliban's atrocities for decades. It will keep them in power," Firash said, his voice rising with anger. "And it will ruin an already broken land further. Years of war and now this? The world means to rape Afghanistan once more. Only not with their rifles and bullets this time. No, now they will use the guise of charity . . . charity!"

"I know. The corruption is so widespread. We need to make a *real* stand. Something unmistakable!" Her delicate fist pounded the metal table with each word. "Those in power are ruining everything. Draining our resources on pointless 'fixes' that do nothing but cost us millions."

"There is an ex-professor from here," Firash had started tentatively. "She has sold her soul to the very corruptors you're talking about."

Maggie's eyes had lit up. "Who is it?"

His heart soared as they talked about stopping it, seeking revenge on those involved, exposing their lies. And then when he could no longer keep it from her, Firash had confessed that he was not a student. Not anymore. Flashes of places where he had hidden around campus came to Reed in rapid succession. The hot mist of the gym showers, the smell of 'homestyle' food in the cafeteria, the cold of empty dorms for sleeping. He had been ashamed to tell her, but Maggie had found it mysterious, adventurous, and it had been their secret affair. She had made him feel like he was more than just a lost boy from a broken land. He was a warrior, a rebel, like her. And they would take back their future together and make them pay. Starting with Iris.

And then Maggie appeared next to Reed, kneeling next to him behind the hedge of lavender, a pair of binoculars to her eyes, the warmth of her arm against his as she whispered what Iris was doing in the Briar Ridge parking lot. Firash had almost told her then, Reed realized. Warned her. The intent was there, the words slipping through the memory like silk.

Not everything is as it seems. You must stay far away when the time comes. I could not bear to see you—

But then Maggie looked at Firash . . . at him . . . and smiled. And it jolted Reed to see her moving. Alive and not pale, cold, and still like when he'd first seen her. She was talking, but the scene was already changing, the yellow flowers behind her growing brighter, longer, the sky darkening. Maggie's face changed. The life bled out of her in streams of gutter water that poured from her open mouth, taking the pink from her cheeks and the light from her eyes. She froze, her gaze going black, and then she tilted her head up to the churning, gray sky and screamed. The flowers connected, becoming yellow tape dancing in the wind, tied to a tree trunk. Barring students from the crime scene.

The floor rumbled and the brick and sandstone facades of Seattle City College jutted up from the ground, rising around Reed, taking him back to that day. He saw himself from behind the crimes scene tape leaning over Maggie, talking to Nat. The feel of Firash's fingernails digging into his own palms, the stifling ache of sorrow squeezing his throat. He'd come to tell her everything. Reed's pulse raced in his ears, and he couldn't breathe. Firash's anguish, his grief, his lost love tightened around Reed's chest like a steel band, squeezing until he lost sense of time and of place, until he wasn't sure if the pain he felt was his own or Firash's. And then Slater crossed Firash's vision and sudden rage scorched through Reed at the sight of him watching the scene from behind the crowd of students.

It was him, Firash shook where he stood. Wanting to attack the man, send his drones to pierce his eyes, to cause him pain. He killed her. He and Danzig—the name floated through Reed's mind, and he latched onto it, thinking of those eyes, the tone of his voice and then he saw it. The network files, streaming in pale blue down the screen. A torrent of information. A vast ocean of corruption and connections. But the pain of seeing her burned brighter than everything around it and all Reed could see was Maggie.

The flicker of the camera drone hovering over her prone body sent shards of fire through Reed's eyes. The strobing flash grew brighter, lasted longer, and then a roar of thunder blew the scene apart like ash. Lightning streaked across the inky black of the sky and then he was running. His hands taped behind his back, teeth chattering, as he stumbled along the lip of the embankment. Glancing back at the call of his name, Reed saw himself running after him. Gaining, grabbing for him.

The rain river swallowed him, and panic ripped through Reed as he realized he couldn't swim. Had never learned, not even at Gloria's. He flailed, slapping at the water, feeling its pull. And then Reed was looking down into his own eyes as the water rose up around Firash's face. Reed saw himself through the surface of the water, heard his own muffled screams, as the numbing cold of the water dragged Firash further into himself. Lightning scratched a jagged line across the night and then Firash drifted back up into consciousness, saw the woman detective leaning over him, yelling at him to stay. He felt the pain of cracked ribs, but it was already fading. Until there was no cold. No anger. There was only the sky and the light and the roar of eternity coming for him.

A desperate, terrorized wail bubbled up out of Reed. The cold blasted down onto him, shaking him, stealing his voice. He was being dragged, and he fought for his life, certain that death had him by the heel. The sound of his own name, of Reed's name being screamed assaulted him from the edges of nothingness, tugging at his mind and he followed it, grasping for it.

"Reed! Pull out of it!" Nat's voice punctured the shroud, and then a searing pain pierced his thigh yanking him back to the present.

He gasped, his eyes flying open. Ice cubes bounced off his face as Coyote threw another bucket at him. Blurry-eyed, freezing, his body wracked with frigid cold, he coughed, the vestiges of the memory falling away like scales. Reed stared at the bathroom ceiling, shivering, confused. He was on his back in the tub. Water and ice rippled around him. Nat and Coyote stared down at him a bucket in her trembling hands.

"Are you back? Are you okay?" she breathed, her eyes wide.

"I-I'm back." Reed coughed, his chest still aching from the CPR Nat had given Firash.

"What the hell was that, Morgan? You nearly boiled in your own skin." Coyote extended a hand and Reed crawled out of the bathtub, hugging himself. His T-shirt and sweats dragging down with the weight of the water. "I nearly called an ambulance."

"What?"

"You spiked a fever out of nowhere. Nearly one hundred and five. I think you might've even had a seizure."

Nat grabbed a towel from the bar over the toilet. But instead of handing it to Reed, she slapped him with it on the chest with every word. "Stop. Trying. To. Die!"

"I'm okay, Nat," Reed said softly as he caught the towel. She let it go, folding her arms across her chest and staring at him with more worry than rage. In fact, she looked downright scared. His thigh hurt and blood oozed from a puncture in his sweatpants. "Did you stab me?"

She dropped the large safety pin. "I saw it on a medical show. For like comas and stuff."

"Wait a second." Something occurred to Reed. "You're not supposed to be here. How did you find me?"

"Your friend over here bought his burners in bulk. From a vendor known to cybercrime to be dirty. And you called me on it to leave that horrible, cryptic message. Took me five minutes to trace yours here."

Coyote looked at her with admiration. "Seems like I've been shown a chink in my security precautions."

"That wasn't helpful advice," Nat said, rolling her eyes. "I was saying it was easy to find you."

"And I'm saying it won't be next time, Detective De La Cruz," Coyote said as he leaned into Nat's space, clearly enjoying the repartee despite Reed shaking like a belly dancer.

"Guys . . ." Reed said.

They nodded, leaving him to change into something Coyote had tossed him from Reed's go-bag. He once again failed to get completely warmed back up but walked out into the condo living room to their back and forth bickering about pizza toppings.

"Fever?" he asked as he wandered to the kitchen. He could feel their eyes on him.

"I think you over-clocked your brain," Nat said.

The oven clock read three in the morning and Reed stilled, his stomach dropping. He turned to Coyote. "How long was I out?"

"Almost four hours," Coyote said and shook his head. "I must've used all the ice in the complex. Nothing worked until Detective De La Cruz's little parlor trick with the safety pin."

Hours? It had felt like seconds. Maybe a minute and yet also an eternity. Time worked differently inside the memories.

"So, was it worth it?" Nat asked. "Did you find anything helpful in the void?"

"I think so." Wisps of images and sounds still echoed in the back of Reed's mind. He dug around in his bag for his notebook. Then he remembered. "Ah, man. I had my notebook in my back pocket when I went into the ravine."

"I can hit an art place in the morning," Coyote checked his phone. "Well, later this morning. They should be open in a few hours."

Reed dug in the drawers of the kitchen. "No, I need something faster. Everything's slipping away. I need something to draw with. Like a notepad or some stationary."

"This is basically a safehouse, man. People don't send out notes from a place they're hiding in."

"Oh, oh! Hold on," Nat said and ran out to her car. When she came back, she held up a pair of VR goggles and two controllers. "I can do you one better. Had these in my trunk to return to cybercrime."

Ten minutes later, while scarfing down a piece of cold, semi-burnt pizza, Reed fought to retain the image of Sepulcher as he waited for her to set up the equipment. The hate in his eyes, the tilt of his scornful lips. They had to find him. Despite Firash's death, an accomplice meant nothing had changed. Reed thought about the holiday traffic, the bridges and tunnels travelers would use, and countless public transportation venues that could be in danger. The events and gatherings to celebrate with hundreds of spectators. His gut knotted, too many targets to vet. He had to find evidence to convince Tig that something was coming. That somewhere in the city, a deadly trap was about to snap.

37

Nat stood in front of Reed and showed him how to adjust the virtual reality goggles on his head. She wiggled the ones on her own forehead and then held up her own brush controllers.

"Think of this as the stripped-down mobile version of the Virtual Depot experience you had earlier with Gerald's autopsy."

"But with no connection to SPF."

"No, these are training sets. They run off that mini hub." She pointed to a black cube the size of a softball on the coffee table. Its internal lights streamed across the middle like a digital horizon. "They're part of a pilot program for field use with the bomb squad, SWAT, even rescue rigs for use in situations you might need to visualize a 3D model, but funding issues put the program on hold for a bit. Which means I get to play with them. But I promise, everything done on here is stored in the mini hub, totally separate. No one will have access."

Reed slipped the goggles down and the sensors brought the field into view. An endless pale blue world with white grid lines.

"You've got the standard controllers," Nat's voice sounded in the earpiece. Her avatar appeared in front of him. Almost her exact clone except for the not-quite-human way it moved. Too flowy, like a drunk balle-rina. She gestured and an oversized controller appeared in front of him.

The buttons and joysticks glowed bright as she explained them. It wasn't as complicated as Reed had thought. It took a few minutes to get used to the VR goggles, but the controllers, the brushes to be exact, were intuitively designed. The brush and pen strokes he used in real life yielded similar results in the virtual one.

"Okay, what kind of medium do you want? I've got clay, mosaic, some oil paint programs that saturate really well. Oh, there's also ready-made forms like furniture and stuff you can throw into place like 3D stickers and then add layers to customize. What do you need?"

"Can I get a solid field. Like a sketchpad. Maybe cream or sepia?"

"Do you want a wraparound world of it or an easel in front of you like in real life."

"I'll take the wraparound."

"Hey, did either of you go through this kid's backpack?" Coyote's voice, sounded outside of the virtual world.

"Yeah, I did," Nat said. "The revolver has no serial numbers, so hand it over and let me take it into ballistics to get any further."

"To what lab? Didn't the ME's department get burned down?"

"Not down, but yeah, damaged when whoever covered up Slater's death torched the place. We're sending things uptown for now."

"I'm keeping it stashed for now. I don't know people up there well enough." Reed said. "And the lanyard?"

"Just a cheap card holder you can get at any office supply store. It says 'staff', but that could mean anything."

"But he was using it to get *in* somewhere, right?" Coyote asked.

"Which makes the attack at an event more likely than say a random skating rink or something," Reed said. "So, we're closing in."

Nat's avatar waved her hand, getting Reed's attention. "Need anything else?"

"I need some colors. Warm fall, not too bright. I kept seeing a shape. It was painted orange, I think. Though it could be an umber . . . brown, maybe?"

Nat showed him how to access other features via the drop-down menus, and then winked out of the virtual space "Ok, you're all set. If you want to manipulate the image, use this menu. Oh, and see if you can work on the accomplice's face first. That' something concrete, a suspect I can take to Tig. I'll upload it to him and get him to issue a BOLO."

"What're you going to tell him it's for?"

She hesitated. "I'll think of something. I'll call Imani and we'll both do a search for the alias, Sepulcher. We'll see if anything pops."

Nat had set him up in a world of softly muted paper lit from behind. Raising his hand, he tested out the first curving strokes of the image in his mind. Sepulcher, the man in Firash's memory, wore his hatred on his features. His shaggy hair hung low on his neck, its medium-brown color unremarkable. Long hair with a middle part when he'd turned in the memory to Firash, revealed dark blue eyes, set back in his head. Flashes of that moment played behind Reed's eyes. How he moved on the balls of his feet, shoulders rolled, like he was used to looking over his shoulder. He held the promise of violence behind his sneer.

Reed worked the image for almost an hour. Trying to capture the features clearly, feeling the feedback from the system like texture underneath his charcoal pencil. The program offered facial feature suggestions, and the sets of eyes, various noses, and mouths floated midair in front of him. He tried drawing the mouth and had the AI try different voices saying the same, 'They'll never know what hit 'em.' line Reed remembered from the memory, but nothing jogged more detail than he already had.

Sepulcher had patted the delivery from Firash, and Reed strained to see past him. There was that shape again. The swirl from the material he'd seen in the shed behind Gloria's house. He tried to draw it, pulling from experience the natural direction of the pattern, the filigree details, pushing for a breakthrough.

Reed shoved the sketch of Sepulcher aside. It drifted in the serene emptiness of the paper world. He moved on, trying to capture the fractured images he remembered from when he looked through the windows of the shed. The table and floor beneath it rose out of his charcoal etchings in the air around him. A deep rendering of the shed, and what Reed had seen slowly filled the space. He pushed at the edges of his recollection, trying to see what he'd missed.

A rounded edge of a cylinder, the bulbous curve of metal, a silky, tent-like material with a filigree pattern. Reed slowly spun the images like coins in his palms, looking at each shape from several angles. The larger one, the soft arc of it, bothered him. It wasn't familiar in that he had seen it before, but the form *fit*, somehow. Reed just didn't understand why. The stun gun barbs, and chloroform messed with his memory of what happened at the shed and what he'd seen. The events faded in and out of black, from being dragged along the ground to waking up duct taped to a chair in the garage. An impression floated to the surface of Reed's consciousness. Sound and movement. The snap of material in the wind.

And then he was pushed forward, hit by the swell of the shouting crowd that surrounded him, running as one from the explosions as Firash's memory tore through Reed's mind. Another explosion detonated so near, he flinched. He yanked off the goggles, his breath coming in hitches. Coyote and Nat stared over at him, frozen.

"You all right there, Morgan? You look a little twitchy."

"I'm fine." Reed had been at it for almost two hours. Maybe staying so long in another reality wasn't the best idea.

"Is there lag or something?" She asked, her gaze narrowing.

"No, I . . ." Reed tossed the controllers and goggles on the couch and paced a little, clearing his mind. The heat of the blast still warmed his cheek and neck. "That thing's just a little disorienting, that's all."

Nat looked at him for a beat and then waved him over. "Come and take a look at this while you're taking a break." She motioned to the map she and Coyote were looking at on the coffee table.

"Where'd you find an actual paper map?" Reed asked, walking over. It was a map of Seattle and the surrounding area, including the islands in The Sound.

"My buddy owns a used bookstore. They have maps of everything. Also detailed plans of public buildings and the city infrastructure itself, if we need it." He gestured toward a bundle of rolled paper on the sofa.

"Sounds completely legal," Nat murmured, glancing at her phone. It had buzzed and she frowned at it but shoved it back into her back pants pocket.

"Well, when the city digitized all of that precious information and locked it behind firewalls, they forgot to make sure the old archives had the same kind of security." Coyote shook his head. "Human error. Gets 'em every time."

Nat glanced at Coyote, a weird look on her face. "It does."

"I've seen the most elegantly designed, sophisticated security systems rendered useless in the face of abject human stupidity."

"Thank you," Nat said, genuinely into the conversation. "I mean, do you know how easy it would be to swipe a low-level IT worker's badge, work your way in via his info—"

"I do indeed. There's a whole other layer of this world if you're smart enough to see it." Coyote flashed her his wicked grin.

Reed rolled his eyes. "What are we looking at?"

Coyote rapped his knuckles on the map. "The thing is, there's an insane amount of things going on in the city this weekend. It's the last day before Thanksgiving so we're looking at the parade over by Ballard. It runs all the way up to sixty-second, I believe."

"We've had traffic detoured since yesterday," Nat said, glancing at her phone again. "We also have that thing at the Seattle Public Library, the central one. They have that carnival going there all day. The big hotels over there are involved with little train rides, food trucks, all sorts of activities inside the library itself. I think there's a visiting children's choir, even. I mean . . ." she shook her head. "It's a nightmare if we have to evacuate."

"What's Tig saying?"

"Nothing because I've been avoiding him like he's an ex. Like I literally saw him in an elevator as it was opening and ducked into a stairwell."

"That's the opposite of being my eyes inside," Reed said.

"Well, I'm worried he's going to tell me they found a—" she glanced at Coyote.

He leaned over and gaped at Reed. "Another one, Morgan?"

"Alright, listen," Reed threw his hands up. "I didn't cause *this* one either. Not directly."

Nat looked from Coyote to Reed and back. "How is it you guys know each other, exactly?"

"Long story," they both said at once.

Reed slid his fingertips across the map, searching for possible targets. "We're sure there aren't any other possibilities?"

"Well, I mean, SPD is already all over the trains, the tunnels," Nat nodded to Coyote. "You know how bad it is out there, right? Tell him."

"What's buggin' you about all this?" Coyote asked Reed instead. "What's got you stuck in neutral?"

"The parade, the library's holiday festival, those are all soft targets," Reed murmured. "Firash had a love for Gloria, I know that for sure. And he got them out after I left, presumably to protect them."

"Or hide his assault on an officer," Nat said, with a frown.

"What else?" Reed asked, letting her comment go.

Coyote tapped the map. "That's it for today, but tomorrow, on Thanksgiving Day, we've got the brunch for the city put on by that church alliance. That pulls a huge crowd of mostly marginalized people. The poor and homeless."

"Other than that, Thanksgiving is known for people going to the movies, we've got early bird shoppers . . ." Nat's arms flapped at her sides. "Most of these things are for families. Which is terrifying."

"Hell, all he'd have to do is wait for Black Friday and he'd have most of the city out in shopping malls," Coyote replied.

Nat's phone pinged again, and she looked at it, this time frowning.

"Are you expecting news?" Reed asked.

"You said that in Slater's memory, they thought that Alastair Kuntz the weapon's dealer had sold Firash Ferrin."

"Wait, I did?" The memory burst forward from Slater's meet with Danzig. Crowding his head and spiking his pulse. "I, uh . . . don't remember telling you that."

"You yelled it. While still stuck in the memory or whatever in the server room. At least I thought that's what you yelled, I couldn't be sure. You could've said 'ferrets' and I wouldn't have been surprised given your state at the time. And no one wanted my opinion on anything anyway at that point. But then you didn't tell Tig, and I wondered why. I assumed it was on purpose."

"It wasn't." Reed scratched at his forehead absently. How could he have forgotten so much already? "It must have slipped away before I talked to him."

"Well, I asked a chemist friend of mine to run some models for me. Specifically, scenarios in which Ferrin would be an efficient weapon."

Coyote gave a low whistle. "That'll raise some red flags."

"My friend works for an artificial intelligence modelling lab. They run complex simulations of disaster scenarios for research. And he didn't even have to run one from scratch. It's a scenario they'd already run. And it's bad, Reed. We have to bring in Tig."

"But I didn't know what form, right? They hadn't known." Reed tried to reach into memories that weren't his but there was nothing. Like ghosts on the outskirts of his mind, they floated just out of reach. "I think there's granules, maybe powder?"

"Doesn't seem to matter," she said, and tossed him the phone. "In powder, if it gets in the ventilation system or in an enclosed space, we'd get a lot of casualties. It burns the skin, if it gets inhaled it causes damage akin to breathing in a fire. There's lung tissue damage, nasal passages, eyes . . . it's horrible. It was outlawed ten years ago after that massacre in the Sudan."

Reed nodded. "Do it. Tell him what we have. It might be enough to do another security sweep at the least."

"Okay but hurry up and finish that sketch of the suspect. I have to move it from the hub to my tablet to upload it, but it needs a secure signal code, or it won't transmit. I have those back at cybercrime."

"Really sell it, Nat. We're too far behind on this one already." She nodded and stepped into the bedroom to call.

Coyote sat casually back on the sofa watching Reed.

"What?"

"This is . . . forget convincing your boss. We need to start calling in some of the alphabet gang. We're above our pay grade by an order of magnitude, brother. Let the FBI handle this apocalyptic crap."

"I can't give them a credible threat. I have memories my partner ripped out of a drowning victims' head." Reed paced the living area. "I've been suspended for 'health' reasons. You tell me what kind of response I'll get on a holiday weekend."

"We could call in an anonymous threat to their tip line. I'll bet your brainiac partner over there could make you invisible."

He was right and Reed knew it. "Okay, we'll call in, see if we can trigger a response. Tig's not taking my texts or calls. So, I need to think about some things for a few minutes. Because given straight, my explanation for why I think there's a public disaster coming sounds insane. I need a better story." Reed slipped the goggles back down and the 3D drawing flickered back into view. "But I like the call idea. I'll talk to Nat when she comes back in."

Reed handed Coyote the goggles. "Does this look like anything to you?"

Coyote slipped them on for a second and then pulled them off. "Shaving cream can?"

"I thought so too," Reed said and tossed the goggles back on the couch, dejected. "Why would that memory be important but not what I need?"

"Reed!" Nat yelled as she burst back into the room. She stood in the threshold, gaze locking with his as he lifted the goggles. Her hand gripped the doorknob with white knuckles.

Reed moved toward her. Saw that she shook slightly, though whether it was in fear or adrenaline, he couldn't tell. "What happened?"

"They found something along the parade route."

"You're kidding me," Coyote said, and he shook his head at Reed. "Man, I hate it when you're right."

"What is it?"

"I don't know. That was a buddy at my old precinct. He said maybe a backpack or a duffle bag. He said details are murky right now because something is off with communication. They think there might be a signal blocker somewhere along the route messing with cell phones. Bomb squad's checking it out." She looked at Reed hopefully. "Maybe we stopped it."

"Yes," Reed murmured. "I hope so."

"They're calling for all hands on deck. SPD is saturating the area in case we have to evacuate." Nat grabbed her coat, a sympathetic look on her face when she glanced at Reed. "I-I gotta go."

He hooked her wrist with his fingers, gently stopping her stride. "Hey, no heroics, okay? I'm not breaking in another partner this month."

"I mean, with a teacher like you, how much trouble can I get into?" She said with a smile that didn't reach her eyes. Nat slipped from his grasp. "I'll keep you posted."

He watched her leave, feeling the churn of trouble in his gut. He dug his hands in his pockets, his mind racing. Reed pushed around the fragments of Firash's memories, the emotion that went with them, the attention. Nothing ever felt like the indiscriminate carnage of a bomb. Firash was focused. Wanted to stop something specific.

"Your gears are churning so fast I see smoke coming out of your ears. What gives, man?"

"It just feels wrong."

"What?"

"All this time, all that planning, and they find one backpack?"

"You think there's more?"

"Maybe. I think so. This all is just . . ."

"Listen, I know you've got a soft spot for this kind of kid. Lost boys, damaged, like Butter. It's your particular kind of poison. One I'm sure will be the end of you one of these days."

"Your point?" Reed asked, though he already knew what Coyote was going to say.

"Plenty of people go through hell same as this Firash kid and don't lash out at the innocent. You remember that."

"I remember it every day, man." Reed stared out the window at the shards of pink escaping the horizon, morning breaking through the darkness. "I just wonder about fate, you know?"

"Well don't. And I told you that philosophy major was going to mess you up."

Reed's focus narrowed inward as he sifted through his impressions and interactions with Firash. "This kid had finesse, Coyote. He was exacting, disciplined. And a bomb at a family event is indiscriminate, messy. It's just not what I thought he'd do. At all. . . ." Reed shrugged, looking at Coyote. "That's all I got."

"And you know this guy because you hunted him."

"Yes, like back in—"

"Yeah." Coyote regarded him silently as he tapped a cigarette pack on the heel of his hand. "You know, it would be perfectly legal for a common citizen to attend said parade, if they were so inclined."

"Just . . . drive over?"

"Why not? Just like any other Seattleite might do this fine morning. Who's stopping you?"

"What happened to calling in the FBI?"

"Those glory grabbers always have all the fun," Coyote said with a dismissive wave of his lit cigarette. "Besides . . . we're just going to take a quick gander. No harm."

Reed checked his watch. It was nearly six in the morning. "Parade goers line up along the streets at four in the morning to get a good spot. There must be hundreds of people there already with more coming."

Coyote shrugged on his leather jacket and flipped his hair back with a hitch of his neck. "Well, I guess we better hurry, then."

Reed headed out but paused, looking at his friend over the hood of the car. "You sure?"

"I'm getting into the car, aren't I?"

"I think you should know that I have no idea what I'm going to do."

"Yeah, I know. That's what's always made you so damn scary, Morgan."

38

They stopped at Reed's house first to grab a set of walkie-talkies and his off-duty weapon before heading into downtown along fifth avenue. Construction to fix flooding from storms earlier in the year had pushed the parade along a different route than normal. According to a quick search on his phone, the parade was supposed to begin at eight in the morning with a muster point in the downtown area, ending further north near the public library. With the museums and galleries in the area also open for the holidays, the traffic was worse than disaster movie gridlock.

Nat had left the VR hub when she took off and therefore, his sketch of the accomplice behind and Reed rode shotgun, trying to transfer from memory of what he'd worked out in the VR world onto a sketchbook he grabbed from his desk. The stop and go of traffic made it hard to get a good likeness.

Coyote cut off a bus, flipped off the driver when he honked, then glanced over from the driver's seat. "You think that's going to help?"

"I can take a picture and send it to her. She'll get it out to patrol from there. Best I can do, but this signal blocker might make it pointless" Reed looked up from his sketchbook. "I don't even know if she's getting anything I'm sending. When I call, it goes straight to voice mail."

"We're still about a half-mile from the parade route," Coyote said. "Maybe when we get closer."

They inched down the street. A patrol officer stood in the intersection letting one side go for a while and then another. Reed was checking the emergency frequencies on the walkies, scanning for Nat's voice when his phone trilled, it was a call from her. When he answered he heard her voice, but she broke up, like a tuning radio skipping through channels. In the background, he heard loud conversation, band music, and the gun of engines. The parade.

"Nat, can you hear me?" Reed shouted into the phone. "What's going on?"

"Yeah, we cordoned off the muster point down south. Comms are going in and out. We found two dampeners already spanning the route. They're consumer grade. You can get them online for thirty bucks each, but they're effective. Imani is down here with a sensor and she says there's got to be a couple more still. I had to run over a block away to get through."

"Firash left a backpack on the street?" Reed rubbed his forehead, thinking. "The Bomb Unit confirmed it?"

"No, you know how these guys move at a snail's pace. Buncha jittery dudes," Nat said. She yelled at someone to settle down and then was back. "We're trying to keep things low profile to avoid panic until we know for sure. They said the x-ray points to pipe bomb, but we don't know what the trigger is. Patrol is moving the perimeter street detours further out. We'll start to evac slowly. People are gonna start asking questions though when they see the disposal guy in his giant getup."

Reed plugged his ear to block out the sound of horns honking on his side. Someone had broken down, slowing things further. "I have a sketch. A workable one. It keeps failing to send though."

"Text it again. If I can hear you, I can receive messages. You won't get through here anyway. We're blocking all new entrances until they clear the backpack. Could be nothing, but . . ."

"We're on radios in case you need to get ahold." Reed looked at Coyote who held up four fingers. "Channel four. We're inching along third avenue if it doesn't work I can always meet you and give you the physical sketch."

"Got it," Nat said. "I'll call back if nothing comes through, but send it now. I gotta get back."

"Be careful," Reed said, but she was gone.

They passed a detour route and Reed sat up. "Turn here."

"That's away from the parade."

"We can loop around the Central Library and approach the parade route from the end point up north. We'll double back up Fifth."

Coyote took the turn, and they rolled along side streets, going by memory, finding a path. The carnival at the library wasn't underway yet, but there was a huge crowd.

"Not exactly your family friendly looking bunch," Coyote said.

Backpacks, hoodies, posters, gas masks. Reed took in the throng of people walking together up the street with growing apprehension.

"Have you heard anything about a protest?"

"Now? Over what? Turkey rights?" Coyote asked. He honked at the stream of people crossing the intersection despite green lights. "Damn menace."

Reed put the window down and yelled at a group of kids in the crosswalk. "What's going on? What's happening?"

A girl with her hair tied into Viking warrior looking braids pointed ahead at a group of municipal buildings. "Uh, the Gage Appeal. The verdict is coming down at noon."

"I don't know who that is," Reed admitted. "What's he on trial for?"

The girl shook her head, a frown wrinkling her freckled brow. "No trial, an appeal. He was railroaded by the corrupt justice system."

"Ah, gotcha." Reed glanced at the groups of people walking up Fifth. They looked like they were going on a hike or to a sporting event. Running shoes, backpacks, hats pulled low over their foreheads. Reed realized many of them carried water, oven mitts, and gas masks. "What groups are set to show up for this protest?"

"You're not cops, are you?" Viking Girl's friend, a young guy with a bandanna worn loose around his neck walked up to the car. He had on a white sweater with images of life-sized faces looking in different directions, profiles, just the eyes, laughing mouths. Reed recognized it as an adversarial pattern to avoid AI facial recognition.

"It's not illegal to protest." Reed said.

"Yeah, not yet," Viking Girl said. "That's why we've got to fight the man. Stop them from stealing our future."

"The future, right." Reed repeated, something about her phrasing snagged the back of his mind. "Take it back . . . starting with Iris."

"What?" The girl asked. "Who's Iris?"

The crowd crossing the road had thinned and the car behind them honked for Coyote to go.

"I'm getting out here," Reed said and pushed open the door. "I'll meet you in a few. I just want to check this thing out."

"Suit yourself," Coyote said, winked at the Viking Girl, and drove off.

Reed walked with Viking Girl and Sweater Guy who turned out to be named Misty and Jay, siblings. They joined the ass end of a group up ahead and Reed tried to listen in on their chatter while pumping Jay and Misty for more info.

"So what's this Gage guy saying he was framed for?" Reed asked, shoving his hands in the front pocket of the hoodie he was wearing. His sweatpants did little to stave off the wind chill whipping down the avenue.

"You really should have some protection on." Misty handed Reed a bottle of water. "Keep it for your eyes. What about a mask?"

Reed put his hands out. "I'm just going to go take a look. I'm not joining."

"Yeah, the cops totally make the distinction," she said and tossed him a bandana.

He tied it loosely around his face and then pulled it down around his neck for now. "So are you for or against this guy going to jail?"

"Oh my God, against," Misty gasped. "Obviously."

Reed glanced at Jay. "Elaborate . . ."

"Okay, so Gage Hill is the founder of Second Wave. That's us," Jay pointed to him and his sister. "We're working to keep the government accountable. I mean the corruption in Congress alone . . ."

Reed listened absently, glancing down at his phone as he did his own research online. This kid was spewing media talking points like he'd read it off a blog.

Gage Hill had sent a package bomb to a Washington State senator as a protest against the recent introduction of a bill to allow law enforcement to pay online prescription service businesses for customer information that would give the most recent pick up or delivery location of a suspect. It bypassed HIPPA altogether because the prescription drug service was a private business and not a hospital or medical center. Gage saw it as a betrayal of privacy, they went back and forth online, via podcasts, and even mainstream news shows. Then the senator was killed.

"He sent him a bomb. What's the confusion?" Reed asked as they climbed the steep incline past grand old hotels and restaurants squatting next to the taller, sleeker corporate high-rises.

Jay shook his head vehemently. "It wasn't a bomb. It was a fake one, to scare him."

"He died."

"Of anaphylaxis," Misty piped up. "It was filled with a glitter powder that was just supposed to get all over the senator right before this morning show, but the anticaking ingredient Gage used just happened to be the one thing the senator was allergic to. Like deathly allergic. It had peanut shells in it or something. But Gage never meant to hurt the guy. It was just a symbolic protest. First amendment stuff and all that. They tried him for manslaughter anyways."

"They're reading off the appeal decision today?"

"Yeah, and this congresswoman is showing up to gloat. She was on the prosecution team in the original trial before she ran off the conviction. She's trying to build a career over taking our rights. We're here to heckle her when she tries to spout her strong on crime bullshit." Misty's face turned red as she pontificated.

"Yeah," Jay said. "And it's set to get crazy out there."

"What do you mean?" Read finished off a second article as they crested the hill. People were moving in from the west. Families pushed out of the parade area by foot-traffic detours hiked up toward the Nakamura Building after evacuation. "Whoa."

Jay laughed. "Yeah. It's a party."

Reed thanked the kids and hurried up the hill. He radioed Nat.

"De La Cruz, come in."

"Go ahead for De La Cruz."

"Have you heard of the Gage Hill case?"

"Yeah, I think it's over."

"Well, we've got people mustering up by the Federal Courthouse over here with riot gear."

"That's not on anyone's radar. It's supposed to be small with the holidays and everything."

Reed crested the hill and walked up the courthouse's vast lawn. The largest in the city, it was a popular public gathering place for picnics when the weather was nice. Right now, it was crawling with college kids, families, people with banners and flags bearing various logos and mascots, and no police presence. The noise of the rally grew as he approached. Air horns blasted periodically, somewhere a rock anthem played, and above it all, the din of hundreds of people. It looked like a music festival. "Not small, Nat. Huge. I think half the parade goers wandered up here."

Reed wove through the gathering crowd on the lawn and steps of the grand building. Despite the recent structural renovations, it still looked like it had when he was a kid. Ten stories of sleek vertical rise and recessed glass gave the Neoclassical façade a feeling of lift like a cathedral. The faux abstract colonnade now extended into a columned portico after recent structural renovations. Large oaks and manicured hedges provided shade and shelter from the wind blowing off Elliot Bay in the distance. Huge granite planters flanked central stairs that rose up to the building, which sat back from the street almost thirty feet. Families displaced from the parade sat on the steps, under the porticos, on top of retaining walls. Kids played on the grass. And more were coming as they waited for traffic to ease up so that they could go home.

"I'm watching various groups meet up. Some of them are decked out in gear and masks like they're expecting rubber bullets. Meanwhile, there's little kids and pregnant mothers thrown in the mix. I don't like where this seems to be going."

"No, no. Tig briefed us this morning. It's supposed to be small, peaceful. The last one was not a problem. A lot of first amendment people, counter protestors calling for Gage's head as a domestic terrorist, your garden variety college kids, that sort of thing."

"I met a couple of them," Reed said. He caught sight of a security guard leaning against a tree trunk and started over. "See if you can redirect some of our patrol over here. I'm getting bad vibes off of all this."

"I'll see what we can do but we're spread thin, Reed," Nat's voice crackled from his radio. "We found two more backpacks along the length of the parade. We're evacuating everyone. There're patrols trying to get cars going out of this gridlock down here."

"What about the library? It was having that holiday thing today, right? It's just down the block from here. Do you have anyone working the area right now?"

"Hold on," Nat said, and then came back a moment later. "We're sending a unit your way. Two patrol guys. That's all whose close enough."

"I'll take it," Reed remembered what Misty and Jay had told him and asked, "Have you heard of Second Wave? It's a political group."

"Uh, I don't think so." Someone was shouting on her end. "Find the patrol guys, I'm heading your way. Your sketch didn't come through and we need it. I'll meet you on the front steps of the courthouse," Nat said and was gone.

Reed walked toward the guard who stood up from the tree when he saw him approaching. The guy's plastic name tag read, Pico.

"Where are all your buddies?" Pico asked. When Reed looked at him funny, he said. "You're a cop, right?"

"I am."

"How come I haven't seen one black and white out here all morning. Look at all those people."

Reed settled next to Pico under the oak. "Did you guys know this crowd was coming?"

"No way. All we heard was some hippies might show up with signs. But my supervisor is over at the east entrance, and she says we got a lot of parade people getting pushed up here." Pico had Caesar-like haircut and tattoos in Old English Lettering on his knuckles. "The stupid college kids moved all the safety cones so now everyone is just . . . everywhere." He pointed down the slope of the lawn to the street.

Groups of orange cones nested on top of one another at the corner.

"Great," Reed said. More chaos. "He wiggled his phone in front of Pico. Is your cell working? I can't get any data."

"No one can. Not even the floats." Pico pointed up.

Reed's gaze rose to the sky, and he tilted his head, puzzled. A mini blimp, a small one used by the media to grab aerial views of the parade route without being obtrusive listed lazily overhead, drifting in the wind. It was designed to blend in with the floats and giant balloons so that it could grab action shots of the floats, marching bands, and giant balloons of the parade without getting in the way. About eight feet long and propelled via a small motor running semiautonomous navigation, it still had to redirect via signal. One that was likely blocked by the dampeners they hadn't located yet.

"That's the second one to escape," Pico said with a chuckle. "Damn cameras probably cost more than my house and they don't even work. I heard that whatever is messing with comms is messing up their receivers, I think. I heard one ended up landing on the stands."

Reed was barely listening as he flicked through articles on his phone screen. He'd picked up Wi-Fi from the courthouse and did a search of Second Wave. It was a post about a previous altercation uptown at the US District Courthouse last year where several sister groups, Second Wave, Citizen Cavalry, and Restoration Republic clashed with counter-protesting groups at a hearing.

Reed stilled. Firash and Restoration Republic were connected to this protest. *This* place, not the parade.

His gaze snapped to the growing number of people gathering on the courthouse lawn and steps. Strollers, kids, young adults . . . all in one small area. Reed turned to the security guard and spoke calmly. "Pico, can I talk to a supervisor or head of security?"

"She's on a conference call with the press. They're having a hard time getting here with the mess out there. And I heard there's some VIPs arriving, too. They got a nice tent though, so they don't have to be out on the grass like the rest of us. But I can get her if you want."

"I can't express how much I need to talk to her immediately."

"Yeah, you think maybe somethings going to pop off out here?"

Reed nodded. "The sooner the better."

Pico called on his own shoulder radio for his boss. Reed tried to raise Nat and Coyote on his own while they waited. A few minutes later an older woman walked toward them from the east entrance in a wool skirt and jacket, her sensible heels sinking into the still wet grass. She had salt and pepper hair, horn rimmed glasses way too big for her, and a nervous pinch to her lips. She extended her hand as she approached.

"I'm Vanetta Brown, Mr. Pico says you need to speak with me, Detective?"

"A situation might be brewing here. How many guards are on duty here?"

"Well, just the four . . ."

Nat's voice came back first on the radio. "Checking in, Reed. What's your status?"

Reed shook her hand. "One moment, Ms. Brown, I have to take this." He stepped away and said to Nat, "I just found out Second Wave is a sister group to Restoration Republic."

"Oh, crap! How did we miss that?"

"Restoration Republic is not as big, and the other two groups are based out of different states. Most articles only mention Second Wave because that's the group that Gage is the head of, but that's the connection, Nat. Firash's group is here to protest. His accomplice is here."

He stepped back over to Pico and Vanetta, and Reed's eyes fell to the lanyard around her neck. It read, 'staff' and looked just like the one in Firash's bag.

"Nat get people down here now. I think—"

Reed spotted a name on some of the posters waving in people's hands, *Joshi for Justice*. Firash had mentioned the name to Iris's assistant, Mika. She'd said he'd yelled it. Reed wrongly assumed it was a first name. Congresswoman Joshi. Iris's 'in' to push the Ghanzi project through for Danzig. A photo of her face on one of the signs sent a jolt of hatred soaring through him. Black bob, bright white blazer, a huge smile on her face . . . familiar somehow. Firash's memory tore across his vision. He'd read about her corruption in Danzig's Special Project's files. Her vote. Her tainted conscience, would decide the fate of his people. She was here.

Reed twisted from the memory, ripping himself from it. "It's the Congresswoman Joshi. She's the target."

"Is she here?"

"I don't know, let me check." His gaze snapped to Vanetta and she jumped. "Pico said VIPs were—"

"Fight for freedom, fight for the future!" A guy yelled through a megaphone as he jumped onto the stone planter base. He screamed it again, pumping his fist and then another guy joined. Then another. The shouts spread through the gathering like wildfire. Signs rose up, and people shouted together, chanting louder and louder. Counter-protesters jeered and booed, their signs equally as vibrant as they bobbed them up and down, pushing their way up the steps to drown out the others. The bullhorn guy lowered it from his face and Reid froze. It was Sepulcher. He shouted about being stripped of his rights, corruption, and greed, all the greatest hits, but it was what he held in his hand that made Reed move. Sepulcher waved an orange cannister, like a shaving cream can, over his head as he yelled. Reed pushed through the crowd, fighting to get to him.

"Give them a taste of their own medicine this time!" Sepulcher pulled the tab from the cannister, and black smoke spewed out of it. "They can't arrest us if they can't see us!"

A dozen cannisters arched through the air trailing black smoke. They seemed to come out of nowhere all at once, landing in the heart of the crowd, a coordinated volley. Reed's pulse paced up as he traced the trajectory back to a group of people under the courthouse portico. They wore gas masks and black field uniforms, some even had riot gear. They screamed with the crowd, banging on their chest armor like barbarians in battle. Where had they come from? Next to Reed, a man holding a baby gasped, his eyes going wide with fear. He backed up, dragging his stroller with him. Reed grabbed his radio.

"It's breaking loose, Nat! Where are you?"

"The patrol guys are there, at the west entrance. There's some injured kids in that area. I'm almost to you, coming up the street on the east. One block," she panted and Reed realized she was running.

"I need them at the Fifth Avenue entrance. We've got bad actors whipping people up over here. I smell a riot."

"I'm in contact with the incident coordinator. They're working on it!" She yelled back.

Coyote's voice came through. "Morgan, where are you? I'm stuck down by the library. I was trying to double back."

"Get to the courthouse. It's going down any minute."

"On my way."

The energy had changed. Cheers turned to shouting as more cannisters flew through the air at the courthouse, littering the lawn and stairs. Black smoke rose up out of them like demons escaping from hell. The wind spread it, creating a murky fog. Counter-protesters ran to grab them with their oven mitts and tossed them back. The air filled with the cloying, dark smoke. The crowd churned, growing agitated, and all around him kids cried, frightened.

Pico started coughing, and he turned back to look at Reed from further up the lawn. "They must be using pepper spray!"

"Get all the families and kids downwind. Get them to the street," Reed yelled, pulling his bandana over his mouth and nose.

But Pico didn't move. He stood ramrod straight, staring at the sky.

"What the hell is that?" Reed followed his gaze up the ivory façade of the courthouse to the blimp now hovering directly over it. "Do you see that? How is it still here in this wind?"

The small blimp didn't move in the lazy bobbing manner of before. Instead, it centered itself over the spire of the building and lowered slowly, inexorably down. Reed held his breath as if waiting for an alien tractor beam to slice down onto the crowd. Instead, as it lowered, the design pattern came into sharp focus. A delicate filigree border lined the bottom of a 'Happy Thanksgiving' message emblazoned across the blimp's surface. Reed's blood went cold, and he reached into his boot for his weapon.

"We have to get people out of here," Reed said. All around him, voices died down, murmurs of confusion as everyone watched with rapt attention. He keyed his radio. "Nat, do autonomous media blimps have a lost protocol or something? Because this one's acting bizarre."

"They'd land as soon as possible. Why?"

Everyone flinched when four small bursts, like pops from a cap gun, exploded from beneath the blimp releasing the curved, burnt orange undercarriage. It dropped down from the bottom of the aircraft.

"Watch out!" Reed shouted. The metal fuselage crashed to the bricks of the steps. The crowd scattered, screams erupting as five disk-shaped drones flew out from the inside blimp under carriage and raced low over the crowd, razing inches above their heads. Several people toppled to the ground, stumbling over each other. Four small crafts and one larger one, maybe two feet across circled the group.

"Take cover!" Reed ran toward the fallen piece of metal fuselage. This was what he'd seen. The curve of orange, the paint. Firash had hidden his devices in the blimp. The drones looped back toward the undercarriage and Reed dove behind a retaining wall near some hedges. He peered over the edge and by the formation alone, he knew the big one was the problem.

The four smaller drones flew outward to the edges of the throng. The larger one, a few feet across, hovered over the center of the crowd. Four metal appendages folded out from underneath the frame of the drone like insect arms. Propellers the size of hands extended over a group of huddled teens and their hair rippled in the rotor wash. A water bottle flew at it from the edge of the lawn, the large drone surged upward, its light grid tracking the bottle and then it let out a shrill tone.

Without warning, the four smaller drones fired pellets at the crowd. They vaporized upon impact sending plumes of burning powder everywhere. Those who got hit, screamed in pain, pawing at their skin, and coughing. Everyone ran, some breaking for the streets, others tried to make it to the buildings, but the drones herded them like cattle. Impossibly fast they zipped through the air, directing the melee by firing at the ground, pushing them toward each other. Their high-pitched motors vibrated the air. People trampled one another, crawling over each other in the fight to get away. More rapid-fire pops rang out as small pellets slammed into people's chests, faces, and legs.

"Reed!" Nat shouted as she ran up from the street, breathless. He pulled her down behind the wall with him. "What the hell is going on?"

"It's Firash. He set up drones to do . . . something."

"What?" She peeked over the wall at the lawn and then sank back down, shock on her face. "Oh, you gotta be kidding me. I'm seriously getting traumatized. I lock my stupid robot floor cleaner in the garage at night now because those things creeped me out so much."

"The backpack, the parade . . . I can't explain though," Reed said, checking his weapon and counting his rounds.

"You're going to love this," Nat said. "The pipe bombs were fake. All four of them."

"It must have been a diversion. To get us spread thin." Reed peeked around the side of the bricks. "*This* makes sense. *This* is him, not bombs."

"Yeah, and what exactly is this?"

"His final lesson." Reed shook his head. "We need to fight back."

"We should wait for backup. They're on their way, Reed. Traffic will make a way through for them."

"We can't wait. He's using Ferrin," Reed said, rising up, looking for a chance. "He's burning people. We need medical here. And those Fly-net shotgun shells you guys have."

"I'm gonna go check the patrol cars on the street for those."

One of the drones flew down the center of the crowd firing, the muzzle flash pulling Reed back to Kabul. Fire from the sky, black smoke from the flaming trucks and buildings, the screams of those around him. A chain link fence strobed into place before Reed and he reached for it, his hands closing on nothing. Firash's voice echoing in his head.

You will know that fear, that pain . . .

Next to him Nat shouted into her radio snatching him back to the lawn. "I repeat, they are herding everyone and firing something . . . like a mustard gas. We need water, we need burn kits, we're looking at mass injuries. Roll more busses, grab academy trainees if you have to. And we gotta have some Fly-net shotgun shells stat, there's a drone swarm kicking our asses up here! We need help!"

The armed crafts stopped suddenly and hovered at the edges of the lawn in a strange back and forth movement that reminded Reed of a hockey goalie. Then the larger drone glided over the cowering people. Green light grids beamed down from its belly and slid from face to face. Two cameras, crisscrossed the crowd, scanning.

A wooden bat swung up from one of the protesters, arching toward the drone but it was too fast. It evaded the blow and then a shot rang out over the lawn as a blast knocked the man backward. Screams tore out of the throng as a circle widened around the body. A bullet hole in his chest spread crimson across his light sweater.

Complete chaos erupted and Reed ran toward the larger drone, already pulling his weapon. He came up behind it, saw the two cameras panning back and forth, and fired just as a screaming kid ran right into him, bouncing off his chest. The shot went wild and one of the cameras pivoted backward, locking onto him. The entire drone whipped around, and the light grid slid across Reed's features. The lines turned from green to red, and Reed's arm came back around, re-aiming . . . not fast enough. It shot him.

39

The round seared past Reed's ear and white-hot pain surged through his scalp. He fired as he stumbled sideways, the weapon bucking in his hand over and over as he ran, he missed every shot. The drone flitted back and forth, blazingly fast, firing back at Reed. Its gridlines seeking him as he leapt over bushes and scrambled up the steps toward the front entrance and the cover of the large oaks. The crowd burst apart, scattering, running each other down in their panic. A woman tried to use a lighter and a can of hairspray to fend off one of the smaller drones and caught some bushes on fire. The flames spread to the dry fall leaves and branches, flaring alight. The large drone closed in, flanking Reed. It chased him, gaining. He ran past a couple of guys wearing all black as they used a flag to whip at the small drones, they hit one and it wobbled off kilter, slamming into a pylon near the steps, disintegrating.

The large drone fired, and the round slammed into the front door of the courthouse. Reed ran in a crouch, veering left along the front, heading for the corner. He wove in and out of the support columns, the drone right behind him. Out of the corner of his eye he spotted the shadow of it on the wall. It slipped along the white façade, closing in.

He rounded another corner to the back of the courthouse. The trees were thicker there, and the drone was too large to follow. It rose abruptly over the treetops. Reed crept sideways, his back to the wall of the building, keeping his eyes on the drone through the branches as he tried each door-knob and window he passed. Everything was locked in anticipation of the protest, but the upper windows bled smoke into the crisp air. The fire was spreading.

The drone's tracking grid flit from opening to opening, calculating trajectory, the rotors shaking the dry leaves. He panted, his hand to his head as he fought a wave of dizziness. His palm came back bloody. The scalp just above his temple throbbed and he touched it gingerly and felt the ragged edge of a wound. A space between the tree canopy left him open to exposure and he glanced back the way he'd come, debating. Slowly, he moved his hand to his radio. He turned down the volume and then moved further out from underneath the cover of trees, his eyes on the sky.

Propellers whined above him, and the larger drone moved over the branches and then hovered as if it were waiting. Then he saw it. One of the smaller drones rounded the corner. Dented and flying skewed, it fired pellets wildly down the path. Reed shot it down and then another one dropped down from between the branches. Undented and with perfect aim, it charged Reed who turned and ran. The pellets vaporized against his back and arms, the fine powder made it through the athletic material and burned his skin like nothing he'd ever felt. The ground at the rear of the building sloped down toward the street and became a second lawn behind the courthouse. Reed slipped and slid down the grass. The drone, unable to track his frantic movements, sent pellets whizzing past him as it followed.

A first aid module sat on the back lawn of the building. Set up for possible injuries, it had translucent machine-printed walls and thick plastic flaps for doors with circle windows at head height. Light but sturdy in the wind, it wasn't exactly a place for VIPs. To his left, a few doors he hadn't tried. Reed debated. Pico had mentioned the press and announcement guests had their own area and this was the only 'tent' Reed had seen so far. He decided to check it out and ran through the front flaps. He cut off to the side of the opening, waiting. The high-pitched rotor of the mini drone sounded close, and its movements cast light changes through the trans-parent siding. It wouldn't come in. It just bobbed up and down at the window as if caught in a loop. Then in a flutter of falling leaves, it flew out of sight.

Reed stepped away from the wall and then backed up slowly, his gaze on the entrance. He wondered if they'd given up or were regrouping. Either way, he had to warn Joshi. A portable air conditioner hummed in the corner and a single button light stuck to the plastic ceiling lit up the space. He pulled off his hoodie, glancing at the burns on his arms. Red welts with white centers created a patchwork along his triceps. He recognized chemical burns when he saw them. Water bottles littered the grass next to toppled cases and Reed opened one and doused his skin, looking around. A couple tables, some metal chairs, and a gurney lay strewn around the inside as if hit by a hurricane. Reed pulled his radio, raising the volume just enough.

"Coyote, Nat, do you copy?" Reed hissed.

Nothing came back but clicks and then, "Copy good, Morgan, where are you?" Coyote answered.

"I'm hiding in a first aid module behind the courthouse. I pissed off the mothership when I shot at it, and it chased me down, but now I don't see it. Firash must have loaded it with facial rec because it was scanning people. Looking for Congresswoman Joshi. She's supposed to be here with some VIPs, I think. I don't know if they arrived. But I do know everything that happened, the riot, the Ferrin, is all a diversion for an assassination. It's hunting for her, Coyote."

"Please don't make it sound so alive. What do you need?"

"I need you to find Congresswoman Joshi and warn her this thing is gunning for her. Get word to Nat. I haven't heard from her. Over."

"I saw her by the squad cars. She shot one of those smaller ones down with a shotgun."

"Okay, that's three down that we know of," Reed said. "I took one out back here and I saw another one crash."

"That leaves one small, one large."

"I'm going to try to find the supervisor I talked to earlier and see if Joshi made it. I don't want to go to her in case that thing is still following me—"

Metal clanged at the far door of the tent. Reed's weapon came up. A sink station wobbled over on the grass and the top of three heads sat huddled behind it.

"I'm a detective with the SPD." Reed said, walking over. "Who's there?"

Three pairs of eyes looked over the top of the cabinet at him and one arm rose.

"I'm Joshi," a soft voice said. She stood and Reed thought she looked exactly like her picture on the posters. His blood ran cold. She was in the worst place possible. Next to him.

Two others rose. They were young, wearing blazers, one still clutched a leather folio. Blond and brunette, the two men couldn't be more than twenty-four, and likely her interns.

"Joshi's with me," Reed said into the radio. "We gotta get her away from here, man."

"I'm on my way to you now, coming up Fifth."

Reed signed off and turned to Joshi. "You have to run. Toward the street. My . . . colleague is driving up. I want you to run for the road, I'll cover you from here, and jump in the car. He'll get you to safety."

"I can't leave!" Joshi held his gaze. Frightened, but firm. "Not without my daughter. Kimmy was on the front lawn with my head of security, Angus. She was going to watch my speech."

Reed's stomach sank. The front was chaos and fire. "Are you sure she's even still there?"

"We had to drag Joshi in here when we saw the drones," the brunette assistant said. "But I last saw Kimmy out on the stairs."

"Regardless, we have to stay far away from Kimmy, Congresswoman." He looked over at the staff members present. "In fact, we have to get away from all of your people."

"What? Why?"

Reed pointed out the window. "That weapon was searching for you. You're the target and if they happen to be near you then they'll die too."

The two aides stared at her with horror.

She looked at him with frightened eyes. "But Kimmy is out there . . ."

"You get to the car. I'll get your daughter. What is she wearing?"

"I'm going with you," Joshi said, pulling her blazer off and dropping it to the floor. She kicked off her heels. "She won't go with you. Not without me."

"You need to get to safety—"

"I'm getting my daughter!" Joshi snapped, her hands shaking despite the determination in her eyes. She started for the tent door. "You coming?"

"You're likely to die if you go after her." Reed stepped in front of the tent door, blocking the congresswoman's path.

"It's a risk I'm willing to take."

"You put yourself anywhere near her and your daughter becomes collateral damage. Her life's in your hands. Are you willing to gamble it?"

She hesitated. "Is this . . . is this Danzig?"

"No, it's . . ." Reed caught shadows shifting through the white plastic of the roof. One or both drones were back. He lowered his voice. "This is Firash."

"Who?" Her voice rose.

Reed put his finger to his lips, pointing up. "The guy trying to derail your deal with Iris."

"How . . ." she backed up, her gaze sliding to her assistants. "I-I was blackmailed. My older son . . . he has a drug habit. He got in trouble. Danzig threatened his life in lock up. He said he'd have him stabbed to death—"

"I'm not here to bust you. I'm here to get you out of here. Firash found out what you and Iris were doing, and he built that thing to hunt you down. We have to get as far away from other people as possible. Are any of the doors to the courthouse unlocked?"

"No, we tried them," the brunette piped up. "That's why we're in here still."

"Please, Detective, I need to get to my daughter. I don't expect you to understand, but there's no way I'm leaving without her," Joshi tried to move past Reed again.

"Ok, stop. If I can't convince you otherwise, then we're doing it my way." Reed handed Joshi his hoodie. She shrugged it on and pulled the hoodie down over her face, nodding. To the assistants Reed said, "We can't go through the building, so we'll have to make a run for it. Joshi and I will split off and you two head for the parking lot."

The blond assistant looked at him with abject terror. "No, way am I leaving this module. Not after what you said. I'd rather take my chances in here."

"There're drones out there now. Won't be long before this place becomes a kill zone," Reed whispered harshly. His gaze snapped to the shifting light overhead. They hadn't given up. He didn't know if that meant once targeted, they stay with you or that they knew Joshi was in the module. Neither answer seemed promising. "You're not safe here. No one is."

Joshi put her palm on the assistant's forearm, her smile reassuring. "It's okay, I'll be okay."

"How could this be happening?" The brunette asked, his face twisted with anger.

"We'll get to the bottom of this. I will absolutely not allow whoever did this to get away—"

A low tone from the drone cut across her. Red grid lights snapped alight and glowed through the roof as an audio fragment played in Joshi's voice. *I will absolutely not allow our city to be overtaken with crime.*

Joshi froze. "That's from my campaign speech."

The voice replayed over and over. *Absolutely not. I will . . . absolutely not.*

"How can it do that? How . . ." she went blank, and the color drained from her face.

Reed locked eyes with the two interns, then made a running motion with his fingers. The blond one nodded. The other one gingerly picked up a section of the fallen IV pole from the grass and swung it like a sword. He nodded once. Reed checked his weapon. Four rounds left.

Joshi spoke, her voice full of disbelief. "I'd heard about what Danzig had access to, but this is . . ."

"Be quiet," Reed mouthed but it was too late. Overhead, the grid lights darted from side to side, searching for her at the sound of her voice. Reed grabbed Joshi by the shoulders, making her look at him. "Go, now!"

"But I—"

"Don't look back!" He shoved her toward the door just as rounds punched through the plastic roof and slammed through the gurney, the metal chairs, the water bottles.

He and Joshi burst out the back going toward the front of the courthouse, the interns ran the other way. The drone stayed with Reed. Joshi whimpered as she ran, keeping her head down as they cleared the corner. They skirted around the side to the front walkway toward the lawn.

The rally had turned into a full-blown riot with groups clashing on the grass. Bloody lips and red eyes. The black smoke still seeped out of cannisters littering the ground. Everywhere people coughed and spit, some even threw up as they fought the Ferrin gas overtaking them. Sirens blared from the back streets, honking for a path to get to the victims.

Reed pulled the bandana that Misty kid had given him over his mouth and nose as they ran. Joshi stumbled in front of him, and he caught her elbow, righting her as they jumped onto one of the oversized planters. Reed scanned the crowd, two drones shooting at a man and his dog stopped abruptly and raced toward them.

"Do you see her?" Reed asked, aiming at the front runner. "Do you see Kimmy?"

Joshi's gaze flitted across the lawn of the courthouse, tears streaming down her cheeks. She gasped, pointing with a shaking hand. "There! Oh, my god. I think I just saw her run behind that retaining wall!"

Reed pushed Joshi down and fired at the small drone. He hit it, and it careened into the courthouse, breaking a window as it crashed. Black smoke spewed from the second floor, obscuring his view. The second one flitted over the roof and was gone. Reed coughed, squinting at the smoke blackened sky. He'd lost track of the larger drone.

"Nat are your ears on?" Reed yelled into his radio. "I need cover at the courthouse. Parking lot!"

"Please! We're so close. We have to get to her," Joshi cried and tried to run, but he held her by her upper arm.

"If you run to her and it'll identify you. Once that happens, all bets are off. You'll be a marked target. You go after your daughter and you'll draw the drone to her, do you understand?"

"Then make sure it doesn't identify me." A stubborn defiance etched deep lines in the congresswoman's face.

Reed could see no point in wasting more time arguing the contrary. The only option was to control her as best he could and hope it would be enough to keep them all alive. "Right now, the drone will only have picked up your voice. I have no idea if that's enough for it to target you so, if we're going to do this, you have to keep your head down. Do you understand?"

As they prepared to move, a shadow crossed over them and Reed looked up. The larger drone dove down through the smoke, its grid locking onto his face. Its arm swung down. Reed fired up at its belly. It wobbled, but quickly righted itself, the armed appendage swiveling to aim. Reed dove with Joshi, throwing them under the portico of the courthouse. Rounds cracked into the pavement and sent shards into his face. He shoved her behind him, coming up on his knees, returning fire. He hit it again, this time a bullet finding its mark and shattering one of the cameras. The other drone banked sideways and swung around, the light grid stuttering as it panned the area, searching for them. They crawled behind the hedges, putting distance between them and the arial threat. The drone shifted up and down, jockeying for position.

"That's her!" Joshi gasped.

The retaining wall sat between them and the parking lot. And Reed spotted pink jeans and a flowery shirt sticking out from behind some bushes.

"I see her."

"Where's Angus? Why is she alone?"

"Joshi, you need to focus. The best thing you can do right now is to keep a clear head. Understand?" She nodded, her gaze flitting to her daughter. Reed redirected her eyes on him. "I'm going to provide some cover fire. When I do, I want you to run straight for the blue car. Hide your face from view. Grab Kimmy as you pass her, but don't stop. Whatever you do, don't look back," Reed whispered.

She looked at him, suddenly uncertain. "What if it follows me?"

"I'm going to give it a reason not to. You just get your daughter and get safe."

Joshi nodded, her face pale. "Run. Get Kimmy. Blue car. Don't look back."

Satisfied the congresswoman's bulletized recounting of the next critical steps in his plan were received, Reed stood and ran toward the drone. He let out a controlled burst from his weapon as he charged. "Go!"

Joshi ran, slipping and sliding down the hill. The large drone fired, pushing him back toward the building. Reed ducked behind a support column, firing back. Chewing up his ammo as he scanned the street in the distance. He spotted Coyote gunning it toward them in the blue car. Joshi scrambled down the grass with her daughter in her arms.

The drone shot up and out of view. Reed seized the momentary lull in the battle as his opportunity to make his break. He exploded into a dead sprint, running to the lifeline Coyote's getaway car provided. He'd nearly made it to the tree line. The curb where Coyote's car idled was just a few feet away when the larger drone burst from behind the oak branches over-head, raining leaves and twigs down on them. The little one's motor whined as it accelerated. It must've run out of pellets because instead of shooting, it flew down around their feet, trying to trip them. Joshi stumbled with Kimmy in her arms, just barely righting herself before hitting the ground.

Reed made a beeline for Joshi. He sighted in on the low-flying drone. As he ran, Reed timed his steps like he'd done in playing soccer a million times before. He could hear the whir of the drone hovering above the ground in front of him as he slammed the instep of his right foot into its side, punting it against the retaining wall. He heard the crash but couldn't tell if the damage had ended the threat because his eyes were set on Coyote's car speeding toward the curb as he continued his relentless sprint forward.

"We're almost to you," Reed shouted into the radio. "Be ready."

"I see you, Morgan. You still got one on your six. Hang tight. I'm coming for you."

"Negative. Negative. I'm handing off Joshi and her kid. Get them out of here."

They stumbled to the asphalt, the low hum of the large drone's rotors vibrated the air near Reed's head while Coyote screamed on the radio. "You can outrun that thing better in the car."

"I'm running to you with Joshi and her kid. Get them safe. I'll lead it away if I can," Reed shouted as he got ready to cut away from her. And then Joshi looked back, and the drone's light grid flashed to her face. Reed dove with her behind a tree, a second before bullets slammed in the trunk spit-ting up bark and shards of wood. Reed turned and fired, hitting its side. It swerved and got caught in the tree. One of its extendable propellers snagged on a branch and Reed used the moment to break for the sidewalk.

"Get to the car," Reed shouted.

Coyote drifted the car sideways, skidding against the curb. He leaned over and popped the door open, and Joshi tried to scramble into the car, but the little drone appeared again and swooped across the roof of the car, zooming at her. Joshi swatted at it, protecting Kimmy's face. In her fending of the relentless drone, Joshi's footing faltered, sending her staggering backward. She yelped as the drone swooped forward. Coyote managed to yank them both into the passenger seat.

The little drone fired pellets at the window, cracking it. Reed snatched it out of the sky, slammed it into the sidewalk, and shot it. He went to close the door when the large drone dropped down from the sky, blocking their escape, hovering just in front of the car. Its light grid flared inside the dark of the car, settled on Joshi's face, its weapon pivoting on target.

Reed leapt across the hood, his body acting as a shield for Joshi and her daughter as he slid in front of the windshield. He felt the kick of his gun as he released a rapid succession of shots at his robotic enemy. The drone rocked backward, but not before its rounds slammed into the steel of the hood, punching through the metal and shattering the glass behind him. A hot stabbing sensation seared through Reed's shoulder. He rolled off the hood, dropping to the asphalt alongside the car. He slapped the driver's side window and screamed for Coyote to go. The car tore away, the larger drone turning to follow.

Reed shot to his feet and spun around, as he planted his boots, and fired his last shot. His round pinged off the metal propeller extensions. The drone veered up then dove for Reed, plunging toward him in a strafing run. Reed swerved into the street and leapt onto the bumper of a car parked at the curb. One in a long line going down Fifth Ave. He ran up the back over the top of the hood and roof, and then down the back. He leapt off the trunk to the next car, his eye on the drone as it sped along him. There were more people here, possible collateral damage if he didn't get it away.

The drone pulled up next to Reed as he leapt to another car and its targeting grid flickered at him. The barrel of its weapon locked onto his face, and he had no choice. Reed sucked in a breath and flew at the drone from the car roof. Pain tore through his damaged shoulder as he grabbed onto it midair, tackling it to the ground. They tumbled together on the asphalt. A shrill tone tore out of the machine. Both weapons swinging around. Reed swapped his gun into his good hand and grabbed the drone's barrel with the other. The machine's engines whirred as it fought to pull from him. It fired aimlessly. He shouted in agony as he battled for control.

All of the death. The lies. The loss. It coursed through his veins like molten lava as Reed wailed on it, shouting in anger. The second camera shattered, and he dug his knee into the elbow of the propeller extension. The weapon pivoted in his grasp, and he shook with effort. The hydraulics whined as it aimed. A round shot into the ground a foot from his head. The next one at his ear, he yelled, twisting against the pain in his shoulder.

"Reed!" Nat stumbled down from the lawn, breathless. Blood seeped from her nose as she rushed toward him with a shotgun in her hand, her eyes lit with adrenaline. "Watch out!"

The shotgun blasted the drone backward. Coyote ran up from the parking lot with a bat as Reed scrambled to his feet and then the two of them beat the machine until it stopped moving, exposing its gears and wires like disemboweled entrails. Reed stood there, panting. Blood dripped down from the bullet trail at his temple, and he wiped it from his eyes. His back and shoulder throbbed, crimson streaming down his bicep. The drone quivered once more as its last propeller tried to spin.

"Is it dead?" Nat asked, racking the shell out and loading another.

"Dead as any robot can be." Reed kicked the motionless machine with his boot.

Coyote dropped the bat, his hands shaking. He looked at the drone and then back at Nat. "I'd still shoot it."

Without hesitation, she blew it to oblivion.

CHAPTER 40

The full force of the SPD descended on the scene, and it took almost a week to sort out how badly everything had gone. No actual bombs were found at the parade, and it was determined to be a diversion for Joshi's assassination. Firash knew how to play them all. He moved them like chess pieces, clearing the board for his attack. The mayor swooped in, worked the press, and sold the story of a disturbed young man who built a weapon. No mention of Firash's connection to Slater or any of the staged suicides. And not a word was spoken about Danzig or Firash's theft of the technology from High Rock Holdings that made the drones so deadly. They tied it off clean.

A week after the incident, Reed met with the Office of Professional Conduct and given all that he knew and all that they wanted to keep others from knowing, he was reprimanded for insubordination and ordered to meet with the therapist. Nat came to see him at the hospital when he was getting his arms checked for chemical burns. She told him that Petraeus had needed surgery to fix a bleed in her brain and the procedure had destroyed the evidence of the halo on her scalp. A post-op MRI showed strange, thread-like lesions snaking through her brain tissue, but nothing else. When he asked if she was going to recover, Nat shook her head. She wasn't ever going to be the same.

Representative Joshi resigned for health reasons, citing the trauma of the event, and being shot at by a flying robot. Nobody blamed her, and Reed hoped Danzig would let things go. She was found unresponsive in her garage with the car running a few days later. Reed went to the funeral though it rained and watched them lower a glossy black casket into the muddy ground.

On a Thursday evening, two weeks after Thanksgiving, Reed sat in his recliner by the big picture window in his living room and read Firash's journal on Maggie's missing tablet. He'd found it while cleaning up the garage after Firash drowned and hid it from Nat. It made him feel guilty, but he needed to know. What had gone wrong?

It wasn't what he expected. Firash had written on the screen with a digital pen and his flowing script spelled out the heartache and confusion of a man in love yet crippled by hate. He'd simply been snooping in the High Rock Holdings files. As an engineer, he'd heard of the technology rumored to belong to the company and simply wanted to take a peek. It was during one of his unauthorized jaunts into the Special Projects files that he'd stumbled onto Iris's name. The rabbit hole of information Firash fell into led him to the conspiracy connecting Danzig to Slater's kills and the horrific weapon being used on the innocent.

He'd also learned of the plan to place a compromised Joshi on the Congressional Committee on Foreign Investment. Working with Iris Abernathy at Briar Ridge they planned to push through a restructuring bill that would grant a contract to Danzig's company to build infrastructure in Afghanistan under the guise of the government restoration of roads. In reality, it was a plan to pave the way for Danzig's mining operation. Firash swore to stop another rape of his country's treasures. He'd wanted to make a statement and joined the Restoration Republic organization when his plan to take out Joshi had formed. Unable to get past her security, he needed pandemonium and so created it.

Firash wrestled with his feelings for Maggie and his dedication to the mission until he witnessed Slater throw Alastair in front of the train. That had moved the plan to purpose. It was the moment Firash had decided who he was and lost his way.

Reed set the tablet down and sipped his coffee. None of it was admissible. Almost none of it believable to the common person. Especially the Memory Bank. If he hadn't seen it, experienced real ripped memories with his own mind, he'd wouldn't have believed it either.

On a run the next day, he stopped by Caitlyn's favorite spot by the water and tried to remember the color of her eyes. In his memory, they looked like a storming sky. On the way home, he thought he saw a car following him. Then a guy at the grocery store seemed to look at Reed a little too long. Nothing sure. But a hint of unease settled in Reed's gut. That night, he dreamt of trains and sparkling brooks and laughing with his friends on summer break. But then a shadow swallowed up his world, destroying everyone in its path and he woke panting, panic clawing at his throat.

Danzig walked through the crowd of gala attendees. A sea of tuxedos and gowns in the opulence of the arts center. Museum exhibitions donated by prominent families and corporations lined the dais. The soft light caressed the masterpieces as party goers strolled with champagne between them. He nodded to a couple, rolled his eyes once past, and walked between his security guards to the terrace. They shut the doors behind him, and he strolled to a waist-high railing and lit a clove cigarette. The soft waltz from the party wafted through the French doors and he stared out at the twinkling lights of Seattle. Danzig took a long drag, letting the exhale float out of the side of his mouth in a rivulet of smoke.

The scent was sweet, like honey and Reed let the cloud of smoke drift past him before raising his weapon. Danzig froze with his hand halfway to his mouth as Reed stepped out of the shadows.

"Stop reaching for your weapon," Reed said. "Just pull that other hand back out of your jacket."

Danzig looked at him and then smirked, complying. He completed his drag off the clove before speaking. Lithe like a swimmer, his cobalt eyes slashed in the fake torchlight of the wall lamps. "You are everything I was told you were," he said. "No one gets past my security."

"Our government was kind enough to gift me with the know-how. And other skills I'd be happy to share with you, should you be so inclined."

Danzig's brows furrowed. "How did you know I'd come out here?"

Reed kept his weapon on Danzig and leaned against the railing. He tilted his head, taking in Danzig's sharp nose and cleft chin. A patrician face. The kind you'd see on a coin. "I smelled smoke on your breath."

"What?" Danzig tossed the clove off the terrace and turned to Reed.

"Toss the weapon. And the panic button."

Danzig complied, setting them on the railing. "We've never met face to face."

"Sure, we have. In a hangar. When you ordered Caitlyn's death."

"You weren't there . . ."

"No, but Slater was."

Danzig's eyes went cold. "No one will believe you. You have nothing even remotely admissible. Drug induced hallucinations after an explosion are a hard sell to the powers that be, as you've found out. Especially this election year."

"You seem to think I'm building a case." Reed pushed off from the railing getting in Danzig's space. "But the law is one thing. War is another. And I am *much* better at the latter."

"Is that what you're here for? To declare war?" Danzig stepped around Reed and folded his arms. "With what? There doesn't seem to be anything left of Slater's misdeeds. Or, as I hear it, your career. Maybe that's what this is about, hmm, Detective Reed?"

"Maybe." Reed shrugged. "Or maybe your mercenaries are just that. Maybe you murder enough people for someone you start gathering insurance against your own."

"Anything Slater may have had, if you were to believe his rantings, was likely destroyed when his home unfortunately burned down yesterday." Danzig smiled. A stiff, angry sneer. "You have nothing."

"I have what Gerald had." Danzig stilled and Reed clicked his tongue. "Slater forget to mention that? Yeah, that genius had squirreled away a whole lot more than evidence of purchase of the MER-C system by your Spectre Group. Slater, it turns out. Stored personal files on a server at Neurogen. Files he'd taken from your network. Including what Firash infiltrated in your special projects. Names. Dates. Big fat files." Reed tapped his head. "And I learned something from Petraeus. I have everything set to disseminate to multiple sources via a kill switch. In case something unexpected happens."

Danzig's brows furrowed with feigned surprise. "Why would anything happen to you, Detective? After all, you did exactly what I wanted. You kept our Congresswoman alive."

"Then why did you kill her?"

"I didn't. Guilt did. I would've found a way to get that 'yes' vote back." Danzig held Reed's gaze. "Do you even know what you did? Trillions of dollars. With the eco-lunatics blocking the Salton Sea's reserves this was a chance for the US to gain an independent Lithium reserve. Our defense department alone—"

"This isn't about national defense," Reed cut across him. "Power and money. That's all this is about, so cut the shit. And I didn't do anything. Firash Nuri, a war orphan, ruined your plans to exploit his country. A nerd with a keyboard against your entire operation. That's got to just burn a guy like you."

"Assets or enemies. That's all anyone is." Danzig said evenly. A mask of calm on his face. "Right now, you seem to be a bit of both."

"What the hell does *that* mean—"

The French doors opened, and in that millisecond, Danzig snatched his gun. They faced off with each other, Reed's back to the railing as Danzig backed up toward his men.

"It means this impasse won't last. And when it does, when no one is looking or even remembers your insight held any weight . . . you'll pay for what you cost me. This isn't over."

When they left, Reed lowered his weapon, then turned and looked out over the twinkling lights of the city.

"You're right," he said to the darkness. "This is far from over."

RETROGRADE FLAW
A MEMORY BANK THRILLER
by Brian Shea and Raquel Byrnes

In a world of high-tech deceit, where memories are weapons and truth is a fragile illusion, Detective Morgan Reed must decipher his own past to survive.

Detective Morgan Reed is back on the force, but the digital landscape he once knew has evolved into a treacherous realm of shadow games and shifting allegiances. Thrust into an investigation surrounding the enigmatic High Rock Holdings and Spectre Group, he soon discovers the Kraken—a next-gen tech weapon with chilling accuracy.

Yet, the deeper Reed digs, the more personal the stakes become, with ties to his own haunted past and a murdered friend, Dontae Black. Teamed with the astute Detective Natalie "Nat" De La Cruz, the duo unravels a tapestry of betrayal, crime rings, and covert tech conspiracies.

But as the truth edges closer, Reed must confront a harrowing question: In a world where trust is just a byte away from betrayal, who can you really believe?

From Raquel Byrnes and Wall Street Journal bestselling author Brian Shea comes *Retrograde Flaw,* where every digital footprint leads to an unexpected twist, and the line between ally and adversary is but a click away. A must-read for fans of Michael Crichton and David Baldacci.

Get your copy today at
severnriverbooks.com

ABOUT BRIAN SHEA

Brian Shea has spent most of his adult life in service to his country and local community. He honorably served as an officer in the U.S. Navy. In his civilian life, he reached the rank of Detective and accrued over eleven years of law enforcement experience between Texas and Connecticut. Somewhere in the mix he spent five years as a fifth-grade school teacher. Brian's myriad of life experience is woven into the tapestry of each character's design. He resides in New England and is blessed with an amazing wife and three beautiful daughters.

Sign up for the reader list at
severnriverbooks.com

ABOUT RAQUEL BYRNES

Raquel is the author of critically acclaimed suspense series, The Shades of Hope trilogy, Gothic duology, The Noble Island Mysteries, and epic Sci-Fi Steampunk series, The Blackburn Chronicles. She strives to bring intelligent characters with diverse backgrounds to the forefront of her stories.

When she's not writing, she can be seen geeking out over sci-fi movies, reading anything she can get her hands on, and having arguments about the television series Firefly in coffee shops. She lives in Southern California with her husband, six kids, and beloved Huskies.

Sign up for the reader list at
severnriverbooks.com

Printed in the United States
by Baker & Taylor Publisher Services